SWEETER
THAN
SIN

ALSO BY SHILOH WALKER

SECRETS & SHADOWS E-NOVELLAS

Burn for Me

Break for Me

Long for Me

SECRETS & SHADOWS SERIES

Deeper Than Need

Available from St. Martin's Press

SWEETER THAN SIN

SHILOH WALKER

St. Martin's Paperbacks

This is a work of fiction. All of the characters, organizations, and events portrayed in this novel are either products of the author's imagination or are used fictitiously.

SWEETER THAN SIN

Copyright © 2014 by Shiloh Walker.
Excerpt from *Darker Than Desire* copyright © 2014 by Shiloh Walker.

All rights reserved.

For information address St. Martin's Press, 175 Fifth Avenue, New York, NY 10010.

ISBN: 978-1-250-03241-6

Printed in the United States of America

St. Martin's Paperbacks edition / October 2014

St. Martin's Paperbacks are published by St. Martin's Press, 175 Fifth Avenue, New York, NY 10010.

10 9 8 7 6 5 4 3 2 1

*For Tim and Marty M. —Tim, thanks for all your help.
Marty . . . just thanks.*

*For all my readers, who kept asking when I'd do another
suspense, here you go. I hope you enjoy.*

*For Nicole, who is always answering legal and lawyer
questions. I know I drive you nuts. Thank you.*

For my husband and my kids, I love you.

AUTHOR'S NOTE

This series had a false start . . . and stop . . . before I finally got around to really working on it. The first idea ended up getting trashed and I had to start from scratch when I was finally able to start working on the project.

It started with the idea of a body, found under the floorboards of an old house, inspired by something I'd read online. It trigged that old 'what if' game that happens to so many writers.

Right about the time that I got to working on this project the second time, events surrounding the molestations of numerous underage boys came to light and the entire world watched as Jerry Sandusky, a retired assistant football coach, was arrested and eventually went to jail for child molestation.

Not long after I sold the series and while the Sandusky trial was still very vivid, a teenager was raped, her assault captured on video and shared via social media. Her attackers were found guilty. Indictments against school officials, related to tampering with evidence and failure to report child abuse, later followed.

For every victim who finds justice, though, hundreds do not.

Very often, it seems where we live in a world where

victims of assault have no voice. The Secrets & Shadows took on a life of its own, where people of power manipulated and abused some of the most helpless among us.

To those who have known such pain, may you find peace.

If you or somebody you know has been a victim of rape, abuse or incest, you can find support at RAINN. Rainn.org

CHAPTER ONE

It could be said that Adam Brascum loved women.

It *could* be said.

But it would be off-target. Adam didn't love women—he didn't *hate* them, but he didn't love them, either. He needed them.

The soft curves, the scent of their skin, the husky voices as they whispered to him in the night. If he worked it right, he could spend the night with any number of them and he wouldn't have to be alone unless he wanted.

Wouldn't have to be alone, with just the voices in his head, the memory of a phone call, the memory of a smile, the memory of the girl he might have been able to save.

If only he'd done something.

Now, years after, when it was far too late, he was doing something. Drowning his sorrows between the thighs of just about any woman who would have him.

There had been a time when he'd drown his sorrows with a woman, along with the help of his good friend Captain Morgan or maybe some Jack Daniel's, but that had all stopped on a cold, wintry day. He could still remember the soft, sad words spoken in his ear, and at the foot of a grave he'd made a promise.

He didn't make them often, but when he did, he kept them.

So the booze was gone.

His only vice now was women.

Lately, though, that vice wasn't doing it for him anymore.

He barely knew the name of the woman in bed next to him. She was beautiful, a long, sleek woman maybe ten years older than him, and she had left him feeling like she could put him through his paces for the rest of the night. He'd slept maybe thirty minutes, her neck tucked against his chest, her hand resting on his stomach.

And then the nightmare hit.

He was standing in front of the house.

Just standing there.

It was dark.

It was cold.

The dimly lit windows mocked him. If he moved any closer, the lights would go out and he'd find nothing.

But he could hear her. Her voice, whispering his name.

Adam . . . why didn't you help . . .

Why didn't you . . .

Why didn't you . . .

He came awake, choking back the oath. He'd learned long ago that when he made noise, whatever partner he had in bed with him tended to ask questions. Questions weren't the kind of thing he liked to entertain in bed, so he eventually figured out how to strangle the groans, the curses . . . even the screams.

After all these years, it was second nature.

Next to him, there was a long, soft sigh. He froze, listened.

After years and years of slipping out of beds, he'd all

but perfected it to an art and he could almost tell to the second when a woman was about to wake.

She shifted, rolled onto her belly.

Adam turned his head, stared at her in the dim light filtering in through the skylight. Her face, all but lost in the darkness, was a clean oval, her skin a warm, rich brown, her lips sweet and full. She had a wicked laugh and she'd looked at him like she had more than a few ideas about any secrets he might harbor. She'd looked, and she hadn't cared.

I just divorced a son of a bitch who'd been cheating on me for eight years. I knew, and I couldn't leave him. Now I can. She told Adam that, sitting across from him at the sports bar he owned, staring at him with clear eyes. *This is how I burn those bridges.*

He'd lifted an eyebrow at her. *Just how do you burn them, Jez?*

He was the only man I ever shared my bed with and I plan on changing that damn fast. I'm almost fifty years old and I don't want the only man I've slept with to be a lying, cheating son of a bitch.

Adam was a son of a bitch, but he couldn't be called a cheater. He'd never married, never even had a serious relationship. Again, it went back to promises. If you didn't make them, you didn't have to worry about breaking them.

I might be a son of a bitch, but I'm clear on the rest of it. She'd smiled at him.

They'd ended up in her room at the B&B, not the big one in town but a smaller, quieter one out near the river, and she'd all but turned him inside out. A hungry woman, a hot woman . . . who should have left him too burned-out to dream.

But here he was, on the edges of a desolate nightmare. While Jez slept on.

He leaned in, brushed her cheek with his lips. "Find somebody who'll do more than just share your bed, Jez," he murmured.

She made a grumbling sound under her breath and then sighed, a faint smile curving her wicked, delicious mouth.

Then she shoved her face into the pillow.

He was gone in less than three minutes.

But he didn't go home.

Instead, he drove out to the house that had haunted his nightmares. Yet again.

It stood there, a silent sentinel on the river. What secrets it guarded Adam didn't know.

It hadn't yielded an answer in all this time.

And now there was a new owner. It wasn't likely any answers would ever be found. A new owner—pretty lady, from what he'd heard. A young kid. Blowing out a sigh, he put the car in reverse and did a three-point turn.

He hadn't gotten answers in all this time.

It wasn't going to happen now, either.

Chicago

She had a ritual.

Get up in the morning.

Run three miles. Come back home. Do one hundred push-ups, two hundred sit-ups, shower, brush and braid her hair and then sit at the computer and take care of business before she went down to work. After work, she'd come up here, check her email again, read and then eat. Sometime around midnight or so, she would go to bed.

And all the while, she waited and she worried.

This was her life.

This was the only life she knew.

It was boring.

It was lonely.

It was safe.

It was comfortable.

Sometimes she hated it, but mostly she needed it.

Needed it because she remembered a time when she hadn't *had* the safety. Nights when she hadn't even had a bed. Days when she hadn't had food in her belly. Days, weeks, months that had passed in a blur of nothingness, all because she had to forget, had to bury who she *thought* she was.

You can do anything you set your mind to, baby. . . .

She'd been told that from the time she'd been just a little girl. Was it arrogance that she'd believed it? She hadn't thought so at the time. But looking back, she'd realized those words had just been encouragement from an adult to just convince her to *try*.

She'd thought she could do extraordinary things; she'd set out to do just that. Then came the one thing that seemed so simple.

In the end, it had been huge, an insurmountable wall, and although that wall needed to be scaled, she just wasn't strong enough to do it.

Instead of changing things, she'd ruined her life and the lives of how many others?

She couldn't even begin to count.

So she didn't try to change things in a big way anymore.

She focused on little things. If a guy needed food, she'd give him food. If somebody needed clothes, she'd find a way to give him clothes. More than once, she'd taken the shirt off her back—she always wore two around here, a T-shirt and a bigger outer shirt, a flannel in the winter, a work shirt in the summer. If she came out with fewer clothes than she left with? No big deal.

When she first started this new . . . life . . . if that was what she had to call it, somebody had told her, *Keep your head down. Don't cause trouble, don't look for it. Don't attract attention.*

So that was what she did now. She helped in small ways, because she hoped it might balance out the scale eventually. But she avoided trouble. She worked hard and she kept her head down.

It wasn't enough, but she tried to pretend it was.

She wasn't going to let anybody get hurt over her again.

But then the day came when she couldn't keep up her nonexistence. The day, boring as it was, started like any other. She could hear the rattle of the L outside her window, smell the scent of coffee, bread from a bakery down the street. Car horns beeping and she rolled over, stared up the window with a sigh.

It was never quiet in Chicago. She'd long since gotten accustomed to it, but she missed silence, even now. After a minute or two of lying there and letting her brain wake up, she rolled out of bed, hit the floor and headed to the bathroom.

Five minutes later, she was out the door and ready for her run.

It was miserable hot, even at six a.m., and she dodged the commuters, the people rushing to and from the subway. Businesswomen in pretty suits with sensible shoes they'd swap out later. Some brave souls already wore their toothpick heels even to navigate the streets of Chicago, and that always made her smirk a little.

She was more at home in her boots and tennis shoes, but some of those heels did fill her with a wistful sort of envy, made her remember a time when she'd had a small—very small—hoard of pretty clothes. She'd had to bust her tail to get them, but she'd cherished them that much more. She'd loved just being a girl, pairing this shirt with that skirt, messing with her hair, playing with makeup, spending a ridiculous amount of time in the bathroom as she got ready for the day.

These women reminded her of who she might have become. Their sharply cut suits, the way they moved through life. They had a sense of purpose.

She envied it.

She had no purpose anymore. She hadn't had purpose in far longer than she cared to think about. No purpose, no goals. No goals, other than maintaining the status quo.

You can't worry about him now. You need to rest up, heal.

Those words echoed in her mind, even now.

She wished she could banish that voice.

Wished she could just silence it, forever.

But that wasn't going to happen, and she knew it.

While memories chased her, she ran, her feet pounding the pavement, her breathing sawing in and out of her lungs.

She consoled herself with the knowledge that the monster responsible for *all* of this was dead and the evil he'd spawned had also died. It wasn't good enough and it didn't undo what he'd done.

It wasn't much, but it was all she had.

The memories still haunted her and her impotence, her fear, chased her, choked her.

So she ran harder.

That was part of her routine, too.

Life was just routine, and it had been for a good long time.

Her routine crashed to a halt that hot, muggy day.

It was at precisely 7:42. Eighteen minutes before she was supposed to be downstairs, when she took over the store.

Her life went straight to hell . . . all because of a Google alert.

Clifty Drive.

The words jumped out at her, quick as a snake.

She knew that name. She'd tailored this search down to catch only the things she needed.

And this was something needed.

It was an announcement in the paper. A small paper, from a town in southern Indiana. A place so small, most people had never heard of it.

She had, though.

The announcement was short, simple and to the point.

All about a house, one that had sat empty for years.

And now it wasn't.

Somebody had bought the damn thing.

Leaning back in her chair, she rubbed her hands over her face and tried not to panic.

Somebody had bought the old Frampton place.

That didn't have to mean anything . . . did it?

CHAPTER TWO

As it turned out, it meant everything.

She didn't realize it until later.

Several weeks later.

Part of her had already been prepared. She had money stashed. No bank accounts. She hadn't had one of those in decades. But she did have money, some saved, and then there were people who owed her. Those who could pay she tried to collect.

The people in her life she cared about, she made sure she visited them, one more time.

She'd learned the value of that. The hard way. You never knew just when might be the last time you got to see somebody you cared for. The final memories should be good ones.

She didn't let herself admit she was saying good-bye.

Not at the time.

But deep inside, she knew what she doing.

Then the day came when she read about the discovery that rocked the little town.

A body, discovered in a cellar, in that small town on the Ohio River.

In a city like Chicago, the discovery of a corpse wouldn't even make most of them blink or pause for more than a second. Some might murmur about what a waste, might wonder who the victim was, but it wouldn't slow life down, not a bit.

It would bring the little town of Madison to a halt.

She haunted the website for the town newspaper, day in and day out. Had a few messed-up moments when she was skimming the archives and discovered an article about a body found in a submerged car that had been pulled out of the river.

Who—

But then she made herself stop.

Don't, she cautioned herself. The body had been in the river for years, but she wouldn't let herself think negative things. *You can't think it. If you think it, you might make it happen.*

Once, she hadn't believed in such a thing. Paranoia had been something she would not let herself dwell on. She'd always believed that if she just pushed hard enough and did the right thing it would make a difference.

She'd been wrong.

Bad shit happened and nothing she did or said could stop it, and sometimes that bad shit just kept right on rolling.

And this was that bad shit, in force. It was like dominos. One thing after another happened.

The body in the river, the one in the cellar, the fire . . . and then the arrests.

She'd read about *those* with a mix of horror, despair and rage, her hands shaking, her vision blurring to red, while part of her wanted to rage and shove the computer to the floor.

No. No. No. This wasn't happening—

Except it was.

That was when she understood.

She couldn't hide anymore.

It didn't *matter* if she stopped thinking about the bad shit, because the bad shit had never stopped and she'd been up here, blissfully unaware, while monsters continued to exist.

You'd promised me, she thought, half-desperate as she read through the article, reading the disbelief in the reporter's words even as he tried to be objective:

Years of rape and abuse . . .
Going back for generations . . .

She dropped her head into her hands as darkness crowded in on her.

She barely remembered anything from that night so many years ago. All of her memories came from after, nearly two days later while she was recovering, her head aching from a concussion that had left her with headaches that haunted her for months. There was also shock, from her injuries, from what she'd seen, what they'd had to do.

Memories of blood, pain and screaming had taunted her.

And when she came out of the darkness, all she'd heard was a voice.

I know you're still healing up, but it's not safe here. You have to go.

That low, steady voice, so full of certainty and so steady, as she tried to argue. *Go?*

No, what she needed to do was *find* him. Had to help.

It's too late to help now. You can't. And if you stay, you'll be in trouble. You didn't do anything wrong . . . you just tried to help. But nobody will believe that—

Setting her jaw, she pushed all of that aside and continued to read, hoping that somehow the words on the screen would change.

But they didn't.

*The depravity appears to go back some fifty years,
spanning across generations. The Cronus Club, as
reports have called it, allegedly consists of several
well-known families, all men, and their sons are
inducted into the club through acts of sodomy and
sexual molestation that start in their early teens and
last for three years—*

That was all she read before the need to puke hit her.
Hard and fast.

She bolted for the bathroom and emptied her belly.

Heart racing, head pounding, the violent spasms racked
her body for endless minutes, but she didn't mind—she
almost welcomed it.

The Cronus Club.

Son of a bitch.

It hadn't stopped.

Everything she'd left, everything she'd walked away
from—her father, her friends, her *home*—it had all been
because she thought they'd managed to *stop* it. That one
good thing had come out of that night.

And it had been *worth* it. Even the nightmares, vague
bits of memory that she would never fully recover, all
those faded bits and pieces of a night she'd never understood. Even the misery of the next few years, when she'd
lost herself, *that* had been worth it.

It had all been a trade-off, a lousy one, but in the end
a trade-off she could live with because it had stopped.

Only . . .

She closed her eyes.

"We didn't stop anything," she whispered, her voice a
stark echo in the small bathroom.

She didn't get it. The men who'd abused David were
dead. She knew that.

A string of accidents had befallen them in the years since

she left Madison. She'd tracked their deaths, watching the newspapers over the ass-backwards Internet, tracking things down in a way that would have done Lois Lane proud.

They were *dead*.

So how had this started again?

"Look at the facts," she told herself, her voice hoarse. Her mind worked furiously, though, processing the information she had to work with.

Apparently David hadn't known all of the men involved. Her head pulsed, pounded with that information. *Fuck,* how many of them could there be? It wasn't like Madison was that big. There couldn't be *that* many people who'd been involved in this, could there?

In the end, the only thing that mattered was that they hadn't gotten everybody. The one thing that had kept her sane all this time, and it was a lie.

Sweat broke out over her forehead as she hunched over the sink, washing her hands, rinsing out her mouth.

It took every last bit of will she had to force herself to go back to the desk and sit. It took even more strength than she thought she had to focus on the monitor and make herself read. Almost desperate for something to cling to, she fished out the key she wore around her neck and gripped it, the rough edges biting into her palm as she made it through once, then a second time, then a third, reading between the lines all the things that hadn't been said.

Then she leaned back and rubbed her hands down her face, swallowing the bile rising up her throat.

Hiding was no longer an option.

Lana Rossi was going back home.

Damn it to hell and back.

"Damn. You mean I get to just *stay* here?" The guy staring at her looked like he'd been given the keys to the kingdom.

She smiled at him from the mirror as she wrapped a band around the end of her ponytail. Already a few strays of her hair had worked free, wispy brown strands coming loose to frame her face. She needed to decide what to do about her hair, she thought. She'd started dying it brown not long after she'd left Madison—the vivid red curls were just too noticeable. Did she stop coloring it now? Keep it up? She didn't know.

What was she going to do with her clothes?

Too many decisions to make, not enough time.

And the man across from her just continued to watch her with confusion in his eyes. She forced herself to smile, remembering how she'd felt when Deatrick had shown her this place.

"Yeah, you get to stay here, Jock . . . but not *just*," she said quietly. "I talked to Deatrick down at the store downstairs. You have a job waiting. It won't pay you a lot, but it will keep you in food and the rent is part of your wages."

Jock blinked and then shook his head, backing away. "No . . . no, ma'am. Ain't no place going to hire me. I'm a fucking junkie and—"

She turned around and caught his arm before he could vacate the premises. "So was I."

Shoving up the sleeves to her shirt, she bared her forearms and showed him the needlemarks on her arms. Fourteen years ago, she'd been one of the ones living not too differently from Jock. Deatrick had been her knight in shining armor, dragging her out of the streets when she'd tried to pick his pockets. The asshole hadn't called the cops when he'd caught her, either.

He'd dragged her kicking and screaming back here. Fed her. Told her the next meal wouldn't be free, but she could have a meal any time she wanted . . . *if* she'd work for it.

A week later, she'd come back. He'd made her scrub

the damn toilets. Then he'd fed her chicken and dumplings.

Four days later, he had her mopping up the stockroom in the little convenience store he ran with his parents. He'd fed her beef stew that night.

The pattern kept up for over a month and then one night, instead of feeding her, he'd brought her up here and shown her this little apartment. It had been his, but she didn't know it at the time. *You need a job,* he'd told her. *I need somebody to help out in the store when my folks retire. You can have the job if you'll get clean. You have a month and I've got friends who'll help you.* Then he'd told her if she used, even once, after that month, he'd kick her ass out and never feed her again. If she ever stole from him, he'd turn her in.

He didn't know it—or maybe he did—but she'd been chasing her death almost ever since she ran away from Madison.

Guilt, the memories she couldn't uncover, the nightmares, it all plagued her and one night, when the dreams got to be too much, she'd given in and accepted a pill from a guy she'd been flopping with. She'd woken up with him inside her, and instead of freaking out and pushing him away she'd clung to him because she hadn't been alone and the pills made her not care about anything else.

It didn't get any better from there, and the guilt, the shame, all of it, piled up and she couldn't outrun that any better than the memories.

She thought of Noah, the boy she'd left behind, the boy who'd loved and valued her, and how she'd never be able to look at him after what she'd done . . . and it only made it worse.

She'd been spiraling down, so hard and fast, and the spiral lasted for years.

It was a miracle she hadn't ended up dead or sick.

And if her spiral hadn't crashed her into Deatrick, she probably would have ended up dead, sick . . . or worse.

He'd probably saved her life.

He'd definitely saved her soul, and for that she could never repay him. He'd given her a lifeline when he offered her that job. Now it was time to pass that lifeline on to somebody else.

Under the scruff and the street dirt and the punches life had thrown at him, Jock was a good guy. He'd take this chance and make something of it. She knew he would.

Right now, he was staring at the scars on her arms with something like shock, though. Then it moved to sympathy as he shifted his gaze to her face.

"You're sick, aren't you? That's why you're leaving."

"No." Man, if *that* was the burden she carried, she'd almost be ready to shoulder it. At least then it would only be her life she'd screwed up. She'd almost be up for that. Instead she had this one. *How many lives—* She pushed the thought aside, stared at Jock. *Brood later.* This had to come first. She didn't leave things undone. Not anymore. "I'm not sick. Got lucky on that front. Only used the needle a few times; the tracks got infected and I had a bad trip. Decided pills were better."

She usually chased those pills with alcohol, ended it all up with sex. Sometimes not necessarily in that order. It didn't matter as long as she got out of her head for a while. But the needles . . . no. She hadn't been able to keep up with the needles, and after those first few guys she made everybody she slept with use a rubber, too.

She was looking for oblivion or death, but after she'd seen some sad souls wasting away from AIDS or other diseases, she decided that wasn't the best way to die. If she needed death that bad, she could jump into the river. It would be a lot quicker and less painful in the long run.

While he continued to stare at her, his gaze considering, curious, she tugged her sleeves back down.

"You know the guy downstairs who runs the store?" she asked.

"Yeah. Your boyfriend. He's a bruiser."

She smiled, a little sadly. Deatrick wasn't her boyfriend. For a while, she'd thought maybe she was in love with him, and for a very short while, they'd been lovers. But Deatrick liked fixing broken people, and once he'd helped fix her, she'd lost her appeal for him.

Even as the thought circled through her head, she felt ashamed. That wasn't fair to him. The man had saved her life. If he hadn't pulled her off the streets, she might not be dead, but she definitely wouldn't be somebody who could stand to look at herself in the mirror.

"He's not my boyfriend." She shrugged and moved over to the beat-up couch. Dark hair fell into her eyes and she shoved it back as the broken-in cushions closed around her. The couch was about the best thing in this place. Her one contribution to this sad, safe little haven. Absently she tugged out the necklace she wore. Deatrick had given it to her all those years ago, back when she was still trying to find her feet. Find herself. She was still looking.

He had more faith in her than she did. Sighing, she rubbed her thumb over the message written on it. It had only one word. *Strength*.

You always had the strength to survive, sugar, Deatrick had told her when he gave it to her. *Don't forget that.*

Stroking the chain between her fingers, she studied Jock. He'd been a vet, served back in Desert Storm in the nineties. She knew that, knew his wife had cheated on him, gotten pregnant while he was risking his life, and when he came back she welcomed him home with divorce papers. He'd tried, he told Lana. Had tried hard.

But the job he'd landed dried up after a year.

There had been another one, but problems with post-traumatic stress started creeping in and the nightmares . . . He'd started self-medicating with drugs.

Compared to him, Lana's nightmares were like a walk in the park, but she'd done the same thing. She understood just how tempting it was to self-medicate, to hide away in a fog of drunkenness or pills, how easy it was to silence the dreams when they screamed and raged.

But then it got to where the dreams screamed even louder and the blood shone redder and one pill wasn't enough; then two weren't.

Aware that Jock still watched her, she crooked a smile in his direction, her memory winding back down the road that had led her here. "Fourteen years ago, I tried to pick D.'s pocket."

"Girl, that was a damn stupid thing to do."

"Actually, it was the best mistake I ever made." She looked down and studied the key, remembered. She'd seen the guy around. Deatrick was big, standing at six two, skin a deep, warm brown and black hair that he shaved every week on Thursdays. She'd seen him, judged him as a sap because he was always going around and handing out food to people on the corner. A sap with money, too, because she saw in the paper that he'd won some serious cash in the Lotto.

So she'd watched him.

Waited until she had an idea when he'd make his daily trip to the bank with the money from the store.

She'd bumped into him, had her fingers on the money pouch. Then he had one big hand clamped around the back of her neck.

Was wondering when you were going to try it, sugar, he'd said, and his voice was sad.

She'd been so scared when he dragged her off the street

and into the store, through a back door, though, not the front one, where people might see.

"He caught me," she told Jock. "I wasn't as clever as I thought and he was much *more* clever than I'd realized. He caught me and dragged me into the shop. You can probably figure out what I thought he was going to do. Instead, he dumped me at the big table in the back. You know the one. You've eaten there a few times."

Jock looked down, plucking at a ragged hole in his jeans.

"He gave me one meal. Just like I gave you. After that, everything he gave me, I had to work for . . . just like you have. And now you're getting the chance he gave me." As his eyes jerked up to meet hers, she said quietly, "He'll give you one month to get clean. That's what he gave me. One month, Jock. He's got friends who can help you through it. After one month, if you use, you're out. And he'll know. Deatrick always does. If you use, you're gone. If you steal—"

"I'm not a thief," Jock said quietly, and the pride in his voice was unmistakable.

She smiled at him. "Then you're already doing better than I was."

Standing, she reached into her pocket and held out the keys that Deatrick had given her all those years ago. "So it's your call. Do you want the chance he gave me?"

"What's the catch?" Jock watched her suspiciously.

"There isn't one," she said honestly. The weight on her shoulders felt a little lighter as she saw the glimmer of what might be hope in his eyes. *A difference,* Lana thought. It wasn't saving the world, but she could still make a difference. It was the only thing that kept her sane sometimes.

"It's possible one day you'll have to leave—or you'll want to." She looked around, fought the sting in her eyes as she rose and moved over to stare out the window at the bustling life of the city. The noise of the L filled the room and she rested her head on the window, listened to it one more time. "If you leave, you can maybe find somebody to pass this on to, like I am. Or you can let Deatrick do it. He's good at it. The only thing you have to do is work for what's being given to you."

Jock took the keys, his eyes lingering on her. "Are you going to be okay?"

"Sure."

They both knew she lied. And they both smiled.

She walked out of the room with just the clothes she'd bought for herself over the years and the key hanging on a chain around her neck.

It was harder than she'd thought it would be.

And one of the hardest things was the first stop she had to make . . . saying good-bye to the man who'd pulled her out of hell.

CHAPTER THREE

"I'll tell ya what, Preach, that place is going to take a little more than a hammer and nails and a few more boards to fix it up."

Adam joined Noah Benningfield at the edge of the property and stared up at the house. For years, the people of Madison had just called this house the old Frampton place.

Generally, people avoided it. Unless you were a kid . . . then you might come out here on a dare. Or at least lie and pretend you had.

Plenty had lied, because they all knew if Judge Max had caught you hanging around this place he *would* call the cops, he *would* press charges and your parents would *not* be able to talk him out of it. Judge Max wasn't a bad guy, but he had a pretty straightforward sense of right and wrong. The *No Trespassing* signs were clear enough in his mind.

But then he'd managed to sell the house.

It wasn't much of a house now, though.

Adam rubbed his jaw, careful to avoid the burns along the right side of his face. They were healing, as were the ones on the outer part of his right arm. He'd received them when he tackled the boy who'd set the fire.

There was still a huge, gaping hole in the side of the house. Police tape surrounded the property. It had only been ten days since the explosion that could have killed Noah and his new fiancée.

If Adam thought about it for too long, he just might get sick. Easier to joke about it.

"I don't know." Noah slanted him a look, and there was a glint in his eyes that said he understood. He shrugged and reached up, scraping at the stubble that darkened his face. "I'm pretty good with a hammer and nails. I'll grab a few rolls of tape. Duct tape is always good."

They both laughed. It felt good to laugh.

They hadn't done enough of it the past few weeks, and that was a fact.

There wasn't going to be a whole lot of laughing in the near future, either. Not for Adam, not for Noah. Hell, most people in town had taken this like a punch to the face.

Every time Adam closed his eyes, he saw that fire. He closed his eyes and he remembered a chat between a couple of kids. . . . That fire had *led* to this. It could have been so much worse. Noah could be dead. Trinity could be dead. That kid of hers—funnier than hell and whip smart—he could be left without a mother. Yeah, it could be worse. But this was still pretty bad.

"The town is better off, I think," Adam said abruptly, folding his arms. The wind kicked up off the river, blowing his hair back from his face. He needed to get it cut, and he probably would remember . . . in another month or so. For now, he had his hands full, running short staffed at the bar, covering some extra nights at the forum while Noah dealt with everything he needed to do for a shotgun wedding.

"Yeah?"

As Noah looked over at him, Adam jerked his shoulder

up, tried not to let Noah look at him too closely. "Yeah. How much just downright *messed-up shit* has been tied to this house?" Adam lifted a hand and ticked the events off, one by one. "Frampton murders his wife, beats her to death with his own hands—that's been what, fifty or sixty years? Old Max probably put himself almost in the poorhouse trying to keep this place up and nothing ever came of it. Turns out those sick fucks were using this as their playground while they hurt kids." Rage boiled inside Adam, an ugly, nasty brew that made him want to hurt anything and everything. But he couldn't. If he gave in to that fury, he was going to lose himself; he knew it. He had come too close to that edge before. He couldn't go risk coming that close again. He might never come back. Hard to balance on that sort of precipice when there wasn't much on this side to hold him steady. Once the red had cleared from his vision, he continued. "This is the place where something happened to Lana. To that kid David. Maybe even his folks. We don't know. We'll never know. Maybe it's one of them that was found down under the floorboards, maybe not. Trinity moves in here and she has an absolutely *brilliant* start to her new life here in Madison, right?" He ticked off another finger. He couldn't quite wrap his mind around how awful it must have been, crashing through rotting floorboards and coming face-to-face with a dead body—the skeletal remains had been down there who knows how long.

Bile climbed up his throat as images tried to shove their way into his mind.

Lana . . . it's Lana. . . .

No. Absolutely no, and he wouldn't let himself think about it, either.

Forcing himself to go on, he said, "Then, after *all of that,* two kids nearly get themselves *and* you *and* Trinity killed. Yeah, the town is better off."

He kicked at the dirt. "We should tear it all down; that's what we should do."

A caustic voice added, "Salt the earth?"

Adam closed his eyes. *What the hell.* Sometimes he thought God was mocking him, throwing this guy in his path all the time. The man standing on the walk wore simple clothes—most of the Amish did. He had the typical ugly-ass haircut, although he hadn't grown out the beard that a lot of the men from that lifestyle did. Might be because he wasn't married. Adam thought the beard went with marriage but he wasn't sure. Apparently none of the women could tolerate the bastard. Which just showed how smart the ladies were.

Caine Yoder was nothing but a grade A asshole.

As he joined them, Adam bared his teeth in a mockery of a smile. "Nice seeing you here, Caine. Hey, it's Sunday. Don't you have church or something?"

From under the brim of his hat Caine studied Adam for a long minute. Then Caine looked at Noah and nodded. "I wanted to talk to you, see if they ever told you what happened."

"What happened?" Noah rubbed a thumb down his cheek. "Well. I was upstairs . . ." He pointed in the general direction. "And two kids outside decided to try and torch the place. They didn't know we were inside. That pretty much sums it up."

"Does anybody know why?"

Adam snorted and then turned, reaching in through the open window of his car. The car was his baby, the one and only thing he took pride in, a classic rebuilt '68 Corvette that had belonged to his dad. Adam had had to finish the restoration himself after his dad's death and it had taken him three years to even be able to *do* it, but it was done now and the car was his.

The morning paper was in the backseat. Grabbing

it, he shoved it toward Caine and then went back to staring at the house. "If you folks would actually *read* shit from time to time, you might know why, Caine," Adam said.

"Oh, we read."

Adam slid Caine a narrow look. Caine gave him a patient, polite smile, but his eyes seemed to say, *Fuck off.*

"Yeah? What have you ever read besides your Bible?"

"Well." Caine took his time, acting like he was thinking it over. "I like picture books. The ones with the really bright pictures and the cute little kids. And sometimes, I like mysteries. There's this one . . . with a bunny. All the vegetables in the house are mysteriously turning white. You ever read that one?"

Adam had been the butt of more than a few jokes in his life. He had no doubt it was happening again, but he had no idea just what Caine's game was. Adam opened his mouth to fire something back at Caine, but before he could Noah stepped between them.

"Enough." Then Noah nodded toward Caine. "Caine. Not sure what game you're playing, but Adam's head isn't a good one to screw with . . . he barely knows what *he* is doing half the time. There's no way he can explain anybody else's rationale, and you're not going to find the answers in the paper anyway."

Caine rolled up the paper and held it back out to Adam, all without looking at him. His gaze stayed locked on Noah. "How is Caleb?"

"Caleb . . ." Noah drew it out and then he blew out a breath. "Caleb is a mess."

"They aren't going to put him back with his family, are they?" Caine asked.

"No." Then Noah sighed. "And beyond that, I don't know anything more I can tell you."

Yeah, he did, Adam suspected.

But what Noah *knew* and what Noah could *say* were two different things.

Adam understood that feeling. There were things he knew . . . and couldn't say.

But he sure as hell would like to know just what secrets Noah harbored about that hellhouse. "Tear it down," Adam murmured. "It's not a bad plan."

"I think it's a fine plan," Caine said, his voice quiet. "I would even find the salt."

Noah looked at him, and then they both glanced at Caine. But that man was already moving off, in the direction of the ruined house.

You people.

It made him something of a hypocrite, Caine decided as he parked the truck. He could hear singing.

It had been years since he'd attended church with his family.

It got his back up, though, having a prick like Adam Brascum taking digs at the Yoders, or people like them, based on what he thought he knew. It was those digs, more than anything else, that had Caine here.

There were close to two dozen buggies gathered around the small, simple building. He had missed much of the service and he didn't really care. For some reason, he wanted to see Abraham.

Maybe it was a need to be in the man's calming, restful presence.

There had been *nothing* calming or restful in Caine's life for a good long while now, and the past few weeks it had been worse.

It wasn't even the fire.

Or what had happened after. . . .

His lids drooped as he moved through the bodies and settled at Abraham's side.

What happened after.

You don't belong here, a scathing voice said in the back of his mind. He ignored it and focused on the voices, on the familiarity and the peace of them. He wouldn't find God here, but he did find peace.

"You were late," Sarah Yoder said hours later, putting the plate of chicken down in front of him with more force than necessary.

He nodded and waited until Abraham had served himself before he filled his plate. "I'm sorry, Sarah."

Sarah was three years older than him. She looked like she had him by a decade, though. It wasn't the simple dress the Amish wore, and it wasn't the way she scraped her hair back from her face. It wasn't even the plainness of her features. When she'd been younger she'd been kind of pretty, he thought.

But Sarah scowled.

A lot.

She glared at people; she snarled. She never laughed and she preferred to accuse or threaten rather than ask or request.

All that bitterness weighed on her, and not in a nice way.

He had a mouth full of mashed potatoes when she said, "You need to leave Madison and come back home. It's an evil town, all the things happening back there. If you keep working there, being around those people, you'll be as evil as they are."

"Sarah," Abraham said quietly, catching his daughter's eye. "That's enough."

A mutinous look crossed her face. "You know what has taken place there. It's vile."

"That's enough," Abraham said, shaking his head. "I won't hear another word on it. I spend little time with Caine as it is."

A tense moment of silence passed and then Sarah left the room, thankfully taking some of the tension with her. As the back door slammed shut, Caine rubbed the back of his neck. "I didn't mean to ruin the day."

"You didn't." Abraham smiled, his worn, tired face softening. "I think Sarah is the unhappy one today, not you." The old man leaned back in his chair, his expression thoughtful. "You aren't particularly happy yourself, Caine. What troubles you?"

Sourly Caine laughed. "Life?"

He tore a chunk of meat from the chicken breast and popped into his mouth, chewed it without really tasting it as he stared outside. "I find myself wanting to do bad things lately," he murmured. He could trust Abraham. Caine's words would go no further, and the other man wouldn't judge him, either.

"The police are involved," Abraham murmured.

Caine shifted his gaze to Abraham and then shook his head. "Is it enough? Will they *believe* those boys?"

"You do."

Caine nodded. "Yes. I do."

Then he sighed and tossed the rest of the meat down on the plate. His appetite fading, he wiped his hands on a simple white napkin and leaned back in the chair. "Even if they arrest all the men involved, what good does it do? It doesn't undo the damage, does it? It goes too deep, goes back too far."

"Yes. But there is nothing *you* can do, either. Let God sort it out, son."

Caine shot him a look.

It was respect more than anything else that made Caine keep his mouth shut. But he'd stopped believing in *God* a long time ago.

* * *

It was the second time in the span of just a couple of months that they had to dig a vehicle out of the river.

That was pretty unusual even for a big city.

Madison, Indiana, was *not* a big city.

What was even more fucked up was the fact that this vehicle, just like the first one, had a body inside it.

This body, though, wasn't old.

Charlie Junior had been missing only a few weeks.

The last time he'd been seen was the morning he clocked out just after the big fire at the Frampton house.

His wife was currently on the bank of the river, half-drunk and clutching at her mother while they continued to work on the truck.

It was tricky business pulling a vehicle from a body of water.

If Chief Sorenson had his way, Missy Sutter would be removed from the area, and if she started screaming again she *would* be removed, whether she liked it or not. Damn the idiot who'd called her anyway. That was the problem with living in a town like Madison. Somebody had reported the truck and the call went out on the radio. Somebody had heard and given Missy a call—she'd gotten down here only a few minutes after the chief.

He didn't want to think about what might have happened if she'd gotten here *before*. She might have waded into the river herself.

As it was, she had done nothing but yell at them to hurry, to help Charlie.

She didn't understand her husband was past that kind of help.

Once she saw him . . . yeah. She was going to scream.

Sorenson knew what he was seeing.

Charlie was still behind the wheel of the truck. The fish had been having their way with him, although that wasn't

going to keep the medical examiner from finding out just what had put Charlie in the river.

Sorenson suspected there were no natural means involved. Charlie had been the fit sort. He didn't think Charlie had a heart attack, and the truck wasn't too messed up, so he didn't think there was a wreck involved, either. Nor did he think Charlie had decided to up and kill himself.

If Sorenson had to make a call, right then and there, he'd go with his gut and say somebody had helped Charlie find his way into the river.

Not that he'd make a judgment call like that.

Smart cops didn't do that sort of thing. He'd just say . . . *suspicious death,* because of course it was suspicious, seeing as how trucks don't naturally find themselves in the water like that.

Behind him, Missy started to shriek.

Sorenson lifted his eyes to the sky.

Please, Lord. Just give me patience.

He felt for the poor woman; he surely did.

But he'd tried to get her to leave. And she'd insisted she had a right to be here.

Now she was going to live with this image in her head.

"I shoulda listened."

Missy moaned it again, for the fifth time, over a cup of coffee.

The cops around her had taken the little flask she'd tucked inside her purse. She'd tried to pop Jensen Bell for doing it, insisting it was just a medicinal tea she used to steady her nerves.

Jensen had rolled her eyes while pouring the vodka out. "Medicinal tea . . . I've heard it all now," she'd muttered.

"Missy."

Missy looked up, her eyes dull as she stared at Jensen.

"Can you help us here?"

"I want Charlie," she whispered. "I want my Junior."

"I know," Jensen said, nodding. "I know. But we need you to help us help him now. Who could have done this?"

"Nobody." Missy reached for coffee and lifted it, her hands shaking. "Everybody loved him. He never hurt anybody and everybody loved him."

Over Missy's bent head, Sorenson met Jensen's eyes and then nodded.

If Jensen had any reservations at all, she never showed it. "Are you sure about that?"

Missy lifted her head. "What do you mean by that?"

"We have his name down as one of the participants in the Cronus Club."

Missy's face went white, then red. "I don't know what in the fuck that means."

Oh, yes, you do, Jensen thought, seeing the denial, the disgust, the confusion, all the emotion Missy tried to hide.

"It's a club, a boys' club of sorts . . . where the men meet up every month or so . . . and they rape their sons, trading them back and forth," Jensen said, pasting a vague smile on her face as she said it. Like she was discussing the weather or what she might wear to Shakers that night. *Yeah . . . this is just a thing here. Let's talk about it. . . .*

She saw Missy's hand and moved just in time.

The scalding coffee would have felt really nice.

"You crazy bitch!" Missy screeched. "You fucking *evil* bitch! My Charlie didn't do that. And those boys are just a bunch of fucking *liars*! If they say anybody *raped* them, they are wrong!"

CHAPTER FOUR

You know you'll have a place to come back to, if you ever need it.

Those words haunted her sleep.

Those words taunted her waking hours.

Even now, as she slowly walked down Main Street, Lana had thought about Deatrick's calm offer and part of her wanted, more than anything, to take off and run back to him. It would be so easy.

She didn't have to *be* here.

The cops were working the case now and it didn't look like they would turn away from it. Not *this* time. They'd turned a blind eye to it once, but Chief Sorenson didn't appear to be cut from the same cloth as Andrews. Sorenson was actually digging into things, arresting people. People would burn over this.

Did they *need* to know what had happened twenty years ago? How much could she tell them anyway? She didn't remember anything beyond trying to get David to leave. And she couldn't share his secrets—they were his to share. They wouldn't help, and none of it was admissible.

How could she help? Even if she *could*, did anybody even *care*?

She didn't know.

Her gut was in a tight, nasty knot just then and she eyed the lovely, elegant memorial erected in front of the Methodist church where Sutter had preached. That evil, manipulative bastard.

On Saturday nights, he met up with his boys' club.

Then on Sunday mornings, he'd stood before his faithful flock.

And this town honored him with a memorial.

They mourned his loss.

She reached out and traced the elegant scroll of David's name.

True enough, they mourned David, too.

But Peter Sutter shouldn't be memorialized.

She wanted to find something sharp enough, hard enough, to ruin the elegant lines of both his and Diane's name.

As far as Lana was concerned, the names of monsters should be wiped from the pages of history, and this town put this bastard up on a pedestal. If they had any idea the things he'd done, they'd probably bury their heads in the sand and refuse to believe it.

That was what people *did*.

Their idols fell, and instead of acknowledging it, they blamed the victims. A girl got assaulted by a couple of football stars and instead of blaming *them,* they pointed fingers at her. A powerful football coach systematically abused boys for decades, and instead of dealing with it, *stopping* it, people helped hide it.

The abusers were protected and sometimes revered . . . while victims were shunned, mocked or abused even further.

The rage she felt inside turned into a vicious scream. Everything, breathing, thinking, functioning, past that rage felt like a battle. And some part of her, that weak part, wanted to go back to the peace she'd known just a few weeks ago. Before she knew what was going on here.

Maybe *that* part of her understood. That part of her understood the apathy that let others turn a blind eye to evil.

It was so much easier to just look away.

Deatrick would let her come back. She could find another place to hide, another job. He'd help her.

But if she did it, she'd never be able to face herself again.

Turning her back on the memorial, she headed back to Main Street. She'd see it through this time.

She never should have left.

Injured or not, afraid or not, whether she even remembered what had happened, she should have stayed, and she should have fought.

Hooking a left, she headed down the street. Her belly rumbled as the scent of food caught her attention. She hadn't had much to eat and she was tired, hungry and ready to crash.

She had no place to sleep, although she'd been prepared for that.

First, though, she needed to get some food.

The last thing she'd eaten was a burger from McDonald's and that had been hours ago.

She'd hitchhiked her way from Louisville, clutching a sleek six-inch blade against her thigh the entire time in case the friendly-faced truck driver who'd given her a ride decided he wanted to do *more* than give her a ride.

She'd had to fight her way through that sort of thing, more than once. She'd probably have to do it again. That didn't make it any easier to think about, and she'd been glad once he left her off at the top of the hill. *I can't go through downtown. It's a mess and a half right now thanks to construction and I need to get this delivery made. . . . Can you make it okay?* He'd looked worried as he let her out.

She'd promised him she'd be fine and she'd breathed easier once he'd driven off.

He hadn't recognized her.

She knew his name.

That was Vernon Driscoll, and for a while in school he'd been a horrible bully. Something must have changed for him, because he'd been pretty polite there. He had a wedding ring on. Maybe it was that. Maybe it was just life. She didn't know. He'd been four years older than her, but even *she* had heard about what a jerk he'd been in school.

Of course, Madison was a small town. Word traveled pretty fast.

And he hadn't recognized her . . .

Or what if he had?

Now, even though it had been nearly an hour since he'd let her out of the cab of the truck, she was panicking. What if he had recognized her and that was why he'd let her out—

A cop car drove by and it took all of her nerve to keep from bolting down the street.

Instead, she calmly turned and walked in the door that had just opened.

It was loud and packed and rowdy and she could smell food.

If anybody *was* looking for her, she could lose herself in here and she'd eat, figure out her next move.

Keenly aware of the cop car still cruising on down Main Street, she made her way over to the bar and wedged herself onto the seat at the end, keeping the front door in her line of sight. She'd already noticed where the other exits were, where the bathroom was, and if memory served right—she'd check her GPS to be sure—she knew which route would be the best to take if she had to try and evade the cops.

It was sad that she had to think about this shit.

It was sad that she had to think about running.

It was sad that she'd spent the past twenty years of her life in hiding—

"What can I get you?"

Now that . . . that wasn't sad.

That voice was practically a wet dream, in and of itself. The man's low, lazy drawl stroked over her skin like rough velvet and she dragged her eyes up to meet a pair of dark, dark brown eyes.

Well, I can think of one thing. . . .

The punch of lust was visceral, unexpected. Heat rushed through her, centered low in her belly, as she sat there, wondering just how long it had been since she'd responded to a guy.

A while. A very long while.

A faint smile tugged the corners of his mouth. Such a nice mouth. She knew without a doubt he knew how to use that mouth. As the faint smile warmed just a little, she squeezed her thighs together and returned the smile, tried not to stare. If she stared, people might stare back, and that would get her noticed.

But oh, oh my . . . how she wanted to stare. Brown hair spilled into his eyes, silky and thick, the kind of hair a woman could fist her hands in as she pressed her mouth to his, or maybe as he kissed his way down her torso, lower. Her peripheral vision served her a little too well and she saw the black T-shirt, stretching across a solid pair of shoulders, perfectly sculpted. Just like the biceps visible under the short sleeves. And . . . wow. Tatts. He had tattoos going up and down both arms.

She'd like to study them. Instead, she forced herself to glance past him to the bar, keeping her tone distracted.

If she kept staring at him, like she wanted to, she'd be breaking one of her cardinal rules . . . attracting attention. And *here,* in Madison, of all places.

"I'll take a beer, whatever you have on tap." She'd drink it and hate it, but she knew she'd stand out if she didn't have something, since she'd wedged into one of the few spots at a crowded bar, and a cocktail would cost more.

He nodded and turned away, and she took advantage of the moment to study him from under her lashes. Probably a stupid move, because he made her mouth go dry. The face, the hands, the way he moved. She felt a hot little tug down in areas she'd been ignoring for way too long. As he put the beer in front of her, he leaned his elbows against the bar. "Looking for anything to eat tonight?"

Would it be really, really inappropriate to ask if he was on the menu?

Yes. Probably. So instead, she smiled again. "Hungry enough to eat a horse."

"We don't serve that here. . . . You'll have to settle for a burger or wings." He grinned and she felt a rush of warmth straight to her chest at that smile.

And he probably knew it.

Pieces clicked into place. That smile. That was all it took.

That smile had fueled her teenage dreams, right up until she tumbled straight into the arms of Noah Benningfield.

Son of a bitch—

She swallowed and had to fight the urge to bolt off the stool and take off. It was the last thing she could do, because drawing attention was bad. Very bad. And Adam would notice. Adam had always noticed everything.

Adam Brascum. Son of a *bitch,* why did she have to plunk her ass down in front of one of the very few people who just might recognize her, even after all this time?

His eyes roamed over her face and she took great care to look bored, uninterested. He'd always been a hellacious flirt, and if she gave him any sign he'd pick up on it. And she wouldn't be able to hide from him.

At the subtle shift in her attitude his brow went up and a faint smile crossed his face. She wanted to punch him. The need to hit him was gut-wrenching and she couldn't even understand why, but it was there. Instead of giving in to it, she just looked down at the menu he pushed in front of her. "Now that I think of it, horse doesn't sound all that appetizing anyway. I guess I'll just go with a burger."

She gave him a polite smile and handed him the menu, looking away.

You're dismissed, bye-bye now.

He read the message loud and clear. From the corner of her eye she could see how his expression changed, and she breathed a little easier as he tucked the menu away and rang up her meal.

The friendly smile stayed on his face, but she'd bet it was the same friendly smile he had given the guy sitting next to her. All business, it seemed.

She tried not to feel the sting.

She needed Adam not to notice her, so it was best if he wasn't flirting.

Flirting, not good.

She caught sight of the name emblazoned over the mirrored wall across the bar and she could have kicked herself. *Shakers. Shit. His parents' place.* She should have paid attention when she ducked inside, but she had been more focused on getting away from cops.

Although really, considering where she was and the size of the town, she was likely to see people she knew everywhere.

What she had to do was not react.

And eat her food, so she could get out of here without him figuring out who she was.

She had a mouth he wanted to taste.

Adam had thought maybe, just maybe, he could get over the month long self-enforced dry spell. Ever since he'd left Jez sleeping in her bed over at the B and B outside of town, he hadn't enjoyed a woman in weeks.

He wasn't going to include Layla.

Layla hadn't been about escape or release.

She'd been an . . . aberration.

That was all there was to it.

Yeah, he wouldn't have minded seeing just where things might have led with the pretty lady with the big eyes and that top-heavy mouth. That mouth. He was going to think about it more than once, but *thoughts* would have to suffice, because he'd gotten that message loud clear.

In the blink of an eye, she'd turned *hello, honey,* to *Get me a burger, kthxbai.*

Too bad, because standing next to her had done something to him that he hadn't felt in a good long while. She had a narrow, fox-like face, and those cute retro glasses made him think of sexy, wicked schoolteachers, and he'd just love to have a lesson or two from her . . . or give her the lessons.

But there wouldn't be any lessons. Nothing to be done for it.

Adam knew his way around women too well and he knew that look. It was entirely possible he could charm his way into her panties. He'd done that more than once, but the past few years he'd given it up. He'd rather walk away from a woman knowing she wasn't glaring daggers into his back, looking at him with disgust in her eyes.

He woke up and saw that look every time he looked in a mirror. So he'd rather leave the women with a smile.

A short time later, he served up the burger and chips and offered her another beer. She smiled, shook her head and went back to pretending nothing else in the world existed.

Except the door.

She hid it well, but she watched the door like she expected it to disappear. Oh, she wasn't overt about it. She just made sure nothing stayed between her and the escape route. It was a sort of readiness, like she knew she might have to bolt at any given second.

He'd been working here since he was sixteen, running the place for the past fifteen years, since his parents died in the accident when he was twenty-five. Adam could spot a drunk from a mile away and he knew when somebody was trying to make a drug deal in his place, when a fight was about ready to break out, and he knew when somebody was trying to hide.

That hiding thing was the easiest thing to spot, for him, at least.

He also knew how to hide. In plain sight, even. He didn't even know if anybody had ever seen past the mask he wore, but he knew the signs.

So he saw the signs on her well enough. Travis Nevins sat down next to her, an admiring look in his eyes, and he struck up a conversation, or tried to. She made the right sounds, nodded, and as soon as she could she ended it, and Travis, being no idiot, cut his losses and vacated the stool.

After he was gone, she shifted around so that she had her back to whoever might take the seat next.

Polite, subtle . . . *Leave me alone.*

Through it all, she watched the door.

When somebody cut in front of her and blocked her view, she changed her angle. And kept her watch on the door.

If she hadn't worked so hard to downplay it, Adam might not have even noticed. But she worked too hard to hide it, and that, in and of itself, made him notice.

Shakers was packed. That wasn't unusual. It was Friday; people were ready to blow steam. But the atmosphere in general was . . . tense. That was putting it mildly.

He knew why, too.

He'd caught the whisper of the name earlier.

Charlie Sutter, missing for a few weeks.

Not missing, now. Dead, in the river.

Dead how? Adam had overheard one of his servers asking the off-duty cop at the bar.

Beats the fuck out of me. The cop shrugged, but Adam had a glimpse of his flat eyes. Adam would bet the night's receipts that the man knew, all right. He just wasn't saying.

They had another corpse and it was hotter than hell outside.

All sorts of people were going to be edgy and pissed.

No wonder Adam had already had to break up two near fights. If he got through the night without calling the police, it would be a miracle. He wondered if the cop might be talked into hanging around awhile. Luther did enjoy his wings. Maybe a free order would do the trick.

A raised voice from the far end of the bar caught Adam's ears and he sighed. Every damn person had his tail in a twist tonight.

Adam didn't have to speculate about just what the problem was. It wasn't just the discovery of Charlie Sutter's body, either. It was more. A lot more.

That fucking club.

Somebody had pried the information out of somebody at the police department and given it to the local news. The *Cronus* Club. They couldn't call it the *I Rape Little Boys* Club.

His hand tightened on the neck of the bottle and Adam had to remind himself to calm down, pull back. Mixing up a hurricane for Hank's wife, Tina, Adam took that and the beer down to the end and put them in front of the couple, leaning against the bar and taking a minute while there was a brief lull. Hank smiled at him. Adam just nodded.

"You hear about Junior?" Hank asked, his eyes troubled. They'd spent some time working together when Junior had hired Hank to help with a side project a few years back.

Adam nodded.

"I . . ." Hank stared sightlessly at the wall in front of him. "I can't believe it. Just can't wrap my mind around it."

"Charlie. The Blue family." Tina rested her head against Hank's arm, dragging her finger through the condensation gathering on her glass. "I mean . . . I know Leah. She's kind of . . . uppity and weird, but I can't believe she knew what Glenn was doing to their son—"

"It's a bunch of bullshit."

Now Adam was used to that vehement protest. Used to it, fed up with it. But the last person he expected to hear it from was Rita Troyer. It caught him off-guard, so off-guard that he just stood there for a second as one of his best waitresses propped her tray on her hip and all but got into Tina's face and snarled. "It's *bullshit,*" Rita said again. "You hear me?"

"Rita," he said, shoving off the bar while, next to Hank, Tina's face went red and her eyes widened. She ducked her head and focused on the drink while Rita swung her head around and glared at Adam.

"That's enough," he said calmly. It was hard to keep your voice level and be heard without shouting in a place as loud as Shakers, but he had a lot of practice.

"I'm tired unto *death* of all this bullshit," she said,

glaring at him. Her eyes practically shot sparks as she looked back at Tina, her face pale save for two flags of color high on her cheeks.

Hank wrapped his arm around his wife's shoulders and shot Rita a dark look. "Back off, Rita. The conspiracy theory shit kind of goes to hell when even the guilty ones are confessing that it's true."

She opened her mouth to argue, but Adam caught her arm and bent his head. "If you want to still have a job here, you'll drop it."

The fury that darkened her eyes seemed to lift and she stopped, shaking her head. "What—" A sigh escaped her and she looked around, nodded. "Hell." Swiping a hand over her mouth, she glanced at Tina. "Sorry, Tina. All of this just cuts too close to home." Rita reached behind her and tugged at the strings on her apron. "I need to take my break."

As she lost herself in the crowd, Adam caught Buck's eye and jerked his head at the bar. While the other bartender nodded, Adam headed out. As he passed by, Luther looked at him and lifted his glass. Adam blew out a breath and the older cop's mouth curved in a smile as Adam continued after Rita.

Something was eating at her. If he wanted her in any condition to work, he needed to figure out what it was.

He found her outside with a cigarette, staring up at the sky.

"You want to talk?"

"No." She stared straight ahead. "I came out here to be alone."

"This ain't easy on none of us, sugar. Hurts the whole damn town." Uneasy tendrils curled through him, teasing his gut, making his hair stand on end. In the back of his head, he all but heard a voice going, *It's not over. It's not over. It's not over . . .*

Instead of saying anything, he waited. Rita wanted to talk. This was where they came when they wanted a word away from the club. If she'd wanted privacy, she would have gone to the roof, where he wouldn't go. That was what she always did.

Moments ticked by; the breeze kicked up, bringing with it the scent of the river, alcohol and food from the grill. He could hear the noise from the restaurant and the muted sounds of cars as they occasionally passed by.

And a shaky sigh from Rita.

Without moving his head, he shifted his eyes to her.

She had her head pressed to the wall, the cigarette hanging forgotten from her fingers as she stared off into the night, tears streaming silently down her cheeks.

"Rita?"

She turned her head and stared at him.

Pure hell shone in her eyes.

"My father," she said softly.

Tension slammed into Adam. He didn't let it show, but it was hard to stand there, relaxed, noncommittal, when he knew exactly where this was leading.

"Harlan?" He hooked his thumbs in his pockets, kept his voice easy. "Is he okay?"

She laughed bitterly. "Okay?" She lifted the cigarette, studied the glowing tip and then took a deep, deep drag. She blew out a smoke ring, watching as it dissipated in the air, tears still glittering on her cheeks. She didn't look back at him as she answered, "No, Adam. He's *not* okay. He's a sick, evil bastard. Always was, but I'm just now figuring all that out."

Muscles locked, tight, he stood there, staring at her as she lapsed into silence, puffing on the cigarette and then using the wall to put it out. After a minute, she looked back at him.

"He had this thing. When I was a kid. Did it less often

as I got older, as he got older. But he had his 'boys,' as he called it. He'd go and hang out with his boys once or twice a month. Pete Sutter disappeared and you'd think his entire world had shattered."

Closing one hand into a fist, Adam fought the rage as it built inside him. Rita continued to watch him, like she wanted him to just . . . *know*.

And he had to hear, as much as it sickened him, as much as he wanted to cut his ears off, cut out his brain. He had to hear and she had to tell him. And when it was done, he was going to do everything he could to convince her to call the cops.

"It was a guy thing, he'd always tell me. Sometimes I think he hated that I wasn't a boy, because he couldn't bring me into his little *club*," she said, her mouth twisting in an ugly snarl. "And I hated that I couldn't do it. Dad never spent much time with me and I never could understand it. I loved to hunt, fish. But did he ever take me hunting? Fishing? No. I learned it on my own. Mom never did get it. One year, for Christmas, there was a bow and arrow and I was so excited—I thought they finally *got* it. Turns out the bow and arrow set was from her folks. They got me better than my own parents did. Dad . . . he was never there. He spent so much time with that fucking club."

She dropped the butt of her cigarette into the garbage can Adam kept out there for employees and then just stood there, her hands slack, her eyes dead, her face empty. "He ignored me, you know. And focused his energy on them. He just loved helping those boys become men." Slowly, she lifted her head and stared at Adam. "They called it the Cronus Club."

"You look familiar."

Lana cocked her head and gave the man in front of her a puzzled smile. "Yeah? I get that a lot." She went to brush around him, heading to the bathroom, since he'd placed his very fine body between her and the side exit.

She needed to get out that exit door. Something fucked up was going on, but she couldn't risk catching a lot of attention when she did it. So the bathroom for now, and then she'd disappear after she got away from this guy.

"You from around here?"

She pushed the door open and paused, looking back at him. The light fell on his face just right and she realized she knew him. She didn't know how, but she knew him. He was younger than she was—probably in his late twenties or early thirties, so he would have been just a kid when she disappeared—but that didn't mean much. Giving him another one of those vague, puzzled smiles, she shook her head. "No. From Chicago. Just passing through." She kept her answer short and clipped, talking fast. Indiana might not be a southern state, but in a lot of the smaller towns, especially this far south, a lot of people tended to have a slower, lazy drawl. She'd have to make sure she didn't let that creep back into her voice.

His eyes were dark and shrewd on her face and he continued to study her. The weight of his gaze lingered on her as she disappeared through the bathroom door. Just before the door swung shut behind her, she heard somebody shout and the name had her wincing inwardly. "Hey, Tate!"

Shit.

Tate.

Was that Tate Bell?

Knowing her luck? It was entirely possible.

The age would be about right. The kid she'd babysat had been around nine or ten, she thought. Locking herself in a stall, she sighed.

She had shit luck.

That much was certain.

Shit luck.

The door swung open and a couple of women entered, their voices a fast, excited buzz.

"—you hear what Rita was saying? I couldn't hear for shit."

"I don't know. They were outside talking, then went into his office—"

Lana grimaced and moved over to the toilet so nobody came banging on the door, but it didn't seem like they were in there to use the bathroom any more than she was.

"Jensen's in there. She just showed up here with her brother and sister. Isn't she the one handling most of these abuse cases?"

"Abuse?" The second woman snorted. "This is *more* than abuse. Those boys were raped, for years. You don't think Rita's daddy was involved, do you? I mean, Harlan Troyer is like . . . hell, he's in his sixties. He's on the volunteer committee at the Methodist church and everything."

Blood started to pulse through Lana's head, roaring in her ears. *Harlan. Harlan Troyer.*

The articles she'd followed over the past few weeks started to flash through her mind and she recalled, in detail, everything she'd read.

Jensen. That would be Jensen Bell.

She was the cop in charge of the investigation. And, incidentally, Tate's sister.

Son of a bitch.

She had to get out of there.

The nausea grew, and grew, the guilt and misery taking huge bites out of her as she listened.

One of the women, her voice soft but full of disgust, said, "As long as this has probably been going on, can you believe *nobody* spoke up?"

Just one more nail in her own personal coffin, Lana thought dully, staring at the wall in front of her.

* * *

"It's best if you don't come back."

She stared at the blood that stained the clothes. She didn't remember. None of it. "I can't just leave. I have to make sure it stops."

"That will be taken care of, but you can't stay here any longer, and if you're here everything just gets worse."

Worse? She didn't see how that was possible.

"Does he think I should?"

Kind eyes watched her. "Who do you think is the one telling you to leave?" A neat stack of clothes was placed beside her. "There's another set of clothes. Money. It will last awhile if you're careful. You have to go. Now. But away from here. If you go back to town, you'll be arrested."

Her belly cramped. Arrested. Dazed, she shook her head. "I don't understand. Where's David? I want to talk to David."

She shoved the memories back, strapped down the guilt and pasted a blank expression on her face.

Lana had hid behind that blank mask for years.

She couldn't afford to let it slip now.

As she'd moved onto the sidewalk, she'd seen the unmarked cop car.

There was somebody sitting inside the car, too, so if Jensen Bell was in Adam's office that meant she'd put in a call for the unmarked.

Who knew what was going on inside Adam's office?

He was back behind the bar and hadn't even glanced at Lana as she came out of the restroom, casually placed herself behind a group of three other women. Before she slipped out the back, she lingered a moment, saw the way his gaze kept straying to the back hall. Watching. Waiting.

With nerves dancing along her spine, Lana kept her

pace unhurried and sauntered down Main Street like she hadn't a care in the world.

Tate had still been in Shakers when she left. Nobody seemed to notice her at all. She planned on keeping it that way. If anybody stopped her, she planned on lying through her teeth and saying she was staying at the inn just off Main. If anybody asked why, she'd elaborate further and say she was a journalist from a Webzine and her editor wanted some pictures of the town and a write-up on Madison and the weird shit going on. Then she'd get all nosy and intrusive.

It wouldn't endear her to people, but she'd already seen a van from a news channel in Louisville. Madison had turned into a treasure trove of secrets and no doubt the media would trip over themselves to find the *next* story.

If she had to stay hidden in plain sight while she figured out her next step, so be it.

CHAPTER FIVE

Jensen was still locked in Adam's office with Rita. He'd known she'd show up—the Bells had a regular table here on Friday nights and had for years. It was just a matter of getting Rita to *talk* to Jensen. But Rita had been more ready than he'd expected.

The rest of the Bells and their assorted partners were grouped at their table, tense, quiet. Waiting. They waited for Jensen. Adam waited for Rita. And even though he was wasting his time, he was sort of waiting for the woman who'd disappeared into the bathroom.

He had a feeling she'd already slipped out without him realizing it, though.

He'd been watching the doors and hadn't seen her leave.

She had, though. He'd bet his right nut on it.

That slow smile continued to tease him.

Adam wished he could figure out why.

It wasn't just because he wanted to taste that mouth.

He'd kissed more women than he could remember and he had taken a fair number to bed. If he ever stopped to count just how many, the number would probably leave him a little ashamed inside. Well, if he could find it in him to care. That wasn't likely to happen. The part of him that could feel shame was twisted up over things that mattered more than the fact that he couldn't keep his dick in his pants.

Agitated, he wiped the bar down with more force than needed, focused on filling the drink orders and keeping busy. And watching, just to make sure. Another twenty minutes passed before he acknowledged the fact that she had most definitely left.

It was another thirty minutes before he caught sight of Rita and Jensen in the hallway.

Rita joined him behind the bar, her face pale, but her hands were steady as she tied her apron back on.

"You want to head on home?" he asked, taking a tray of empties from Katie. They were past the busiest point of the evening, and even if they weren't, Rita's night had to suck.

"No." She gave him a wan smile. "Home is the last thing I need."

Her eyes had a haunted look.

Under his lashes he caught the sidelong looks coming their way, and he sighed. "You certain *this* is what you need tonight, sweetheart?"

A sad laugh escaped her.

"No. But being alone isn't the answer, either."

Two lousy hours passed before last call.

Shakers was almost empty, just a few stragglers here and there, and they left within a few minutes. As Adam locked up behind them, he wanted nothing more than to go home and just crash.

Not an option, though. Yet.

A headache pulsed behind his eyes, and as he took care of the cleanup his hands practically shook with the need for a drink.

It was nights like this when he knew he was a glutton for punishment.

An alcoholic who owned a bar was just a man begging for bad things.

Jaw clenched, he finished up and moved away from the siren call of booze. Money. He could deal with the money and be steady.

"That was a lot of fun."

Rita's voice was low and throaty—she had the voice of a porn star. Normally, all he had to do was guide his mind in that direction and he could be ready to do all sorts of dirty things with her.

She didn't have a memorable face—actually, she did. She had a long face, her mouth just a little too wide, her eyes a little too deep set, and her brow was too heavy. Rita wasn't particularly attractive, but she was a fucking fire in bed and most nights, when the demons were too strong, he'd be more than happy to let her chase those demons away. And he'd help chase hers away. He had no doubt the demons were going to be bad tonight.

A hand brushed down his spine and he glanced over as Rita leaned against him, her cheek against his arm. "I don't know about you, but I really don't want to be alone with myself tonight, Adam."

Guilt twisted inside him.

He didn't want to be alone with himself, either.

But he didn't want to go home with Rita.

He was a lousy miserable son of a bitch, too. Alone was the last thing she needed, and he understood that.

She was an unselfish lover and she gave all of herself in bed, asking nothing. Adam, however, asked for a hell of a lot, gave next to nothing, and sex was just a way to drive the demons from his mind. He didn't really even enjoy it anymore, but if it blanked out his mind and relaxed his body that was all he needed.

Rita knew his heart wasn't involved in anything.

That made it easier.

But as her hand rested low on his hip, he felt nothing. Not even the desire to lose himself with her.

He could bring himself to do it, though.

She'd had a lousy night.

She didn't need to be alone.

As she slid her hand down and cupped his through his jeans, Adam pressed his mouth to her neck.

Nothing.

Rita sighed and her hand fell away.

"Not tonight, huh?"

A vise gripped his throat and he reached up, skimmed his palm down her back. "I can come over for a little while. We can watch a movie." And he lied through his teeth as he bent over and pressed his mouth to her collarbone. "Maybe I'm just tired and you can wake me up."

She snorted, the sound full of cynicism and humor. "If you're that tired, you're probably close to dead. Nah, I'm probably lousy company anyway. I'll just go home, get wasted—" Then she grimaced. "Sorry. That's was stupid of me."

"Nah. It's human. After the day we've had, I feel like getting wasted myself. Your day was a lot worse than mine."

He eyed the bottles, gleaming like a rainbow behind the counter.

"Why do you do this?" she asked, her voice quiet. And he knew she knew. She could tell that it was on him again, the urge to reach for one of those bottles.

One drink . . . just one . . .

Yeah. Right.

"It's just what I do." He shrugged and turned away, finished up behind the bar. "Besides, it's a reminder."

Now that the bar was empty, he could name names, but he didn't have to.

Rita had been forced to pry the keys from Geoffrey

Potter earlier, a man who'd been a teacher at the school, once upon a time. A good one, too. Now he was lucky that he could hold a job at the Walmart, and if he got caught driving drunk one more time, he'd lose his license.

Another regular had stumbled out the door earlier. Eddie McKenna. Once Eddie had been so shit faced, he'd walked *into* the door and busted his head wide open. Old Eddie had started drinking after his wife decided she'd rather be with a lady from her book club. Not just discussing books, either. Only she didn't want a divorce. She liked the insurance, and since she wasn't going to marry her new girlfriend, why shouldn't she stay married? And then she moved her new girlfriend into the house where she lived with Eddie . . . into the bedroom, while Eddie was moved up into the bedroom they'd once planned to use as a room for the kids they'd never been able to have.

Eddie didn't have the balls to just file for divorce on his own, so he drowned his sorrows in the booze.

Adam understood all about that. He'd spent years drowning his sorrows and he'd have continued to do just that if he hadn't lost his parents. They wanted him sober. After they'd died in a car wreck, the one thing he could give them was that last wish. So he sobered up—going on fifteen years since he'd had a drink and damn if he still didn't have to fight it.

Those who had never had to fight that fight wouldn't understand. But Adam understood it, all too well. Instead of drowning himself in alcohol, he lost himself in work, in women and in a long, exhausting workout five or six days a week. He worked about sixty hours a week, and if he wasn't working he was very often running or pummeling a heavy bag . . . or fucking a woman.

What little free time he had aside from that was spent in front of a computer where he moderated, anonymously, a board for the kids here in Madison. Those who might, or already did, feel the urge to do the same stupid shit he had. Numb themselves with alcohol. Sometimes he felt like the world's biggest hypocrite, because if he hadn't lost his folks, he knew he'd still be burying himself in the bottle at the end of the day. Who was he to tell anybody to stay sober, that life didn't get any easier behind a haze of alcohol?

But then something happened.

He'd made a difference.

Finally.

After twenty years of being a miserable fuckup, he'd finally made a difference.

Yeah, mostly because Blue—

Blue.

Blue . . . that poor kid. Blue had been a hero that night. Too bad nobody had been around to save him. Just how bad things had gotten for Kevin Blue, Adam didn't know.

But Glenn Blue, his father, had been arrested. Bail had finally been granted, but after he'd tried to talk to his son it was revoked and Glenn was back in jail. *He ought to rot there.*

Him and the rest of the bastards.

Thanks to Blue's quick thinking, two lives had been saved a few weeks earlier and seven monsters were under investigation.

One was in the ground. Jeb. Monstrous, miserable excuse of a human being. Jeb Simms had worn a badge, pretended he was here to protect the people of this town, and look at what he'd done.

Then he'd put a bullet through his brain. Too easy, really.

But at least he was dead, dead and buried, just like the rest of them should be.

If Adam had his way, they'd all be in the ground.

"Knowing everything we know anymore . . ."

He caught the sad, bitter tone of Rita's voice and he looked up, forcing his own thoughts back to the present.

She wasn't looking at him, though. She stared out the window at the empty street; her slim fingers worried the necklace she wore. "I don't want to be here, Adam."

"Rita, if you need to take time off, just—"

"No." She shook her head, and finally she looked over at him. "I don't mean work. I just mean everything."

Her words sent a shiver down his spine. "Rita, come on now. . . ."

"No." She leaned in and pressed a kiss to the corner of his mouth. There'd been a time when that would have sent interest humming through him, even if it was just ingrained, like his body had been trained to react to a female. Now all he wanted to do was study her face, her eyes, make sure she wasn't planning to do something stupid. She moved away, though, evading him. With a smile, she shrugged. "I'll be all right, sugar. I'm just morbid these days. Too much going on. The talk with Jensen. Everything I had to tell her about my dad. I'm just depressed, I guess."

He closed the distance between them. "You come to me," he said, reaching up to cup her face. He knew what it was like, to swing so low, it seemed like you'd never climb out of the hole you were in. "You hear me? If things get too rough and you need to talk, you come to me."

She reached up and patted his cheek.

"Sure, Adam."

Sooner or later, he'd stop worrying about her, he told himself.

It was nearly three, and Adam had yet to reach that point.

His mind was still spinning and his muscles were bunches of coiled knots and he couldn't shut down.

It wasn't just Rita, though.

It was everything.

The fire.

That awful, terrible discovery when he'd learned what was going on with Blue and the others.

And Lana.

Always Lana.

Sometimes those memories were a scream in the back of his head.

Other times just a devil's whisper.

See . . . I saw what you did there. I remember, even if you try to forget. You had a chance, and you could have saved her. She called you, but because you were trying to be somebody you're not, you failed her. And look what happened—

His lips peeled back from his teeth in a snarl and that night spun through his head all over again.

". . . 's this . . ." Adam kept his face buried in the pillow, because he was almost positive it was a wrong number and he wasn't going to exert himself over that.

". . . help."

The voice, low and raw, cut through the fog of sleep. Slowly, he pulled the pillow off his head, his attention focusing on the voice, so faint, as she whispered his name: "Adam, are you there?"

He pulled the phone away from his ear and stared at it as he flopped over on his back and pinched the bridge of his nose.

"Lana?"

"Yes." Her voice, still shaking, came over the phone. For once, he didn't have to think about how her voice undid him. She was still just a kid, in school. Three years younger than him, in high school, and she had a boyfriend. . . . He had no business noticing her, but he did; he'd always noticed her even though he knew he shouldn't.

Then he'd thought maybe it wasn't so awful for him to

notice her. She was older. Seventeen wasn't really a kid anymore, right? He was twenty. It wasn't like he was looking to run off with her. Just ask her out, maybe. Except it wasn't going to happen now.

She went and found herself somebody else.

Noah, of all people. Straight and true Noah.

There wasn't anybody nicer than that boy, and while envy ate at Adam, she still called him up, chatted with him, like they were friends, just as they'd always been.

Trying not to let anything he felt show in his voice, he sighed. "Fuck, what time is it?"

If she'd had a fight with Noah, Adam was going to have blue balls again. All night. Because she'd want to come over, or meet somewhere, so she could curl up against him, not crying, just sitting there, where he could feel the warmth of her, the soft curve of her tits, smell her hair and her skin—

Fuck. He was going to have another one of those dreams, and the next time he saw her his dick would be hard as a rock.

"Adam, I need to talk to you," she whispered.

He shot a look at the clock, sitting up and hanging his legs over the edge of the bed. The bare wood was cool against his feet and he blew out a breath as he saw the digital clock. Midnight. Hell. *"Lana, it's already past twelve."*

"I . . ." Her voice quavered, steadied. "I know. I wanted to call Noah, but his parents would answer."

"And what's the problem there?" Adam asked, jealousy chewing through him. Noah. Yeah, that nice PK she was dating . . . that preacher's kid probably didn't think about the sort of things that Adam did. Noah treated her a hell of a lot better than Adam ever could, too. Would be able to do more for her. So why did Adam hate the thought of them together? Because he *loved her. Had always loved her.*

"I can't talk to anybody but Noah. I don't want his folks to know—" Her voice broke off, catching on a sob.

Worry started to burn in Adam.

Okay. *There was a problem here—a big one. He needed to yank his head out of his ass.* "Lana, what the hell is going on? Are you in trouble? You're not hurt or anything, are you?"

"Adam, I . . . I'm in trouble—"

There was another voice in the background, deep and low. A man's voice.

That worry turned into a full-scale alarm and then the phone went dead.

Shoving upright, Adam stared at it, his heart racing.

"Son of a bitch," he whispered.

Dashing the back of his hand over his mouth, he tried to think through the past few minutes, replay the conversation out in his head, stripping away what he *had been thinking, and focus on what* she *had said.*

Call the police, *he thought. That was what he needed to do. He'd call the police, then head over to her dad's place across the street. Jim Rossi didn't much like him—he had a feeling the old man knew Adam had a thing for his daughter—but something fucked up was going on.*

Reaching for the clothes he'd discarded, he replayed that conversation one last time.

She'd sounded—

"Scared," he whispered. Yeah. She sounded scared. *He mentally braced himself to make that phone call. She was going to be pissed, but he didn't care. If she was scared, there was a problem and Lana could hate him, but he'd do what he had to do to make sure she was okay.*

The phone started to ring before he could pick it up.

He didn't even have it to his ear when he heard her voice.

"Forget I called," Lana said, her voice cool and remote,

a thousand miles away from what it had been only a moment ago.

"What?"

"Just forget I called. Don't tell anybody and if you . . ." She stopped and sighed. "Look. I have to leave. I don't know when I'll be back. I may not be back. You're probably going to hear some things, see some things. Nothing you hear is going to be true, but I need your word you won't say anything about me calling tonight. No matter what."

"I don't think so," he bit off. Now the worry was a scream in his head and he clutched the phone so tight, it bit into his hand. "I think it's time you tell me what's going on, Lana."

"I can't." She laughed and the sound was unamused. "You know how you always told me that sooner or later, I'd bite off more than I could chew? Later has happened; now I have to deal with it. Don't tell anybody, Adam, not if we're friends. If anybody can lie about this, it's you. Hardly anybody even knows we're friends anymore except your folks. . . . I'm counting on you."

If anybody can lie—

He stumbled to a halt at the very edge of the sidewalk and bent over, his lungs burning, the muscles in his thighs quivering, and his heart felt like somebody had ripped it out and torn it to shreds.

Just how did a man live with the knowledge of that kind of secret inside him? For twenty years?

I'm in trouble. . . .

You're probably going to hear some things, see some things. Nothing you hear is going to be true. . . .

Not a whole hell of a lot had ever been *said* about Lana.

People speculated that she ran off.

People speculated she'd done something stupid, although *stupid* wasn't exactly Lana's style. Determined, full of bravado . . . sometimes misplaced. She'd been out to change the world.

Instead, she'd just disappeared and he'd quietly died a little inside, bit by bit, day by day, as he waited for her to come back.

She'd said she didn't know *when*. He'd took that to mean it would take a while.

He'd never expected that he wouldn't see her again. That she was gone . . . forever. She'd said she might not come back, but he hadn't really expected her to mean it.

Over the years, though, he'd realized that just might be the case and he had forced himself to live with it.

Realized that maybe, just maybe, she'd run off with David Sutter, thinking about how he'd seen the two of them that one time.

Lana and David . . . nah, it had never clicked.

But maybe Adam had read it wrong. Read *her* wrong, because he'd been so stupid-crazy over her. After all, if she was the woman he'd thought, she'd never have stayed away from Jim like she had.

And it was easier, really, to think about her out there somewhere with David. Or anybody else. Alone, even, than to think of her *gone*. For real gone. So Adam told himself that what was had happened, that she'd left with David, even though part of him knew better.

The discovery of the body under the Frampton house had just about torn him apart, and he had to keep that quiet misery buried inside.

But somebody had died. Somebody had *killed*.

She'd said she'd done something . . . that she had to leave.

Had *she* killed somebody? That alone was what kept Adam quiet. If she'd done something, hurt somebody, she'd done it for a reason, and he wasn't going to be the one to drive a nail in her coffin.

But fuck, this was killing him.

Who was it?

David's mother? Diane had never been worth shit, and if she was the one Lana had been trying to get David away *from* . . . she probably needed to die. There were worse scenarios, one that dug deep, ugly slashes into Adam's soul and made him want to destroy something, hurt something.

"Son of a bitch!" he snarled, spinning away from the river and driving the heels of his hands against his eyes. Images of blood danced across the back of his eyes like a stain.

He'd discounted *all* of it. Every damn thing, because Lana had asked him.

And now there was a body. A body . . . and worse. His gut told him there was more going on than just that body. Blue, Caleb. All of it connected to that house. That knowledge had festered inside Adam ever since he'd learned about Caleb and his connection to the Frampton place.

What if she *wasn't* out there somewhere? What if she hadn't been out there, trying to help David?

Could it be her?

What if somebody had forced her to lie to Adam on the phone, to mislead him, and he'd just let his one chance to help her slide by him?

Memories of that smile haunted him, that taunting, unintentionally seductive smile—even back then, she'd been like that. She'd just been a kid and maybe only three years had separated them, but it felt like a lifetime. He'd wanted to put his hands on her then, his mouth . . . but he'd waited. Because she was so much younger, and then he'd waited too long.

Now she was gone.

What if, instead of being off someplace doing God knows what for the past twenty years, she'd actually been *dead*?

A sob tried to rip its way out of Adam and he fought it down.

But that smile—

Memories of it teased him. Taunted him . . . that crazy-sexy smile, with its top-heavy upper lip and the way her eyes had that wicked glint.

He could call her smile from the back of his memory with practiced ease and all he had to do was just *think* of her.

And he did just that.

But when he closed his eyes and pulled her face to mind, he saw another one.

Dark hair, framing a thinner, narrower face. A pair of dark, sleek glasses perched on an upturned nose and grey eyes that he'd hadn't seen without eye shadow and mascara . . . at least not since she'd figured out how to put it on.

"Fuck," he whispered, staggering a few steps while his mind whirled and stumbled, merging to the images.

A huge, towering oak was there, and if he hadn't flung out a hand, he just might have fallen, face-first, down the short embankment, straight into the water.

She saw him running.

Lana didn't know if she should stay where she was or just grab her stuff and hope for the best, sneak away once he was out of sight.

If he'd just gone on the other way, she wouldn't have worried about it, but then he came to a stop at the river and stood there, first bent over like he had to catch his breath.

Then, slowly straightened and she'd thought he'd leave.

She couldn't see him from this far away, but she had a bad feeling she knew who it was.

He'd sent her too many measuring looks while she'd been in the bar and now—

Abruptly everything about him changed and she caught her breath as he took off running, yet again.

But this time, he was running right toward *her*.

Oh, fuck.

He couldn't see her, could he?

She didn't have a fire.

She'd found a strange sort of shelter, a pretty little gazebo that had tugged at something deep inside, and the flowers planted around it had pulled at her heart. Knockout roses, baby's breath and daisies bloomed in a chaotic rush of color, making her think of the flowers she'd planted around her dad's house. She hadn't had a lot of money to do it, but those flowers had been cheap and easy to maintain, so that was what she'd gone with.

Now, hidden by the panels of the gazebo, breathing in the air perfumed by the roses, she stared at the sleek form as he pounded the pavement. Barely daring to breathe, she waited.

He'd go by.

Right?

He'd go by and she'd have to make sure she stayed out of his way while she figured out the next step. The pain in her head increased as he barreled past her, not even looking her way.

She couldn't even explain why she did it.

Rising to her feet, the sleeping bag puddled around her, she crossed her arms over her chest and said his name.

"Hello, Adam."

He was twenty, thirty feet away and moving—

He stumbled to a stop and swung around, his eyes unerringly seeking her out in the shadows. She couldn't see his face clearly, not in the velvety darkness, but she could feel that gaze raking over her.

Her heart lunged up into her throat as he came back, not

running this time but moving awful damn fast. She tensed, ready to jerk away, as he stopped just a breath away.

His chest was heaving, moving in ragged, uneven bursts, but she had a feeling like it had nothing to do with his run. Her belly clenched, almost painfully, as a rush of need tore through her. Insane. Absolutely insane. Not here. Not with this man. Nothing could happen here—

He lifted a hand.

A gasp locked itself inside her throat, her eyes cutting to his hand.

There was a time when she'd loved to be touched. She'd bounced into her dad's workshop to wrap her arms around him while he worked, had climbed into his lap even when she was too old to do it. She'd hugged her teachers, hugged her friends, hugged strangers because they said something kind. Adam, how she'd fling herself at him whenever she saw him, happy just to see him, wrap her arms around him until he hugged her back, even if it was just to get her to leave him alone.

And Noah . . . she'd loved to touch Noah.

But in the past twenty years, she'd learned that a touch wasn't always a kindness. Sometimes a touch was a cruelty. Sometimes a punishment was as simple as taking a touch *away*. That had been her own self-inflicted punishment . . . stripping herself away from the comforts she'd once taken for granted.

Twenty years of that changed a person, and she was no longer the girl she'd been, was not the woman she might have become.

But as Adam lifted a hand and pulled her glasses off, she held still.

"Son of a bitch," he said, his voice flat.

Unwelcoming.

Then he shoved the glasses back at her.

"Welcome home, Lana. Thanks for letting me know you were still alive."

The confusion on her face pricked at his consciousness.

The sleeping bag on the ground grated at him.

And he wanted to grab her and pull her against him and rub his face against her neck, bury his hands in her hair and do everything he'd never been able to do.

So much for hoping he'd outgrow it.

Relief, need, confusion and anger, they all combined to form a superstorm inside him, and he didn't know if he wanted to laugh or scream, cry and rage. One thing he *did* want, and wanted bad, was to grab her and strip her naked. The floor of the gazebo would work. She was slender, her body sleek with slight curves, and he had no business pounding her into the unforgiving wooden floor. That was okay, though. He could be on the bottom and she could take him instead.

His dick was hard as a pike and he wanted nothing more than to do just that. Touch. Take.

Finally.

Not in dreams and not in fantasies.

But for *real*.

Maybe then he'd believe what he saw in front him—he could believe she was real, that she was alive, that he wasn't hallucinating or dreaming.

It wasn't exactly the socially acceptable thing, though, and she wasn't looking at him like she'd welcome that approach, either, so he lashed everything down and got it under control. Or he tried. Putting a few feet between them, he tried to think. Gaze locked on the night-dark river, he let himself actually think it.

Lana was here.

She was *here*.

Alive.

Lana was *alive*.

He sucked in a desperate breath and waited until he knew he could speak in a normal voice. Then he turned to look at her. His foot caught on the sleeping bag, the material rustling.

That just jacked up his anger and some of it spilled out in a snarl. "Why are you sleeping out here?"

"I don't have much of any place else to sleep," she said, lifting a brow. She tucked her hands into her back pockets and looked around. "It's not as bad as some might think. Weather is decent. It's quiet. I'll be up before dawn so nobody can complain."

Fury punched a hot fist through his gut and then twisted. But he managed a somewhat neutral voice himself as he said, "Sounds like you might have done this a time or two."

"Sounds like." She angled her head, studying him. She still held the glasses he'd taken from her, not bothering to put them on.

"You need those glasses or you just hiding behind them?"

She smiled, but it was a caustic, bitter thing. "It's not so much hiding as just . . . distracting. Makes things a lot easier."

"A pair of glasses won't distract anybody for too long." He looked over his shoulder, staring at the dark, quiet town. The occasional car ambled by on Main Street, some blocks back, but other than the traffic down the main strip, most of the town slept. And waited. "You have no idea what's been going on around here, sugar. You'd be better off just leaving. Showing up now, with everything that's going on, is just asking to get caught up in it."

"Adam."

Slowly, he turned his head. The words carried a heavy, tired weight and her eyes were somber when she looked at him. "I am caught up in it. . . . This is why I came back."

Prick.

Layla Chalmers leaned against the crumbling brick wall and watched Adam as he hung a left on Main Street with some chick. The woman had a bag slung over one shoulder, dark hair that hung in a fat braid halfway down her back, and the one glimpse Layla had gotten of her face revealed a pair of glasses.

She was pretty.

That smart/sexy kind of pretty that Layla despised. Guys seemed to dig that kind of look. Layla didn't see why. Uppity bitches like that always thought they were *better* than everybody else. Whatever.

Of course, there was Adam, unable to peel his eyes away from her. He'd probably have his dick buried inside her within thirty minutes. If that. Not like he was particularly discriminating. He'd banged everybody from Rita to that gossipy bitch Meg over at the salon. She was in her fifties for fuck's sake.

He'd fuck that dried-up hag, but he jerked away from Layla like she had a disease.

Hypocrite.

Adam had years lost in a bottle but thought he could get self-righteous on her just because she liked to get high every now and then. It wasn't like she'd been doing it on the job. She hadn't even been using when they were fucking. She just kept it on hand when she was around her sister, because *nobody* could be straight around Sybil.

"Uptight bitch," Layla muttered.

It was Sybil's fault, really. All of this. If she hadn't come in and woken Adam up a few weeks back, Layla would have been up and moving, able to get those pills stashed away before Adam noticed.

Now she was out of work, about to get kicked out of her apartment, which meant she'd have to go back to living in that house with Sybil . . . and the kid. The kid.

Because it hurt to think about Drew and the disappointment Layla always saw in his eyes, she chose not to. Turning away from the vague shadows that were Adam and his current fuck buddy, she started down the street, tottering on her heels as she made her way to the apartment she was renting from Bo Grady. She had to pay the rent in another week.

She'd find a way to come up with the money somehow. She didn't know how, but she always figured it out.

A familiar rusty laugh caught her ears and she eased into the shadows as Rita Troyer came around the corner.

Rita. Horse-faced Rita.

Adam's favorite fuck buddy . . . and she wasn't alone tonight, either.

The wide-brimmed hat hid his face, but Layla knew those shoulders, knew the way he walked.

Caine . . .

She smiled a little as a tug of heat arrowed straight down her middle to lick at her core.

Caine was one of those boys she'd just never been able to catch. Nothing made her more determined than that. She'd get him, sooner or later. She'd figured out his poison. She'd already tumbled that sweet kid who followed around in his footsteps—Thomas. He blushed now every time he saw her, but Tommy didn't need to worry about her. She'd gotten what she wanted and now he'd have a few things to show whatever sweet little Amish girl he married.

Laya would figure out what button to push with Caine. Sooner or later. Just like she had with Adam. Catch Adam on a day when he was so tired, he could barely see straight. Get him mad. Talk dirty. Anger could flip to lust damn fast, especially once she had her hand on his cock.

Nobody could make a man burn hot like she could. All she had to do was find Caine's switch. But right now he was guiding Rita down the street to her pretty little white house with the neat little picket fence.

He wasn't into *Rita,* too, was he? Layla's gut burned, even thinking about. It was bad enough seeing the way Adam and Rita were in the back room at Shakers, but now, as Layla saw Caine tip his head down to talk to the other woman, something cold and small ripped through her.

It might have been a stab of rejection, but she wouldn't let herself acknowledge it as she continued to watch them. Rita leaned, drunkenly, against Caine, and while her voice was loud and raucous, Caine's was low and steady, too quiet for Layla to follow.

A few moments later, they were inside the house.

She ought to just go home. Dig up one of her stashes. She still had a few left. That or find one of the bottles she'd bought when she managed to sneak some money off the guy she'd been with a few days ago. What was his name? She couldn't even remember, but he'd had a fat wad of cash in his pocket and he wasn't going to miss what she'd taken.

If it was a problem, then maybe he shouldn't carry so much and maybe he shouldn't go to sleep with a strange woman in his bed.

But instead of doing that, she crossed the street and ducked between the houses, her spiked heels digging into the wet soil. She eyed the windows, all lit up and bright, beckoning to her.

Rita had one of the older homes, but it was down on the river and with fall coming, she did what a lot of the other people down here did, left the windows open to the breeze. Layla crouched in the shadows, listening to the voices drifting out of the house. Rita's was thick and slurred, and she wasn't a happy drunk.

"I had to tell the cops," Rita said.

Layla arched her brows and eased in closer, staring up at the window, but she couldn't see a damn thing, just that square of light and shadows moving back and forth.

"It will be okay." Caine, that voice of his low and steady and soothing.

"Okay?" Rita, half-shouting. "How can it be okay? You know what he was doing all my life? Raping boys! My father is a monster. I'm going to have to talk to the cops again. I'm going to have to tell them what he said about that club and he'll call me a liar or say I'm confused . . . that I'm depressed . . . and it won't even be a lie." She hiccupped and started to sob. "I *am* confused. I *am* depressed. Caine . . . how can I tell them? How can I do this?"

Their voices went lower, softer.

And outside the window, Layla muttered, "Son of a bitch."

Inside the house, they went quiet.

Her heart jumped up into her throat and she couldn't breathe. There was a shift, the floorboards squeaking. "What was—?" Rita's voice went quiet.

Instinct kicked in and Layla took off, pausing only long enough to remove her shoes and carry them as she pounded down the street, using the heavy shadows to hide herself as the front door of Rita's house opened.

Layla reached her own place, but instead of going inside, she waited.

Her heart lodged in her throat as Caine moved out onto the porch and looked around.

Long seconds passed before he went inside.

Layla could swear she felt his eyes continue to watch.

So instead of using the front door, she crept, silent as a mouse, along the porch and eased off the side, heading around to the back.

She didn't turn on a single light.

And the entire time, she smirked to herself.

Rita's daddy, upright, do-gooding daddy, was one of those perverts.

CHAPTER SIX

On the last night of his life, Harlan Troyer sat in his library and smoked one cigarette after another, drinking Crown Royal and trying to figure out just how much trouble this was going to cause him.

They didn't understand, none of them.

They took boys and made them *men*.

They took boys and made them *theirs,* forging a bond that nothing could break.

The boys became men who understood the value and power of loyalty, respect and family—they were all connected and they understood it. They passed it on and those people who didn't understand were just sorry, uninformed fools.

It was their *right* to do this and nobody understood.

His hand shook as he reached for the cut-crystal glass at his hand. The fire burned merrily off to his side, never mind that it was still a muggy seventy degrees outside and his wife had already been in there nagging about how hot it was. He needed the fire. Not just because he was cold, deep down in his bones.

Everything was falling apart. It had been for some time and he'd seen it coming. He'd just missed his brothers, the boys, all of this, so bad after Pete had disappeared.

When they'd decided to re-form the group a few years after Pete and David had disappeared, at first Harlan had thought he'd just move on without it. He'd fallen apart away from it and a number of his brothers had died. It had seemed like they were living under a bad star for a time and he'd held his breath, waiting for his turn. But it hadn't come.

Now, though . . . this was worse.

There was change coming, and none of it good.

Jeb had killed himself and Jeb had been the one to always make sure all the problems would disappear if anybody tried to look too hard at them. There was always somebody who went into law; they made sure of it. There was usually even a lawyer, but that had been Ham and he'd died in a car wreck a while back.

They were careful, so careful, and none of it mattered now.

Change was coming.

And Harlan had to be ready.

He'd gone through his file cabinet the one he kept locked—business material, Business . . . and personal.

The club was personal.

Nobody but a Cronus could understand just how deeply ingrained it was.

The knock at the door made him jump and it pissed him off that he was nervous in his own home.

Had one of them talked?

He tossed back the whiskey and hissed as it burned a path down his throat. Then he reached for the gun he kept in the top right drawer of his desk. Most of the young idiots running the club now had forgotten about him. Every now and then he'd join them, but always under certain conditions, and Jeb had understood his desire for caution.

Of course, Jeb was dead now. *Not good,* Harlan thought. Not good at all that Jeb had decided to just put a bullet in his brain. Things had to be bad for Jeb to make that decision.

If it got to that point as far as Harlan was concerned, he'd be doing the same, but he wasn't ready to do that just yet. If the cops were at his door, he might have to adjust that line of thinking, because he was not going to let others judge what they didn't understand.

If it came to that, he'd control his own fate, as Jeb had.

The knock came again and Harlan moved down the hall, glancing up the stairs. The light to the bedroom was off, Margaret up there, sleeping most likely. Sleeping with the help of a few Xanax and probably some wine. She'd started taking the pills after he'd stopped sleeping with her, but she didn't understand how hard it was for him to touch that body of hers. She'd put on weight and her flabby, soft body wasn't appealing for him. His mind fuzzed out on him as he recalled young, limber bodies, but he had to force his thoughts under control as he peeked through the Judas hole.

The man standing there made Harlan frown.

Even as relief crashed into him. Not the cops. No reason to make that decision yet. If it had been the cops . . .

"It wasn't," he muttered, wiping a damp hand across his brow. "So stop thinking on it."

He slid the gun into his pocket and pasted a smile on his face. Opening the door with a smile, he said, "Well, this is a surprise."

"Harlan. Can I come in? I've got a bit of a problem." The man Harlan called a friend looked worried. Very worried. He darted a look around him and then leaned in, said softly, "I need some help."

CHAPTER SEVEN

The walk to his place was long and silent, a cool breeze coming off the river. She was acutely aware of Adam, that long, rangy body prowling at her side, the heat of him warming her even though inches separated them. Tension practically emanated from his pores and she could all but feel the words he had trapped inside him.

This is a bad idea, she thought, but she didn't know what else to do. She was tired. Going back to the river wasn't going to work. He'd just follow her again, and how was she supposed to avoid being noticed if the two of them were traipsing around well after midnight?

Besides, at some point she had to trust somebody, had to reach out to somebody.

She couldn't get a hotel, not without ID. She had a fake one, a damned good one that she had managed to obtain years ago, but it might not hold up if somebody really, *really* looked at her. She looked different than she used to look but not different enough.

After all, Adam had recognized her.

There were exactly three people in this town she trusted implicitly. Her father was in a nursing home. *Noah* . . . her heart wrenched just thinking about him. The only real option paced along at her side, his anger all but beating against her skin.

Her heart swelled in her throat as they turned down the street where she'd spent the first seventeen years of her life. She stopped for a minute, staring at the house where she'd lived with her dad. The new owner had put landscape lights down, the bright beams falling on the flowers and rosebushes. Tears burned her eyes and she had to turn away before she gave into the years' worth of tears trapped inside her.

She nearly crashed into Adam, his hands coming up to grip her arms. Through the thin material of her long-sleeved T-shirt she felt the strength of him, his fingers pressing into her flesh, solid and real. "Sorry," she said, forcing the rasp out through her tight throat.

"He's not there," Adam said, his voice brusque.

She jerked her head in a nod. She knew that. She knew exactly when he'd left. She knew why. She knew where he was. But she couldn't talk about that now, not if she wanted to make it through the next five minutes—the next five seconds—without crying.

Tugging out of his grip, she brushed past him and headed up the drive toward Adam's house. It wasn't much easier. She had made this trip so many times, she could have done it in her sleep. She paused at the sight of the car in the driveway. Even in the darkness, it gleamed, drawing the eye like magic. She hummed a little, unable to stop herself from reaching out and drawing a finger across the elegant curves. "The Corvette," she murmured. "It's finally done."

"Yeah." Adam's voice was brusque to the point of rudeness and she curled her fingers into a fist, pulled it back to her side as she turned to look at him.

"Is it a problem, me being here?"

"You don't have any place else to go." He shrugged and reached into his pocket, pulling out the keys and heading toward the steps.

She paused, her gut twisting. She was ready to trust Adam, yes. But as much as she loved his folks, she didn't know if she was ready to take that step yet. "Ah, you're back to living in the house?"

"Yes."

Licking her lips, she said, "What about your parents?"

"Don't worry about anybody spilling your secrets, Lana." He shot her a glittering look. "It's just us. Now get your ass in here."

She stared at him, fighting the urge to flip him off. She'd take the surly shit for a while. It was more than deserved, after all. But the snarling was getting on her nerves. Struggling to find some middle ground that wasn't going to result in him biting her head off, she asked, "Since when did you move back in here?"

His voice was flat as he answered, "Since my parents died."

Those words hit her like a punch, right to the heart. She all but went to her knees while he calmly unlocked the door and went inside, ignoring the fact that he'd just blindsided her.

Slumping against the wooden railing, she pulled her glasses off and pressed the heels of her hands against her eyes. *Melanie and Chuck . . .* Setting her jaw, she tipped her head back and stared up at the sky until the urge to cry had faded. The need to sob, the need to give in to the ache that lived inside her, sometimes it was overwhelming, but she coped by shoving it all off into some part that almost felt separate. Sooner or later, that *other* part was going to get too full and it might overtake her. *She* might cease to exist and that other part would take over everything.

But not tonight.

Slowly, feeling like she'd aged a year in the span of five minutes, she shoved off the railing and eyed the door. In the void where she'd held the pain there was now just a hollow sensation. Sooner or later, those bits and pieces of pain that she refused to deal with were going to come chasing after her, determined to have their merry way with her.

But not tonight.

Her boots echoed hollowly on the wooden floor as she moved to go inside. The broad, muscled plane of Adam's back was the first thing she saw. He stood at the sink, staring out over the dark backyard.

Her throat went tight and she was overcome by the urge to move to him, press her lips to his shoulder and just slip her arms around him, hug him. Kiss away the misery she sensed lay inside him.

Twenty years ago, she could have gone to him easily. Maybe she wouldn't have felt the urge to go kissing on the man—but well. Twenty years ago, things had been different. With that span of years between them and so many secrets, she was frozen, though. Unable to go to him, unable to stay silent, she forced herself to say the only thing there was to say. Trite, empty words.

"I'm sorry, Adam."

Adam turned to look at her, his velvety brown eyes narrowed. Seconds ticked by and then he shrugged. Her mouth went a little dry as the movement had the muscles bared by his tank top doing all sorts of lovely, wonderful things, the tattoos rippling.

Her belly clenched as the image of her going to him danced in her mind. This time, though, it wasn't comfort she had in mind. She wanted to press her lips against his skin, yeah. Learn his taste, though. Maybe she could comfort him, but she wanted a lot more than that. She wanted to feel him, skin to skin, study each of those tattoos and then learn the feel of his muscles, his body, as he moved above her.

She couldn't remember the last time a guy's body had fascinated like this.

Maybe never.

And it was utterly impossible.

Adam looked at her like he didn't want to be within ten feet of her, and the more she thought about this, about *him,* the worse her headache got.

A heavy sigh escaped him, forcing her thoughts back on-target.

"So," he said, drawing the word out.

She looked at him just in time to see him crossing his arms over his chest, the muscles in his arms bulging, flexing under that inked skin.

Wary, she rocked back on her heels.

If this was the way he got ready to open up the game of twenty questions, too bad. She wasn't ready to play.

A sardonic smile curved his lips and he pushed off the counter. "You disappear for twenty years. Nobody knows anything. And then you show back up. . . . What's going on, Lana?"

"I can't really talk about it yet." Yeah, not much on wasting words, was he? She looked away, swallowing the knot in her throat, wishing she could just explain, just *tell* somebody. But it wasn't as easy as that. How could she explain anything? Most of *that* night was a fog. The next few days were blurred by the pain from her concussion and fear, adrenaline as she took off running, chased by that quiet, solemn voice. *You can't stay here.* . . .

The solid memories she *did* have were based on what came before and then almost a week later, when she finally slowed down enough to think.

How could she explain any of that to Adam? How

could she explain anything when she didn't really understand herself?

"I think you need to talk about it; otherwise, I'm going to make a phone call and tell a detective I know that I saw you. That's going to throw all kinds of wrenches into things," he said, his voice silky.

Jerking her chin up, she stared at him. "I'm not doing anything *wrong* by being here, you know."

"No. You just did shit-all wrong by disappearing and letting everybody who cared about you think you were dead. Raped, murdered, who knows!" he snapped. He closed the distance between them, glaring down at her. "You have any idea what your dad went through? Noah?"

Me?

Adam wanted to grab her. Shake her.

He'd always loved her.

Always.

And when she reached out to him, he hadn't realized in time, hadn't understood . . . until it was too late. All this time. Staring at her face, he searched for some sort of sign, some lingering echo of the girl she'd been. That girl who'd been ready to fight the whole damn world and change it.

So little about her was the same. He remembered the vibrancy of her hair, almost painfully. He'd dreamed about that hair, red and rich and beautiful, so often, wrapping it around his fist as he kissed her the way he'd always wanted to. Lying down with her and feeling it across his skin as they slept. Crazy dreams, hurtful dreams, dreams that would never happen.

Now her hair was a soft, quiet brown and it irritated the hell out of him, because he *knew* she'd done it deliberately.

Her eyes were the same . . . mostly. Sadder and harder,

a misty shade of grey, framed by spiky lashes. Her chin
was up and she glared at him, all but daring him to do
something, say something.

He could think of a lot of things he'd like to do, and
that monthlong dry spell of his was catching up to him.
He had no problem imagining her naked and spread out
under him, but he'd imagined that a hundred times.

What he wanted the most was answers.

And she was quiet.

Her mouth stayed closed, and when he edged closer, all
she did was arch a brow.

Daring him.

"Didn't you think about any of us or were you just that
determined to take off with David?" he asked softly.

Something flashed in her eyes and then she shrugged.
"If you think you already know what happened, then why
should I bother to answer?"

"How about you *tell* me what happened and then I
don't have to speculate?"

She went to turn away.

He caught her arm.

She spun around, fist flying.

He barely managed to block it, and the force she had
behind that blow left his arm numb. "What the—"

Instinctively he spun them around and trapped her
between his body and the island, his hands trapping her
wrists, holding them behind her back. For one long volatile second, they both held their breath.

Then, slowly, she blew out a breath. Her skin was pale,
her mouth tight, as she glared at him. She tensed, her skin
pale, her mouth tight. "I don't like it when people touch
me," she warned.

"I noticed." Her pulse was racing. Bounding against
his fingers like a mad thing. *And just what happened?* he
wondered. Because the Lana he remembered had *loved*

touches. She had been a hugger, even from the time she'd been a kid.

He'd adored her then.

He'd loved her then.

He'd known her when she was just a rough-and-tumble tomboy, only five years old, when she moved in across the street into the little house where her dad had lived until his stroke.

Adam had loved her when she went from tomboy to coltish teenager, even when he'd been too old—already in high school when she was just in middle school—and because he knew it wasn't right he'd avoided her, putting a sad light in her eyes when he acted annoyed when she came over. Bit by bit she'd pulled away, and he hated it, but he knew it wasn't right for him to want her the way he had.

But that age difference wouldn't have made a difference forever.

And it hadn't stopped him from noticing everything.

The way she threw her arms around her father's neck when he got home from work. The way she hugged her friends. The way she hugged Adam's parents when she saw them. The way she hugged her boyfriend or a teacher she liked.

The way she'd rested her hand on David Sutter's shoulder one day after school. It wasn't the kind of touch a girl gave a guy she liked. Adam had known that then. It was the kind of touch a person gave a wild animal, the kind you gave to a scared child: *Calm down; everything is okay. . . . I'll take care of you.* The slim girl, all of five feet four, with the heart of a giant.

Adam had seen it, even if nobody else had. David had been in trouble, and Lana had known. She'd reached out, ready to help.

Three weeks after that, both of them were gone.

Twenty years later, she was in front of Adam, yet again, and everything was different, but her eyes were the same and his heart still raced as she looked at him, but she didn't like being touched.

"Why?"

She stared at him like he'd spoken another language.

Lowering his brows, he dipped his head and demanded, "Why? You used to touch *everybody*. What happened? Where did you go and why did you let everybody think you were dead?"

"I already told you, I'm not ready to talk about it ye— *hey*!"

He let go of her so abruptly, she lost balance. Guilt punched him, but he shoved it aside as he started to pace. From the corner of his eye he watched her. "Do you know where your dad has been the past year?"

Something in her flickered.

She knows—

Adam stopped pacing and turned to face her, readied himself to hear at least some small truth.

Then she shrugged and glanced past him. "No. You said he wasn't across the street anymore. When did he move?"

Liar. Adam kept it behind his teeth. Then he shrugged. She knew. Somehow she knew. But how?

He figured he'd keep this close to his chest . . . and he'd watch her.

Since she wasn't going to give him any answers, he'd have to find them for himself.

Easily he said, "I lost track of him." Then he turned around. "Come on. I'll show you where you can sleep. You look exhausted."

He could practically feel the daggers she glared into his back.

"Hasn't anybody ever told you that's the last thing you should say to a woman?"

"Oh, sure. But since when did I ever listen to that sort of thing?"

He bypassed the little guest room he should give her. It was on the first floor, quiet . . . close to the door.

He wanted her upstairs. Where he'd hear if she tried to leave. Not that he'd be able to stop her, but at least he'd *know.*

He'd never sleep.

Adam knew it, as sure as he knew his own name.

Sleep was an elusive thing for him, something he'd chased after for the longest time, until he realized that the harder he chased it, the harder it was to catch. But he did need to rest, his dragging, tired body screaming at him to just *stop.*

Not entirely trusting himself to stay upstairs, just twenty feet or so from the room where Lana slept, he settled down on the couch, his gaze locked on the ceiling over his head.

Now she was maybe thirty feet away, but she was separated from him by a flight of stairs and the solid construction of the floor.

Far enough, he thought, that he wouldn't be tempted to go and open the door, stare at her as she slept just to convince himself this was real. That he hadn't started hallucinating again.

He'd done that before, back when he quit drinking—cold turkey is a dangerous thing for a hard-core alcoholic and the DTs had come on hard, followed by freaky-ass hallucinations that were yet another deterrent. That wasn't the only time he'd ever had that pleasure, though. Sometimes he'd go two or three days without sleep, and that was when it hit him really hard. He'd thought for a minute down by the river that he was doing it again. Hallucinating, imagining that he was seeing what he wanted to see, just because he did want it so bad and he was so fucking tired.

But then he had reached out, grabbed her glasses and felt the satin smoothness of her skin and the shock of it went through him like a jolt of pure electricity. He might as well have shoved his hand into a transformer or something, it was so powerful, and it managed to clear the fog of exhaustion from his head.

She'd been *real*.

She'd said his name.

And now she was in his house, in the bed over his head.

She was in that bed, too. That bedroom had a creaky, noisy floor, and if she'd been walking around he'd have heard every single step. Now the only sounds he heard in the still, quiet house was the occasional sound she made as she shifted in the bed.

Where have you been? He wanted to demand she tell him, but he knew Lana, or he *had* known her. Demands had never worked well with her and he doubted that had changed. If he pushed her now, she'd just shut down. If he pushed too hard, she might disappear again.

He heard a faint squeak and closed his eyes as a cold sweat broke out over his forehead. Every time she moved, he had a vision of her shifting on that bed, her sleek, pale body spread across the mattress. Did she still have those freckles? Was her hair still as silky as it had always been?

And even though he knew it was a dye job, he was all but burning to strip her naked and find out for certain, preferably by settling between her legs and studying the curls between her thighs.

Right before he took the things he'd never had the right to take before.

Things he didn't have a right to take now.

Swearing, he reached down and pressed the flat of his hand to his erection.

"You like to torture yourself," he muttered.

Under his hand, his cock pulsed, throbbed. But this was Lana. Whether he wanted to think about her like this or not, it was going to happen. Eyes wide open, he focused on the ceiling and freed the button of his jeans. It was this *now* or walk around hobbled until he gave in. Dragging the zipper down, he winced as he freed his dick, his flesh painfully sensitive.

When he closed his hand around his shaft it pulsed, almost viciously. Dragging his palm up, then down, he let himself pretend, even if it was never going to happen, that it wasn't his hand.

It was Lana.

Riding him, her sleek thighs gripping as she slid up and down, her hair spilling down around them, hiding them in the darkness, while those sexy glasses perched on the tip of her nose.

His muscles tensed, went rigid.

Breath sawed in, out, of his lungs.

Jerking his fist harder, fast, he clenched his teeth against the ragged groan that rose in his throat, choking him. Her cool grey eyes going smoky with hunger, her mouth parted on a broken cry.

He could picture himself sliding his palms up that slim torso, cupping one small breast in his hand. He'd always loved those pretty, elegant tits, the way they curved under the tanks she'd wear in the summer as she worked the garden. Just enough to fill his hands, and he'd spill her onto her back, discover her taste, the color of her nipples—

A hot, twisting chill raced down his spine and he arched his hips up, meeting the thrusts of his fist. A second later, hot pulses of semen splattered across his belly.

Sucking in a breath, he tried to calm the erratic beating of his heart, tried to catch his breath.

Then, reaching down for the shirt he'd dropped down

on the side of the couch, he couldn't resist the bitter laugh that bubbled out of him. How long had she been home . . . a few hours? A day?

And here he was, already in a hot, miserable mess, just like he'd been twenty years ago.

"Welcome home, Lana."

CHAPTER EIGHT

Every morning, Margaret Troyer got up and took a long bath, then got dressed and put on her face. She did love her baths. She also took a nice long, hot soak before she went to bed. After Harlan had put in this fancy bath with the jets, she sometimes thought she might spend a little too much time in here, but he spent so much of his time in his office, she didn't see the harm.

She'd enjoy her baths and her books, as long as she didn't have to deal with his temper, and it was awful. Especially the past few weeks. She understood, of course, that most people in town were feeling a little snappish, what with everything going on in town, but she didn't see why that had to affect her.

It had nothing to do with them, as far as she was concerned, but Harlan certainly did seem worked up over something.

She simply put it out of her mind as she soaked in the tub, head on a little specially designed pillow she'd ordered from the Internet. None of that nastiness needed to darken her "me" time, not as far as Margaret was concerned.

A woman who worked as hard as she did deserved her me time, after all.

Halfway through the bath, it occurred to her, though,

that it was still rather quiet in the house. He hadn't so much as come bothering her for coffee, hadn't nagged her for a shirt.

A mild frisson of worry slid through her, but she pushed it aside. He was probably just worn-out. He'd spent so much time brooding the past few weeks, it must have caught up with him. Worrying about the town. Just like everybody else.

She swallowed, suddenly chilled in the water as a familiar, unwelcome thought pushed itself into her mind. His boys. Harlan used to talk about his boys a lot. The weekends he planned once a month, weekends for just him, the other guys and the boys they mentored.

But . . . that was *mentoring*. Nothing else.

None of this had anything to do with Harlan.

It couldn't.

Her enjoyment gone, she hurried through the rest of the bath and climbed out, drying off with a fat, fluffy towel, ignoring the body that had gone plump over the years. Her once blond hair had turned gray and it was just . . . well, *hard* to see how old she'd gotten.

A lot of things were hard these days. Just thinking about Harlan made her worry anymore.

The club.

The boys.

"Stop it," she told herself, her throat tight and thick. Sniffing, she grabbed a towel from the rod and started to rub at her hair. "Don't be silly. Harlan is hardly the sort of man to be involved in this."

The sudden surge of ragged emotions eased back and she calmed herself enough to finish her hair, fix her face and dress, settling on a bright, cheerful dress of red checks. She'd make them a big breakfast, see if he wanted to go out for the day. They could both use it.

He hadn't been in bed when she woke up, hadn't even

come in to sleep with her, but that wasn't unusual. Sometimes he slept in his office, and that was getting more and more common, the fool man. He needed to take it easy, rest. She'd see that he did it, she told herself as she pushed the door open.

For the first few moments, she was able to tell herself he was still sleeping.

But then she saw the blood.

And the knife in his chest.

Margaret Troyer passed out, striking her head against the doorjamb as she hit the floor, her pretty red-checked dress billowing out around her in a crazy circle.

"Their housekeeper called it in."

As the paramedics rolled Mrs. Margaret Troyer away on a stretcher, Detective Jensen Bell continued to study the note that was none too subtly stuck to Mr. Harlan Troyer's chest. The knife was just a plain, simple hunting knife. She'd be able to buy that thing at any Walmart or sporting-goods store—she even knew the brand, although she didn't know if this was this year's model or last year's. It wasn't anything special or unique, and that would make finding the buyer a problem, unless of course they were lucky enough to find prints.

And that wasn't going to happen.

She already knew it. Jensen was a small-town cop, but she was still a cop and she already knew what she was dealing with—a killer who had thought this through all too well.

There was no sign of a struggle.

Harlan had been sitting down when he was attacked.
Knew him, didn't you?

There was a bottle of scotch on his desk—Crown Royal—and she suspected that was what was in the glass, too. She'd get a sample of the whiskey, from both the bottle and the glass. It was possible the whiskey had been doctored. Either that or Harlan had been really plastered, because it didn't look like he'd so much as put up a fight.

One would think you'd struggle a bit when you saw somebody with a big-ass knife pointed at your chest.

And the knife went through both his chest and the note.

"Think he was drugged?"

She looked over her shoulder at the newly minted Detective Thorpe. To say he had been rushed into his position as detective would be a bit unfair, but they definitely hadn't taken their time. A few weeks ago, he'd been a uniform, brushing up and hoping he'd hit detective.

And now she was training him.

To be fair, she'd been working with him for a while, but it had been more on an as-time-allows basis because, they were short staffed even in the best of times and they couldn't take one of the uniforms off the streets so he could *play at being a detective,* as a former asshole—now dead— had liked to complain. Of course, Sims had a reason to worry about real cops. He hadn't liked her and she knew a lot of that was because she was a good cop. He'd written her off because she was female, sexist son of a bitch.

Thorpe would have been harder for Sims to handle.

Rubbing the back of her neck, Jenson studied their dead man.

"Well, what do you think?"

Benjamin took the question seriously. He was wearing a suit, bless his heart. She barely managed to get out of bed and stumble into a nice pair of pants and a not-too-wrinkled shirt and jacket—granted, Dean had been busy fucking her brains out half the night, so she could write it off to that, but she never bothered to put herself together as well as Thorpe did.

She wondered how long it would last.

His blue eyes squinted as he continued to study Troyer, and then Thorpe looked at her.

"No signs of struggle. No bruising." He pointed to the floor where there was just a minimal amount of blood. "He died here and I imagine we'll find out the knife went straight in, killed him almost instantly. If he had been awake and aware of what was going on, wouldn't he have struggled some?"

She smiled at Thorpe. "Not bad." Nodding at the liquor on the table, she said, "We're already having that analyzed. We'll get his bloodwork, too, see what happens there. But whoever did this knew him. Of course, this is Madison. Harlan knew plenty of people. But Harlan knew this man, was friendly with him. I say our killer came in here planning to kill him. Especially considering that note." She grimaced and added, "We'll have to reach out to the state for help and we need to check the paper, but I bet the note came from here."

She looked over and took a second to study the paper. Heavyweight and a soft, pale cream. Not something you'd find up at the Walmart. She pulled open a drawer on the desk, then another and another, and wasn't surprised when she found a supply of paper that was identical to the paper used for the note.

Jensen took a moment and read it again.

It sent a shiver down her spine, and she was small enough to admit, some part of her was almost viciously happy with what she read. She wouldn't admit it, though. Well, maybe to Dean.

Harlan was just the beginning. Cronus must die.

"And he's not done," she murmured.

Then she looked down at the picture that had been left on the table.

Like the man wanted them to know *why*.

Like he had to make them understand.

I'm not just a killer. I have to do this, he seemed to be telling her.

She picked up the picture, the bile rising in her throat.

It was old, one of those Polaroid type of pictures. The edges of it were burned. She eyed the fireplace, bits and pieces of paper, even a few photos, still partially visible.

Had her man pulled it out of the fire?

There was no way to identify anybody in the photo, but she didn't have to know them to be disturbed.

There was a bench. An older man—she had a bad, bad feeling it was Harlan, although she didn't know if she'd ever known for sure. The image was cut off so all she could see of him was the shoulders down. There was a scar bisecting his left biceps.

His flesh was male and toned.

And he was raping a teenage male, a skinny young man tied up and bound to a bench. Scars, both old and new, marred his narrow back. He was faceless, nameless, head turned away from the camera.

Whoever that man in the picture was . . . *yeah.* Her personal thoughts were that death just wasn't good enough. But her personal opinion couldn't come into play here.

"Think it's Troyer?"

She looked at Ben as she slid the picture into an evidence bag. "I don't know. If he has a scar like that, we'll know after the ME looks him over. If it's not, we need to figure out who it is, because he'll be one of the next victims."

Her stomach twisted even thinking it. She didn't want to help save a man who'd rape a child.

She wanted to kill him herself.

She dreamed.

Arms closed her around and she wasn't afraid.

You came back.

The voice wasn't familiar, low, rasping in her ear, and the sound of it made something low in her belly go all tight and fluttery.

As a hand opened low on her hip, she tried to turn, but he nipped her shoulder.

Be still.

I want to look at you, she argued.

No . . . I've waited, too long. I get to do what I want now.

What he wants. The promise of that made her shiver. Made her want to whimper with want and need.

Squeezing her knees together, she tried not to moan as he nudged his cock against her ass and started to rock against her, the rhythm unmistakable. Warmth rushed through her, preparing her.

He slid his hand between her thighs and she gasped, arching.

Take a breath, he said. *You'll need it.*

She almost laughed. She couldn't breathe. Couldn't even think—

Then he flipped her onto her belly and her face was shoved into a pillow. A hand tangled in her hair, held her pinned there.

You think you can come back now? His voice was an ugly, hateful snarl. *How many lives will you ruin this time?*

She struggled against his fist, tried to claw against his hands. *Please. I only wanted—*

But she couldn't speak.

Couldn't even breathe . . .

Lana came awake, choking the scream back by shoving a fist against her mouth. She'd learned, long ago, how to hide the sounds of her nightmares. It had been ages since she'd shared her bed with anybody—not since Deatrick, years ago. But even if she woke screaming, people talked and word got back to him and he started worrying.

Before him, it had been problematic in other ways.

Eventually, she'd learned to hide it for other reasons. It was just easier. Better this way.

But as the screams died inside her throat, tears leaking from her eyes while the nightmare faded, she lay shivering on the bed, feeling more alone than she'd felt in her entire life.

She was home.

Just as she'd wanted for so long.

But nothing was the way she'd hoped it would be. She'd come back under a lie. And nothing was any different than it had been a year ago. Six-months ago. Rolling onto her side, she curled her knees up and hugged them to her chest, waiting for the ache to fade, the raggedness of her breaths, the erratic beat of her heart.

As it faded, she grew aware of the serene, blissful silence.

It was another brutal blow that Lana hadn't been prepared for. For years, her life had consisted of routine, routine and more routine. She'd wake to the sound of the L, the rush and clattering of the trains on the elevated railroad that cut through Chicago. She'd smell the familiar scents of the bakery across the street, fried food lingering from the store she managed and other scents she associated with the city. She'd wake in the dark, because she woke up early.

She knew her routine.

But her routine was broken and she felt broken along with it.

The scent of coffee filled the air. Golden streamers of sunlight slanted through the window to fall across her face, and as she lay there she could hear the music of birdsong. She hadn't heard anything like that in far too long. It almost hurt to think about it. It almost felt like a dream.

She let the simple pleasure of it chase away the ache of the nightmare, staring at the golden light shining through the tree branches. She caught her breath, almost afraid to move for fear that the dream would shatter.

When nothing changed, she dared to let the oxygen trapped inside her lungs out and then she let herself think. That, though, was a mistake. Everything caught up with her at once and the few hours of sleep she'd allowed herself, the confusing night, the fear, the worries of what was going to happen and just *being* here, it all hit, and it hit *hard*.

That hollow space inside her where she shoved dreams and nightmares and fears and misery just . . . exploded and all of it came rushing back at her. As everything slammed into her, a sob rose up to choke her. She shoved a fist against her mouth to muffle the sound, still staring mesmerized at the sunlight streaming through the trees.

Home—

Home—

Her father, in a nursing home because of the stroke.

How many times had she ached to be here, just one more time, to be in that house, hear his big, booming voice and sit at the table with him while they had dinner? To walk along that river? To hike through the park or stroll down Main Street? *Home.*

Now, as the ache threatened to rip her in two, she knew she had just what she'd wanted, that one last time—she *was* home. She could see her dad, if she could figure out a way.

Noah . . . another sucker punch. He had moved on with his life, but how many times had she wished she could just see him, tell him she was sorry?

David. Where *was* he?

Adam . . . She flinched, thinking of the anger in his eyes.

How many lives will you ruin this *time?*

That voice rose out of her dreams, haunting her.

Oddly enough, that was the memory that had the torrent of misery ebbing inside her. Yes, she'd ruined lives the last time. But she hadn't been the one who'd been responsible for the systematic torture and abuse of children. Peter Sutter had headed that club and *he* was gone.

His wife, that cold, callous bitch, was gone.

Lana had been a stupid, terrified kid and she'd believed a man who said he'd make sure everything stopped.

Now she knew it hadn't. She'd come back to put things to right.

You're arguing with your conscience, Lana.

Sighing, she sat up and swung her legs over the edge of the bed, the T-shirt she'd slept in caught up around her thighs. Her mouth was dry, her belly a shriveled little knot, and she wanted a shower.

Rising off the bed, she stretched, arms high overhead, while a headache from the crying jag settled at the base of her skull and started to pound. And the hair on the back of her neck stood on end.

Swinging her head around, she found herself trapped in the brown velvet of Adam's gaze. He leaned against the dresser, his arms crossed over his chest, brows low. For a second, as she stood there staring at him, his gaze left hers, dropped low to linger on her bare legs before traveling back up to stare into her eyes.

"What in the hell are you doing?"

Instead of answering, he pushed off the dresser and paced toward her, his face unreadable. "You do this a lot?"

Blood rushed up her neck. Lana could feel it, staining her cheeks red, the heat of it suffusing her entire face. No point in asking what he meant. He'd been in there while she broke and cried like her heart was broken. "I don't think it's any of your business, is it?"

"Twenty years," he murmured, like she had not said a word. "You come back to town, you won't say why you've been gone. And you spent the past thirty minutes crying like you've had your heart ripped out. We used to be friends. Some part of me feels like it should be my business." He reached up, caught a lock of her hair in his hand.

She tensed and immediately his hand fell away.

The glittering look in his eyes sent a shiver racing through her, though, one that left her skin feeling over-heated while her nipples drew tight and pressed against the front of her shirt.

"Twenty years changes a lot of things, Adam," she said, casually folding her arms over her chest.

His lids drooped low, shielding his gaze. Somehow she didn't think she'd fooled him. Not on any level. "Does it really, Lana?" Then he shrugged and turned away. "I brought you some coffee, but it's probably getting cold. Come on downstairs and I'll see what I can salvage from breakfast. "

Then he was gone, shutting the door quietly behind him.

A long-sleeved black T-shirt had never looked so sexy until twenty minutes ago.

He hadn't meant to intrude, but he'd heard her and he couldn't have stayed away if he tried.

But the way she huddled there on the bed, rigid, her spine so stiff, he hadn't thought she'd welcome his touch. And other than that one ragged, harsh breath he'd heard as he passed by the door, she worked very hard to keep him from hearing her tears, practically choking in her effort to keep silent.

He absolutely hated that.

He'd planned to say something, but then she stood up and his brain melted, just melted and died as he caught sight of long, sleek legs, strong muscle and sleek calves.

The black lace of her panties had peeked out from under the hem of her shirt as she stretched and his blood had rushed to his cock so sudden, it was a miracle he hadn't passed out from it. And when she'd turned to face him, her nipples had gone from soft to ready for him, ready for his mouth, in a blink.

And it was for him. He'd seen that lambent heat in her gaze, even if she wasn't about to give in to it.

Attraction was easy, passing. It didn't surprise him that she wasn't the type to give in to it at the drop of a hat.

But the thought of those sweet little tits, nipples tight and ready for him, was going to haunt him.

Not as much as the expression on her face now, though.

She sat there like a shadow, her skin pale, her hands fisted in her lap, while she stared out the window at nothing.

She had nibbled at the bacon he'd put in front of her, taken a bite of toast. That was it.

Now she just . . . sat there.

He wanted to yank her out of that chair, push her up against the wall and kiss her stupid. Then he wanted to yell at her. He wanted to go to his knees and beg her to tell him what was wrong. He wanted to get lost in her . . . and then maybe beg her to . . .

Hell. He didn't know.

He wanted a resolution.

He wanted answers.

He wanted *her*.

He had *always* wanted her, but she'd always been untouchable. First she was too young and then she'd been gone.

Now she was like a shadow and life was a fucking monstrous mess.

And he was . . . ruined.

She slid him a glance and he fought the urge to look away. Every woman he'd touched over the past twenty years, he'd either pretended he was touching *her* or done it to forget her.

Every drink he'd taken had been to dull the pain or to punish himself for not saving her.

Because he *knew.*

Not right away, no. If he'd known the second she was calling that she'd needed help, he would have been there, found a way to get it out of her, called the cops . . . something. But after that second call, with a leaden weight and fear in his gut, the suspicion had grown and then the days bled away and there was no news from her.

The rumors flew and the fear grew and he just knew.

If he'd been a better guy, if he hadn't been pulling away from her, if she'd trusted him . . . something, anything. If he'd just been . . . better, he could have saved her. If she had trusted him the way she trusted Noah, he could have saved her.

That knowledge was the one constant in his life. Maybe he'd stopped reaching for the bottle, but he still hadn't forgiven himself for that.

And now she was here. Sitting there and watching him with unreadable eyes, her face blank.

Like she had no idea.

Like it didn't matter.

Like the hell he'd lived with—

Fuck.

It's over. Ancient history, he told himself. Twenty years of it. What he needed to do was just distance himself from her. He couldn't have exactly just left her sleeping on the street, but that didn't mean he had to put himself out there for her, right?

He'd just mind his own business and try to fix the mess that was his life. Somehow. She was alive and that meant one of his nightmares hadn't come true. Time to move on from that.

Forward. Away from her. Starting now.

Good plan.

He congratulated himself on that idea. All he had to do was get up and walk away without really engaging with her.

"What do you plan on doing today?" The question seemed to form without him even giving himself permission to *ask* it.

Lana blinked, a slow, almost lazy lowering of her lids, a faint smile on her lips as she shrugged and looked away.

"Oh, I don't know," she drawled, lifting her coffee cup and curling her hands around it. She didn't drink, though, just held it and stared down into it. "Maybe I'll sightsee. Catch up with the people who think I'm dead. What do you think?"

He snorted. "I think you'll stay here and hide."

She lifted a brow. "I'm not hiding." A quiet sigh escaped her. "If I wanted to hide, I never would have come back to Madison. I just need to . . . figure out my next step."

He thought the next one was obvious.

She should go see her father.

But Adam wasn't going to suggest it.

He already knew she was going there.

She'd been checking the map online when he walked by his computer earlier. Although she'd shut the window down the second she'd heard him, she hadn't been fast enough—he saw what she'd been looking up.

There was only one person in there who would interest Lana.

Lana had powerful memories of her father.

He had always seemed larger than life, working long hours at the electric company, then coming home and helping her with her homework, spending evenings in his workshop, where he crafted rocking chairs and rocking horses and bookcases by hand, selling them at flea markets and the like on weekends, anything he could do to make sure he provided for her.

She'd been his world, and for the longest time he had been hers, the one solid person she could count on. Her mother was a nonentity, somebody who had run off when Lana was just a baby. She had made herself stop caring about her mother when Leanna Rossi hadn't come to the mother–daughter day in sixth grade. Dad had come, though. He'd switched shifts, and when people eyed them oddly he'd told Lana, *People may look at you weird your whole life. It's up to you whether or not you'll let that affect you.* She had already noticed that people gave him odd looks sometimes. If he didn't let it bother him, she wouldn't let it get to her. It had been one of those defining moments in her childhood.

He had stood so big and tall and handsome as he walked with her to her table in the middle of the cafeteria, and more than a few of the moms had blushed when he spoke to them in his gruff voice.

Now he was a thin, pale shadow of himself sitting in his wheel chair in the courtyard. Watching him made an ache settle in her heart and she had to bite the inside of her cheek to keep from saying anything, had to lock her knees to keep from going to him.

There was the softest sound behind her and she tensed, spinning around to see Adam standing there, just a few inches away.

"Didn't know where he was, huh?" He stood there, thumbs hooked in his belt loops, legs spread wide, his head cocked as he studied her. He looked rough and ready . . . for anything. She'd been able to see the tattoos clearly earlier—the tattoos and the healing burns on his right arm—the burns left her gut twisting, because she knew how he'd gotten them.

From the fire. She'd read up about it, how he, Noah and

some guy she didn't know how been there when that hell house went up in flames. All because of a couple of boys. She suspected she knew why, but she didn't let her thoughts linger on it, not yet.

She wanted to stroke a hand down Adam's arm, ask if he hurt. She wanted to learn the lines of those chains, link, by link and the thought of it made her mouth go dry. What did those chains mean? They wrapped around him from the wrist up. So many links, such heavy chains.

If she were the girl she'd been, she would have asked him about the burn, about the fire. She would have asked him about the chains and whatever it was that bound him, because she knew Adam too well to think he'd just picked that design randomly. But she didn't have the right to ask him anything these days.

Because he continued to stand there watching her, because she could feel the strength inside her wavering, she reached for the attitude that had pulled her through so much shit over the years. Heaving out a frustrated sigh, she gave him a pained look. "You never used to be the creepy stalker type, Adam. Let me clue you in on something. No matter what books might try to sell you, in real life that shit is never sexy."

She went to go around him, refusing to let herself give her father another look.

Adam stopped her, a hand on her shoulder. "Aren't you going to say hello?"

"I—" The lie caught in her throat, stuck there. *Don't look back, don't—*

But she couldn't stop herself. Slowly, turning her head until she caught just the edge of his profile, Lana shook her head and then looked back at Adam. "I can't. Not yet."

"Why?"

"What's it going to do to him, if I go to him now, and then have to disappear again . . . or, worse, end up in jail?" She knew it was a possibility, a knowledge she'd carried inside her all these years. There was no real evidence; there couldn't be. But even after so many years, people still had the Sutter family on a pedestal. While she was forgotten. If she was the only one to return after so much time, she knew what people would think.

It was a price she'd pay, but she wouldn't bring her father any more pain.

Adam caught her chin, studied her face.

To her surprise, he swept his thumb across her cheek and that light touch sent a ribbon of heat curling through her. "And what will it do to *both* of you if he strokes out in five minutes? The next one is likely to kill him." Adam's eyes narrowed on her face. "But somehow I think you already know that. Just how do you know that?"

She jerked her chin out of his reach and looked away.

"I can't—"

"You can. Just go over there. Whatever else happens, all he has wanted for the past twenty years was a chance to see you again. Can you tell me you haven't wanted the same?"

Lana shoved her hands through her hair and spun away, staring back toward her father. "I can't do it out here."

"That's easy enough." Adam shrugged. "Just give me a few minutes and follow me. If you're ready to stop running. Isn't that why you're *here*?"

She closed her eyes. Hugged herself. Then slowly, she lifted her lashes and whispered, "Yes."

In the next moment, he was gone, striding toward Jimmy Rossi while Lana waited there, in the shadows. Watching. Waiting. Praying she wasn't making yet another mistake.

The walk to his room lasted just a few minutes and she trailed behind, keeping out of sight, listening to the rushes of voices around them. With her head down, she watched everybody from under her lashes. She'd slid inside with a group of kids and adults—probably some kids from the nearby elementary school coming to read—but she wasn't sure if her luck would last or not.

It did.

As Adam pushed her father's chair into his room, he cast a look over his shoulder, and when he met her gaze something eased in his expression, like he hadn't expected to see her there.

The insane urge to stick her tongue out at him almost overtook her.

He evidently saw something of it echoed in her eyes, because a reluctant grin flashed across his face before he disappeared inside the room. She crept closer, pausing just outside the door only to freeze in her tracks as a familiar voice, deep and low and steady, came rolling out of the room. "Now what in the hell is this, Adam? I spend enough time in this damn room. If I gotta sit on my ass, I might as well do it outside."

He might be a shadow of himself, but that voice hadn't changed, she thought. Big as life and just as strong.

"I told you, sir. Somebody wanted to speak with you."

Lana closed her eyes. Swiping her hands down the front of her jeans, she slid inside the room. Her heart slammed against her ribs, her breathing ragged and uneasy. *This isn't normal. This isn't routine. You have to stick to your routine! You have to be careful!* In the back of her head, the voice that had guided her life tried to shout at her.

In the end, though, that voice was the very thing that made it easier for her to move deeper into the room, to stop just a few feet away from her father, to dart a look around the room before stopping, finally, to stare at him through her lashes.

Fuck her routine. Fuck normal. Fuck *careful*.

Maybe if she hadn't been *careful,* she would have realized the problems were still happening. Maybe she would have stayed or come back and she might have been able to stop it before more kids got hurt. But she'd thought it had stopped, and she'd stayed safe, she'd been careful . . .

And nothing had been *normal*.

Normal was a lie.

Squaring her shoulders, she lifted her head and looked at him, seeing all the changes brought on by twenty years.

What if he doesn't recognize me?

For a long moment, there was just silence.

She stared at him.

He stared at her.

But there was no question.

In the glittering depths of his eyes, she saw it. In the harsh intake of his breath, the way his mouth fell open and the way his good hand tightened over the arm of his chair.

Slowly, he reached out a hand. Lana remembered when those hands had been big and strong, how he'd sat at the table helping her with algebra and geometry and how he'd groused when she'd struggled with chemistry because it was too dang hard for him. Now those hands were gnarled and bent and it hurt her heart to see him reaching out for help.

She started to move forward, but Adam was already there, helping Jim to his feet, and that massive ache in her chest spread.

She hadn't been here. The dull, painful knowledge twisted in her like a blade.

With slow, uneven steps, Jim Rossi crossed the tiled floor and stood in front of her, leaning heavily against Adam for support. Jim's voice when it came was soft but firm. "I knew you were alive," he said softly, staring at her like he was trying to see every single change that had happened over the past two decades. He saw past the glasses she didn't need, the dyed hair that annoyed the hell out of her, saw differences that time, heartache and grief had left written all over her. "I knew it."

"Daddy . . . I . . ." She swallowed, unsure of what to say to him.

He shook his head. "I don't to need to hear. Not right now. You got trouble on you; I can see it. Are you in trouble now?"

She hesitated, uncertain how to answer that.

He arched a brow. "Just answer the question, Lana. I raised you to face it if you did something wrong, not to run from it. You never had any trouble facing it, no matter what kind of mess you got caught up in. So just tell me . . . are you in trouble now or is everything okay?"

I raised you to face it. . . .

Translation: *Whatever happened, I believe in you.*

Something she didn't fully understand—shame, maybe hope, maybe fear, maybe all of it—twisted inside her. Flashes of the blood, echoes of the lingering pain, the fear, the faded bits of memory that continued to haunt her.

Part of her wanted to cry because that message was one she'd needed so badly over the years, but she didn't know if she was worthy of it. *I believe in you. . . .*

He believed in her, but did she deserve that trust?

She didn't think she did.

And there was nothing really she could offer him.

"I . . ." She paused and took a deep, slow breath. "I don't remember a whole lot of that night, Dad. I ran because I thought it was the right thing to do—the only thing. At the time."

It was, mostly, the truth. It was also the only truth she could offer, for now.

He studied her for a long moment and then nodded.

He reached for her and a second later she was folded in his arms. And the strength was still there. He was weaker, but there was still strength in him and she let herself lean on him for just a moment.

Lana swallowed the sob that caught in her throat. She wouldn't cry again. Not here. Not now. But damn if she wasn't going to take a few minutes.

CHAPTER NINE

Get your ass in here.

Adam scowled at the text message from his manager, then turned the phone off and pushed it into his pocket. Whatever was eating at Troy's ass had big, ugly teeth, because he never bothered Adam this much.

But he did have to get to the grill.

He hated to do it, though. Leaving Lana alone just didn't seem to be the right thing to do. She sat at the table, looking empty and tired and broken, and all he wanted to do was pull her up against him and hold her.

Not an option, though.

Not only had she brushed his hand aside when he tried to just touch her; she hadn't even wanted to speak with him. Shutting him out, completely. *Fine, then.* He had a business to run anyway. Interviews lined up and that position to fill—they'd been running short ever since he'd fired Layla, and they couldn't keep it up.

Saturdays were also busy as hell, and there was no way he could take the time he wanted. Well, maybe if she'd acted like she wanted him to . . .

She didn't. Move on. Deal with it.

She still had the spare key. His gut told him she'd be

back, even if she wasn't around when he got in from work.

And if she wasn't, he'd just find her. He had questions and he was going to figure out what the hell had kept her away, and scared, for the past twenty years.

Whatever was going on, though, she was here for a reason.

A mission, he thought. She wasn't just here because she'd missed home. The way she'd sobbed into the pillow had been telling. She'd missed home, a lot. She'd missed her father.

Something had kept her away and something had drawn her back. Considering all the shit exploding in town, including the body and the fire, the ties to the Frampton house, Adam had a bad feeling about how all of this might be connected.

At the same time, he knew it meant she wasn't going to walk until she'd seen this through.

He was still brooding over Lana and the puzzle of her when he let himself into his office roughly twenty minutes later. The place was buzzing and all the chatter was an annoying hum in his ear already. He just wanted a few minutes of peace.

And he wouldn't get it. He hadn't even had a chance to put his butt in his chair when his manager appeared in the doorway of Adam's office. *What shitload of problems is he bringing me now?*

Troy, his daytime bartender and assistant manager, stood there, his ruddy face tight with strain. "We got a problem."

"Yeah, I got that idea after the first ten texts about me getting my ass here. However, I pay you to handle problems when I'm not around . . . so . . . deal with it," Adam said sourly, although he already knew Troy would have already *done* that if he could. That was why Adam had put Troy in that position—he knew what needed to be done and he did it without complaining and came to Adam only when he couldn't fix things on his own.

A headache brewed at the base of Adam's skull, threatening to take a big greedy bite out of him. He eyed the big box on the floor near the door. A new rum he was trying out in the bar. He had visions of opening a bottle and just having a drink. Or five. But it never stopped with one—*or* five. Jerking his chin to the box, he said, "Get that put up for me, would you?"

"Later." Troy planted his hands on his hips, deep grooves bracketing his mouth as he stared at Adam. That look never spelled good things. Usually Troy only looked like that when he was having man troubles.

Hell. Adam didn't have time for this. "Look, if you and Drake are having problems, too fucking bad—"

"I dumped his ass. Be quiet a minute. I didn't want to text you about this and you weren't answering your phone, so just shut up and listen. Rita's dad was murdered last night," Troy said, cutting him off.

Adam closed his eyes and dragged a hand down his face and then looked back at Troy. "What?"

Dropping into the seat across from him, Troy leaned forward and pinned him with a level stare. "You heard me. That's what everybody is in there yapping about. Her mom is in the hospital. Passed out or had a heart attack or some shit. But Harlan Troyer is dead." Then, dropping his voice even though there were just the two of them, Troy said, "I heard rumors that he was one of them. I . . . uh, well, I know one of the medics who was called out to the scene. They're keeping it quiet, but he knows she works here and all. He gave me a heads-up."

Adam barely even registered that.

He was too busy remembering last night . . . and Rita. The hour she'd spent locked in here with Jensen.

"Son of a bitch."

"Yeah." Troy leaned back in his seat and stretched out his legs. The faded T-shirt went tight over his paunch and it seemed the grooves around his mouth and eyes had gotten deeper.

For a moment they lapsed into silence, and then Adam covered his face with his hands, scrubbed them up and down. He lowered them, half-hoping that Troy would be gone and this would all turn out to be some exhaustion-fueled hallucination. Adam had had them before.

But not today.

Troy was still sitting there, looking tired and strained and pissed. He ran a hand back over his balding head and then got up to go look at the box of rum, staring at it like he didn't know what to do with it. "They found him this morning. My buddy tells me that there was . . . well . . ." He grimaced, shot Adam a look. "It's a pretty good chance he was in on that fucked-up shit. If you know what I'm talking about."

Adam gripped the arms of his chair, thought about punching the monitor in front of him. "Yeah. I know." He blew out a sigh, rotating his neck as tension gathered there and settled in for a nice, long party. "So Rita won't be in. We'll deal. Anything else?"

Troy was quiet.

Adam blew out a breath. "What happened with you and Drake?"

"The dick was two-timing me again and, on top of that, acting all crazy every time I talked to anybody. Got tired of it. I don't need anybody that high maintenance."

Adam studied him for a minute. It wasn't Drake, but something still had Troy all wound up. "If it's not him, what is it?"

Troy opened his mouth, then snapped it shut and shook his head. He bent down, hauled the box of rum up, straining until he had it settled in his arms. His face was red with the effort by the time and Adam almost told him to put it back down, he'd move it later. But he needed that rum out of there.

Now.

After a second, Troy spoke again, his voice edged. "Somebody needs to check on Rita." That was all he said, but it was the unspoken words that left Adam unsettled.

"Why?"

Troy looked past him, staring at the wall. "I just think it needs to be done, Adam. And trust me, you don't want me doing it."

Troy and Rita didn't get along, at all, but the look in the other man's eyes had Adam worried. "Did she call in?"

"No. One of the girls tried to call, check on her, after we heard. It was Rhonda. They are pretty good friends. Apparently she called Rhonda last night, or early this morning . . . whatever. Rhonda said she sounded drunk off her ass and was talking crazy. I . . ." He blew out a breath and shook his head. "Look, somebody needs to go out there, okay?" He jerked a head at the door. "Get that open or you get to sit in here and torment yourself some more with this shit. You go out and see Rita. I'll deal with the interviews. But I don't think this should wait."

It was, he mused, a bad, bad day.

He'd had to kill before, but the circumstances had been very, very different. He'd served his country, and as a soldier sometimes had to do, he'd taken lives. That wasn't the only time he'd been forced to kill, though.

The men he'd killed here in Madison years ago, he truly believed, had been killed as an act of justice. He hadn't planned to kill more than that, just the names the boy had given them.

It never would have happened if the cops had listened to young David, investigated as they should have. Those men should have been arrested, had their day in court. Instead he'd sent them off to face God's justice and he'd thought he was done.

The system hadn't protected the boy, so he'd taken the job on himself. If he had nightmares over it, he'd bear that burden. Eventually, he had been able to cut himself from that period of his life. It was, as he'd viewed it, a necessity.

Sometimes a man had to take extreme actions or others suffered. It had been one of those occasions.

So for that brief period of time, he'd let himself become somebody else, just as he'd done when he'd served his country.

The problem was that it wasn't done.

All this time, he thought, brooding. He'd thought it was done. He'd had their names. He'd taken care of them.

But it wasn't isolated. It was a spreading cancer that was going to eat this town alive if he didn't excise it. This time, they'd all go down. Either he'd catch them or the police would

A few short weeks ago, he'd had to kill again. It was harder that time but still, mostly, an act of passion and he had less time to think, more time to act. All the thinking had come after the fact.

Now, though, now . . . there was plenty of time to think. Time to think and worry and brood. And plan. There were plenty of plans to be made, because he knew there were more to come.

The question was . . . how many?

He'd gotten four names from Junior, right before he'd put him in the river. That was what he should have done the first time around, gotten names from each of them, discovered how much they knew. He'd learned from his mistakes.

A couple of those men were already under investigation. The law wouldn't fail this time. Jensen Bell wouldn't allow it; neither would the current chief. The wheels of justice would turn. It was a different time. People couldn't hide behind their names as easily as they could twenty years ago, even ten years ago.

The biggest concern was uncovering all of those involved. Junior had said he didn't know all the members, especially the older ones. Junior only knew Harlan because Harlan had been the one to help *initiate* him all those years ago, and he rarely came to the meetings these days.

More names were discovered going through the files in Harlan's office—Harlan's thoroughness was going to be the downfall of quite of a few. The man thought he was careful—oh, the fire had burned up quite a few pictures.

One hadn't burned, though, and he knew from that scar that it was Harlan in that image.

Stupid, arrogant old fool.

The autopsy would confirm, if the cops were worth much of anything. Jensen was worth about ten of the cops in town, as far as he was concerned, so he suspected things would get along just fine as far as that was concerned.

Harlan's journals and "minutes" were proving to be very useful. And very disturbing. They'd kept minutes, the sick bastards. They actually kept minutes and notes.

We discussed inducting Abel's son, Glenn, at the next meeting and decided it would wait until summer.

Abel—Abel Blue, dead quite some now.
His boy, Glenn. Glenn Blue, who was currently in jail.

He'd been one of the victims once. Now he was an abuser, awaiting his day in court.

Perhaps he should feel bad for him, and he could pity the child Glenn had been. But now he wanted to murder the man.

Did they note down the atrocities they committed or just keep it circumspect?

If nothing else, when he started to falter or lose sight of the goal, all he would have to do was look at those notes, written in a spidery scrawl, and he'd find his strength again.

Killing Junior had been harder than what he'd done all those years ago. Last night had been the hardest yet, because he'd had to think it all through and plan. He was under no illusions that this would be easy. But he would see it through.

He'd find the others, and they'd all die.

Rita lived in a pretty little old house, surrounded by a white picket fence, the gleaming ribbon of the Ohio unfurling just behind the backyard.

The house had seen better years, but she'd been working to fix it up.

She'd even conned him into helping out here and there and they'd spent more than a few lazy Sundays splattered in paint or sawdust as they fixed this room up or worked on the deck or added in those bookshelves.

Just then, he wasn't thinking about any of that.

Worry gouged deep grooves into his mind as he threw his truck into park and climbed out. The gouges turned into canyons as he slammed a fist against the door, the sound of it echoing through Rita's quiet house.

A chill raced down his spine. The quiet . . . it screamed like a banshee to him. Rita didn't do quiet. She had music playing at all hours when she was home. During the day it was as loud as it could get without her getting in trouble, and at night it was a low, soft thrum coming from speakers he'd helped her install throughout the house.

The silence didn't have to be a bad thing. Maybe she'd gone for a walk.

There was no reason for him to be this worried, he told himself. The healing burn running down his arm itched as he lifted his hand and banged harder, longer. "Come on," he muttered. "Come on. . . ."

He knocked again.

"Damn it, Rita, open the fucking door!"

Nothing.

He looked over at the driveway. Her run-down Accord was parked there.

A breeze kicked up and he listened, eyes closed.

That quiet scared him. More than anything else. Swearing, he took a step back. From the corner of his eye he saw somebody walking up the sidewalk, but he ignored it.

His gut was a raw, bloody mess and he knew, as surely as he knew his own name, that something was wrong.

Gritty-eyed from lack of sleep, Caine pulled his toolbox out of the trunk and glanced over toward Rita's house.

Last night had been an eye-opening occasion.

Not just for him, either.

Madison was one fucked-up town, a fact he'd known for a while. Others were just now cluing in to to the fact, but even he was sort of surprised at just how deep the filth ran.

Strain and exhaustion pulled at him and all he wanted to do was just go back to his place, pull the curtains to block out the brilliant sun blazing down on him and sleep. For a month, maybe. He was tired enough that he thought he could get a few hours without the nightmares, the vivid memories and screams and pleas ringing in his ears.

He had to be ready to drop before he could sleep worth shit.

After last night, he thought maybe, just maybe, he was almost ready to get some rest.

"Damn it, Rita, open the fucking door!"

Frowning, Caine turned his head and stared at Adam Brascum pounding on Rita's front door. It wasn't quite noon, but between his and Rita's house there were two kids running around playing. Brascum needed to watch his mouth around kids, Caine thought.

Besides, he didn't think Rita was going to be opening that door to Brascum.

He needed to—

Adam kicked the door in.

"Well, hell," Caine muttered, tugging his hat down. With a sigh, he put his toolbox back into the trunk and slammed it shut before jogging down the walk toward Rita's house.

It wasn't hard to find Adam. Caine just followed the sounds of the shouting.

And found them both, in Rita's bedroom.

She lay on her back, a nightshirt that usually reached her knees rucked up halfway to her thighs. Her skin was pale, unnaturally so, Caine noticed. Adam had his arm under her shoulders.

"Damn it, Rita. Come on . . . say something, sweetheart," Adam said, his voice harsh and ragged. "You don't get to do this—"

Something like a sob escaped Adam as Caine knelt beside them. He cocked his head, studying the empty prescription bottle and the gleaming glass flask that had once held Jack Daniel's, some of Tennessee's finest. The stink of whiskey hung in the air, mingling with the stench of death and waste.

Her eyes were fixed on the ceiling.

She was gone.

He could see it, and he knew that Adam could, too.

The difference was that Adam wasn't ready to admit it.

"Rita, come on!" Adam shook her.

"She's gone," Caine said, reaching out to touch Adam's shoulder, still looking around the room.

The phone, half ripped out of the wall.

Adam sucked in a ragged breath and then dropped his head, pressing it to Rita's brow. "You stupid woman," he whispered. "Why did you do this? It wasn't your fault."

Silent, Caine rose and moved away, studying the room, the whiskey, the phone. He shot Adam a glance, but the other man was caught in a world of his own and didn't even notice as Caine got the phone.

As he started to dial 911, he looked back behind him and saw that Adam had put Rita on the floor, flat. The dispatcher came on the phone just as Adam started to blow into Rita's mouth.

It was too late for that.

But Caine supposed Adam had to try.

Caine left the man to the sad, grim task and spoke softly to the woman on the other end of the line. He had a cell phone for work, but he'd never gotten in the habit of keeping it with him all the time, never did understand why anybody would want to be in contact with people all the damn time.

"Did you say Rita Troyer is dead?" the lady on the other end of the line said.

"Yes," he said levelly, still watching as Adam moved to pump on her chest. "It looks like she took pills and drank some whiskey. I think she's been gone awhile."

"I'm calling the police; please stay on the line—"

"Just get them out to her house. I'll wait here," he said,

cutting her off. Then he moved back into the bedroom and stood watch as Adam tried to revive Rita.

You knew it wasn't your fault, Caine thought, studying the lifeless woman.

But there was no answer.

CHAPTER TEN

Betrayal wrenched at her heart.

It's best if you don't come back.

That low voice. The promise that it was over and done, it was all that had kept her sane—or close to it—for so long. It was why she'd given everything up, why she'd made herself accept the truths he'd told her, how she'd lived with what she'd done. What had happened.

Is that fair to him? Hasn't he been through enough?

Swearing under her breath, she tried not to think about the selfish, bitter thoughts that had eaten at her over the years. *What about me? What about what I went through?*

It did no good.

She'd come back to make things right, like she should have done years ago. Maybe they wouldn't want to have believed her *then*. But she'd make them believe her now. Considering how many of the mighty were falling in Madison, was it going to be a surprise that she had more names to add to their list? Yeah, the people *she* knew about were dead, but she knew things about the Sutter family.

She could do *something*.

That urgency thrummed inside her mind, but her thoughts stumbled to a halt as a familiar form cut across her line of sight.

Adam—

She'd left his house earlier, her hair flatironed, hanging straight to frame her face, the blunt bangs and the retro-style glasses a basic—and effective—disguise. She hadn't worn makeup since the day she'd left Madison and her skin seemed paler with the dark hair, the dark lenses. She'd already learned that people saw what they expected to see.

Nobody expected to see Lana here anymore.

So nobody did.

Maybe that was why it was so easy to spot Adam. She kept expecting to see *him* everywhere lately. And there he was, moving across the street with his head bent, his hands jammed in his pockets. Everything about him screamed, *Leave me alone.*

He ducked inside the restaurant and her heart wrenched at the sight of him.

She'd heard the news, sitting there in the middle of the coffee shop, surrounded by familiar voices and unfamiliar ones. Listening to the gossip and the chatter, she'd heard one woman's horrified voice as she talked about the tragedy that had befallen the Troyer family. The father and daughter, both dead. One murdered, one lost to suicide.

Go to him. . . . a little voice in the back of Lana's head whispered.

Go to him. She hunched in her seat, bent over the paper she'd picked up after the previous customer had left it at a nearby table. *Go to him and do what? Say what? I'm sorry you're trapped in Hellsville, USA?*

No. She had to do better than that, and if she was going to talk to him, it wasn't going to be just because she felt the insane urge to offer him comfort. Comfort or whatever else he wanted.

She really had to get her mind out of the gutter.

Forcing her mind back to the here and now, she studied

the people around her from under her lashes. Maybe she'd be lucky. A clear sign, telling her *what* she should do, *how* she should do it and *when,* would fall right out of the sky. Although hope was something she'd given up on, she shot a peek outside. The sky was clear and blue—nothing falling. No rain and definitely no signs.

She'd come home because it felt right. Now that she was here, though, she felt lost. She needed proof, somebody to go to, somebody to talk to. The only *proof* was David. Or the disc they'd made.

She had no idea where to find him, or the disc.

But she did know who to talk to, she realized. If she hadn't been so shaken by the very prospect of being here, she would have already figured it out, too. Biting her lip, she shot another glance around the coffee shop, hoped nothing she felt showed on her face.

She wanted to grab everything on the table, dump it in her bag and lunge for the door.

Instead, she casually started to put things away, drained the rest of her coffee. *Nothing much going on here . . . finished my coffee . . .* She kept the mask she'd worn for so long firmly in place, but then, as she went to push back from the table, somebody came through the door and her heart jumped up into her throat.

Out of all the faces she'd seen in here today, a few had looked vaguely familiar, but nobody had set her internal alarm buzzing.

Not until now. As the woman came striding through the door, Lana's spine went tight and her heart ached. Too many seconds passed before she figured out who it was.

For one moment, just one, she almost started to cry. *Nichole*—

The closest thing to a mom Lana had probably ever had. She'd heard about the disappearance, after it had happened, and everything in her had screamed out in denial. It had sent her careening down another spiral as she thought about the Bell kids, growing up without a mom, just like she had.

She thought about Nichole's wide, wicked eyes and that amused grin.

She thought about Doug's solemn, serious smile.

Her chest ached and ached until she had to remind herself to take a breath.

That woman wasn't Nichole. Because Nichole had been killed fifteen years ago, her body only recently found. But if that wasn't Nichole . . .

The woman moved to the counter, placing her order while Lana watched, breathing slow, steady. *In. Out.* Breathing really wasn't that complicated. She went to push her jacket to pull out some cash and that was when Lana saw the gun.

The dots connected.

Jensen. The cop. Jensen Bell.

A detective here in Madison.

Any second and Jensen would turn her head, Lana thought. Jensen would turn her head, look at Lana, and she'd know. There were probably only a handful who would see through the disguise, simple as it was, but Jensen was probably one of them. Even as a kid, she'd been clever.

Stay cool. Lana just had to stay cool. She continued to casually put up her stuff, keeping her body half-averted, her head tucked low so that her hair hung in her face.

There was a guy with Jensen. Some part of Lana was aware enough to appreciate that guy. He was gorgeous, his skin a warm, soft brown, with dreadlocks tied into a neat tail at his nape. The suit he wore looked like it cost a mint. Jensen sat with her back to the wall and her gaze passed over Lana, lingered for a moment and then moved on.

Don't look at her. Don't look at her. Don't look—

Hitching her bag onto her shoulder, she headed for the door. Her knees were knocking, her belly twisting. *Don't look. Don't look. Don't look.* Pushing through the door, she held her breath, convinced every second of the way that Jensen would call out her name.

It didn't happen.

When she hit the end of the block, she turned and got the hell out of sight, her gut a hot, angry snarl.

She wanted to go back to Adam's, bury herself in the bed and just stop breathing for a little bit. Stop thinking. Stop existing.

Except she'd done that. For twenty years.

She knew where to start now, knew exactly where to go.

It was time to face the man who'd sent her away all those years ago.

If anybody knew where to find David, it was him.

He sat on the porch.

She'd imagined this moment so many times over the years, when she was scraping by, living in cardboard boxes, in shelters, flopping in some guy's house because he'd said he'd help her score if she'd just let *him* score. She'd spent years in what felt like hell, all because he told her it was best that she leave.

And he'd spent those years here. Even now, he was on the swing, pushing back and forth, staring out over the water. Like there wasn't a thing wrong in the world. Like the entire world hadn't shifted on its axis twenty years ago, like it wasn't crumbling under her feet, just now.

Maybe it wasn't, for him.

And that, frankly, sucked.

It wasn't fair.

Her father had suffered a series of strokes that left him confined to a nursing home.

She was a shadow of herself.

Twenty years had all but rewritten who she was. There were days when she didn't even recognize herself. She'd spent more than two hours sitting in a coffee shop on Main Street in the middle of the town where she'd been born, where people had said she'd either remake the world or ruin it. But nobody had recognized her. Nobody even seemed to remember her.

She'd ruined Noah's life. It looked like he was just now finding something that might make him happy.

She thought of the Bell family, how many years they'd wandered, waited, spent nights with no answers.

She thought about David and the hell he'd gone through. Even now, he was still out there, somewhere. No justice for him, no justice for so many other kids.

People *mourned* his parents. Those monsters. People mourned them.

So many other things wrong in this town. But there he sat, rocking on his porch.

Yeah, that pretty much sucked.

. . . It's best if you don't come back. . . .

She started toward him, those words echoing through her head. *Yeah? Well, guess what?* She came back.

She saw it when he realized he wasn't alone, a fine tension racing through him, and slowly his head lifted. He turned, looking toward her, and sharp, watchful eyes narrowed on her face.

She felt the impact of that gaze right down to her toes, but she wouldn't let herself look away.

She'd given up twenty years of her life.

She wasn't giving up anything else.

As she mounted the steps, he sighed and started to fold the paper he'd been reading. It rattled, the noise grating on her ears. He tucked it under his coffee cup before looking over at her. "Why am I not surprised to see you here?"

"You were always the intelligent sort."

He looked away from her, staring out into the distance. Then he nodded to the empty space next to him. "You might as well sit. I suppose you didn't come by for nothing."

"No."

She sat in the seat and crossed her legs while her mind spun with hazy memories of the last time she'd seen him.

Those memories were too fragile to be trusted—whether it was the head injury, the trauma, the fear, she didn't know, but the first few weeks were a blur and she barely remembered *anything* but the first few minutes when he'd stood over her.

Come on, Lana. You have to get up. You have to move.

A rush of panic, fear . . . and then again his hands gentle and kind, his voice soft and reassuring. *Everything is going to be okay.*

Except it hadn't been okay.

Nothing had ever been okay again.

Minutes ticked away and neither of them spoke. The wind kicked up, blowing her hair back from her face. Despite herself, despite the heaviness in her heart, she had to smile. She'd missed this place. This town. *Home.* She'd always dreamed about leaving . . . for a while. Just to see the world. Then she wanted to come back. Marry Noah. Have a family. And do things that mattered.

That was all she'd wanted.

She'd managed to do one of those things. She saw the world.

That was about it.

Feeling the weight of his gaze, she turned her head and meet his familiar blue eyes. The steadiness of that gaze had been one of her clearest memories for a very long time. When everything else was a daze of blood and fear and pain, she remembered those eyes.

And the promise.

A broken one.

Coolly she said, "You're a damned liar."

"Am I now?"

"I was half out of my head—sick from the pain, the way my head hurt. But I remember you standing over me, telling me everything was going to be okay." Her lip curled as she looked away. "How in the hell can you call *this* okay?"

His quiet sigh drifted to her. "Well now. That is a question. I was an arrogant fool. I thought I could handle it on my own. I had the names, you know. David gave them to me. I took care of them, each one of them. On my own."

Startled, she swung her head around to look at him.

"You . . ." She blinked and rubbed a hand over her mouth. "You took care of them? There was a heart attack. A car crash."

"Easy enough to make it appear that way. If you know how." He shrugged. "I knew how."

Stunned, she stared at him, processing what he'd said. "You . . . wait." She pressed the heels of her hands against her temples as all of that settled into place. It didn't want to fit and it left her head pounding. *You killed them. All of them?* She chanced another look at him. His face was serene. And she realized she didn't doubt a word he'd said.

But it wasn't good enough. Surging to her feet, she started to pace. "It's not enough, damn it. It's still *happening.* How can it still be happening?"

She was just as angry with herself as she was with him, but it was easier to throw this out, to force the anger on somebody else.

And he let her.

"If I had the answer to that, I'd give it to you, Lana," he

said quietly, staring out over the river. "I thought it was over."

"You *thought*?" She threw the words out between them like a challenge. "Something that fucking ugly and you *thought*? Everything I left behind? Everything we did and tried to do and you *thought*? Everything we went through and you *thought*? All these boys that have been suffering and you *thought*? That's not good enough. It's not—"

"You're right," he said gently, his quiet, level voice cutting through her fury like a bucket of cold water. "I killed the men that David told me about, but I never looked any deeper, never thought to look. And I'll carry that regret to my grave. If I can find each of those boys and apologize, I will gladly do so. But I had the names of the men David knew, besides his father. I thought it was done."

Staring at his back, she curled her hands over the railing and then looked away, trying to figure out what to say next, what to do. She'd come back for a reason, and this time, no matter what it took, she'd see this through. "I'm not leaving again."

"Of all the times for you to come back, girl. You had to pick now." He shook his head, his sigh drifting away on the wind. He slanted a glance at her, a thick brow rising. Those insightful eyes probed her, seemed to see straight through her. "I take it you heard about the body. You know they found her."

"I . . ." She gulped, spit drying in her mouth and turning her heart to lead. As it sank like a stone to settle in the pit of her belly, she forced herself to speak. "I know. It doesn't matter. I heard about the arrests. I know it's still going on. Nothing else matters. I have to see it through, make sure it stops this time. No matter what."

"No matter what." He tugged off his hat and ran his fingers through his hair, staring down at the floorboards, studying the toes of dusty worn-out boots. "And when you're connected to what happened all those years ago, girl? What are you going to do when they start pushing for answers? Plenty of people tried to connect you to their disappearances. You aware of that? Have you thought it through that far?"

"No." The word came out faint, weak, and she had to clear her throat before she could say anything else. "No. I haven't through it through. But I can't just sit back and turn a blind eye when I know what's going on here. If I'd stayed . . ."

"If you'd stayed . . ." He paused, his words trailing off as he stared off into nothing. "A lot of ifs. Twenty years gone, no way to know what could have happened. They'll have questions for you. A lot of them. And you'll have to be the one to answer some of them."

He turned, leaned against the railing. "If it comes to that, so will I."

Guilt lodged in her throat, weighed down on her like a stone. "I don't have to tell about you."

"Horseshit. I'm involved. Same as you." Those shrewd eyes lingered on her face and she had to fight not to squirm. "What can you tell them about that night?"

The pounding in her head increased, that ache that always got worse every time she tried to figure out an answer. She just shook her head. "Next to nothing. Most of it is a jumble. A few bits and pieces of you. There was David, before she showed up. And then her . . . once she showed up, everything moves too fast and there was the gunshot. Pain. Then it's all a mess and I don't have anything clear until . . ."

She stopped, looked away. If she kept talking she'd start to rage at him, and that wouldn't accomplish anything. She wanted to yell, wanted to demand answers. Why had he shoved her away like that?

Why hadn't he . . .

Something of what she felt must have shown on her face. She saw the change come over his face, saw it as he prepared to say something. Before he could, the door to the house opened. Lana froze and ducked her head, staring at the floor as a woman's soft, questioning voice drifted to them.

Feeling the weight of the woman's curious stare, Lana turned around, staring back over the river as the man and woman talked.

Then Lana turned away, giving them her back.

A moment passed and the door shut.

Swallowing the knot in her throat, she glanced over at him while a war waged inside.

Now what?

She wasn't sure what she'd hoped to accomplish here, but she'd come hoping he'd have answers. Insight.

Something.

But there was nothing here, she realized.

Whatever she was going to do, she'd be doing it alone.

"You don't need to go stirring things from the past up," he said gently. "All those people are going to pay for what they did. It's all coming to light now. You don't need to be involved in it."

"Involved . . ." Bitterly, she smiled. "I've been involved from the get-go. There's only one other person *more* involved than in this than I am." She turned and gave him a hard look. "And I guess he's not wanting to do jack shit about it."

There were a hundred questions she should ask—so much of that night was a fog, and so many of her memories were muddled.

She could ask those questions. She would try to get answers. But the rage inside her was clawing to get free and one thing she had learned—she knew better than to do anything unless she was completely in control.

Since she was veering into that area where she just might lose control, she pushed off the railing and left.

He stayed behind, watching and waiting.

CHAPTER ELEVEN

He felt like he was moving through a fog.

Death did weird things to people, and he wasn't talking about the deceased. All fucking day, Adam had been forced to deal with nosy questions, false sympathy and, even worse . . . awkward, *real* sympathy from people who weren't really sure what to say. Rita had a lot of friends, but not many of them had been close.

She'd been a lot like him.

A loner.

In a few weeks, other than her mom, he might be the only one who even thought about Rita much.

It hurt. A lot. She should be remembered, somehow.

Moving down the street, he stopped in front of her house and leaned against the fence while his mind struggled to work.

It didn't add up. None of it added up; none of it made sense.

I want this to make sense.

But there wasn't any sense to make of it. How could he make sense of her death, though?

The past few weeks had been miserable, but why had she killed herself over something her father had done?

Had she slid that far down into that pit of depression

again and he just hadn't seen it? She'd fought those demons before, but he could usually see it coming on.

This . . . this mess with her father had been different.
Had it come on that fast, that hard, and he just hadn't seen
it? Yeah, she'd asked him over, and there'd been a shadow
in her eyes, but it wasn't *that* look. He knew *that* look.
That darkness, that desperation.

If he'd seen that there, he would have gone home with
her. Would have been there.

But it had been there anyway, and *he* hadn't been.

She'd been alone, completely alone, and she'd killed
herself.

"Fuck," he snarled, driving the heels of his hands
against his eyes in a desperate attempt to blot out the image
of her, her pale form sprawled against the carpet, her eyes
sightless, the bottle of Jack a few inches from her hand and
the empty bottle of pills just a few more inches away.

That memory spun around in his mind like a deranged
child's toy and he couldn't stop it, couldn't wash it away.
If he kept standing there, he was going to find a way *to*
wash it away. Preferably with his own bottle of Jack.

Because the call was damn strong, he turned away and
started up the road, heading toward home.

It wasn't a long walk, but each step was dogged with
guilt and grief. Hands jammed into his pockets, he refused to look toward Shakers as he crossed Main and
headed west. His house was just a few more blocks away,
and once he hit his street, he breathed a little easier.

He hadn't given in, hadn't succumbed.

One more night.

He'd made it through one more night.

At the sidewalk, he paused, staring up at the house, so
dark and quiet.

And empty.

Completely empty.

Son of a bitch.

Lana wasn't there.

One hand curled into a fist, tight, useless, impotent, as it hung at his side.

She wasn't *here.*

Somewhere deep inside, he realized he'd been holding on to some halfhearted hope that she'd be here when he came home. That he wouldn't have to come home alone.

And she wasn't here.

The windows were dark, staring out at him like dead eyes as he stood at the foot of the walk. What little strength he had left all but drained out of him and he almost went to his knees.

Abruptly the desire for that bottle of Jack returned, with a vengeance. *Why the hell not . . . ?*

He'd done it for his folks, but they were long gone and they'd never know if he lost himself in a bottle again. The one person he really did need was never going to be his. She'd probably leave again anyway, so what did it matter?

What the *hell* did it matter if he fell inside the bottle and never crawled back out?

Because you owe it to yourself.

At this point, though, that wasn't much of an anchor.

Lana stared out the window of the room Adam had given her.

He looked . . . lost.

He looked empty.

And as awful as it sounded, she wanted to go down there, wrap herself around him and just lose herself in him.

She understood the need for seeking comfort in physical contact. She'd done that a *lot* when she'd first hit the ground running. Although maybe *comfort* wasn't exactly the right word. She'd just been looking for something.

Looking to find herself. Looking to lose herself. Looking for something to hold on to so she didn't just . . . fade away. Just looking.

She'd never found what she was looking for, although she'd come close with Deatrick.

Now, though . . . she wasn't just aimlessly yearning.

Looking at Adam, she actually *wanted*.

It was the first time she'd actually *wanted* somebody since . . . hell. Since Noah.

She didn't just want the physical contact and she wasn't just looking to scratch an itch. She wanted to strip those battered jeans away, that faded black T-shirt. She wanted to learn the hard muscles under the clothes, with her hands and then with her mouth. She'd already spent far too much time learning him with her eyes, but she'd damn well like to see how he looked when he wasn't wearing a stitch of clothing.

Preferably when he was crouched over her, his hands fisted in her hair as he came inside her.

A pulse of hunger hit her square in the middle and rippled through her entire body. Loose, liquid warmth spread through her, turning her limbs to putty, pulsing through her core, while her nipples drew to near-painful points. Just from thinking about him. No. Not *him. Them.* Together.

This was insane.

Lana didn't care. She wanted to grab it, grab *him,* and ride that insanity all the way to the end.

One day.

She'd only been back one day and the crazy need was threatening to eat her alive.

But then again, some part of her had always belonged to Adam.

He'd been her first crush.

He'd been her confidant.

He'd been her closest friend, for the longest time.

And when she'd seen him running along the river, some part of her had felt . . . *safe.*

She didn't want safety now, though. She wanted to stroke away the misery she sensed inside him and she wanted to wrap her arms around him, guide his head to her breasts and promise him that it was going to be okay.

Even if it was a lie.

She wanted to *make* it okay. Not just for her, but for him, as he stood down there, looking like his entire world was falling apart. Then she wanted to do something completely selfish and make him focus on something other than his grief. She wanted him to focus on her.

"You are a selfish little tramp," she muttered.

Look away, she told herself. If he was grieving over Rita, she should leave him to it. She should curl back up in the bed and get back to trying to piece through the notes she'd been making, articles she'd been researching online, bits and pieces of what she remembered from years ago.

She'd spent most of the afternoon on it, not that she'd learned anything. David hadn't been able to really give her many names. The men were careful about how the boys were brought in, but he'd mentioned, once, that he thought he knew who a few others were. One of them had been Glenn. Glenn Blue. And that son of bitch had become one of them. Now he had a son of his own.

They had tried to *break* it and then that bastard had just up and remade it. There had to be more. Other connections, other ties that she needed to see, but she couldn't drag her eyes away from Adam.

All she could think about was him. She wanted to tell him she was sorry. For so many things. For his friend. For the hurt she'd caused him.

Lifting a hand to the window, she watched, wondered, worried. And as she watched, he lifted his hands to his face. Broad shoulders rose and fell in a ragged rhythm.

The sight of it made her ache and the tears he didn't seem willing to shed rose inside her.

"Adam . . ." she whispered, lifting a hand to the window.

And it was like he heard her.

Adam didn't know what drove him.

He didn't hear anything.

He didn't see anything.

But awareness rippled through him, his skin prickling as he slowly lowered his hands and lifted his head, staring up through the night at the darkened house before him.

There, at the window of the room he'd given her. He saw nothing, save the ripple of the curtain, the pale material pulled back.

Then, something shifted and Lana appeared. All he could see was her hand as she lifted it, pressed it to the glass.

The next few seconds were just a haze on his memory. He didn't remember crossing the sidewalk, unlocking the door. He might have run, raced the entire way, and he could believe it, because when he came to a halt in the doorway of her room it seemed like an eternity later, like an instant later, and his breath came in harsh, ragged pants.

She stared at him.

If she'd looked worried or nervous or startled, he could have turned and walked away.

Lana just stared at him, the sexy, sleek horn-rimmed glasses a shield, hiding those luminous grey eyes. In the dim light of the room he couldn't clearly make out her face, but he didn't need to. Every feature was etched on his memory. From twenty years, from hours, ago. He could recall her in detail.

He crossed the floor to her, his boots thudding on the floor, his heart thudding against his chest and his breath still coming in harsh, uneven rasps.

He reached up and pulled the glasses off, waited for her to do something, say something.

She *should,* he thought. She *would.* Lana wasn't one of the women who came to him for this, who know what he was—

Suddenly shame twisted in him.

Rita had needed just that from him last night. Comfort. A friend in the night. If he'd let her turn to him, maybe she'd be alive. But he hadn't been able to give it to her and now she was gone.

And he didn't *care.* Oh, he cared about the fact that his friend was gone, but instead of mourning her like he knew he should, what he wanted to do was just reach for Lana and have what he'd wanted, needed, all these years. As he worried, as he wondered, as he needed and prayed and tried to lose himself in everybody but the one woman he always wanted.

Adam looked down, stared at the glasses he held. *Walk away.* He needed to do that.

He needed to walk away, if for no other reason than because he needed to be able to live with himself in the morning. He was used to being used. He had used plenty of women. He had to do something to numb the pain, smother the guilt. But he couldn't use Lana—she was the source of his pain, his guilt, his need . . . his everything. And it would kill something inside him if she just wanted to use him.

Swallowing the bitter ache that had settled in his throat, he blindly shoved the glasses at her.

She caught his hands. One gently took the glasses.

The other curved over his wrist.

He stared, mesmerized, as she slid a hand up his fore-arm, pausing to scrape her nail along one of the chain links he'd inked onto his skin over the years. His skin burned under her touch. *Walk away . . . walk . . .*

Only he didn't know if he could. Not now. He would lose all self-respect in the morning, but he had so little left anyway, what did it matter? It would kill something inside him, but there wasn't anything there worth saving.

As she slid her hand higher, over his biceps to grip his shoulder, he wanted to growl, push her back up against the wall and rock against her. Feel the softness and the curves and the strength and the heat.

"You had a lousy day, I think," she murmured.

He jerked his head up, staring into her eyes.

A sad smile curved her lips.

Sympathy.

This was sympathy.

Somehow she knew about Rita.

Stupid ass. She doesn't want you, a sly, ugly voice in-side him whispered. *She never did. She had somebody else back then . . . somebody better. All she wants to do is pat you on the head and give you stupid, empty words.*

And being the desperate fool that he was, he would take it. He knew. If she wanted to rock him and hug him and just let him cry his eyes out while she held him, he'd take that and be pathetically grateful.

He had no pride when it came to her. He'd take any-thing she would give him.

The only thing that kept him from grabbing at her was the fact that he didn't know how he'd hold himself to-gether when she left.

Looking past her shoulder, he stared out the window into the dark night. "Yeah. You . . . I guess you heard about Rita."

"Yeah. I hid in the coffee shop. Scared somebody

would see me, recognize me, but everybody was talking about what happened with her, her dad." Lana eased a little closer and slid her arms around his waist, resting her head on his chest.

She fit there.

He closed his eyes and tried not to let himself relax, to cuddle her closer to him and breathe her in and lose himself in her. He needed that, so much. But that wasn't his to take. *Lana* wasn't his to take.

So he kept his hands at his sides, kept his body locked in a rigid line and just shrugged. "The whole damn town's gone crazy the past few months."

"The past few months, Adam?" She tipped her head back to stare up at him. "You think this just started a few months ago? No."

She pulled back and turned back to stare out the window. "This has all been a long time coming. And there's going to be a reckoning."

Those words filled him with foreboding. And because the want in him, the heat, the hunger, the love he'd felt for her all his life had to be denied, it tripped out of him in a rage he just couldn't silence. "Yeah?" A snarl curled his lip and he watched as she turned to look at him. "Why don't you just tell me about that, sugar?"

The rage wasn't exactly unexpected.

But how he'd gone from raw misery to raw rage in the blink of an eye, it caught her off-guard.

"I don't think I'm ready to talk about that yet." She turned away from him but hadn't taken even a step before she was spun back around. Instinct warred with fury and logic and compassion. Muscles bunched, clenched, ready to strike out, but she didn't do anything as he loomed over her, his face all but lost in the shadow.

"And when are you going to be ready? You show up

out of nowhere after twenty years and you won't say a damn thing. *When* are you going to talk, Lana?" he murmured, reaching up and pushing a hand into her hair. "*Are you going to talk or are you just going to disappear again?*"

Her skin prickled at his touch.

She looked away from him, away from the intensity of his eyes, and tried to breathe. It had gotten hard in the past few seconds. Probably had something to do with how hot it had suddenly gotten, or maybe the fact that her heart had short-circuited and was racing away at about two hundred beats a minute.

The hand in her hair tightened as he tugged, guiding her gaze back to his. "No answers?" The smile on his face was just this side of cruel. "Why am I not surprised?"

"I can't give you answers I don't have, Adam," she said, keeping her voice level.

And her gaze off his mouth.

She really, really wanted to feel that mouth against hers. All of a sudden, it seemed very important, like the center of her world. It might even be the most important thing *in* the world in that very moment.

"What can you give me?" he asked, his voice low.

She was imagining the need in his voice. Imagining it because she *wanted* to hear it there. Except when she forced herself *not* to look at his mouth, she noticed that he was looking at hers.

Hunger lashed at her like a whip and she curled her hands into fists to keep from reaching for him.

"What do you want?" she asked, her voice hardly more than a whisper.

His lids drooped low.

Silence hung between them, heavy, taut, sharp as a blade. Then, as it stretched out for almost longer than she could bear it, he reached up and rested his hand on her hip. "I want things I shouldn't. I always did."

His thumb slid beneath the hem of her T-shirt and Lana could feel her breathing hitch in her chest. This was insane, the way she wanted.

This was insane, the way she needed.

But then again, she'd taken one look at him behind the bar and she'd wanted. Each second since then seemed to draw that need even tighter and now, standing there, practically surrounded by him, she felt like she was coiled like a spring, just ready to snap.

Maybe it was stupid. Maybe it was insane.

But she didn't care.

She'd been *careful* for twenty years.

She'd shut herself down for twenty years.

She could have one damn night when she didn't have to worry about anything and everything, couldn't she?

Slowly, she lifted one hand and rested it on his chest. Through the thin material of the shirt he wore she could feel the heat of him, and it scalded her. His heart hammered against her palm, hard, fast beats that seemed to echo the rhythm of her own. Swallowing, she dragged her eyes upward and found herself caught in his gaze. Caught, held.

"What do you want?" she asked softly.

He just stared at her.

And when she leaned forward and pressed her lips to his, he held still. Almost like he was frozen. But she felt the hunger, like it was a beast, snarling from within. It practically vibrated inside him and she pressed closer, desperate to unleash that hunger and just *feel*.

To let go for a little while and have somebody else—no. Not somebody else.

To have *Adam* with her while they both enjoyed the ride.

She stroked her tongue across his lips and he just stood there.

She caught his lower lip between her teeth, tugged, and he just stood there.

She kissed her way across his cheek, his jawbone, and down his neck. He just stood there. His pulse raced under her touch, but he didn't do anything. Didn't even show any sign that he wanted her.

Other than the fact that she could *feel* it.

Doubt started to whisper inside her and she went to pull back.

That was when he moved.

Her breath lodged in her throat as he spun them around. Her head was still whirling and then her heart stuttered to a stop as hard, calloused hands closed around her waist and boosted her up, settling her butt on the edge of the bureau that took up nearly half the wall. She opened her mouth to say something. Anything. She didn't even know what she might have said, though, because Adam's mouth caught hers in the next moment and anything she might have said just . . . died.

His kiss consumed her.

It was as though he breathed her in and just . . . consumed her.

His hands cupped her head, held her steady, and that touch might have been the only thing grounding her, too, because she felt like she was about to fly into pieces just from the kiss.

His tongue rubbed across hers, a sensuous, teasing rhythm that sent a low, demanding pang through her. Groaning, she arched against him, and he responded by sliding an arm around her waist and pulling her up against him, firm and tight so that nothing but their clothes separated them.

Too many clothes . . . through those layers, she could feel the heat of him and the strength of him and that hunger that vibrated inside him, barely held in check.

With teeth and tongue he all but devastated her, with just that kiss. And then he shifted his attention, working his way down to her neck, and she fell back, slamming her hands down on the bureau. Dazed, dizzy, she stared up at the ceiling as his teeth raked over the sensitive curve of her neck. "Adam . . ."

His hand curled over the hem of her shirt. "You asked me what I wanted."

"Yes." She sucked in a desperate breath of air and watched as lifted his head, staring at her through his lashes.

His hand skimmed up along her torso. She felt her heart bump against him as he passed over her chest, and then he stopped, his palm curved over her neck. "And what if I want this? Do I get this?"

Heat flooded her.

She should say no.

Logic should step in and she should think and she should push him away.

Instead, she reached for the hem of his shirt and pulled it up.

He let her. She dropped it to the floor and reached up, resting her hands on the wall of his chest. He had a light smattering of hair between his nipples, running down the middle of his torso, disappearing under his jeans. She wanted to follow that line with her mouth. Her throat went dry as she reached up and traced her fingers along the ink. Here the chains were broken, like something had caused the links to break, just along his powerful shoulders.

The sexy, sexy tattoos. She had such a weakness for them.

Biting her lip, she traced her finger down his chest, studying the dates written in scrolled ink. They started above his heart and continued down the lean line of his torso, stopping shy of his hip bone. Three dates, in bold, scrawling font. She could barely read them in the dim light. Easing in, she cocked her head, studied them. "Why the dates?" she murmured, pressing her lips to them.

"To remind me."

She lifted a brow. "Yeah? Wouldn't a calendar be better?" she teased.

He hissed as she touched her tongue to him, one hand coming up to curve over the back of her flesh.

"Some things are more important than that." He tangled a hand in her hair and tugged her head back. "Open your mouth. I want to taste you."

She groaned and he swallowed the rest of the sound down, his mouth slanting over hers.

Against her chest she could feel the raging rhythm of his heart, and when she closed her mouth around his tongue and sucked, his heart rate jacked up even more, his arms tightening around her.

"Bed," he growled against her lips a split second later, pulling back just enough to press a line of kisses down her jawline, along her cheek, up to her ear to catch her lobe between his teeth. "We should move to the bed."

"Sounds good to me." She angled her neck and shivered as he scraped his teeth across her skin. That was . . . bliss. Yeah. *Bliss* described it. She hadn't felt alive like this in, maybe, ever.

Instead of either of them moving to the bed, though, they fumbled with their clothes. He stripped her jeans away while she fought with the zipper of his. He kicked off his boots and she hurriedly unlaced hers.

He came back to her in the dim light and reached for the hem of the shirt she still wore, but she evaded him, smoothing her hands across his torso, studying the tattoos she couldn't quite make out.

The dates written in scrolling ink down the left side of his chest and abdomen, while on the right side of his chest what looked like a firebird that stretched across his skin, the wings edging over his shoulder, the flames meeting and appearing to melt the chains as the wing continued on down his back. It was like the giant bird had mantled his wings over Adam and settled into his skin. There was an odd design in the bird's chest, one she couldn't make out in the light. She rubbed it with her thumb and leaned in, but instead of trying to study it, she found herself kissing Adam, pressing her mouth to his chest, seeking out the flat circle of his nipple and biting him lightly.

Adam groaned, the sound hoarse and broken as he wrapped his arm around her waist.

"Bed," he muttered again, his voice more urgent.

She laughed, clinging to him as the room whirled around him. The sound died in her throat as she found herself sprawled on her back, staring up at the ceiling as he came down over her. His mouth, hungry and hot, caught hers, his hands going to the inside of her thighs and pushing wide.

She fumbled with his jeans, all but panting as she finally freed the thick, heavy ridge of his cock, a rush of want arrowed through her and she felt feel herself getting wetter. Wet and ready and so hungry for him.

Closing her hand around him, she dragged her palm up, down, felt him throb under her touch. As she reached the crest, she circled her thumb around the tip and felt the bead of fluid there. She spread it across his head and watched his face as she stroked back down.

He jerked in her hand and she smiled, staring up at him. A snarl crossed his face and she did it again, and again. He started to push against her hand and need twisted inside her, almost painful.

"Lana . . ." he whispered, the sound shaking and rough, almost reverent. Then, abruptly, he was gone and she shivered, sitting up and staring at him as he snagged something from the ground.

She blinked, feeling a little dazed, and then understanding dawned as he pulled out his wallet. Something that might have been humor tried to work free as he tugged a rubber from somewhere inside the wallet.

At any other time, she would have made a flippant remark.

Just then, she was only glad he had something with him.

She heard the foil tear and she reached for him as he came back to her.

He reached for the hem of her shirt and she caught his hand out of instinct, held it down. Those were questions she wouldn't answer. Catching his head in her hands, she tugged his mouth to hers. His hand stroked across her torso, back up her neck to rest there, and his gaze bored into hers as he moved up and pressed against her.

Her breath caught and she shifted, spreading her thighs and curling her arms around his neck.

A shaken curse slid free as he slowly pushed inside. "You . . . fuck, Lana. You're so tight and hot." He stroked a hand down her thigh, seeking out the rigid knot of her clit, and she jolted as he started to stroke. "Easy, girl . . . relax."

Relax? She sucked in a breath. Was he insane?

He rocked against her, pushed a little deeper. "You're so wet . . . that's it. . . ."

She whimpered, rocking against his hand, unconsciously working him a little deeper inside her.

"Fuck, that's good . . . more," he muttered. "Take more."

She shuddered and did just that, arching and moving against him, feeling bruised from him, but she didn't care. It didn't matter; nothing mattered but getting closer, taking more, just like he'd asked.

He slid a hand under her, tugged her closer as he rotated his hips and sank deeper inside. The thick pillar of his cock stroked against sensitive flesh, stretched too tight, and she shuddered as he swiveled his hips, changing his angle so he hit her just *there,* right against her G-spot, and she cried out, arching her spine and moving against him again.

The hot, heavy wall of his chest moved against hers as he crushed her closer. "Like that?"

"Yes. . . ."

He did it again and she cried out again as he found his rhythm, each stroke taking him deeper. It had been so long for her and she hung on the blade between pleasure and pain, so desperate for him, for more of this. Watching him, feeling him moving inside, getting lost in his eyes, was too much.

All of it swamped her and she closed her eyes, desperate to center herself, even a little. A hard, warm hand came up, circled the front of her neck.

"No," Adam said, his voice guttural and harsh. "You said I could have this . . . that includes you seeing me. Me seeing you . . . Look at me, Lana. *Look* at me."

She groaned and forced her lashes up. He retreated and then surged forward, flexing his hips and driving deeper inside. And he watched her . . . the whole time. It felt like he was staring straight into her soul and all the secrets, all the darkness and the fear and the misery, was just laid bare for him to see.

Shaken, she tried to grab some of it back, hold it inside even as she held his gaze.

She didn't want to share that much of herself. Her body was one thing. . . . Everything she'd held trapped inside was something else.

She scrambled to pull back from him. Adam could see it.

He might not ever have anything else, but he'd have this. Hunkering down over her, he canted her hips higher and watched her, holding her gaze captive with his as he took her mouth.

A shaken, broken noise fell from her lips and he swallowed it, groaned as she wrapped one arm around his neck and sank her nails into his flesh.

Her legs wrapped around him and it wasn't enough.

Shoving upright onto his knees, he reached for the hem of her shirt.

Her eyes widened and she resisted.

This time, he ignored her and stripped it away.

For one second, just one—the scar on her ribs was all he saw.

Old and faded. Laying his hand over it, he shifted his eyes up, met hers.

She stared at him, the heat fading from her eyes, the color in her cheeks bleeding away until she was just pale.

Feeling a little sick, he pulled out and went to his knees, shifting until he could press his lips to the long, thin mark.

Adam had taken more than his fair share of cuts, scrapes and bruises in his life. When you made it your life's mission to fuck as many women as you could, fights tended to happen. Especially when you didn't care if the women were married or not. Guys took offense to that sort of thing. One of the worst moments of his life, one that had actually *almost* made him get his act together, had been when Little Tom Naughton had come after him when he realized that Adam had been sleeping with his wife, Judy, while Tom was out on the road. Tom had been sleeping with a lady up in Seymour, Indiana, and everybody knew it, except Judy. But Little Tom hadn't much liked it when Judy decided to turn things around on him and he'd come after them both with a knife. Adam had taken the knife instead, pushing Judy behind him.

The knife had just grazed him and he hadn't need

stitches, just a few butterfly bandages to hold it closed. It had left a scar . . . sort of like Lana's.

Only the scar on Lana's torso was much, much bigger.

This one was so faded, he knew she'd had it a good long while.

Pressing his lips to it, he told himself he wouldn't ask. Yet.

But she'd damn well tell him.

Her hands lay fisted next to her hips, her face averted.

Settling between her thighs, he caught one small, tight fist in his hand and drew it up beside her head as he pressed against her. Rubbing his lips against her cheek, he whispered, "Kiss me, Lana."

She said nothing, still staring off to the side.

He sighed and kissed his way down her neck, across her shoulder. "I'll just kiss you, then. Everywhere."

The smooth slope of her pale shoulders. Her breasts, small but full and firm. He opened the front catch of her bra and groaned as he caught sight of her nipples, plump and pink and practically begging for him.

Dipping his head, he caught one between his teeth and tugged on it, listened to her breath catch. "You like being kissed there, I think." So he did it, again, and again, and watched as her breathing grew ragged once more.

He spent several minutes doing nothing but playing with those pretty, pink nipples, but a man had to keep his word, when and if he gave it. And Adam had promised to kiss her everywhere. He slid his lips back up over her collarbone and started down her biceps. Her muscles tensed. He barely noticed as he scraped his teeth along toned, sleek skin. "You're so fucking gorgeous," he muttered. "You don't . . ."

His lips brushed over a ridge.

He might not have noticed except there wasn't just one. There were several of them, on her right forearm.

And as he lifted his head, he felt the tension radiating off her body. Her face was flaming red, but she stared at him, her gaze all but challenging him, her chin up, daring him.

She shoved the other forearm at him. "You're in bed with a fucking junkie. Am I *still* gorgeous?"

His heart broke a little at the pain he saw hiding in the backs of her eyes.

And he thought of all the tokens he had thrown in the back of the drawer of his desk. Thought of the tattoos she'd been kissing on his chest, the links on his arms. She thought she had cornered the market on demons, huh?

He could give her lessons, he'd bet.

Pressing his lips to each scar, he whispered, "Gorgeous."

And then he covered her body with his and cupped her face in his hands. "You said I could have this . . . you backing out now?"

Her eyes, shocked and wide, locked on his.

Her throat worked as she swallowed. Then she jutted her chin up. "You that fucking hard up you'll screw a junkie, Adam?" she jeered.

He laughed and pressed a kiss to the corner of her mouth. "When was the last time you used, Lana?" Wrapping his arms around her, he turned, stopping when he had her sprawled on top of him. For a second, one sweet, blissful second, he let himself enjoy the hot, wet pleasure of having her wet, hot pussy rubbing against his aching dick and then he focused on her face, on the insanity of the situation. She was still glaring at him, even though her gaze had gone a little unfocused. He arched his hips and smiled a little as she whimpered, her teeth catching her lower lip in an effort to silence the sound.

"No answer?"

He eased her into an upright position and slid his hand

down, sought out her clit. "I'll tell you what . . . you think about it and I'll just get you off. I'll watch."

Her lids drooped, her head falling back. It lifted her breasts and his mouth watered. He wanted to taste her again, wrap his mouth around those tight, pink nipples and lick her, suck her, until she sobbed out his name and gasped for breath.

"You . . ." She rocked against his hand as he stroked her clit. "What are you . . ."

He plunged two fingers inside the slick, wet well of her pussy and twisted. "I'm going to make you come. I'm going to be either fucking you or doing it like this, but I'm going to make you come. If you want to think about the answer to that question while I'm doing this, fine . . . or you can just ride me and fuck the answer. I think we both know you're not using now. So stop using it as an excuse."

It was damn hard, he decided, to carry on any sort of conversation when he had her naked on top of him. Naked, and she was tight and hot and wet around his fingers.

And then she was shifting, pulling back and grabbing his hand.

"You're an asshole, Adam. When did you turn into an asshole?"

If she pulled away from him, he was going to cry, he thought. He knew it.

But she closed her hand around his cock and held him steady, started to sink down on him.

"Oh, I've been an ass for a while," he muttered. *Twenty years . . . give or take.* He reached up and gripped her hips. "Ride me, Lana. I want to watch you come. And then I want to do it again. And again . . ."

Morning came slow and easy.

Adam kept his face buried in her hair and refused to

think about the fact that he shouldn't have spent the night in her bed.

He rarely spent the night with a woman. He couldn't say *never*.

But he tried to avoid it.

And he hadn't ever had a woman sleep in his home. This was one thing he should have avoided. Lana was his weakness, his drug, his cure, his strength. His poison.

His everything.

She always had been.

A soft grumpy sound left her and she snuggled back against him, her ass firm and soft and perfect against his dick.

His dick approved.

He didn't need to note the approval of his dick, though.

What he needed to do was get out of bed and go shower, maybe try to grab another hour of sleep or two in his own bed and then figure out how to handle this.

He'd slept with Lana.

That wasn't *exactly* a problem.

Adam had slept with . . . well. More women than he could really count.

The problem was Lana herself.

The scar on her side. The scars on her arms were just as big a concern to him, although probably not for the reason she thought.

His gut told him that he knew where the knife scar had come from. Or at least *when*. She'd been hurt that night. Was that why she'd called him? Instead of letting him help, why had she lied and why had she run?

Where had she been all these years?

And *fuck*, Lana had been using drugs. Just what had pushed her to that? She'd been the straightest, most level person he'd ever known, but something had pushed her over.

If he was smart, maybe he should worry about whether or not she was clean, but that was the least of his worries. Just like he wasn't worried about whether or not she was using anymore.

The woman he'd spoken with over the past day or so was sober and clean.

He knew addicts. Nobody knew an addict quite the way another addict did.

She wasn't still using. He knew users. He'd known Layla was using when he hired her, but as long as she wasn't high when she worked he was willing to give her a chance. It had set him off, though, when she had drugs in the same house where her kid lived.

Lana, though, he hadn't caught that vibe off her. It had been years since she'd used; he'd bet his life on it.

She made another one of those grumpy sounds and then she sighed. "You think awful damn loud. How in the hell did you get to be a Lothario if you're like this in the morning?"

That startled something of a laugh out of him.

An embarrassed laugh, but a laugh none the same.

She rolled onto her back and glared at him.

"You think it's funny. I'm trying to sleep and you're laughing."

He stroked a finger down her cheek. "Lothario?"

"Yeah. A man-whore. You went and turned into an asshole and a man-whore."

He winced, and this time there was no denying the embarrassment. Sighing, he pulled away and sat up, staring out the window, although the curtains kept him from seeing much of anything.

Behind him, Lana sighed.

"That was mean. I'm sorry."

He glanced back over his shoulder at her. "Why? It's the truth. Just like the fact that at some point you went from being a goody two-shoes to using drugs. I turned into an asshole and I fuck my way through town. Although I'm kind of curious how you figured that out. *You* haven't been around."

"I keep tabs on things," she said vaguely, shrugging.

You kept tabs on things. He ran his tongue across his teeth and tried to keep a grip on the edge of fury that sliced through him. Tried to control the hurt. "You kept tabs on things . . . but you couldn't find a way to let me know you weren't dead. To let your dad know. Noah. Didn't we deserve that courtesy?"

She sighed and the bed shifted as she rolled onto her back. "It's not about courtesy, Adam. I couldn't let anybody know. There were reasons."

"Yeah? I asked last night for you to share some of the reasons with me."

He turned on the bed, bracing one hand on the other side of her, staring down into her face. Her hair, dark and dense, spread out on the pillow. He knew now, for a fact, that it was definitely a dye job. The curls between her thighs were a dark red and he found himself missing all the things that she'd forced herself to change.

He had to know why, had to understand.

"What are you hiding from, Lana?" he asked quietly. "How much of this has to do with that fucking Cronus Club?"

Her lashes flickered. That was the only sign she gave.

But she said nothing, turning her head to stare at the wall.

"His dad was one of them . . . wasn't he?"

A sigh gusted out of her and she shut her eyes.

Then, even as he told himself that she wouldn't tell him, she swung her head around and met his gaze. "This isn't my secret to tell," she said, her voice low, while misery turned her eyes to smoke.

"Maybe it's not your secret to tell, but it's time the truth came out," he said, shaking his head. He laid a hand on her face, sighing. "If the truth had come out all those years ago, think about how many kids could have been spared hell."

"You think I don't *know* that?" She averted her face, staring at the wall. "I thought it had stopped. It was the only reason I stayed gone. I thought it had stopped."

CHAPTER TWELVE

"You look like you're doing well, Caleb."

Caleb shrugged and looked around, his expression that patented bored look that so many teenagers excelled at.

But he looked . . . almost happy.

Noah hadn't been sure if this was the place for Caleb, but it was hard trying to *find* the right place for him.

When Jensen had suggested they put Caleb with her dad, Noah hadn't known what to think.

They needed somebody who was definitely *not* part of the evil that seemed to stain the town, and Jensen trusted her father, completely.

They needed somebody whom the boy could connect with.

Family was out of the question in this case.

Too many of the families connected to Cronus had actually *known* what was going on . . . or they'd just been willfully blind—wives, sons, cousins, grandparents. It was a poisoned web, stretching back so many years.

Fury punched at Noah and he had to work to hide it. Hide it until he could work it out, because that fury wouldn't help this boy. But a calm hand, acceptance and love . . .

It seemed he'd found it with Doug Bell.

Out in the driveway, Doug listened to Tate argue with Jensen. No, they were *discussing* the proper way to grill up some steaks. And off to the side, Chris and Dean were watching. Dean looked amused by it all. So did Doug.

"If she lets Tate do it, you'll be eating a steak that's tough as rubber," Noah said, watching as Tate lifted a bottle of beer to his lips, smirking at his younger sister.

"She won't let Tate do it. She just likes to let him think he'll win." Caleb had something in his voice that sounded just this side of adoration, and he watched Jensen with the hot, intense focus of a boy in the throes of young love.

Jensen made a rude noise in Tate's direction and everybody laughed, including Caleb.

"You think maybe you'll come to church Sunday?"

Caleb jerked his thin shoulders in a shrug. "I dunno. I don't much like church, Preach."

"Yeah. I know." He reached up, watched as Caleb instinctively tensed. But the boy held still as Noah rubbed him on the shoulder. "But maybe someplace else would be different. Doug comes to the same place I go. You might find some peace there."

"Peace." Caleb looked older than his years in that moment. "I don't want peace. I want those fuckers dead." Then he flushed and looked away. "Sorry, sir."

Noah squeezed Caleb's shoulder gently and then lowered his hand. "It's cool, Caleb." He blew out a breath and prayed he'd find the right words. More than most, Caleb needed the *right* words right now. "I won't claim to understand how you feel. I can tell you that I've spent a lot of my life angry."

Caleb's gaze cut his way.

Noah smiled and leaned back against the worktable behind him. Crossing his arms over his chest, he met the kid's gaze. "You look surprised. You know that memorial over in downtown near the Methodist church? For the Sutter family?"

The boy's thin shoulders jerked in a shrug. "Yeah. They do that dumb candlelight thing there every year."

"Yeah. They do." Noah lowered his gaze, staring at the dusty toes of his boots, waiting for the resurgence of his anger. All the vigils for the Sutter family. Nothing for Lana.

Every time he'd thought of it, he felt the surge of anger, resentment.

Now he felt only sadness.

He'd finally let her go. Let go of her, and all the rage that had lived inside him for so long.

"They disappeared, the entire family, twenty years ago. But they weren't the only ones. . . . My girlfriend disappeared that night, too."

Caleb blinked, a look of surprise passing across his features. "What?"

"Nobody talks about her," Noah murmured, sighing. He skimmed a hand across his head. "It was why I started drinking. It was the only way I could sleep at night, get through the day." Slanting a look at the boy, he added, "*That* is something I understand. Booze was how I buried the anger, how I coped with the hurt. I started not long after she disappeared. I never could bury the pain, but a drink at night helped. Then one wasn't enough . . . then two. I couldn't drink during the day, at least not at first, but I found a way later on. That anger, it was always inside me, though. If a person even looked at me wrong, I went half-crazy. Almost got myself expelled more than once. Broke my parents' hearts time after time."

Now he shoved off the worktable and moved to stand in front of Caleb, watching him closely. "I understand anger, Caleb. And misery. Feeling alone, and lost. I know how it can all eat you up inside. I understand the need to hurt something, somebody. I lived with that and let it destroy me for a very long time; then I had to remake myself."

The angry tears and the defiance on Caleb's face just about tore Noah in two. "And while I don't understand how you feel inside right now, I can tell you that I have *never* wanted to commit an act of violence as badly as I have since the night you told me what was done to you, and to others."

A sob broke out of him and Noah reached out, caught Caleb against him. Noah thought Caleb would tear away, but he didn't. Caleb clutched at Noah like a drowning, dying child, a terrified one. "But they've done enough to you, kid. You can't let them take anything else from you, and trying to hurt them now would take even more from you. It's time to let somebody else handle it."

"And what if—" The boy's voice broke and then steadied. "What if they get away with it? What if nobody believes me and they just get away with it?"

Noah stared at the wall, clenching his jaw as he fought to steady his own voice. "I promise you. That's not going to happen."

Monday morning found Lana bent over the table making notes, an iPad propped in front of her. Adam stood in the doorway, watching her, fighting the urge to move up behind her, press his lips to her neck.

She hadn't shared his bed again.

He hadn't really expected her to, but there was still a hollow ache in his gut, while his dick throbbed, pulsed. He felt it had been years since he'd touched a woman instead of just hours.

He could lose himself in her twice a day, every day, for the next ten years and he knew he wouldn't lose the need he had for her. He didn't have ten years, though. He probably didn't have one more day—just those hours from that one night.

She sighed, reaching up to rub her eyes, and he saw how pale she was, the strain in the set of her shoulders, the way she gripped her pen. *Talk to me.* He wanted to go to her, demand she tell him something. Anything. Everything.

Once, she'd been willing to tell him her secrets.

But that had been back when they were friends.

He wasn't sure what they were now, but Lana seemed to have forgotten how to share bits and pieces of herself. Although maybe *forgotten* wasn't the right word. She just didn't let herself do it anymore. She didn't trust herself, or she didn't trust him. Both, probably.

Instead of pressing his lips to the delicate curve of her neck, instead of sitting down close to her, he just moved into the kitchen, moving loudly enough that her head came up. Her eyes moved to his and the faint smile on her face hit him square in the heart. He'd do almost anything to keep that smile on her face.

He might even cross out the *almost*. What would it take to take the misery from her? He just might be willing to do anything.

"Good morning," she said, her voice husky, soft.

"Morning." He focused on the coffee she'd brewed, giving that simple task far more attention than it deserved, but he wanted to be in control before he sat down in front of her. It was kind of nice, he mused, having somebody sitting at the small table with him in the morning.

Especially today. He wasn't ready to be alone in his head. A few minutes ago, he'd taken a call about the funeral arrangements for Rita. One of her cousins had called, wanting to make sure he knew about the visitation and the service, but halfway through that conversation her mother had overheard and she'd yanked the phone away, screeching at him like a harpy.

By the time it was done, she'd threatened to have him arrested if he even showed his face. Adam didn't know what he'd done to make her hate him, but he definitely didn't want to think it through and brood alone.

"You don't look like you've slept," Lana said. There was something nervous in the back of her pale-grey eyes.

He wondered at it. He'd seen her yesterday morning before he'd had to leave for work. When he came home yesterday she'd already been tucked into her bed, and although he'd wanted to climb into the bed with her, that seemed a little presumptuous. Okay, a *lot* presumptuous.

Hadn't stopped him from wanting to do it. Just to hold her. Wrap his arms around her and feel her next to him as they slept, to know, *finally,* that she was here, that she really was safe and alive. That whatever had put that mark on her side hadn't taken her away from him.

A hundred things danced on the tip of his tongue and he couldn't say any of them. A hundred questions, a hundred demands. Since none of them were the right thing to say, he just shrugged. "I never sleep well."

"I didn't crash until almost midnight. You weren't home."

He grimaced and shrugged. "Comes with owning a bar." He could turn the late nights over to somebody else. Step into the daytime work, stop being so hands-on, but the thought of being in the house, alone, through the long, endless hours of the night was just plain torture.

Lana didn't answer, but the weighted silence coming from her seemed too tense for her to be done. Studying her, he realized she was looking at something. Something small, cupped in her palm.

A ragged sigh slipped out of her, and then finally she put it down.

He wasn't even surprised. The sight of the round token, a dull bronze, sitting there on the table didn't surprise him at all. He couldn't see which one it was, and what did it matter, really? If it had been bright enough in her room, she might have figured it out when she saw more of his tatts, but there was no hiding it now.

Besides, if she was around town long enough she'd hear.

The chip she'd laid on the table was one he'd picked up from countless meetings. He'd stopped attending the AA meetings on a regular basis years ago, but he'd still hit one from time to time if the urge hit him too hard. Sometimes he'd drop in if he thought somebody he knew might need a familiar face.

The shame, the frustration, the guilt, shouldn't those be gone by now? He'd dealt with what he'd done. Hadn't he? He'd climbed out of that hole. Yeah, he still had to fight the need, but he was winning.

Usually. But there he was, fighting the twisting, ugly crawl of guilt in his gut, the hot rush of blood as it crept up his neck as he stared at that token.

Even as he continued to fight with the urges.

She knew. Knowing that she knew *hurt*. It hurt his heart, his soul, his pride.

"How long?" she asked softly.

He dragged his gaze away from the token and met her eyes. "How long what?"

Pushing away from the table, he moved over to stare out the window at the backyard. He had to spend some time out there soon, dealing with the flower beds, weeding, all that shit he hated. He did it because that yard had been his mom's pride and joy and he'd take care of it for her. And it was easier to think about that than to think about this conversation that Lana apparently wanted to have.

"How long since you stopped drinking?"

He looked back at her. "Fifteen years, give or take." He didn't tell her that he had hit the bottle, hard, about the same time her boyfriend had started hitting it. Adam had been quieter with it. He hadn't gone out, gotten into fights. He just went to work at the grill, came home. Got drunk. Day in, day out. That was how he dealt with every day without her.

His parents saw it before anybody else. Adam had very much been a functional alcoholic. Nobody had seen it until the last few months before his parents died, when he'd started needing more and more. That was when he started getting in trouble, picking fights, causing trouble wherever he could.

If it hadn't been for what happened to his parents, he would have drank his way into an early grave, he suspected.

"Adam?"

He turned and looked at Lana, standing there, holding that damn token. That tarnished little coin. He'd always thought that he and Noah were just like one of those tokens, two sides of a twisted coin.

Noah had gotten himself good and fucked up, but then he'd pulled himself out of hell. Adam had gotten himself good and fucked up . . . and then he'd stayed that way, sliding from one hell into another.

And nobody but Lana would understand why.

Now she wouldn't even *tell* him what had happened, why she'd run, why she'd made him lie.

She rubbed the back of her hand over the back of her mouth. "Fifteen years . . ." She licked her lips. "Was . . . was it your parents?"

"They'd wanted me to sober up for a long time. It was the one thing I could do for them, so even though I did it over their graves, that was the final gift I gave them." He shrugged and looked back outside. "It wasn't much of a gift, but it was all I could do."

Silence was a dark, ugly weight and then the chair

squeaked across the floor and he turned to watch as Lana crossed the floor to him. She stopped a few feet away, her eyes troubled. "I don't understand. . . . You didn't start drinking then? When they died?"

Then? He stared at her.

Then he looked away. "I grabbed my first drink the day I had to lie about your phone call, Lana."

He went to go around her, intent on changing into some work clothes and sweating himself to death out in the backyard. Manual labor would feel good. Damn good.

"Adam."

Her voice, soft and shaken, stopped him before he hit the door.

Closing his eyes, he rested a hand on the wall. "What?"

"What . . . what phone call?"

For the longest time, he didn't look at her.

He stood there, his back to her and his head bowed, one hand braced on the wall. Tension wrapped around him, practically vibrating from him—she could see it in the rigid muscles of his back, the stiff line of his spine and the way his hand clenched into a fist as he slowly turned to face her.

His jaw bunched as he stared at her and she felt she was seeing the face of a stranger.

Not a boy she'd chased after as she grew up, not a boy she'd secretly had a crush on throughout most of school. He'd all but broken her heart when he'd brushed her off as he got older. But she'd been stubborn and refused to give up. He'd been too old for her and she knew that. Just because she couldn't *have* him didn't mean they couldn't be friends, though, and she wasn't about to give up on her hero so easily. And Adam might have been a grouchy teenager, but he hadn't been cruel. He'd been pulling away from her, but he wouldn't outright turn his back on her,

and when she'd plunked herself down next to him at the
table in his parents' house he'd just rolled her eyes and
listened as she chattered.

Now, though, she felt like she was looking at somebody
she didn't know.

And not just because of the twenty years when she had
disappeared into nowhere.

"What *phone call*?" he demanded, his voice slicing
through the silence of the kitchen, as brutal as a back-
handed blow.

She flinched and then, as anger started to trickle through
her, she stiffened her spine and stared at him. "Yes. What
phone call?"

Two long strides closed the distances between them
and he shot out a hand, closed it around the front of her
T-shirt and jerked her against him.

He stared at her, his brown eyes hot, molten. The
breath jolted out of her, and to her utter and complete surprise she felt something stir down deep inside her belly.
Hot, potent lust. Part of her wanted to shove her hands
into his hair and pull his face to hers. Part of her wanted
to lick and bite at his mouth and turn that anger into a
passion of another kind.

Furious with herself and with him, she shoved her
hands between them and her body shrieked out in rage as
she managed to put a few inches between them. "Jackass,"
she snarled, trying to twist away.

She never managed it.

He caught both her hands in his and pinned them her
back. That brought his pelvis in line with hers and she
had to swallow a moan. *Oh. Oh my.* She bit her inner cheek
to keep from groaning and it was sheer will that kept her
from moving against him. For that moment, at least. Because in the next moment the hunger withered away and
died as shock grabbed her.

"The phone call," he said again, his voice throbbing, full of anger. "That call from you the night you disappeared."

Then he shoved his face into hers while she gaped at him. "*Two* phone calls, actually. The one where you first started to ask for help, then you hung up. A minute later you called again and told me to forget you'd called. When you told me to *lie* for you. Ringing any bells yet or has it been too long?"

She stared at him, feeling the strength drain out of her legs.

PHONE CALL—

She'd called him . . . ?

Swallowing, she shook her head. "Adam . . ."

"You made me *lie* for you, damn it," he snarled. "You have any idea how hard it was to look at your father and tell him that I hadn't talked to you? How much he suffered? Everything he went through? And you still won't tell me *shit*."

"Adam—"

"I want to know what in the fuck happened that night!"

"I don't remember!"

The words tore out of her, an almost-panicked scream, and she twisted violently against him, desperate to get away, and this time she managed it. Her lungs screamed for oxygen. The simple act of opening her mouth to drag air in was almost impossible. Stumbling away, she collapsed against the counter and slammed her hands flat against it. Head bent, she forced in one breath. Her throat felt like it was lined with razor blades, and that one act of breathing in was excruciating. She held the oxygen in for a few seconds, then blew it out, did it again.

None of the panic clawing inside her receded, but she did manage to think it through.

She'd called him.

Sometime that night, a night she'd never remember, she'd reached out . . . not to Noah. Not to her father.

But to Adam.

Squeezing her eyes closed, she whispered soundlessly, *I'm so sorry*. No wonder he was so angry with her. No wonder he watched her with mistrust and apathy.

Licking her lips, she forced herself to turn and stare at him. Her palms were slick with that cold, nasty sweat, the kind that came from shame, fear and humiliation. She felt all three now, crowding up her throat until she thought she might be sick.

His eyes cut into her, his face hard as stone. She had to give him something. Twenty years he'd lived with this and it had torn into him. She didn't even understand how deeply, she suspected.

"I don't remember," she said again, keeping her voice level, although her voice was raw, her throat aching.

Adam was quiet.

Her heart thudded in dull, heavy beats against her chest, making breathing almost impossible. "You already know about Cronus," she said.

She hadn't—couldn't—really share what she knew. It had been David's secret. His horror. His fear. He hadn't even known who all was involved. None of the other boys had wanted to speak, not after a very public example was made of David. He'd tried to get help. For himself. For the others.

He went to the police.

When Cronus was done with him, that night he had been nothing but a bloody pile of bruised and battered bones. It had taken four days just to get out of bed and it was more than two weeks before he could return to school.

The official reason for his absence was that he had the flu.

The beating had been recorded and he'd been unmasked, forced to watch as they caught his humiliation, his beating, his rape, on video, one that he was told would be shared with the other *initiates*.

So no other child makes your mistake, son. It grieves me to do this. That was what David had been told by his father.

She closed her eyes, thinking about the scared, panicked words he'd whispered to her the night he'd finally agreed he had to leave, just a month after that brutal beating.

Leave, because going to the cops, trying to get help, just wasn't an option. He'd tried that, already, and he'd suffered for it.

One of the club members was a cop.

Another had been a doctor.

And David's daddy had been a preacher.

Yeah, the town had a cancer inside it and they were blind to the sickness.

The sickness had survived for more than twenty years. She swiped her damp hands down her jeans and took a deep breath, remembered the look in David's eyes that night. Blank, unwilling to even hope.

"I . . . I *can't* tell you all of this. It's not my place to tell you. But it was about . . ." Her voice trailed off.

"David." He bit the word off. "I'm not an idiot, okay? I can put two and two together. You don't have to tell me the details, but I know it was about him. Was he finally going to run away?"

His voice was raw, ragged.

Swearing, she covered her face with her hands. "Fuck. *Yes.*"

Gentle hands closed over her wrists and guided them down.

Although the last thing she wanted was to look into those angry, dark eyes, she found herself unable to stop it.

The anger, though, was gone. He just looked . . . empty.
Drained.

He looked the way she felt.

"Tell me," he said, his voice flat.

"We had it all planned out. He was going to run away.
He had . . ." She paused, wondering how close she could
come to the line without violating David's trust. "We
wanted to stop it. But he had to get out of town. Then . . .
everything went wrong."

It all got blurry after she'd pushed the backpack into
David's hands. She did remember seeing Diane, but the
order of events was jumbled, hazed.

She *knew* what happened, technically.

She'd been told.

Diane was dead.

Her blood stained Lana's clothes, her hands.

Lana had killed her.

"Just *what* went wrong?" Adam asked.

"I don't know." She shrugged, feeling impotent, useless. All those big plans. The determination to see it
ended. "I gave him the backpack. He . . . well, David had
proof. That was how he was going to stop it. I remember
that. And then . . . there was a sound. I have flashes of
blood." She tugged her hand from Adam's, touched the
old, faded scar on her side. "I woke up and I had this, plus
a knot on the back of my head. And . . ."

She stopped, uncertain where to go from there.

Guilt was an old friend of his, but just then it was taking
a bigger chunk out of his ass than Adam was used to.
Brushing her hair back from her pale face, Adam cupped
her chin. "You don't remember."

"No."

She tried to look away, but he wouldn't let her. As he

searched her grey eyes, that guilt twisted inside him, tighter and tighter.

All this time, he'd waited for her to reach out, to somehow let him know.

But she didn't even remember.

Head injury, shock, fear. He didn't know. And all the anger he'd been struggling with, it was useless. Misplaced, maybe. He should be pissed at the people responsible—Diane, who was probably dead, the evil fuckers of Cronus—and he was ready to kill all of them anyway, but now he had another reason.

Dragging his thumb down the smooth surface of her skin, he sighed, the sound ragged and broken in the silence of the room. "You sounded scared," he said, still watching her. "When you called. You were terrified. I hadn't ever heard you sound like that. I was about ready to call the cops, your dad. Then, barely a minute later, you called me back. Told me to forget you'd called, told me to lie if anybody asked about you. And you don't even remember."

It wasn't a question, but she answered anyway. "No." Under the thin material of her red shirt, her shoulders slumped. "No. I'd hit my head pretty hard—probably should have been in a hospital, but . . ." She shrugged. Her pulse beat a wild tattoo at the base of her neck. "I had a concussion—I've had them since, and once you have them you can't mistake that feeling. The headaches were awful, and I lost a lot of that night. Memories that won't come back, nausea. It was a couple of days before I could think clearly. By that time, I had to . . ." she stopped and blew out a sigh. "Had to leave."

"Had to leave," he said slowly.

Lana winced, nodded. "I was in the area for a few days, and then . . ." She closed her eyes and rubbed the back of her neck while a headache pounded. Those headaches

always came back when she tried to think about that
night, tried to pull it more clearly into focus. "I'd been . . .
hell. Hiding. I couldn't hide forever, not here, and everybody was saying the worst, right? So I had to bail."

Lies . . . why are you lying to him?

She wasn't lying, exactly. She just wasn't sure what to
tell him yet. Until she knew what she was doing, what she
could do, it was best that she not drag anybody else into
this mess. And she couldn't tell him who all had been
involved. Yeah, he knew about David, but she couldn't
complicate it any more than it already was.

"You had to bail," Adam said, echoing her words yet
again.

She grimaced, knowing how awful that sounded. "You
think I don't regret what happened?" she murmured,
turning to look at him. "You don't think I don't look back
at those days, at that night and wonder if there was a better way I could have handled it? I was a stupid, idiot kid.
My dad always told me I could change the world . . . I . . .
just wanted to make a difference. I wanted to help."

"I'm not pissed about the fact that you were always out
trying to change the world. I'm not pissed about the fact
that you were always out there biting biting off more than
you could chew . . . and I'm sure as hell not pissed off
that you tried to help a kid in trouble," Adam said, his
voice stark and cold. "I'm pissed about the fact that you
called me, asked me to lie . . . and then left me to worry
and wonder for twenty years."

She swallowed the knot in her throat. "I don't remember calling you. I . . ."

She'd called him. Reached out to him. Oddly, now that
she thought about it, it didn't surprise her, not really.
What bothered her was the fact that she had done something that had left him wondering, full of unanswered
questions, for twenty years. She knew what that was like.

The pounding in the back of her head increased and she thought she might be sick. Aware of the weight of his gaze, she looked up, met his eyes. "I don't remember, Adam. If I'd known you were . . ." She stopped and blew out a breath. She knew what it was like to lie awake at night, wondering. She'd done it to herself. She'd done it to Noah, to her father. And apparently to Adam. "I'm sorry. I can't undo it. I can't take it back. I'm sorry."

For a long moment, he said nothing. He didn't move, didn't even blink, as he studied her face. When he did move, it was to turn away. He stared out the window, his shoulders a rigid line.

"Why did you even *go* there?" he demanded.

"Because that's where it all started," she murmured. "That's where they tormented him, where he thinks they hurt the others. It was his idea—he needed to see it, one more time. Face it, I guess. We talked about burning it down, you know. A nice, fitting statement. But we wanted to make sure he had a chance to get away before anybody realized what was up—that was what mattered. He had to get out, find a way to get people to listen, so he could make it stop."

She laughed bitterly, the sound a hollow echo in the brightly lit kitchen. Too dark and too grim for the hot summer morning. "But it didn't. . . . It was all for nothing," she said softly. "We didn't realize it, but it was only getting started. I killed her, you know."

Adam tensed as she turned her head to look at him.

"I killed Diane Sutter."

He just waited, uncertain what to say, what to do.

"I don't know how, or why. . . . I don't know what happened. But when I left that house, Diane was dead and I had her blood all over me. I had two choices. I could either stay . . . and *try* to fight, try to convince people that I didn't *just* kill her . . . and nobody was going to believe

Diane would ever do anything wrong. Or I could run, and give David a chance to get away, find a chance to start over. Because if I went down, everybody would believe he was involved, too."

A bitter smirk twisted her lips. "She made sure of that. People in town *still* talk about it. Even now."

CHAPTER THIRTEEN

Gary Quimby was not a nervous man by nature.

He had no sons, much to his displeasure. He'd looked forward to the time when he could pass that tradition on in the club, but Sandy had never been able to conceive and a few years ago he'd had to bury his sweet wife.

Gary Quimby was a private man. His visits to the club were discreet. He preferred to watch, and when he did participate he tended to be a shadow initiator, wearing a hood and mask, teaching the boys to submit to authority and letting them know how it would be when it was *their* turn to be in charge.

Gary Quimby was a *cautious* man. He understood that many would twist the beauty of the club, find something wrong with it, and he wanted to protect his . . . interests.

His need for privacy and caution had served to protect him, and many of the newer members hadn't even known he was involved. It had been nearly ten years since he'd attended one of the meetings, and he didn't even miss them. It had been going downhill ever since Pete's death, but when Abel Blue had that heart attack and died so suddenly, that was when the situation had really began to deteriorate fast.

Jeb and Glenn had tried to do too many different things, change too many things. The videos, the webcams, all the photos. None of that was needed and all of it was risky.

No, Gary wasn't a nervous man.

Not many people would know that he was a member of Cronus, save for his brothers, the older members of the club.

Most of them knew better than to talk.

It just wasn't done.

Now, though . . . well, it was only a matter of time before the men started to talk. He doubted it would be Glenn. His father had trained him too well. But the others . . . Discipline had been slipping over the years.

It was only a matter of time before the cops found somebody who would rather break than honor his word to his brothers.

It would probably be Sam, because that son of a bitch was a weak one and always had been.

Jeb Sims was dead.

Harlan Troyer had been murdered.

Yeah, there were looking dismal as far as Gary was concerned. He needed to figure out just how to proceed from here, because although he'd been cautious, there were still those who knew his name.

Lately he'd been thinking it might be the ideal time to retire . . . out of the country. It was something he'd researched before, but more and more it was looking like just the thing to do.

The door to his small accounting firm opened and he managed to paste a smile on his face.

When he saw who it was, he relaxed.

Every time it wasn't a cop, he relaxed.

"Well, hello there." He managed, barely, not to sneer. He never had liked the son of a bitch who'd just come to a stop in front of him, but he was very good at hiding that sort of thing. Bastard thought he was better than most folks, Gary included.

"How are you doing today, Gary?" He nodded at Gary, his blue eyes studying the posters on the walls, advice for IRAs and all the bullshit the government suggested. Gary didn't see the point. There wasn't anybody who'd been able to retire these days. If you weren't a rich SOB, you'd work right up to your grave, and that's all there was to it. Gary wasn't a rich SOB, but he had taken out an insurance policy on his wife—if and when he decided to leave Madison, he'd be using that money.

"Oh, I'm doing well enough, well enough." He smiled and nodded back. Had to play the little chat game. Being a small-town business owner meant you had to do that bullshit even if you hated it, even if you hated the person you were talking to.

"I need a new accountant." He blew out a sigh and said, "I've been using Maisy Keaten up on on the hill and I just don't like some of the stuff she was doing with my accounts. All of those suggestions for write-offs and some of the information she needed . . ." He looked around and then asked, "Would you mind getting me a cup of coffee? I need to wet my whistle."

If it was almost anybody else, Gary would have just lied and said, *Fresh out.*

The problem was as much as he disliked this fuck, he was good for local business. He did business with a lot of other business owners, and it was good to play this game.

So Gary just gritted his teeth and said, "Sure. Give me a minute."

And then he went to the little kitchenette in the back of his office, grumbling silently under his breath.

Once he came back out, a minuscule cup of the cheap shit he saved for clients, he put it on the edge of the desk and sat back down.

"Black . . . just the way I like it." He took a sip and sighed, then put it down on the desk. He reached into his pocket and pulled out a bag of M&M'S, popped a few in his mouth. Then he stood up and put a file down on Gary's desk. "See this? It's last year's return. Will you look it over, see if you think you could do any better?"

I think some of you idiots need to understand the fact that the IRS is going to have its cut and you just need to deal with it. But he pulled out his glasses and bent over the file, careful to stay away from the bag of candy. "Try to keep that away from me. . . . Remember my allergies." He said it with a smile but was tempted to tell the jackass to throw the bag away. Just about every damn person in town knew how bad Gary's allergies to shit like chocolate and nuts was. He flipped through pages, scowling at the faint gritty feel.

Gary lifted his hand and rubbed his fingers together, frowning at the dusty sort of feel on his hands. "Are you remodeling or something? It feels like there's dust all over this."

"Oh, I'm always doing something," he said, smiling, an odd light in his eyes as he munched on the candy.

Gary grunted and flipped the page. The itching started almost right away and the coughing fit hit next—manners had him covering his mouth, and that was where he really messed up.

"Son, you look like you need a drink now."

He needed his fucking EpiPen. *Where the hell—*

His throat felt like it was closing up on him and he gasped, sucking the air in. When the glass of water was put in front of him, he grabbed at it and took a drink, tried to say, "Get my 'Pen—"

But then he saw it.

The son of a bitch stood a few feet away.

And he held Gary's EpiPen.

He also held Gary's phone.

And gloves . . . he wore gloves on his hands. Flesh-colored gloves, hard to see unless you were looking, but he was looking now, because the son of a bitch held the cure for the anaphylactic reaction that was killing Gary.

Gary could all but feel the fear busting through him, making his heart race.

He lunged for the bastard but tripped over the briefcase he'd never gotten around to putting away. He hit his head on the metal filing cabinet.

Darkness swarmed around him, and dimly he heard a voice.

"I wasn't sure if this was going to work, you know," the man said tiredly. "You were going to be one of the hardest and I knew it. You don't like me. . . . Now, now, you can pretend otherwise, but we know it's true. And I can safely say I don't care for you, either and it didn't even have anything to do with Cronus."

Gary felt hands on him, strong hands, rolling him onto his back.

Something was shoved into his mouth. Caught between bliss and terror, he realized it was chocolate.

Lots and lots of chocolate . . . A hand clamped over his mouth and he clawed at it, tried to keep from swallowing, but it was so hard to breathe, so hard. While blood roared in his ears, he stared at the man who killing him.

Why?

"You didn't really think you could get by what you did to those boys, did you?"

The last thing he heard was, "Go on now. God and the devil can deal with you."

It wasn't hard, cleaning up. He looked at the office with a jaded eye, making sure to pick up the bag of M&M'S. He'd opened them at home, kept the bag carefully sealed in his pocket.

He kept the gloves tucked away as well.

Gary had no other appointments today. He knew because he'd called.

Gary's wife had died a couple of years ago and nobody would think to look for him until tomorrow.

The door was locked. He'd taken care of that detail when the man went to get his coffee. He checked it again, the one worry in his mind that maybe somebody had seen him come in here wearing a glove on his hand. It was a possibility, he knew. But the glove had been flesh colored. Even Gary hadn't noticed.

The risk was a small one, but one he'd have to take.

Gary's office wasn't on a busier street, tucked off Second, and he'd made sure to park several blocks away.

Now he just had to let himself out the back door and head away.

After, of course, he left the note.

People had to know.

These men weren't being targeted in vain and they weren't being killed for fun.

There was a reason for each of them.

And they'd all die for what they'd done.

He left the note on Gary's chest after he'd waited a few more minutes. Just to be sure.

The man's eyes were wide and fixed and his pulse was gone.

He was dead, sure enough.

The note read:

> *This one raped Glenn Blue. Glenn might tell you the truth; he might not.*
> *Quimby also raped countless others. He's not the last, either.*

Sybil Chalmers was pissed.

She didn't have time for this.

She'd spent half the morning dealing with Layla's mouth and still had to figure out how to handle the money she owed the IRS. Why in the *hell* did they want so much when you were self-employed? They made you *pay* for providing a job for yourself. That was some messed-up shit there.

And if Quimby wasn't here for her appointment, she'd damn sure be switching her business up to that new accountant. Maisy something or other. Sybil couldn't remember the last name, but she wasn't putting up with this bullshit.

Pounding a fist on Gary Quimby's door, she shouted, "Come on, Gary. I know you're there. I saw your car around back. If you'd answer e-mail, I wouldn't have to come by."

It was hotter than hell and she'd walked here rather than drive the two blocks from her house to Quimby's office, but just then she was regretting that call.

Especially since she might have to go back home.

Pulling her phone from her pocket, she found the number and called.

Through the window, she listened for the ring of the phone.

It wasn't there.

Frowning, she moved over and peered through the curtains. She didn't see him at his desk—

Wait.

Was that—

Oh, shit.

Without even thinking, she looked around and when her gaze landed on one of the decorative rocks in the flower bed, she picked it up and moved back to the door. The glass caught in the blinds behind the little window in the door and she used her purse to knock the rest of the glass out of the way before reaching inside and feeling around for the lock. "Gary? Gary, I'm coming inside, okay? Are you all right?"

No answer.

Had he another one of those weird allergy attacks? He didn't go anywhere without that adrenaline thing—

Something crunched under her foot. She glanced down, saw the white tubular device, and dread curled in her heart.

Moving around the desk to where she'd seen his prone body, she found him lying there.

And she saw the answer to her question. Gary was most definitely not all right.

He was dead, and if the look of him was anything to go by he'd been dead for quite a while.

Numb, she reached for her phone and dialed 911.

It was as she was speaking to Dispatch that she saw the note.

For a moment, it didn't make any sense at all.

And then rage exploded through her and she wished she hadn't even *bothered* to try to helping the monster.

He raped Glenn Blue—

"He's one of them," she whispered.

"Syb?"

Swallowing, she turned away from Gary's corpse. "Send whoever you need to," she said woodenly. "But whoever killed him, I'm buying him a bottle of champagne. Gary was one of those fucking rapists."

CHAPTER FOURTEEN

Jensen Bell hadn't had a good morning. The chief wanted her to talk to a couple of scared, unhappy kids who had already been through hell. Wanted her to push them for information she didn't think they had. Wanted her, specifically, to try to find any connection that might help the police figure out who was picking off members of the club. Members he hadn't even realized were connected.

People playing vigilante. They'd drive her insane.

She was out of coffee—she'd had to spend the night at her place, because Dean had to go home to Lexington, juggling his cases like crazy to get it done, but he'd worked minor miracles. It hadn't surprised her. His grandmother was sick, and there was nothing that man valued more than those he loved.

That included Jensen, a fact that never failed to fill her with something like awe. He loved her. Just thinking about that made her morning a little brighter.

Of course, if she'd slept at his place he would have had coffee. He never ran out.

She'd had to settle for the lousy crap from the diner, because she really wasn't in the mood to listen to Louisa's unending attempts to get the good gossip.

Instead of decent coffee, a morning of slow, lazy sex,

Jensen had lousy coffee and had her ass handed to her because she hadn't interrogated a couple of kids. The chief also told her he had faith in her, told her she was a good cop.

Probably trying to psych her up to give those kids grief they didn't need.

Screw that.

A good cop knew when to listen to her gut, and her gut told her that talking to the kids was a wrong move.

Maybe she was looking at it wrong, but that wasn't the avenue she wanted to take yet.

There were other ways. Those kids had talked to others. One other in particular, at least as far as Caleb was concerned. So she'd do an end run around the kid and see if she couldn't get answers another way.

She started to head in through the front, but the large metal doors in the back were open and she veered in that direction instead.

There she paused, and then, without a bit of guilt, she leaned against the wide-open doorway and looked her fill.

For a preacher, Noah Benningfield was definitely a pretty thing to look at it.

She had about forty-five uninterrupted seconds, watching as muscles gleamed and flexed, as fists pounded the bag with undeniable skill. Then he stopped abruptly, his blue eyes cutting her way as he realized he wasn't alone.

And judging by the way his blue eyes went grim, she decided he was also pretty damn insightful. She didn't know if that was a preacher thing or not.

"I can't help you, Jensen," Noah said for the third time. He slammed his fist into the bag again, listening as chains rattled, metal clinked. Leather smacked against leather. Each time he hit the bag, he felt the jolt of it echo up his arm. It was like a vicious, beautiful song, and he wanted more. Needed more.

I need to know if Caleb has told you anything.

Caleb . . . scared, lonely boy . . . yeah.

Noah had been talking with Caleb off and on, and the kid was slowly starting to talk more. He'd told Noah plenty.

But none of it had come soon enough to help Caleb, to save him.

Savagely Noah hit the bag again, harder this time, and he wondered if there was any way to take this weight off his chest. Any way to drain the fury, take out the poison.

He was getting married in four days. Instead of focusing on his wedding and the woman he loved more than his own life, he had a cop in his shop.

Instead of thinking about his upcoming wedding, he was thinking about the kids he'd failed.

Instead of thinking about the short trip he and Trinity were taking, he was thinking about hunting down the few people he knew were involved and *hurting* them. Brutally. Thoughts that should be alien to him, unacceptable. But he couldn't cut them out of his head.

He shifted his stance and spun around, driving his heel back into the bag. The red rage creeping through him didn't lessen. Imagining Glenn Blue up there on the bag didn't help, even when Noah pictured himself pummeling the man bloody. The solemn, quiet voice of his father that usually managed to talk Noah down every time the anger got too loud wasn't there, and right now rage was eating him.

Poor Kevin, the way he'd looked when he'd seen Noah at church. So scared and ashamed.

Noah had asked Kevin if wanted to talk. *You can tell me, you know. If you need to talk, I'm here.*

Kevin had just shaken his head. *They hadn't—*

Then he'd looked away, dull red creeping up his cheeks. *They just made me watch. Everybody was masked. . . . I just . . . Dad wanted me to be prepared, but it wasn't my time yet. I'm okay.*

Poor kid was so far from okay. Made him *watch*? There was no fixing what had been done to him, to any of them.

"Come on, Noah. Talk to me," Jensen said, her voice just a little bit above a wheedling whine. "You know that all I want to do is make things right for those kids."

He shot her a look. "Make it right?" He bit back a laugh.

He knew she wanted to help, knew she probably wanted, in the end, the same thing he did. To protect those kids, to see justice done. He'd known Jensen Bell most of her life. She had been a nosy, bratty tomboy up until her mother had disappeared, and then Jensen had turned into a quiet, pensive near-adult almost overnight. That she'd become a cop didn't surprise him. That she was here didn't surprise him. But he wasn't telling her anything.

He didn't really have much *to* tell her. What little he did know had been told to him in confidence, and unless those boys gave him permission, he wasn't saying anything. Those kids weren't in danger—now—and they were his priority. If he had any names that hadn't already been given to Jensen, he'd do what he could to make sure she had the information, but he couldn't help and he wasn't going to violate a confidence.

"Come on, Noah. You have to help me out. I realize you have this confidentiality thing going on, but even taking that into consideration, when there's a credible threat out there, aren't you obligated to talk to me?" she asked. She also threw in a serious, woebegone look, just to top it off.

Grimly he smiled as he slammed his fist into the bag again. Then he stopped and turned to face her. "Now see, here's where the problem is. If I really felt there was a credible threat, yeah, I'd be obligated to talk." He shrugged and started to strip off his gloves, moving over to the bench where he kept his towel and the water bottle. "The thing is, I don't think I know jack shit that will help. I only know *two* victims . . . and you're already aware of who they are."

"Neither Kevin or Caleb is talking."

"Well, I can't help you there." He'd speak with Caleb. He didn't think Kevin knew much. They'd messed up when they tried to bring in a kid that young. That was what had set Caleb off. He'd tolerated it until they'd gone after somebody too young, somebody he'd known, cared for.

But other than Kevin, Noah didn't think Caleb knew any of the others.

They'd used a cloak of secrecy to protect themselves, to isolate the boys, and it had worked, for a very long time.

"You know I need more," Jensen said, her voice going hard.

"I know you *want* more." Noah shrugged. "We don't always get what we want, though, do we?"

He wasn't about to push them. It could help and he'd explain that, but if the kids weren't ready, they weren't ready. They'd been through enough. If one of them wanted to talk, fine. But if not? Jensen would just fumble through on her own.

"What about your partner on the forum?"

Partner—

Adam's face flashed through Noah's mind and he slowly lifted his head, stared at Jensen. Frowning, he shook his head. "I don't follow."

"Yeah. Is it possible that Adam knows more?"

Noah leaned back against the table, arms crossed over his chest, as he studied Jensen. Absently he reached up and dragged his nails down his face as he studied her. "Just what do you think Adam knows?"

"Look, you know as well as I do that somebody is out there hunting men with a connection to the Cronus Club." Something lit her eyes—there quickly, then gone. It looked like understanding. "Somebody who wants them dead. It would have to be somebody who *knew* about the men . . . somebody who had been told. Maybe the boys told Adam. Maybe he's known for a while and he's been biding his time."

It took a few seconds for her meaning to hit. When it did, Noah shoved off the table and crossed over to her. His heart was still thudding from the workout and sweat was drying to a cool, sticky film on his skin as he met her eyes. "You obviously know a different Adam Brascum than I do. That Adam? He gets pissed off and he's ready to rip your throat out. He wouldn't have information like this and then *bide his time*. Either he'd have been dragging their bodies to you the day he found out or he would have just killed them and left their bodies to rot."

Jensen blinked. "Ah. . . ."

Even as he said it, Noah wished he could yank it back, but it was a little too late. Glaring at her, he shook his head. "Everything I know about cops I learned from watching *Law and Order,* but tell me this: The person who killed Troyer, was it a rushed thing or did they plan it? Because I can tell you this: Adam might be capable of making some very bad judgment calls, but he's almost incapable of *biding his time,* like you suggested. If Adam was going to kill somebody because they were hurting one of the kids from the forum, he would have done it the very night he knew about it."

Her hazel eyes rested on his and Noah fought the urge to look away. Things were bad enough—he didn't need to make it worse. Normally he could make things *better.* For others, at least. *Yeah, not today.*

"Are you *certain* of that?" Jensen asked, her gaze pinning him into place and holding him there. "Absolutely certain?"

Snagging a towel from the workbench, he mopped the sweat from his face and then grabbed his shirt. Once he'd done that, he pulled it on and delayed another minute by circling the workbench to grab another bottle of water. After he'd taken a drink, he leaned over it and met Jensen's eyes. "Yeah, I'm certain. Now here's a question for *you:* Why are you suddenly so focused on Adam? Why do you think my partner is out there playing caped crusader?"

Adam had reluctantly revealed his connection to the forum to the police after the fire at Trinity's place. Both Noah and Adam had been surprised when the cops had downplayed that connection. Jensen had rather bluntly explained, *The forum does a lot of good. . . . We know that. People might get their panties in a twist if they connect Adam to it. I'd rather not deal with it.*

Noah thought back to that conversation now and realized things had changed. So much for them not giving a shit. Although he realized that wasn't exactly fair. It wasn't the forum that was the problem. It was the fact that people were getting killed.

"I never said I thought he was," Jensen pointed out. "But I have to check out those who have connections. He does."

"Adam isn't doing this," Noah said, shaking his head.

"But we still need to talk to everybody involved. He is involved."

"Oh, horseshit," Noah snapped, the curse slipping out of him before he could stop it. Mentally he apologized even as other, less polite things ran through his head. "He's involved the same way I am. A couple of kids trusted us . . . actually they trusted him, because they didn't know who he was. They don't trust adults because they've never had a reason to do so."

"Caleb trusts you," she pointed out.

"Yeah, and I'm not going to give him a reason not to." That trust was hard-won and it wouldn't take anything to shatter it. The boy needed *somebody* he could count on. Noah wasn't betraying Caleb. *Adam* needed somebody he could count on. Noah wasn't going to betray Adam, either.

"I'm not asking you to betray his trust." Jensen sighed and turned away. Under the lightweight jacket she wore, her shoulders rose and fell on a sigh. "Noah, look . . . we have a mess going on here. We're trying to get a handle on it, but we can't even scrape the surface of it. The few men we've arrested won't talk. The boys won't talk. I get that they are scared, but we need to pull this thing apart and keep it from ever happening again. We can't do that unless we can take it apart, from the bottom up."

"You don't need Adam for that."

She looked back at him. "I think Adam is a big boy. He can protect himself, can't he?"

"Yeah, he's a big boy." But he was also one who was walking an edge lately. Having cops push at him would likely push him even closer to falling over. "You really need to go pushing at an innocent man, one who hasn't done shit wrong, one who just lost a friend, saved my life, because you all are coming up empty-handed?"

"I—"

He cut her off, shaking his head as he took a step forward. "I don't want to *hear* it, Jensen. You know why the two of us started that forum. You may not remember how Adam was fifteen years ago, but how about me? He's the one who helped me pull through. We started that forum to give those kids a safe place, so maybe they wouldn't end up the way we did. I don't want you pushing Adam back there."

"Noah . . ." She sighed and passed a hand back over her hair, staring off past him outside. "You see, it's not really my fault the man has a drinking problem."

"No." Noah shook his head. "It's not. But he's my friend and I might not have gotten a handle on my problem without his help. I don't want to see you all pushing him back over a line just because you have nobody else left to push."

Then he turned around and walked away. Just before he locked himself in his office, he said, "Get out of my place of business, Detective. Don't come back about this unless you have a warrant."

Yeah, Adam was a big boy, but Adam had never really made it all that far from the pit he'd climbed out of and his balance had never really returned.

It made it that much easier to fall back in.

Noah wasn't going to stand by and see a bunch of cops push Adam back over because they just didn't have anybody else to push. They could look elsewhere as far as Noah was concerned.

And maybe he'd give Adam a heads-up. That was what friends did. They looked out for each other.

Or if you saw a friend teetering on the edge of that pit, you gave a friend a steadying hand. Adam had given Noah that steadying hand more than once.

Noah had his own pit, one he'd sidestepped for ages, but over the past couple of years it had gotten smaller and smaller. Over the past few months it had shrunken down to the point that he couldn't see it at all.

Now?

It was practically nonexistent, and even though he could almost catch a glimpse of it out of the corner of his eye, he no longer worried he'd fall into it if he had one off-day.

He had Trinity to thank for that.

Adam, though . . . well. If Noah's pit was getting easier to avoid, then Adam's was just getting bigger. The man acted like he was fine, carried on like nothing had changed, but Noah could see it. They'd been friends too long and he knew the signs, knew what he was looking at.

Lately Adam had been edging closer and closer to whatever self-imposed limits he had. Adam's demons kept just getting closer and closer all the time. Rita's death the other day hadn't helped things at all.

Discovering the body in Trinity's basement seemed to set it all off. They had been close, Noah knew, Adam and Lana.

Lana . . .

Noah sighed, that familiar little ache tugging at his heart. None of them had heard anything about the body that had been found. A few rumors were drifting around—mostly that the body was female, but that was it. He knew enough cops to know that since the body was so old, the state crime lab wasn't exactly going to rush things through, so it could be months before they heard any sort of concrete news.

But that was when Adam had seemed to . . . change. He'd always been a moody bastard, yeah, but it had gotten worse and that day seemed to be the tipping point.

It was like Adam really didn't care anymore if he managed to outrun the demons or not. He just didn't care.

Climbing out of the cab of his truck, Noah stared up at Adam's house and skimmed a hand back over his hair. Adam's car was there, a sleek black Corvette that his dad had been rebuilding. Adam had taken the job over after his parents had been killed in an accident, and although it had taken him years, the car was finished. It gleamed, beautiful and black, in the driveway. That car was no guarantee that Adam was home, but it was Wednesday and that was typically the day Adam took off from work.

Noah heaved out a breath and tried to figure out the right way to approach this. He'd put his foot in his mouth with Jensen. He'd been trying to get her to back off, although he knew he hadn't succeeded.

She'd come and pester Adam anyway and there was nothing to be done for it.

So the right thing to do was warn Adam.

And . . . Noah admitted to himself, he was worried.

Adam was probably going to be pissed off at him. Noah knew this. Just then, he didn't care. He just wanted to warn the guy, maybe try to talk him into at least getting a lawyer. If Noah had wedged his foot in his mouth earlier, Adam was likely to shove both feet in clear up to his knees. A lawyer would be wise.

Only idiots believed that if you were innocent you didn't need a lawyer. Adam wasn't an idiot and he'd done dances with the cops before, so Noah hoped he'd see the sense in this.

Hoped.

If Adam wasn't feeling stubborn.

In a cemetery up on the hill, they were laying Rita to rest.

Down on the river, Adam ran eight miles. As his feet pounded the pavement, he thought about the woman he'd known for most of his life, and although he didn't cry, he finally let himself ask all those questions.

Why the hell did you do it, Rita?

Why didn't I see this coming?

Why didn't I get to you sooner?

Why didn't I just go home with you that night?

Dozens of questions, and all of them boiled down to *why.*

Even worse, there were no answers.

Rita had danced with depression before, had even once tried to kill herself. But Adam had been pretty good at seeing when she was sliding down that edge again. Yes, she had even more of a reason that day than any other, but to just up and end it, so fast?

Why?

It just wouldn't settle in his mind.

Of course, his mind was jumbled, too full of questions that had no answers, worries and fears that he just couldn't calm no matter how hard he ran, no matter how far, how fast. Only half of that chaos came from Rita.

He kept seeing Lana's face in his mind. Her face. The scars on her body. The scars on her soul that he had glimpsed in her eyes. Twenty years of her life, all but stolen from her.

She'd run. She'd lied to him. He'd lied *for* her.

But not because she'd wanted to. And it was all for nothing. There had to have been a better way. Maybe the kids they'd all been couldn't see any other option, but he wasn't a kid anymore and he knew there had to be other ways. She was too close to it, even now. It was possible *she* couldn't see any other way, but it had to exist.

His mind spun in circles as he chased the sun and eventually ran himself out, circling back around until he ended up back up on his street, walking until his heart slowed, his muscles like jelly and his hands curled into impotent fists.

Even after his heart had gone back to normal, he couldn't go inside. Instead he moved into the cool, quiet shade of the backyard, staring up at the house, waiting for some of the turmoil to ease.

The door opened and Lana was there.

A different sort of turmoil settled inside him and he clenched his jaw.

Instead of turning away, he nodded at her and figured the best thing to do would be head inside, shower, change, then get the hell out of the house.

It was, really, a good, sensible plan.

Her soft grey eyes met his and he started toward her, too aware of her, the way she watched him, the dark hair she'd woven into a braid, the glasses she didn't need perched on her nose.

He wanted to pull them off, crowd her up against the door and strip her naked. After he'd brought her to climax, when she was weak and whimpering and still panting from him, he'd see if he couldn't get her to talk. It was dirty and sneaky as hell and he was just fine with that if it would finally get him answers.

Oh, he had *some* answers . . . like why she'd been gone. She'd stayed gone because she was protecting David, and that was typical Lana.

But Adam wanted more.

Why had she come home *now*?

What was she hoping to accomplish?

Was she going to leave again?

Had she missed him?

Did she want him?

As he reached the door, she edged out of his way. He caught the scent of her, something soft and gentle, like wildflowers and rain. He wanted to press his face to the curve of her neck and find out just where that scent came from.

Instead, he brushed past her.

Behind him, Lana shut the door.

"There were about ten calls while you were gone."

"Only ten?" He turned the cold water on and bent over, drinking straight from the faucet. The muscles in his legs were quivering and he thought maybe he should have something to eat, sit down. He didn't think he'd eaten breakfast. Or dinner. He was bad about that when he was pissed off or stressed. The past few days, he'd been in that state of mind a lot.

Lana showing up. Rita dying.

"Margaret Troyer called several times."

He pulled away from the tap and looked at Lana.

"She called eight times." Lana grimaced and added, "She left messages, warned you not to dare show your face at the funeral."

"That's restraint for her." He shrugged and turned the water off.

Lana opened a cabinet and pulled out a glass. "You know, you have a good dozen of these. They hold water. They are useful."

"Yeah, but then I have to wash them." He grabbed a towel from the little hook hanging by the window and dried his face off before he turned to look at her. "The other two calls?"

She nibbled on her lower lip. "One was a cop. Ah, Detective Bell."

He shrugged. "I'll catch up with her in town at some point."

"If cops are going to be nosing around here, I need to find someplace else to go."

Everything inside him screamed at the idea.

No.

"No." It burst out of him before he could stop it and she whipped her head around to stare at him.

Clearing his throat, he shrugged and moved over to the cabinet. He wasn't thirsty now, but he'd drink if it distracted her, kept her focused on something other than the cop. Running some water into the cup, he drained it and then rinsed it out, taking his time on each little detail as he formulated a response. "It's not like you can check into a hotel or anything," he pointed out. "And your dad's house has been sold. You don't have a lot of options, right?"

She lifted a brow. "I'll figure something out. I don't need the cops to know I'm here just yet."

"And when are you going to let people know you're here?" he asked softly. Putting the cup in the dish rack, he crossed over to her and touched her cheek. "Lana, you've been here almost a week and all you do is sit inside my house and poke around online. Just what are you *doing* here? Why did you come home?"

His eyes bored into hers and she opened her mouth, the words hovering on the tip of her tongue.

How could she tell him that she just didn't *know* why she was here, what she was doing?

She needed to have some sort of answer. Some sort of game plan. She'd come down here to set things straight, and she was slowly trying to make connections, vague names from her memory to those people still in town. She needed to talk to people, but whom did she trust? Besides Adam, she didn't know.

Licking her lips, she shifted on her feet and glanced up.

He was staring at her mouth.

Her heart stuttered to a stop, her breath catching in her throat as their gazes locked.

"Fuck, Lana," he muttered.

And then he lowered his head, his mouth slanting over hers, his hands pushing into her hair.

Well, that was *one* plan she could get on-board with. That one night kept replaying itself over and over in her mind and now it was a fever in her blood, something that was turning into an obsession.

He was turning into an obsession.

His body was hot against her own, his chest damp and sweaty under the ragged T-shirt, his skin furnace hot. She wanted to peel his clothes away, then her own, and press up against him, have him press her against whatever surface was available and then push inside. Hot, hard and fast. Anything to ease the ache inside her.

Groaning, she slid her arms around his waist, skimming her hands under the hem of his shirt. When she found his skin, silken smooth and hot, she sank her nails into it.

He hissed against her mouth and nipped at her tongue.

That only made it worse and an ache settled deep down inside, panging inside her womb, a hungry, needing little beast that was going to drive her mad.

He caught her face and angled her head up and to the side as he ran his mouth down her neck. "You want to drive me mad," he muttered. "That's just all there is to it."

"We can go mad together," she said, trying to breathe around the raging ball of want inside her.

"Sounds like a plan." He leaned back, grabbed the hem of her shirt.

"Good plan." She started to strip his away.

The little clicking sound didn't register at first. Not right away. Even the light breeze dancing across her flesh didn't entirely click. Not until Adam looked away.

She followed his gaze. And her heart jumped up into her throat and lodged there.

CHAPTER FIFTEEN

The side door was where everybody came and went at the Brascum household. It had always been that way, and even though Noah hadn't known the older Brascums well, he was close enough with Adam that he was in and out of this house often enough that it felt like a second home.

He hadn't knocked and just then, as he stood there, staring, he realized that was an oversight on his part.

His gaze bounced off the brunette at first—there was something familiar about her, but he couldn't place her face, not at first. His gaze moved to Adam's and Noah grimaced, reaching up to rub at the back of his neck, an awkward apology forming on the tip of his tongue.

Adam stared at him, his dark eyes intent and focused.

"Ah . . . sorry," Noah said, forcing the words out.

Both of them just continued to stare.

And they were so quiet, so damn quiet.

They had dual expressions of shock on their faces and Noah looked from Adam back to the woman, and this time his eyes lingered on her face.

"I . . ." The word lodged in his throat as they continued to look at him.

She backed away from Adam, her motions jerky and

erratic, her gaze locked on Noah's face. She went to smooth her shirt down, looking down at the floor for a second before her gaze bounced back up to meet his.

Grey eyes.

Haunted and beautiful.

Those eyes—

Noah's blood started to roar, thrumming in his ears, so loud and fast.

"Noah," Adam said, his voice low and intent as he cut in front of the woman.

Noah had been backing out of the room, but now he took a step forward, then another, barely even aware of Adam. The woman shot Noah another look and he felt his heart slam into his chest, adrenaline crashing through him, hard and fast.

Two decades fell away and he could see that mischievous grin on the face of the girl he loved, the way her eyes glinted as he cupped her face in his hands.

"Just what are you up to now?"

"Nothing." She stared up at him, her face the picture of innocence.

"Uh-huh." Dipping his head, he pressed his brow to hers. "You don't lie very well. Especially not to me."

She poked out her lip. "I lie just fine. *You just don't accept my bullshit the way others do." Lana reached up and pressed her finger to his lower lip. "Look . . . I just . . ." She shrugged. "I just have something I need to do, okay? Something I need to do . . ."*

Now those words echoed in his ears.

Something I need to do . . .

Adam tried to block him, but Noah pushed past him, staring at the woman who'd once been the girl he'd loved.

Lana . . .

"Noah, damn it. Just—"

He couldn't think. He just couldn't think. Shooting out

a hand, he caught the glasses she wore and tugged them off her face. And now, without those masking her features, he could see her plainly.

Lana stared at him and the world that had seemed so steady and secure just a few minutes ago was shaking under Noah's feet. That hole that had narrowed down almost into invisibility swelled up, like the giant mouth of a monster, gaping wide for him to topple straight inside.

Spinning away, he hurled the glasses down on the table and stared at the door. For a long moment, he couldn't do anything. And then, because he couldn't think of a single thing to say, he just strode out.

Lana, shaken, stared at the door as it slammed shut behind Noah.

She was no longer the girl he'd loved; some part of her wished she were. And there was nothing in her that had wanted to see him hurt.

"I need to talk to him," she whispered, passing a shaking hand over the back of her mouth.

But when she went to go after him, Adam caught her shoulders. "Not a good idea," he said, squeezing.

She jerked away from him. "I have to—" She stopped and just stared dully at the door. She had to *what*? Tell Noah exactly what she'd told her father? Nothing? Too many of the secrets she knew just weren't *hers* to share. Tell Noah that she was sorry? Talk about empty words. She *was* sorry, but if she had to do the same thing, in the same circumstances, she might make the same choice. Well, with the exception of making sure she took the sons of bitches down with her this time.

But what could she say?

There was nothing she could offer him.

Adam cupped her cheek and she looked up at him. "You can't have anybody seeing you yet," he said. He cocked an eyebrow and waited. "Unless you're ready to come out of hiding."

"I . . ." She stopped and blew out a breath. "Yeah. I have to find somebody and I haven't had any luck doing it and until I find him . . . well. It's not going to be easy to do it if I end up arrested."

"How likely is that?"

She just stared at him.

Adam groaned and shoved the heels of his hands against his eye sockets. "Okay. For now, you stay here. I'm going after Noah."

"I feel like I should be the one doing that."

"Oh, you should be." He dropped his hands and stared at her. "And don't worry; you still have plenty of explaining to do and I haven't forgotten that." Then he shook his head as he started for the door. "The first thing, though, I need to make sure Noah doesn't go telling anybody he saw you."

"Is . . ." She winced. "Is he likely to do that?"

"No. But then again, he's never been sucker punched like that." He lingered another moment, lifted a hand to cup her cheek. Eyes intent on her face, he pressed his thumb to her lower lip and dragged it across the swell.

Heat gathered like a storm inside her and then he moved in, replaced his thumb with his mouth, soft at first, like he wasn't sure of his welcome. She sighed against him, unable to pull away, unable to even think of it. When she opened for him, he banded his arm around her waist and pulled her flush against him, so that not even air separated them. The heat of his body was shocking and she wanted to curl around him, rub against him like a cat. His mouth ate at hers, his tongue stroking, teasing, tasting . . . and then she was back on her feet while he put distance between them. "This isn't done," he said as he turned away. "You know that."

It wasn't a question.

So she didn't bother answering.

The door banged shut behind him as she sagged against the counter.

She was in so far over her head. And not just because of what happened twenty years ago.

Everybody had a place, that one spot they went to when the entire world had just been ripped away.

Adam's spot was the path along the river.

Noah's was in the park. He liked hiking up to one of the more secluded waterfalls and he'd stay there until the park rangers basically kicked him out. Adam wasn't particularly happy about dragging his tired ass down one of those trails after his run, but as he pulled into the spot next to Noah's truck, he knew there wasn't much choice.

Noah was already on the trail, and if Adam wanted to talk to him, he was going to have to catch up to him.

This really wasn't the kind of talk people had on a cell phone.

It wasn't really the kind of talk people had *anywhere* as far as Adam was concerned. Just how did he approach this?

He didn't know, and in the thirty minutes it took to catch up to Noah, no bright, shining revelations slammed into him, either. Of course, it might be easier to think about if he didn't still have the taste of Lana on his lips, if he wasn't still feeling the sweet weight of her breasts against his chest, the strong, determined grip of her hands on his shoulders as she wound herself around him.

He found himself facing Noah with absolutely no idea what to say. That turned out to be okay, because before he even had a chance to catch his breath, Noah slammed him up against one of the massive, mossy rocks that had fallen away from the cliffs hundreds of years ago. Staring into

Noah's haggard face, Adam stood there, passive and unresisting. Waiting.

"How long have you known?" Noah demanded. His hands fisted in Adam's shirt and he shook him. "How long?"

"Just a few days," Adam said softly.

"Don't lie to me!"

"I'm not." He reached up and closed his hands around Noah's wrists, squeezed. "I'd lie to a lot of people, Noah, but I wouldn't lie to you. I didn't know until I saw her down at the river. She just came back a couple of days ago; I swear."

Angry, confused eyes stared at him.

Then, just as swiftly as Noah had grabbed him, Noah turned away. Without saying a word, he dropped to the ground, harsh, ragged breaths coming out of him.

The logical thing to do was stay inside.

Lana knew that.

She didn't give a damn.

She'd already screwed up, hurting the last person on earth she'd ever wanted to hurt.

Now, before she could do anybody else any damage, she needed to find the man she'd come back here to find.

Nothing could change until she could talk, but those secrets . . . they weren't hers to share and she needed to know if he'd kept the video.

She almost called for the information she needed, but paranoia had been her constant companion over the years and in the end she decided she'd make her request in person. Other than what had had happened with Noah, she was actually pretty damn good at evading notice, and she figured she could get to where she needed to be without being seen.

She should have done it the first day she'd seen him—no,

the first day she'd arrived—but the shock of seeing Adam, her father, the shock of being home . . . all of it. She'd taken a few days to hit her stride, but enough was enough.

She hit her small cache of clothes and changed, going with yet another pair of baggy, wrinkled pants that hung too loose on her hips, a skintight bodysuit and a baseball cap she pulled down low over her face. The clothes were dark, leaving her looking paler than she really was, and she hunted down the glasses, putting them on before she left.

She didn't leave a note, just took the key to Adam's side door and set off.

The old man was going to tell her what she needed to know.

He had to know.

He knew every damn thing that happened in this town. *He didn't know about the club. . . .*

She swallowed the nausea roiling in her gut and pushed that thought off to the side. *No. He hadn't known about that.*

But he did now.

Too many people knew now and they weren't going to be able to brush it under the rug.

There wasn't going to be another kid like David who went to the police desperate for help and instead of getting help, he was beaten, threatened, brutalized even more.

Fury locked her jaw and tightened her muscles.

David got away, she told herself.

It was the one thing that had kept her sane. That scared, skinny kid with bruises and scars and a broken soul had managed to get away. That was the one thing she knew to be true.

Now she just had to find him.

If he was smart, he would have acted on this man first.

William T. Merchant had been a deputy sheriff before he retired and he'd done a stint in the army.

But that didn't necessarily mean much, not to his way of thinking. All of that should have meant Willie T. would be a good, honorable man.

Not a child molester, a brutal, ruthless predator.

But things were what they were. He'd done his own time in the army, and he knew you could find honorable men standing side by side with abusers, thieves and killers.

He would probably be considered an honorable man by many. He was also a liar and a killer. A person could wear many masks.

Willie T. was proof of that. Deputy. Soldier. Protector. Rapist.

The mask was coming off tonight. Even if they both died over this, it was a price he was willing to pay. He just hoped those who loved him would understand why he'd done the things he'd done.

He had known it wouldn't be easy to get inside Willie T.'s house, although when the opportunity presented itself, it had been almost miraculously easy. It had proven to be harder for him to get away from his own. The mid-day was never easy and he had to figure out a way that wouldn't raise suspicion. Sooner or later he would be caught, and he was well aware of that fact. He just wanted to settle as much as he could before it happened.

The way he saw it, he was taking out the men who would either stand a better chance at making a jury believe their lies or find some other way to evade prosecution.

He could see Willie T. taking the same road that Jeb had taken.

It was too easy.

Willie T. needed to look somebody in the eyes and know that he had been seen for what he was.

Then he could die and rot in hell.

It had been a godsend, really, the way Shannon Kirchner had left her key ring at the house. Shannon cleaned the first day she'd arrived—but the shock of seeing Adam, her father, the shock of being home . . . all of it. She'd taken a few days to hit her stride, but enough was enough.

She hit her small cache of clothes and changed, going with yet another pair of baggy, wrinkled pants that hung too loose on her hips, a skintight bodysuit and a baseball cap she pulled down low over her face. The clothes were dark, leaving her looking paler than she really was, and she hunted down the glasses, putting them on before she left.

She didn't leave a note, just took the key to Adam's side door and set off.

The old man was going to tell her what she needed to know.

He had to know.

He knew every damn thing that happened in this town.

He didn't know about the club. . . .

She swallowed the nausea roiling in her gut and pushed that thought off to the side. *No. He hadn't known about that.*

But he did now.

Too many people knew now and they weren't going to be able to brush it under the rug.

There wasn't going to be another kid like David who went to the police desperate for help and instead of getting help, he was beaten, threatened, brutalized even more.

Fury locked her jaw and tightened her muscles.

David got away, she told herself.

It was the one thing that had kept her sane. That scared, skinny kid with bruises and scars and a broken soul had managed to get away. That was the one thing she knew to be true.

Now she just had to find him.

If he was smart, he would have acted on this man first.

William T. Merchant had been a deputy sheriff before he retired and he'd done a stint in the army.

But that didn't necessarily mean much, not to his way of thinking. All of that should have meant Willie T. would be a good, honorable man.

Not a child molester, a brutal, ruthless predator.

But things were what they were. He'd done his own time in the army, and he knew you could find honorable men standing side by side with abusers, thieves and killers.

He would probably be considered an honorable man by many. He was also a liar and a killer. A person could wear many masks.

Willie T. was proof of that. Deputy. Soldier. Protector. Rapist.

The mask was coming off tonight. Even if they both died over this, it was a price he was willing to pay. He just hoped those who loved him would understand why he'd done the things he'd done.

He had known it wouldn't be easy to get inside Willie T.'s house, although when the opportunity presented itself, it had been almost miraculously easy. It had proven to be harder for him to get away from his own. The mid-day was never easy and he had to figure out a way that wouldn't raise suspicion. Sooner or later he would be caught, and he was well aware of that fact. He just wanted to settle as much as he could before it happened.

The way he saw it, he was taking out the men who would either stand a better chance at making a jury believe their lies or find some other way to evade prosecution.

He could see Willie T. taking the same road that Jeb had taken.

It was too easy.

Willie T. needed to look somebody in the eyes and know that he had been seen for what he was.

Then he could die and rot in hell.

It had been a godsend, really, the way Shannon Kirchner had left her key ring at the house. Shannon cleaned

CHAPTER SIXTEEN

He wasn't there.

Lana paced, skirting the edge of the property, knowing if she stayed much longer she was going to be seen.

The car parked in the drive didn't belong to him and she couldn't risk going down there if she didn't know for certain he was there—

A footstep scuffed behind her and she turned, slowly, uncertain of just whom she might see.

Then, as though twenty years had melted away, she felt something warm and sweet shift through her. For just a moment, she was a kid again—sixteen and desperately in love.

Noah Benningfield stood there, looking at her, his blue eyes searching her face.

"Hi."

He looked down at the ground, a sigh shuddering out of him. Silence, heavy and weighted, stretched out between them and she fought the urge to go to him. But that wasn't her right anymore. She'd lost that.

Then he lifted his head and she found herself not seeing the boy he'd been but the man he'd become.

A tired smile slanted his lips and he shook his head. "You've got no idea how many times I thought about seeing you again. Just one more time. And now here you are and I have no idea what to say to you."

"That makes two of us," she said quietly. She glanced behind her, checked around and then eased deeper into the trees. "I . . . ah. Well. I hear you're getting married."

He nodded and the smile on his face changed. *He* changed. The smile, the absolute love he felt, lit him up. Something that might have been jealousy tried to bloom inside, but she smothered it before it could take root. He'd earned that happiness, had fought and paid dearly for it. "Yeah. This Saturday." He grimaced and added, "I'd invite you, but . . ."

"That would be awkward," she said.

"No." He shook his head. "It's not that. Trinity would like to meet you. It's just—well, Adam says you're keeping a low profile."

"Ahhh . . ." She nodded and turned away, wrapping her arms around her middle, prepared for the questions, tried to think up the right answers. She'd never been able to lie to Noah. He saw right through it, each and every time. "Yes."

"Okay."

And that was it. She held her breath, waiting for something more, but it never came. After a full minute passed, she turned her head and stared at him. *"Okay?"* she echoed. "How can you just say *okay*?"

He laughed and leaned back against one of the trees at his back, an ancient oak that towered up into the sky. Around them, the various trees made a very effective curtain. Pine needles cushioned the ground while their scent flooded the air. Not too far away Noah and Lana could hear the rush of traffic, but in this spot here, it was like they were the only two who existed. "If you're not ready to talk, Lana, you're not going to talk," he said, turning his head to look at her. "You were like that twenty years ago. I don't figure that's changed. Now if you *need* to talk . . . I'll listen and whatever you have to say is safe with me. But I'm not going to demand answers. It won't work anyway."

"If anybody has a right to demand answers, it's you," she said, swallowing the knot in her throat.

"No." He blew out a breath and pushed off the tree. "Maybe if I'd kept waiting, kept hoping? But some part of me stopped waiting . . . some part of me gave up hope a long time ago."

And with those words, some part of her died. "I'm sorry, Noah."

They both knew she was apologizing for more than she could possibly put into words.

"Don't." He closed the distance between them and lifted a hand, tipped her chin up with his finger. "I waited. For a very long time. And all the while, I did my damnedest to kill myself. Eventually, I stopped waiting, and I stopped trying to kill myself. But the life I've got now . . ." Some echo of that smile he'd worn when he spoke of his soon-to-be-wife appeared and his eyes all but burned with that love. "I don't want to change anything that put me on this path. Every step we take, it's for a reason. All my steps led me to her."

"She must be something special," Lana said.

"She is." Noah pressed his lips to Lana's forehead. "But then again, so are you. I don't know what I did to have two amazing women in my life."

"Shit, Noah." She pulled back and turned away as the ache inside her spread. "I had you for a couple of years and then I disappeared. I don't think you can call me that amazing."

"I was the one you amazed, so yeah, I get to call you that."

A truck appeared at the end of the road, just barely

visible through the webwork of pine branches. Her heart jumped and she fought to keep her voice level. "Well, whatever you say. I'm happy for you, Noah."

"Thanks."

If she hoped he wouldn't notice her interest in the truck, she was very much mistaken, and she tore her gaze away before he decided to ask. Backing away, she gave him an easy smile. "It was . . . interesting," she decided. "Take care of yourself."

He arched a brow. "When you need me, let me know."

Then he turned and disappeared into the trees.

When you need me . . .

Somehow she suspected that time would come.

Sighing, she looked back toward the house and then started to trail after Noah. She'd have to come back later.

The little park across from the cemetery was a good place for people watching.

Layla wasn't particularly in the mood for people watching, but she was in the mood to find somebody to either give her some money or let her crash with them for a while. She did have a particular man in mind. . . . He was older than she usually went for, but he kept himself in shape, plus he played rough.

That was the only way to play, in her mind.

Plus, once he went out for the night, he went *out*. That left her alone to do whatever in the hell she wanted, including lazing out in the hot tub and getting stoned if she wanted.

The former deputy liked to relax at nights in that hot tub, with a little bit of weed, a nice cold beer. That wasn't a bad way to spend a night, in her mind.

But so far, he hadn't shown his face in town.

If Willie T. didn't show up soon, she just might hunt him down.

He might try to push her out, but all she'd have to do was go down on him and that would be that.

He was a typical man—his brain was always in his dick, and she knew how to handle him.

He was probably her best bet for finding a place to crash for a few days, too. She hadn't been able to make her rent, and yesterday she'd been thrown out on her ass. The landlord had agreed to store her stuff—because he didn't want his wife knowing that he'd taken sex in exchange for rent more than a few times. Layla had tried to barter that again, but Bo wasn't going for it. He'd outright told her that she could either pay him or just tell Betty about the months when she'd given him a quickie in exchange for a cut on the rent, and the look in his eyes said he hadn't been joking.

Since she might need the reference from him at some point, she didn't see the point.

If he wasn't going to back down, he wasn't going to back down.

She was good at reading things like that.

Last night, she'd used her key at the house and slept on the couch for four hours, leaving before Sybil woke up, before the kid could find her there.

She was still tired, cranky, and she needed a hit bad.

But she had to figure out where she was going first.

If she could stand the fucking idea of it, she knew she'd have a bed at her old place. Technically, it was *her* house, too. Mama had left the house to Sybil *and* Layla, but Layla hated that place. Every damn room was a reminder of what a failure she was. Especially compared to Sybil. Perfect, confident Sybil.

Maybe Mama had never pointed that out and Sybil didn't have to, but they all knew it.

No, going back home to the place where Saint Sybil lived wasn't an option. Layla couldn't stand the thought of seeing her sister every day. She could barely tolerate seeing Sybil on the rare occasion when they ran into each other in town.

And besides . . . if Layla was there, she'd have to see Drew.

Sighing, she dug out her cigarette and lighter. Drew, that kid. She loved her boy, but he had a way of looking at her with those big blue eyes that just outright *told* her how much she disappointed him. It wasn't her fault she didn't know how to be a mom. Sybil was so much better at it anyway—

"Well, hello, there. . . ." Layla's attention zoomed in on the man striding up the street. A few dozen yards behind him she saw a woman—the woman Layla didn't know, but the man? Oh, yes. Knew him. Alternately hated and wanted him. Mostly, he just pissed her off, but lately she wanted him like crazy, and it wasn't just because he acted like he wasn't interested. That was bullshit. Noah wanted her. He'd always wanted her; he just tried to hide it.

And right now, he was moving like his ass was on fire.

Smashing her cigarette out on the bench, Layla slid off the bench and moved to cut him off.

He checked himself right before they would have collided, and she sulked privately, just a little. That body of his had just gotten so much better over the years, and part of her yearned to see what he'd be like if he let all that hunger out. He had laced himself up all nice and proper, and she knew that on the inside Noah was *anything* but nice and proper.

Smiling at him, she reached out to stroke a finger down the front of his shirt. He sidestepped before she made contact. Poking out her lip, she said, "Now, Noah . . . you act like you don't want to see me. You aren't still mad at me, are you?"

"I don't much see the point in being mad at you, Layla."
And his blue eyes met hers levelly.

He seemed to mean it. Oh, that made this easier, then.
Taking a step closer, she went to rest a hand on his arm,
but again, he didn't let her touch him. Damn it, this was
like dancing with a cat. "Well, if you aren't mad, how
come you're acting like I'm contagious?"

"Layla." He said her name in a low, quiet voice and
leaned in just close enough for her to feel the heat of him.

It made everything inside her clench up, tight and hungry. Very few of the men she'd been with had ever made
her feel like Noah had. He'd fucked like he had demons
inside him and only fucking would get them out. "Yes,
sugar?" she murmured. "What can I do for you, Noah?
You know I'm up for just about . . . anything."

"You can stay away from me, okay? I'm getting married
in a few days. I'm in love with my fiancée . . . and you're
nothing but trouble. We both know it. So just . . . stay away."

She jerked back, glaring at him. "Nothing but trouble?"

Somebody brushed by them.

That woman.

Her gaze, shielded by overly large sunglasses, lingered
on Noah for a long moment and then moved to Layla.
"Everything okay?" she asked.

Layla went to snap at her, but then she stopped, looking at the brunette. Her voice . . . Scowling, Layla stared
hard at the woman, trying to place her.

Noah gave her a polite smile. "Everything is fine,
ma'am."

The woman nodded and headed on down the street.

"It's *not* fine," Layla said, raising her voice.

The woman just kept on walking.

"You honestly think Holly Homemaker can give you
what you need?" Layla demanded, thinking of the slick,

sexy blonde from New York who was going to marry Noah in a few days. "*Seriously?* She doesn't even *know* you."

"She does." Then he shook his head. "But this isn't about her. Or even me. It's about the fact that you can't stand me turning you down." His gaze lingered on her face, his expression sad. "Layla . . . you deserve better than this. Find a way to be happy with yourself. You're never going to do that by just chasing after every guy you think can give you a good time in bed."

He brushed past her and headed on down the street.

She whirled around and glared at his retreating back.

"Yeah? Like *you* would know shit about giving a woman a good time in bed, you uptight prick!"

The back of his neck went red.

But there was no other response and a moment later he disappeared around the corner.

"Why isn't Mr. Noah here?"

Trinity looked down at Micah and reached across the table to stroke his cheek. "He will be." She showed Micah the message on her phone. "He's just having a crazy day—said he'd join us in another thirty minutes or so." Of course, if she'd seen that message thirty minutes ago she'd have waited awhile before they headed to the pizza place.

Micah pouted, poking his lip out. "I want to see Mr. Noah. I haven't seen him since last night. That's too long."

Trinity chuckled. "Baby, in just a few more days, you'll see him all the time."

Micah's eyes started to shine. "And he'll be . . . like . . . like my dad almost. Except . . ." He looked away and started to scribble harder on the menu in front of him. "What do I call him? He's not Mr. Noah if you're married to him, but I have a dad."

"What do you want to call him?"

Micah never had a chance to respond, because at that very moment an angry, sulky-faced woman plopped herself into the seat next to him. Micah tensed, his eyes going wide as he looked over at Layla Chalmers.

Trinity managed to keep from snarling at the woman and demanding she get the hell away from her baby. It was close, though. Very close.

Especially considering she could see the need for blood in Layla's eyes. Figuratively speaking.

"Layla," Trinity said, keeping her voice level. "Did you need something? We're kind of on a dinner date."

"How sweet." Layla's face smoothed out and she leaned forward, dropping her voice. "I just needed to tell you this: I didn't want you hearing from just anybody . . . or, worse, having Noah just *not* tell you. He might not lie, but he *excels* at keeping secrets."

Oh, puh-leeze. Trinity didn't roll her eyes, but she wanted to. Hard. Arching a brow, she said, "Oh? And just what do you need to tell me?"

"I saw him coming out of the woods with another woman." Layla pasted a look of mock sympathy on her face. "And when I tried to ask him what he'd been up to, he just wouldn't tell me. He was all secretive like . . . Honey, that man was a . . . well. I can't say with a kid here, but let me tell you, he has been around. He's good at hiding it, but every now and then, he slips. Oh, honey . . . how he slips." She gave a suggestive laugh and then slid out of the booth. "Trust me, I know *that* from experience."

As she turned to the door, the bell over it rang.

And Noah walked in.

When he saw Layla, he stilled; then he sighed and shook his head.

Layla gave Trinity a secretive look. "Ask him about what happened in the woods."

* * *

It was a shot in the dark, Layla knew, but as Noah approached she saw his face tighten and she thought to herself, *Score.*

Noah was always talking to people in confidence, or some such shit. And when he did that, he didn't tell *anybody.*

If Layla knew anything about women, that little nagging voice of doubt would eat at his blushing bride and it wouldn't help when Noah wouldn't explain.

As Layla passed by him, she gave him a smug grin and decided she felt pretty damn good about herself.

Now, if she had any luck at all, she could sit here and maybe, just maybe, Willie T. would show up for the pizza he liked to treat himself to on Saturdays. He lived too far out of town for delivery, but he did like his little indulgences, as he'd always called that extra-large pie he bought two or three times a month.

He'd place his order, have a beer . . . and she'd be right here waiting.

And if he was really lucky, he could take *her* home along with the pie.

Plus, Layla had the added benefit of sitting here to watch the show.

"What on earth was that about?"

Trinity managed to keep the question inside until Noah had given Micah a hug and the standard male bonding. Then Micah was off like a rocket to the play area in the back of the pizza place and she couldn't keep it inside anymore.

Noah rubbed his hands over his face, and when he lowered them he looked at her from eyes that looked like they'd aged a good ten years. Worried, she reached over and covered his hands with her own. "Baby, is everything okay?"

He sighed and turned his hands so that their fingers laced. "Have I told you lately how much I adore you?"

"Well, yeah. But it's been ages . . . like a couple of days, even." She smiled. "You can tell me again."

He lifted their joined hands and pressed a kiss to her wrist. "I adore you. Love you."

"Okay. So you've told me. Now . . . what on earth is she up to?"

"She's being . . ." He blew out a breath.

"Herself?" Trinity offered caustically.

"Yeah. Pretty much."

"Okay." She ran her tongue around her teeth. Told herself she wasn't going to give in to the bait. Then she decided, *Screw that.* She'd give in because if she didn't, it would eat at her and that was the entire point of this mess. "She wants me to ask about what happened in the woods. She mentioned it because she wants to get at you. I'm asking because now I have to, but I trust you. You know that, right?"

Some of the strain faded from his face and he reached up, brushed her hair back. "Yeah. And I'm hoping that because you trust me, you'll understand when I tell you that I can't tell you what she's talking about." He paused and looked down, staring at the table for a long, lingering moment. "There . . . well, I did speak with a woman earlier, but what we spoke about was her private business. They aren't my secrets to tell."

Trinity studied his face, saw the heaviness in his eyes. Heaviness, some sadness. But not guilt.

She knew the face of a guilty man, probably better than most.

And more, she trusted *this* man.

Slipping out of the seat, she moved around to join him on his bench. His arm came around her and she snuggled against him. "Will you be able to tell me?"

"I don't know. It depends on her. What she decides to do."

"So I take it that this is a big secret."

A harsh laugh ripped out of him. "She wouldn't say, but . . . yeah. I think it's going to be monumental."

"If you can tell me, then you will." She tipped her head back to look at him.

He rubbed his cheek against hers. "Yes."

"Okay."

It was enough.

They left holding hands.

Layla sat there brooding over her whiskey and Coke—the cheapest shit whiskey around and she could only afford the one. Her credit card was just about maxed out and she had no idea how she was going to pay it. She needed the fucking drink, though, and there was *nobody* in there to buy her a drink, either.

Willie T. hadn't shown up.

And the fireworks she'd expected from Trinity and Noah just hadn't happened.

Trinity Ewing and Noah Benningfield walked out of there holding hands and smiling.

It was sickening.

Fury burning inside her gut, she tossed back the rest of the drink and stood. She wobbled a little on her heels before she managed to get her balance, and halfway across the floor one of her feet went out from under her. She nearly pitched forward flat on her face, but a pair of hands caught her, steadied her.

"You seem to have a shoe problem."

She jerked away, glaring up at Caine Yoder. His face,

solemn and unsmiling, stared down at hers and she sneered at him. "You seem to have an asshole problem," she snapped. Then she looked down at her shoes and could have shrieked.

A few years ago, she'd managed to talk one of the guys she'd been seeing—she couldn't even remember his name, but he'd been hung and loaded—into buying her a pair of red Louboutins. And the fucking *heel* had just broken. She wanted to scream. Bending down, she took off the shoes, staring at the one with the broken heel.

"Son of a bitch," she muttered.

"You can get it fixed."

"Caine." She smiled at him sweetly. "Go fuck your-self." Then she shouldered past him and headed to the door. Fuck waiting for Willie T. to show up. She was heading to his place. He always had plenty of booze, and he had always had weed. Plus, she was in the mood to hurt or be hurt. He was always happy to accommodate on at least *one* level.

Willie T.'s instincts had proven to be rather sharp.

It was a good thing he'd been prepared for that, be-cause he'd hidden himself well. The solid oak secretary on the upper level had protected him from several of the bullets. Several, not all. And he had gotten a good shot off. Willie T. was lying on the floor, gut shot, the dark, ugly blood pouring from him and staining the floor.

His cell phone was by the front door.

One blessing, he thought. Maybe God was with him.

Willie T. was close to one of the house phones—if he got lucky, he might be able to crawl to one.

Of course, he didn't plan on letting Willie T. get lucky and it wouldn't matter anyway. The first thing he'd done when he got inside was unplug the cordless unit and dis-connect the more basic landlines.

"You are a dead son of a bitch when I get ahold of you," Willie T. said from down below.

"Well, you'd have to get ahold of me first," he said easily enough as he managed to wrap a makeshift bandage around his arm. There was blood. He had to figure out how to cover it up or clean it up. There was no way to completely remove blood, but there were ways to destroy it so thoroughly it wouldn't do the techs any good. He had to get out of here, too, and soon. Very soon, or he was going to be discovered. The longer he was here, the more likely it was to happen.

"Boy, you think I can't handle you?" Willie T. said, his voice thin, tight with pain.

In the dim light of the landing, he just smiled. So far, Willie T. was proving to have handled him better than the others. But Willie T. was the one bleeding to death from a gut shot. And he just had a flesh wound. He'd taken worse when he'd been in the military . . . awful years. Just plain awful. But it had taught him a lot. Discipline. How to ignore pain. How to handle a weapon. How to do what needed to be done.

Taking a deep, steadying breath, he braced a hand on the floor and moved into position. He had to get up. He wasn't hurt much. His head spun a little as he started to bring himself to his feet, using the secretary for protection as he glanced around to check on Willie T. Jerking back, he grimaced as wood splintered from the desk.

Willie T. was in fact getting slow . . . and he wasn't aiming well, either. If he had, that would have been his head catching that bullet.

But really, Willie T. shouldn't have fired that last shot. If he was right, the man lying on the floor might have one bullet left in the Glock he carried.

He'd taken a desperate shot, something you did when you saw death staring you in the eye.

Desperation could make you stupid.

Another thing he'd learned in the army.

Letting an edge of mockery show in his voice, he called out, "You're just about out of bullets in that Glock, boy."

"Why don't you come out here and face me like a fucking man?"

"Because you aren't a man. You're a child-raping dog, and I'll put you down like the sick dog you are." He held his breath, listened as the silence stretched out. "What? Nothing to say about that? Aren't you going to defend what you did to those boys?"

"You wouldn't understand, you sack of shit."

"No. I don't believe I would. Nor do I ever want to." Slowly, he stood up, taking a risk, because he wanted Willie T. to see who was acting as judge, jury and executioner.

Willie T.'s face went almost comically blank. And before he could form another word, he lifted his gun. Pointed.

Willie jerked his up, but he was dead before he could even aim.

Put down, just like the sick dog he was.

Sighing, he turned and looked at the blood staining his shirt. He'd have to hide that. There was a spare shirt in his car and he could cover it up, then destroy the shirt once he got home. But first, he had to deal with the blood.

He'd just finished taking care of that when he heard the knock. With the fumes of bleach strong in the air, he straightened, his back groaning as he eyed the front door.

This was a pisser.

He hadn't left his car out front.

He knew better than that.

But it wouldn't matter if he was seen here.

A second later, an angry voice sounded from the porch. "Willie T., open up."

He narrowed his eyes and looked down at Willie T.

Willie T. wasn't going to be opening that door.

And just why was Layla here?

Moving down the stairs, keeping his back to the wall, he eyed the door. It was still locked, but that didn't keep her from rattling the doorknob or banging on it like she wanted to knock it down.

"Damn it, Willie. I need . . ." her voice tripped. "Let me in, will ya? I've had a bitch of a day. I need a drink. I need . . . I just need you to let me in."

Layla never knew what she needed. It was a sad, miserable fact but a fact nonetheless.

And she wasn't going away, either. He grimaced as she kicked at the door and when that didn't yield a response, she started to swear and scream. He headed for the back, but even as he hit the kitchen, he caught sight of her shadow and pressed his back to the wall, watching as she disappeared into the small greenhouse between the garage and the house.

There she stayed.

He tapped a fist against his thigh, waiting, biding his time. Brooding.

Nearly five minutes passed before she came out, and when she did she had a mean smile slanting her lips and as she started toward the back door, she put a joint between her lips.

I'll be a son of a bitch, he thought sourly.

She'd found that out in the greenhouse; he'd bet his right nut on it.

Before the thought even finished, she shouted out, "I hit your fucking stash, Willie T. If you don't let me in, I'll just keep going back." She stumbled past his line of sight and he gauged the distance between him and the back door. There wouldn't be much time—

Blowing out a breath, he moved.

Planting himself between the door and the wall, he waited.

As she came in, he moved.

He tried to catch her before she hit the floor, but he couldn't and she went down hard.

Sighing, he rubbed the back of his neck and then bent down to check on her. Before he left, he disposed of the joint and made sure the note was in place.

Willie T. Number 3. Pardon the accidental rhyme. He was something of a challenge. If you question Glenn Blue, he may or may not tell you the truth, but this man helped initiate him . . . and I believe he also had a hand in harming Lee Brevard. May his soul rot in hell.

CHAPTER SEVENTEEN

She had the taste of a stale joint in her mouth.

Her head pounded something terrible.

And something smelled *awful*.

Groaning, Layla rolled onto her back and stared up at the ceiling while a muddled cloud obscured just about every damn thought she had.

It was dark and she couldn't quite place where in the hell she was.

She'd been coming to Willie T.'s. . . .

Blinking, she went to jerk upright, but the pain in her head screeched and she groaned, reaching up to touch her scalp. She felt something raw and crusty. Pulling her hand back, she saw the dark flakes on her fingers. "What the hell?" she muttered.

Sighing, she shoved upright and checked her clothes, looked around.

"What the fuck is that *smell*?"

She had her purse. Not that she had anything to steal, but . . .

Hitting the lights, she looked around, checked the silverware drawer and lifted up the organizer, saw where Willie T. kept a stash of cash. It was all there, four hundred in cash. Smirking, she slipped out a few of the twenties and tucked them into her pocket. It would take him a few days to realize it was gone, more than likely, and then she'd already have spent it.

Probably on an entire vat of bleach . . . Wrinkling up her nose, she pressed the back of her hand against her mouth and tried not to gag. It smelled like Willie T.'s sewer lines had backed up or something—the stink of shit fouled the air. Well, one thing was sure: She definitely wasn't hanging around here.

Maybe she could—

She stopped in the doorway, her hand falling limp to her side, as she took in the sight before her.

Her brain just didn't want to process it.

The dark stain, almost black, spreading across the floor and drying. The gun that lay beside Willie T.'s open hand.

His eyes were wide open and shocked as he stared, like he couldn't believe somebody had actually gone and killed him.

She swallowed and took another step deeper into the room, unconsciously shaking her head. Her fingers trembled as she dug her cell phone out of the tight front pocket of her jeans and she had to try three times before she finally managed to dial 911.

Her eyes all but burned when she started to read the note.

Layla Chalmers didn't have a lot of lines. She didn't much care about anybody other than herself. Well, herself and her son. And maybe that was why this pissed her off. Because she could so easily see her little boy being hurt. Hurt like—

She cut that thought off before she was sick, right then and there, in front of Willie T.'s dead, useless corpse.

A tinny voice rang in her ear and she realized she'd forgotten the phone in her hand.

"I need the cops to come out to Willie T. Merchant's house," she said, her voice coming in a thin, reedy gasp once the operator came on the line. "He's been shot. And . . . and there's a note."

The operator's voice was a buzz in Layla's ear, but she barely heard it as she lowered the phone and disconnected, staring long and hard at that note. Then she turned and tucked the phone away, striding back into the kitchen. *That son of a bitch.*

She grabbed the rest of the money from the silverware drawer; then she ran upstairs, taking them as fast as she could. She almost fell flat on her face when she saw the bottle of bleach there, open, the stink of it flooding the air. Scowling, she edged around it and headed into the bathroom. Willie T. kept more cash in there, tucked in his shaving kit.

Another cool three hundred. He didn't need it.

And it felt good to take something from him. The cock-sucking monster.

She wasn't really whom he needed to talk with.

He shouldn't talk to anybody just then. He needed to calm down, get his mind in order. Plan the next step.

But Lana appeared at the foot of the steps that night, and judging by the look in her eyes, she wasn't going to go away.

He sighed and rose, walked inside to get himself a cup of coffee and check on things. It was all quiet, the bandage on his arm neatly in place.

So far, nobody had reported Willie T.'s death.

He hadn't hit Layla hard, just a nice, solid knock on the back of her head. She'd been out of it, and considering the life she liked to live, she might sleep for a while. She could probably use it—the sleep, a few good meals. Some plain and simple rest.

Not that he'd been concerned about that when he knocked her out. He just needed to get away from there before she saw him.

Moving back out onto the porch, he found Lana sitting on the lowest step, her elbows braced on her knees, her gaze focused on the water.

She didn't look back at him.

"I missed the river," she said quietly.

"I've had to leave here a time or two in my life," he murmured quietly, thinking about those times. "I never really thought about the river much until it just wasn't there. But I missed it, too. I was always glad when I could come back."

She looked down, then, her gaze on the ground beneath her feet. Her slim shoulders stiffened, and then slowly she looked up and turned her head, staring at him. "You *chose* to leave. I didn't have a choice—you didn't *give* me one. I left because of you. And I never *thought* I'd be able to come back."

He frowned at her. "Just what are you talking about, Lana . . . I didn't give you a choice?"

She gaped at him. "That's what you *told* me I needed to do."

Sighing, he reached up and tugged off his cap, running a hand back of his hair, not quite following. "Child, I don't quite know just what you're getting at, but I most certainly did *not* tell you that you had to leave. You . . ."

He stopped, shook his head. "It doesn't matter now. It's done. I'll say it was harder, if you must know. Trying to figure out which way to go with you gone. David, now . . . he certainly refused to talk and I can understand why, but if *you* had been here, I think he would have found his courage, but you just aband—"

He made himself stop.

She had just been a girl, a girl who tried to do a brave

thing and ended up being put a terrible position, where she saw terrible things. She'd been scared and she ran. He'd come to grips with that and he had no right to his anger.

Feeling the intensity of her gaze, he leaned back in his chair and studied her. Her skin was pale, drawn tight across the bones of her face, while her eyes glowed like the mist coming off the river. "What were you going to say?" she demanded, her voice all but trembling.

He remained silent.

She shoved upright and took the two steps, crossed the porch to glare at him. "What were you going to say?" she snarled.

"I don't blame you," he said gently. "You were scared and you ran. David thought you'd abandoned him, but after a while, he began to realize how convoluted everything had become. I honored your wishes, though. . . . I didn't tell him where you were when you wrote back. He has no—"

"My wishes," she whispered.

She stumbled, sagging against the post at her back.

Reaching up, she went to cover her face with her hands and ended up knocking her glasses askew. Swearing, she caught them in her hands and hurled them down. "I never *wrote* you," she said, her breath coming in hard, ragged pants. "What in the *hell* is going on?"

He heard the tremor in her voice, the confusion. He felt the very same way himself.

Confusion, and the first embers of rage.

"Why don't you tell me everything that you remember . . . from the time I left you that day?"

Lana almost told him to get fucked.

Almost.

But the look in his eyes was one that was too familiar to her.

A look like her father's.

She might be nearly thirty-seven fricking years old, but a look from certain people just had her fighting the urge to snap to attention and go *Aye aye, sir! Yes, sir! Right away!*

So instead of telling him to get fucked, she told him, exactly, what she'd been told all those years ago.

The words were practically stamped on her mind and it took nothing to bring *that* day back into clarity, even though the days that came before were lost to pain and trauma while the years after were wispy and insubstantial, lost in a fog of drugs, fear and misery.

Finally, she finished, her throat raw, like she'd been coughing up razor blades. "I didn't know what to think, really. All I knew was that *you* wanted me gone," she finished. "It was better for David if I was gone—he wouldn't have to answer questions; he wouldn't be in trouble. So I left. I'd done enough damage."

Hearing a hoarse mumble, she looked over to the side and saw that he'd risen from his chair.

Old Max stood there, staring out over the water, his white head bent, his shoulders stooped and frail. Finally, he looked up, his blue eyes faded but still sharp. He pinned her with a hard look. "I *never* wanted you gone. The plan was for you to be here, to heal up, and be there, be steady for David, so when he was ready to go forward, you could help hold him together. He was a mess without you. And when you disappeared—"

Lana's jaw dropped.

"What?"

He smacked his hat against his thigh.

"I trusted a friend, Lana," he said softly, shaking his head. "This town . . . it had poison in it, you know that as well as I do, and I didn't want anything bad to happen to you, not when it looked like the sheriff himself might be involved in what was going on. Not when some of the doctors were even involved. I took you to the *one* place where I thought you'd be safe while I tried to figure out the best way to help you two. . . . I . . ." He closed his eyes. "I was going to make this right. I was going to take them all down. I knew people outside this town, and they wouldn't have been impressed by the sheriff's contacts or Sutter's community involvement. . . . We could have put a stop to it. I was a fucking blind fool. Arrogant, thinking that I could change everything."

Lana blinked, shock rattling inside her at what he was saying. It felt like the entire past twenty years of her life had just been rewritten and she didn't know what to say, what to think, what to feel.

Max passed a hand in front of his face, rubbed at his jaw. "One of my friends with the state police, not a local but from up in Indianapolis, had called me. That very day, when I realized you'd gone and I . . . hell. I had no idea what to say to him. I tried to convince David to meet with him, but David just shut down. He wouldn't talk, not without you there. I didn't know what to tell my contact. In the end, David decided he'd rather stay hidden. All of this because I trusted the wrong person."

He rubbed the back of his neck, shoulders stooped and bowed, looking like he carried the weight of every one of his eighty-plus years.

"I'm going to find out just what happened, girl. I'll find answers for you."

"Answers," she said, her voice hollow. "You're going to find answers. Now. After all this time." She shook her head. "I don't want you to find the answers for me. I'll find them myself. I just want to talk to David."

He stared at her, his eyes faded but still sharp.

"Where is he?"

He arched a shaggy brow. "It's been a long time, Lana."

"Don't give me that."

He sighed, looked away. "I kept in touch with the family who took him in. I'll reach out to them. If he wants to talk with you, he'll get in touch." Then his gaze cut back to hers. "But that's not all I'm going to do. You were lied to. I was lied to. I'll know why."

Lana just shook her head and turned away. It wasn't enough. Not now.

Caine Yoder strode out of the barn, comfortable in the darkness.

There were no lights there.

It was a new moon and the night teased with the coming hint of fall. But the Ohio Valley was something of a bitch, he'd always thought, taunting and teasing like that. It might be two more months before they saw a reprieve from the heat.

Then again, it could drop into the forties over the next week and it could be weeks or even months before they saw a day above sixty again. The weather in this part of the country was fickle, if nothing else.

He'd just finished putting away his tools when he heard the phone inside the house ringing.

He ignored it.

Whoever it was would call back if it was important.

If it wasn't, he had no need to talk to the person anyway.

Caine Yoder's personal number was only given out to a few people. Everybody else called the business line that he'd set up only because he worked with so many of Abraham's family. Abraham had run the family business for many years, but his health had failed over the past few years and he had no son to pass it on to, save for Caine.

Caine didn't want the business.

But he wouldn't let it founder, so he did his best, because while he lacked the ability to love, if he could love he thought he would have loved Abraham.

The phone continued to ring, the shrill sound of it punctuating the night air.

Frowning, he opened the back door. It wasn't locked. He had never gotten into the habit of locking doors. Locking doors did nothing to keep evil from the home or men's hearts and he didn't see the point. It wasn't like he had much worth stealing anyway. The most valuable property he owned was the tools tucked away in his trunk or in the barn, so why bother locking his home?

Shutting the door behind him, the hot, tight air of the house wrapping around him, he moved over and stood in front of the small table and the simple rotary phone. There was no answering machine. His home had only a few electrical appliances and no air-conditioning.

Caine lived a very simple, very basic lifestyle.

The phone rang again. By his estimation, it had rung a good twenty times now.

Reaching out, he lifted it to his ear and waited. He could think of only two people who would be that persistent . . . and he'd just left Abraham's house an hour ago.

"I need to speak with you," Max Shepherd said, his voice blunt and to the point.

Caine's lids drooped low, shielding his eyes. He really didn't want to talk to Max. "I don't want to speak with you."

"I don't give a damn, boy," Max barked.

Caine closed his eyes, dread creeping through him. There were only so many reasons why Max might want to talk to Caine. And if it was why he thought . . . he had things he needed to do. "Fine. When and where?"

"I'll be out there tomorrow as soon as I can make arrangements."

"No. I'll come there." If Caine was right, then he didn't want Max bringing that darkness out here.

"Fine. See that you do it early. This can't wait."

* * *

"Look . . . I just need to go through everything from the top." Jensen fought to keep her face impassive as she sat across from Layla Chalmers.

There were some people who were just hard to like.

Layla was one of them.

Really, if Layla could lose some of the bitterness, some of the pettiness, she could do almost *anything*. Well, that and kick the drug habit. She was smart, she was beautiful and when she set her mind to it, she could accomplish things. The problem was that Layla focused all her talents on men and sex and drugs and pettiness.

A person didn't accomplish much in life when those four things were the goals.

"We've already *been* through this," Layla said, her voice truculent, her eyes locked on the table as she went at her nails with a vengeance. "I found him. He'd shit himself—do people really *do* that when they die?"

Layla looked up at Jensen, waiting.

"Certain things do happen at the time of death," Jensen said vaguely.

"Whatever." Layla rolled her eyes and went back to her nails. "Anyway, he'd shit himself. That's so fucking nasty. The smell was everywhere. The house stank. I smelled it when I woke up." She frowned and reached up, touching the knot on the back of her head. "Somebody hit me. I don't . . . Anyway, I was on the floor, woke up and smelled something nasty. Came in there and saw Willie T. I knew he was dead. He had blood all over his middle, and—"

She stopped and reached up, touched her forehead. "Here. He'd been shot right here. I knew he was dead, had been for a while. I saw the note. Called nine-one-one. What more do you want to know?"

Jensen clenched her jaw, tightening her hand around the pen. But outwardly, she just gave Layla a reassuring smile.

"That's a good start, but let me ask the questions. . . . There are just things I need, in a certain order, okay? Like for instance . . . did he know you were coming over? Did anybody else know?"

Layla gave Jensen a bored look. "You think anybody would have *killed* him if they'd known I was showing up, sugar? How stupid can a person get?"

"You'd be surprised." She shrugged and jotted down a note. "You go over to Willie T.'s a lot?"

"Some." She jerked her shoulder in a shrug. "You'll find the weed when you investigate. I . . ." She licked her lips and eyed Jensen nervously.

"Layla, I'm not interested in Willie T.'s weed or what you were doing with it." It wasn't like everybody in town didn't know about her drug problem anyway. Now Willie T. might come as a bigger surprise, but Willie T. had bigger problems than being a grower of marijuana. His epitaph was going to be *I raped boys*, if Jensen's gut was on-target. "Let's not worry about that, okay?"

"I should get that in writing or something," Layla said suspiciously. Then she shrugged. "Well, I'm not under arrest, so it's not like you can *use* this or anything."

Jensen smiled encouragingly. *Stupid woman.* If she said something incriminating, it could totally be used, but Layla hadn't killed Willie T.

"I wanted to smoke some weed, have a drink. Willie T. is always good for that . . . plus . . ." Layla slid Jensen a sly look. "He's . . . He *was* old and all, but he can get rough. Sometimes that's fun. I was in the mood for that and I headed over there. But he didn't answer the knock. I kept knocking and shouting for him. He didn't answer and I thought he was being an ass. So I go to his greenhouse, thought, *I'll show him,* and I helped myself to the stash he kept out there. He hides the plants he grows, out someplace on the grounds, but I know where he kept a good stock of it and I grabbed a joint, from the slash then headed to the back door." She looked down, rubbed one palm against the other.

Nerves, now, bleeding through, Jensen thought. Getting up, she got a glass of water for Layla and put it down, watching as Layla reached out and grasped at it desperately.

Her hands were trembling.

How much of that was because she needed a fix? How much was from fear?

Layla drained the glass and put it down, then got to her feet—bare feet, her toes painted blue, the polish chipped and peeling. "The back door wasn't locked. Willie T. always has the doors locked," Layla said, staring at the wall. "I didn't think it was weird. Why didn't I notice that?"

"It seems to me you've had a rough few days," Jensen said, keeping her voice neutral.

Layla whipped her head around, staring at Jensen with glittering eyes.

Jensen held her gaze.

Layla sneered and started to pace again. "What the fuck ever. Anyway. I went inside, but . . . I don't remember anything else until I woke up and there was that smell. Maybe there was pain, like something sudden when he hit me. It would have been a guy, right? I don't know. But I didn't see anything, anybody."

"Had you been smoking when you went inside?"

As the temper crawled across Layla's face, Jensen lifted a hand. "I just need to know, Layla. It helps me get the picture, helps me get an idea who tried to hurt you, who tried to set you up for this."

Layla's jaw dropped. "Me?" She pressed a hand to her chest. *"Me?"*

"You were left there at the scene of the crime," Jensen pointed out. She should feel bad about this, really. Nobody had tried to set Layla up, at all. Layla was just in the way when the killer was there and the killer wanted her *out* of the way.

But Jensen needed Layla to cooperate, and Layla only cooperated when Layla got something *out* of it. Suddenly that cooperation was all but flowing from the woman as she settled herself in front of Jensen.

Layla reached out, clinging to Jensen's hand.

"You know I'd never hurt anybody," Layla pleaded, shaking her head. "Not like that."

"Of course." Jensen gave Layla's hand a squeeze. *See? We're friends!* Then she pulled back and focused on her work, the tooth-pulling problem of getting a real statement from Layla Chalmers.

Setting me up—
   Not likely.

Anger gnawed at Jensen Bell, but she kept it under control as she went through everything again with Layla. It was a damn good thing Jensen was such a goody two-shoes. So by the book. Plenty of the cops here would have just tried to pin it on Layla, but Jensen was smart. Jensen had seen what was going on and now Layla could think, could plan.

But she had to push the anger out and focus.

A headache throbbed and her skin crawled like a thousand ants lived just inside it. She needed a fix. The weed hadn't helped. It had been too long since she'd had a decent high and she was dying for one. She'd had a few pills she'd been hoarding, taking just one a few times a day, to keep the edge off, but it wasn't enough and she hadn't been able to take one since that morning.

What she *really* needed was some coke, she thought. That would give her a good buzz, clear her thoughts, and she could think. Get through this, but that wasn't going to happen.

Fuck it all.

She had to grit her teeth and get through it.

Under the table, she closed her hands into fists to keep from scratching at her arms as she continued to answer Jensen's questions. Layla kept a confused, dazed look on her face even as she plotted out how to make this all better. She had to play it smart. Jensen was a goody two-shoes and she liked being the smart cop, but she *was* smart and if Layla laid it on too thick then the bitch would figure it out.

Damn Willie T. Damn his ass to hell and back. For being dead. For being a fucking pervert. For being a monster.

And Layla had let him stick his dick in her. She needed to scrub herself clean. She could never be clean, but she could be cleaner than she was now. But she had to stay here . . . answer these questions—

"And you don't remember hearing anything?" Jensen asked.

Layla stared at her, scrunched up her face. "I was just pissed off, Jensen. I wanted to see Willie T." Then Layla sighed and looked down, pretending to think.

As she did, the events of the past day rolled through her mind and then they stuttered, caught, as one face in particular settled in her mind.

Yeah, she was pissed at Willie T. He had some nerve, up and dying like that. Raping kids like he had.

But she never would have gone out there, never would have gotten involved, if it weren't for Noah.

It was *his* fault she was trapped here, caught up in this mess.

She'd had a fucked-up day ever since she'd run into him, and he was the one who needed to pay.

That was her thinking and she figured it made sense.

He'd given her a day from hell and she was thinking she'd do the same for him.

"Come on, Layla," Jensen nudged, prodding her and nudging her mind back on-track.

Gotta focus. Need to get out of here . . . what were we talking about . . . oh, the noises. Yeah.

"I don't know. I might have heard something. Yeah, I was smoking when I walked in," she said, sighing. She managed to paste a shamed expression on her face, dragged her eyes away like she couldn't stand to meet Jensen's eyes. "You've never done it, I know. You don't know how it is, but maybe after my head clears . . . once I'm not so scared? I think maybe I heard a noise. But I don't know."

She shot Jensen a look, evaluated the expression on the cop's face. Layla could usually read cops pretty well. But Jensen was harder to read. Hard to say.

Take it easy, Layla thought to herself. *Take it slow.*

If she did right, she might be able to find a way to get some payback.

"I think . . . maybe I did see somebody."

As one of the officers escorted Layla out of the station, Jensen leaned back in her seat and met Thorpe's eyes.

He looked at her, and although his eyes were clear, his suit looked a little rumpled. It made sense. It was going on one in the morning and they'd been at it since seven. They hadn't expected to wrap up their day with another murder. They were going to have to call in the state to help with this at this point. Hell, Willie T.'s death wasn't even *in* their jurisdiction, but it was definitely connected— the county boys had been nice enough to let them speak with Layla and Layla just hadn't connected the dots between city cops and county sheriffs.

"You ever get the feeling you're being played? Just like a fiddle?" Jensen asked.

Thorpe nodded solemnly. "All the time. I got three nieces and a nephew and they've turned me into their own string section."

Jensen grinned at him and then looked back at the hallway, watching as Layla flirted with Officer Heaton. She should watch it. Heaton's wife, Roni, would rip Layla's hair out.

Once Layla was out of sight, Jensen turned and looked at Thorpe. "Well, between you and me, I have to say, Layla can outplay your nieces and nephew. We were just played, well and truly. That was some damn fine playing."

"Not so fine." Thorpe shook his head. "There ain't no way it happened like she said."

Jensen closed her eyes. "No. But we have to bring him in." Her heart hurt, even thinking about it.

CHAPTER EIGHTEEN

The house was dark and quiet. Lana pressed her back against the door and closed her eyes, wished like crazy that somebody was inside the house with her. Wished she wasn't alone so she didn't have to deal with the noise in her head. Too much noise, too many thoughts.

If she had somebody with her, she wouldn't have to think.

Somebody . . . no. Not *somebody*.

Adam.

She wanted Adam.

She wanted to feel his arms around her and maybe lean against him. Feel him touch her the way he'd been touching her before Noah had walked in.

Squeezing her eyes closed, she breathed around the knot that just refused to go away. She'd gone to see Max, determined to get answers, because *answers* would make that rawness inside better. That was what she thought. But nothing was going to make that raw, bruised feeling go away.

And now it was even worse.

Now the confusion was spreading and she had more questions.

Max . . .

I never *wanted you gone*.

She shoved a fist against her temple, wishing she could drown out that voice, wished she could wipe away the memory of the past few hours. Even just turn back the clock to when she'd been standing here facing Noah. It had been a brutal, solid punch, but at least *then* she'd thought she understood things.

Instead of looking for clues where to find David—because the judge had been *so* forthcoming about that—she should have gone to Noah.

Explained things, told him she might have to disappear again . . . or, you know, maybe end up in jail . . . *please understand*.

Noah would have held her hand and offered to help her find a lawyer.

Fuck. Actually, her dad would have done that. Noah would have just been a quiet, supporting presence at her back. She hadn't wanted to hurt or disappoint either of those men.

She'd done both.

The floorboards creaked and she shoved away from the door, tensing automatically. As she turned to face the doorway, she let her backpack fall to the floor and then she caught sight of who it was. The tension drained out of her in a rush as she saw Adam, shrouded in half shadows. "I thought you had to work," she said, her voice a soft whisper in the quiet stillness of the house.

He closed the distance between them and reached up, pushing his fingers into her hair. "I thought you might need a friend."

"A friend." She closed her eyes and turned her face into his palm. His thumb stroked over her lip while he pushed his fingers into her hair. "Is that what we are, Adam? Even now?"

He moved a little closer and the heat of his body

reached out to tease hers. She could whimpered, it felt so good. "Do you not want to be friends?"

She dropped her head against his chest. "I no longer know what I want. I don't even know what to think." Her mind was still spinning with what Max had told her.

I trusted the wrong person.

"Things will be okay with Noah." Adam curved his arm around her waist and brought her in close before skimming his hand up her back, resting it on the nape of her neck. "He's confused and upset, but he's a good guy, solid. He'll understand once you're able to talk to him."

"I already did."

Adam's body tensed for a brief second. Oh, so subtly, but then it was gone. "Yeah?" He leaned back and peered down into her face, cocking an eyebrow. "What happened?"

"I was down at the river. In the woods. That was always . . ."

"You always went there." Adam brushed his thumb over her lips again. "I guess Noah still remembers that."

"Yeah." She reached up and touched her fingers to Adam's lips. "Kind of funny. You do, too."

He kissed her fingers and closed his hand around her wrist, his eyes dark and intense on her face. "I remember all kinds of things about you, Lana."

Her heart banged hard against her ribs. That look. The way he watched her. She swallowed, closing her eyes as she tucked her head back against his chest, the cadence of his heart oddly soothing. The scent of him flooded her head and some of the coldness inside her eased back. She felt surrounded by him. Warmed by him. For the first time in forever, she didn't feel alone.

She'd had friends over the years, but Adam had been one of the very, very few who had always gotten her. And nobody made her feel safe the way he did.

"What did you and Noah talk about?" he murmured, shattering that moment of internal reverie.

"Not much." She rubbed her cheek absently against the faded cotton of the Harley T-shirt he wore, opening her eyes to stare off into nothing. "He just . . . I think if I tell him anything, he'll understand."

"He probably will. Noah's good at that." Adam pressed his lips to her temple and that soft brush had her pulse rate skittering in dangerous territory. She tried to ignore it. "You probably need to talk about it, darlin'."

She squeezed her eyes closed. "I can't tell anybody anything, because I don't know anything." Anger twisted in her, exploding through her like a volcanic eruption. She shoved away from him to pace the floor, the edgy tension inside her spiraling higher and higher. *I trusted the wrong person.* "I know even less now than I knew before, too."

"Just what does that mean?"

She stopped and stared at him, and for some reason the glasses she wore—glasses she didn't need—pissed her off. Tearing them off, she turned and hurled them down on the table. "He tells me he trusted a friend," she snarled. "The wrong friend."

Adam had suspected there was a lot of anger inside her.

He just hadn't realized it was this close to the surface, ready to ignite.

Now, though . . .

As Lana started to pace, her face pale, tight with strain, he stayed against the island, forcing himself to relax, not to move any closer. It was hard. Hard not to reach out and touch her as she swung by him, her long legs scissoring as she paced back and forth.

He waited, and waited.

Finally, she stopped by the window, staring out over

his garden, her hands curled over the edge of the counter. "Have you ever had anybody that you just really trusted? Somebody that you put your everything in and then it turns out that faith was misplaced?"

Adam dragged his thumb down his jaw, carefully thought through that question. It was a loaded one, and he could all but see her need to talk, to tell him everything burning inside her.

If he answered this the wrong way, he might never get the answers.

But worse . . . he was going to add to the hurt he could see inside her.

"Everybody places their trust wrong from time to time, darlin'," he finally said. "I'm a paranoid bastard, though. I don't give my trust to a lot of people and haven't since I was a kid. I trusted my folks. I trusted you. I trust Noah. To some extent, I trust a few of the guys I've met through AA. But that's probably about it."

She was silent.

Shoving away from the counter, he moved over to stand behind her. Reaching up, he caught the end of her braid and tugged out the band that held it in place. Slowly, he started to loosen the tight cable. Once he'd done that, he pushed his hands into her hair and started to rub her scalp. "The red is starting to show," he said softly.

"I know." Her head fell forward.

Silence fell and for a moment they just stood there as he rubbed at her scalp. He worked his way down to her neck and she groaned as he went at the tight muscles there.

"I trusted him. . . . I left here because I trusted him, Adam. And the whole time, it was a lie."

He had to fight not to let the tension he felt echo through him. "Why don't you tell me now, Lana?" He let his hands fall away and moved in closer, wrapping his arms around her and pulling her close. Tucking his chin against her shoulder, he murmured against her ear, "Whatever you have to say, it's between us, nobody else."

"These aren't my secrets."

"Maybe not. But these secrets are destroying you . . . Haven't they already taken enough?"

A harsh shudder racked her body.

He closed his eyes and then decided it was time to push harder. Rubbing his cheek against hers, he said quietly, "You've danced around the edge of this . . . but let me take this further, might make it easier."

She was tense under his hands, so tense, he thought she might shatter. He curved his hands over her shoulders, squeezed lightly. "You already told me that David Sutter was abused. . . . I know these aren't your secrets and you don't feel right talking about it. But Lana, it's not right that you tried to help somebody and that your entire life gets destroyed, either. It's a secret that's ruining your life. It's a secret that somehow led to the abuse of more kids, I suspect. It's not your fault, but whoever you trusted could have done something to stop it. None of this is right. It has to end. You know that."

A shudder racked her body.

"Just remember . . . once you get to Indy, you need to find somebody at The Indianapolis Star, *okay? That shithead father of yours likes seeing his name in the news too much—even people up there know who he is."*

Lana smiled at David, tried to show him some sort of reassurance. Maybe she should go with him. Dad would ground her for a month if she just up and disappeared for a few days, but she could call him once they were on the road. . . .

The empty look in David's eyes scared her. He didn't care anymore. He just didn't care. He used to. . . . He'd cared about stopping it. He'd cared about getting out.

But now? He was at the point where nothing mattered. It had gotten worse after he'd tried to go to the police. That had gone over so fucking well.

It was like he was dying inside and he just didn't care. It scared the hell out of her.

"Maybe I should just disappear," David said, his voice dull. "It's not like anybody would miss me."

She shot out a hand and grabbed his arm. He didn't like to be touched, but she thought it was better that he realize not everybody wanted to hurt him. Squeezing his arm, she waited until he looked at her, his eyes just a lifeless void. Softly she said, "I would." Then, slowly, she let go of his arm and pushed the bag into his hands.

He took it, fumbling with it for a minute. His hands had gotten huge over the summer, his hands, his feet, even his shoulders. He'd become clumsy, tripping over his feet, bumping into things, and it was like his hands were greased with butter, because he never seemed to know how to hold on to anything.

He was still too skinny, like he never had enough to eat, and sometimes he made her think of the feral cats she'd catch and take in to the vet. Desperate, and ready to bite.

"I think I should come with you," she blurted. "Dad would be mad for a few days, and Noah would be pissed, but it won't take long. Once we get to Indy and you tell them what you need to tell them, they'll make sure you're safe and I can come back. What do you think?"

David looked at her with eyes that were too old, too wise, too sad, for a kid who was only seventeen. Sometimes it was hard to remember they were the same age. He'd started school a year late, thanks to his crazy-ass mother— it's not good for him, he needs more rest, he was ill as a child, I don't like the environment, *blah, blah, blah. . . .*

That bitch Diane worried about school, and then she let her husband—

Lana cut that line of thought off because if she didn't, she was going to be too mad to think and she needed to think.

"You can't come," he said simply, shaking his head. He went to put the backpack on.

She heaved out a sigh. "Just promise me you are going."

If he gave his promise, he'd keep it. She knew that much.

"I promise." He jerked his head in a nod and looked out, eying his car, waiting for him behind the house.

"Okay, then. Just remember what we've talked about. Give all that shit to the Indy Star. Don't come back here. Don't call, not even once you're on the road. Word will get back to your dad and we can't let him find you—"

Something moved outside.

She knew the sound of this place, knew the feel of it, knew everything about it. There had been a time when she'd even daydreamed about buying the old Frampton house, maybe making it into an inn or something—a haunted one, because of all the stories. But then she'd realized what was going on out here.

But despite that, she still knew this place and she knew that sound outside didn't belong.

Quiet as it was, it might as well have been a siren.

It came from somewhere out in the yard, not close, but close enough.

Somebody was outside.

She jerked her head around and stared at the boy. He was pale, his Adam's apple bobbing in his throat as he stared toward the door.

"Go," she whispered.

He didn't even seem to hear her.

Damn it.

Closing the distance between them, she shoved him toward the hall. "Go, damn it."

He turned and looked at her, his eyes dark, a void in his expressionless face. He'd shut down so much in the past few weeks. She had to get him out of here before he did something she couldn't fix. He reached up and touched her cheek. "What are you going to do?"

"The thing I do best . . . cause trouble. But I can't do it while you're here, and if you don't leave now we're going to get caught." She made a fist and punched him gently. "Now . . . go on already. And don't look back. Whatever you do."

She pushed him to the front door. It faced out over the street, but they'd have to take that chance. That noise had come from the backyard. "I'm right behind you, okay?"

"Diane was there." Lana swallowed and then slowly lifted her head, met Adam's eyes. "She . . . ah, she'd been following David. Watching him. She was obsessed. I don't know why. I don't know what the issue was. But she was obsessed with him and the thought of him leaving, even to get away from what his father was doing, was something she couldn't tolerate."

Something flickered in Adam's eyes. A muscle pulsed in his cheek. But he made no comment, said nothing. He just waited.

"I told Adam to just leave. He had a car. . . . I . . . Ah, well." She grimaced and shrugged. "We'd swiped out the plates on his car with those of an old junker that had just been wrecked. It would make it harder to find his car for a few weeks, I figured. There was a friend of mine in Indy that he was going to crash with. I made all those calls from a pay phone in Hanover, just in case. Everything was set up and ready. David had clothes. He was dying to get out of here. But something clued Diane in and she followed him, listened in. She had a gun."

The arm Adam had around Lana's waist went tight.

Lana closed her eyes as the hazed images from that night started to spin through her head. "She had her phone, held the gun on us while she called Peter."

"The phone records showed a call from her cell phone to their residence that night. It was the only call the police could dig up. . . . People always speculated she'd been out with David and there was car trouble or something," Adam murmured against Lana's hair.

"She was calling him to come get their son. Because there was a problem," Lana bit off. That was one of her clearest memories, the look in Diane Sutter's eyes as she spoke of the *problem*. She'd stared straight at Lana. Diane was going to *deal* with Lana, but she'd leave it up to Peter to take care of David. "A problem. She saw me as a problem—she'd deal with me, and Peter would have to discipline their son. Again."

"Deal with you." Adam's arm was rigid, the muscles all but trembling.

"She wanted me dead." Lana curled her fingers into his shirt. "I saw it in her eyes. She wanted me dead and she was ready to kill me. I knew it, and so did David. He attacked her. Ran at her and knocked her down. The gun went flying. It must have gone off, because I remember glass shattering. She screeched—the sound was like a banshee—and she chased us." Lana touched a hand to her side.

Adam covered her hand with his.

"I don't remember her cutting me. I don't remember it hurting, although I know it must have. Everything was a blur. The blood was so hot on my side. I remember that. But I couldn't stop. I was so afraid for him, because I couldn't let his dad get him. Not again." Slowly she lifted her head. "I remember thinking we had to get out of there. . . . We were running. And then there was the blood. It was so hot. David was on the floor, and his mother was shouting at him, pointing the gun. I . . ." She licked her lips and shook her head. "I don't remember killing her. I think I hit her. I remember seeing her on the floor. But—"

Her breathing hitched, and when she lapsed into silence Adam cupped his hand over the back of her neck and just held her. Held her, and waited. Fine tremors racked her entire body and she stood so rigidly, he thought she might shatter at the first wrong move.

Under his hand, her skin felt cold.

If he thought it would help, he'd take her into the living room and build a fire—screw the fact that it was late August and he'd sweat to death.

But the cold she felt came from within.

He, however, was a raging, burning pit of fury. That anger, scalding hot, didn't serve him right now, but that didn't make it easier to shove it down.

Anger, fear, frustration . . .

And confusion.

She'd called him.

That night.

He knew the ins and outs of every damn thing that happened that fateful night—at least everything that had been made public knowledge. He even knew plenty that *wasn't* public knowledge, information he'd begged and bribed out of people. He'd made it his business to know. That phone call from Diane Sutter had taken place at 10:22 p.m. Lana had called him almost two hours later.

Somebody had spoken in the background. . . . *I trusted him.* . . .

Just whom had she trusted?

Abruptly Lana took a deep breath and it was like somebody had just popped the cork—some of the massive tension drained out of her and she eased away, starting to pace. "I understand why you don't have any booze here," she said, her voice low and rough. "But I could sure as hell use a drink."

"I can go get something for you," he offered.

"No." She shoved her hair back. "I won't do that to you. I just . . ." She closed her eyes and crossed her arms over her chest. "I don't drink much, either, really. For the same reason. I never had a problem with alcohol. It was always pills. But . . . why risk it?"

She opened her eyes and that pale, soft grey gaze locked with his. "Everything from that night is surreal. Huge chunks of it are just gone from my memory. I don't know if it's emotional trauma, or from when I'd hit my head—the headaches were awful and it took weeks for me to recover from it. Whatever it was, though, there are some things that I just *don't* remember—that I *can't* remember. I remember seeing her with the gun. I remember seeing David on the floor. Then he was grabbing me and we were running. He . . . One minute he was fine. Then there was blood all over him and I was trying to keep him upright. I think I screamed. That's what—"

She stopped. Just stopped, and when she opened her mouth, no words would come out. She couldn't force the words to come. Shuddering, shaking, she closed her eyes, pressed her head to Adam's chest and groaned, a low, strangled sound of pure frustration.

"You've come too far to not finish this," Adam said softly.

"I know," she whispered. Swearing, she pulled away from him and paced a few steps away. Turning to look at him, she curled her hands into fists, watched him. "I screamed. And we were at the Frampton house. You know who owned that place, right? People would say it was haunted, that crazy noises were heard from it. Cops would investigate. And the judge . . ."

Her words trailed off.

Realization slammed into Adam. "Old Max," he whispered. "Any time old Judge Max heard a fucking sound from there, he'd be out there with that damn Remington of his."

Lana nodded. "David and I made it onto the porch. I remember seeing the old man. I saw the rifle, but I wasn't afraid. Not of him. I'd always loved that old grouch. I thought he was like the best thing ever. And he saw us. . . . I just knew everything would be okay."

A fragment of memory worked free as she murmured those words and Lana felt herself spinning back.

The judge might have hit his sixties, but his hands were strong and steady as he guided them both off the porch, put them in the little area against it where they'd be out of sight. "Now, you two, stay there," he said, his voice flat and hard. "It will all be okay."

He stood, his thick white hair a halo around his head—he looked like a vengeful angel. Maybe Gabriel would have looked like that, if he was sent to earth and forced to age. A grouchy old fighter. Judge Max climbed the stairs, his face set in a mask as he mounted the steps.

The door opened.

Lana craned her head around and peered up, terror turning her heart into a hammer. It battered her chest and she could hardly breathe as she watched Diane move out onto the porch.

"Hello, Diane," the old judge said, his voice level and easy. Like he wasn't speaking to a woman with blood running down her temple. Like she wasn't clutching a gun in her hand. Like there weren't two scared, bleeding kids on the ground, just feet away.

"Max." She smiled. Lifted the gun. "Please step out of my way."

"I'm afraid that's not going to happen."

"Oh . . . you'll get out of my way, or I'll move *you* out of my way," Diane said, her eyes glinting with madness. "I have a problem with my son and I have to fix it."

"You have a problem sure enough. But you're just going to stay there." He lifted his rifle, pointing it toward her. "Why don't you give me that little phone you're always showing off? I need to make a call."

"No." Diane smiled, a rather dazzling smile. "You know, it's fascinating to me that you want to get involved in my life . . . now. Where were you before?"

The judge sighed. "Does any of that matter now, girl? Give me that phone. Don't make me do this."

She lifted her gun.

The judge moved.

"He moved really fast for an old guy," Lana murmured. She rubbed her hand across the back of her mouth as that bit of memory, lost for so long, settled into place. "He spun the rifle around and just clubbed her with it. She went down, and she went down *hard*. Then he looks at us, tells me that he needs five minutes. I don't know if David has five minutes and I told him that. So he came over, looked at David and made that little grumbly-grunt he makes and said, *He's got five, easy. Just wait here.* Like I could *go* anywhere. He drags her into the house and then he's back outside, moving around quicker than I probably could."

"My dad told me that Judge Max was Special Forces when he was in the army. I don't think you ever really lose that once you get in." Adam brooded, staring out into the night as he turned everything she'd told him over. "Why didn't the judge just take you to the hospital, call the cops?"

Lana swallowed and then, slowly, like her muscles couldn't support her anymore, she sank to the floor.

"Because I begged him not to." She drew her knees to her chest and hid her face against Adam. "You know about Cronus now. How many of them there are, how deep it goes. David had been being passed around for almost three years, and he still didn't know how many there were. A lot of them went masked with him, because he'd gone to the cops once. It turns out the chief of police was actually involved, too."

"The chief." Adam stared at her. He dropped down onto the floor and stared at her, fury knotting his muscles while disgust churned in his gut. "You're telling me that Chief Andrews, the good old boy who attended church Sunday morning, Sunday night and every fricking Wednesday, the one who ragged on my ass because I cussed like a heathen and I dated a few too many of the *wrong* girls and I drove too fast . . . that son of a bitch was involved with the Cronus bastards?"

"Yeah." She rested her head against the cabinets at her back. "So was one pediatrician, an OB/GYN and one of the elders that Pete Sutter was all buddy-buddy with . . . Harlan Troyer. He was one of them."

"I already know about Harlan." Adam surged upright and started to pace, the rage pulsing inside him.

"I think your friend Rita suspected. Or she found something and put it together. She couldn't take the guilt and she killed herself over it."

Adam stopped in his tracks and glared at Lana. "Fuck. Yeah, Rita knew but there was something else going on besides that. There had to be. She didn't do shit wrong, and once it really hit her, she called the cops. She would have found her mad soon enough. Her father wasn't worth her life."

"No. He wasn't." Lana wrapped her arms around herself, shivering, her gaze locked on the floor. "I begged Max, begged, pleaded . . . and David . . . well, he was all but screaming. The thought of going to the hospital turned him into an animal, and even though he could barely walk, he shoved the door to the car open . . . *while Max was driving* . . . and tried to throw himself out. I guess that caught the judge's attention and he asked me just what was going on. So I told him. It never occurred to me that *he* wouldn't believe me."

"I take it he didn't?"

"Oh, no." Lana rubbed her fingers against her mouth absently, staring off into the night. "The judge believed every word. And he started to think, to plan. He had to split us up, he said. Both of us needed medical care, but he couldn't take us to the hospital, because he wasn't going to trust the sheriff—not after what we'd told him. And if he couldn't trust Andrews, he wasn't trusting the city boys, either. The first thing they'd do if we were taken to any of the local places was call David's family, and the son of bitch had a long reach."

"Why not someplace in Kentucky?"

"No place close enough. Even Clark Memorial was almost an hour away, and he didn't want to risk having anybody call the police. Not until *he* had made a few calls, he said." She uncurled her legs and slowly climbed up, moving stiffly, like every muscle in her body hurt. "He knew officers with the state police—up in Indy, not people who were local. Judge Max knew plenty of people who weren't going to be intimidated by Sutter, or involved with Cronus. He was trying to help."

She moved to the coffeepot, reaching for the coffee beans Adam kept in the cabinet overhead. A few minutes later, the scent of coffee filled the air and she turned back to look at him. "Max has . . . well, a lot of unusual acquaintances. I don't know what all happened that night— what I was told was a lie, I think. But Max took David to one of the Amish families, one who had medical training.

I wasn't hurt as bad. Max told me he'd actually helped fix me up—may had been trained as a medic. . . . I guess he has all sorts of secrets about his years in the army. Once he had David settled, he took me to a different family. I remember him walking into the little workshop he had in his garage. That's where I was when the police were searching. I called you from there, I guess. I don't remember that, but I remember him checking the wound, forcing me to drink some water, take some medicine. He told me he had to wait a few hours before he could take me anywhere. Things blur in and out. . . . The next thing I remember was waking up in this little house. No air-conditioning. I looked outside and I saw Max talking to this Amish guy. I thought I was in another world. He came in and talked to me, told me they'd take care of me, that he'd be in touch. He had to see to David." She forced herself to smile, but it faltered, then faded. Turning back to the coffee, she said, "I wanted to go with him, check on David, but he said I needed to rest."

She made a face. "I should have pushed. I never saw David again. I know he's still alive. Max would have told me if he wasn't. So at least I have that much. David got out. And that is the thing that matters the most. I'd fucked up so bad, but at least I didn't get him killed."

Taut seconds passed while Lana sipped from her coffee. She put the mug down, unable to take the silence. Turning to stare at Adam, she saw the hard, angry lines of his face.

Everything inside her went cold.

Here it was, then. Now he knew. Now he knew how terribly she'd failed. Her gut twisted as misery and shame settled deep inside her. Pain grabbed her heart and started to fester there. She'd hoped he would— The cynical voice in the back of her mind started to mock her before the thought even finished. *Hoped he'd what? Understand?*

Understand how you fucked everything up and ran away, while other kids were hurt?

She set her jaw, swallowing the misery inside. There was nothing to understand. She *had* fucked up. There were no excuses. She'd thought they'd stopped it when Peter died, cutting off the beast's head.

But this wasn't a beast. It was like that freaky dragon out of Greek myth. A hydra. They'd cut off one head and three more emerged. Smoothing out her expression, she braced herself for whatever Adam had to say. She'd take it. She'd deal with it.

He paced closer to her, lifted a hand.

Her heart banged against her ribs as he pushed his fingers into her hair, tangled the long strands around his fingers. "Not good enough," he said, his voice low and rough.

"You think I don't know that?" She stared at him, dry-eyed, while her heart turned to ashes in her chest.

He didn't even seem to hear her. "You weren't even seventeen, trying to fix a mess that would bring adults to their knees—hell, look at the town now. Nobody here has any idea what to think. But you tried to take it on, all on your own."

"Ah—"

He cut her off. "And Max just *let* you try to handle it. You tried to take on the world, tried to fix it all on your own, and it bit you on the ass, but you didn't fuck up. The judge fucked up. Old Max ought to be knocked on *his ass* for not doing better by you."

Something jagged and sharp cut into her. She didn't know what it was, but twenty years of poison tried to spill out. "He . . ." She stumbled over the words, licking her lips. "He tried. Things just got—"

"Bullshit. The man was a fucking *judge*. But he goes all vigilante—" Adam stopped, his eyes widening. "Vigilante.

Son of a bitch. He's the one targeting all the members of Cronus now."

"No." Curling her hands into fists, she pressed them to her temples and turned away from Adam. The thought of that cut into her mind, and try as she might, she couldn't push it out.

And a memory rushed at her, just days ago—two? Maybe three?

I had the names, you know. David gave them to me. I took care of them, each one of them. On my own. Max, sitting on his porch, staring out over the river.

You . . . You took care of them? There was a heart attack. A car crash.

Easy enough to make it appear that way. If you know how. I knew how.

"No." She licked her lips and rubbed her eyes, trying to make the images in her head go away. They just wouldn't. Harlan had been stabbed. She'd heard about another death—a man basically poisoned, by chocolate. Allergic to it. A bizarre sort of horrified appreciation rolled through her, despite herself. "Max can't be behind that. He's eighty years old."

"Actually, he's older than that." Adam's voice was grim, his face a stark mask. "It makes sense. He's not taking on anybody young, and he's not doing anything that involves a whole hell of a lot of risk. Troyer was drunk and had Benadryl slipped into his whiskey." He slid her a look and shrugged. "That's not common knowledge just yet. I know a girl who works at the police department. The autopsy came in a few days ago. Once he was out of it, seems like the killer slid a knife into his heart, directly in. Whoever did it knew exactly how to kill. And Max would *know* how to do that. Quimby was taken out just as easy—half the people in town knew the man had major allergy issues. Chocolate, peanuts, tree nuts and eggs. He'd bitch about everything on my menu when he came in, and half the time he tried to come into the kitchen to watch the food get prepared, even though he knows that's not going to happen. They were assassinated, all there is to it."

Easy enough to make it appear that way. If you know how. I knew how.

Easy enough. She swallowed, hard, trying to get rid of the knot in her throat, the bile that kept trying to rise. Dazed, she sank down on the chair. He'd said he'd see it through this time. Why hadn't she already put this together?

"Lana?"

She just shook her head. "I'm trying to picture that old man hunting down those monsters, putting them down like a couple of sick dogs."

"That's what they are." Adam shrugged, looking unperturbed. He grabbed the chair next to hers and swung it out and around, straddling it as he sat down facing her. "Next thing up. What's this shit about you killing Diane? You said *he* took her into the house. Did he kill her?"

Lana crossed her arms over her chest and shuddered. "I did."

"Says who? You said you don't remember. Did *he* say that?"

Swallowing, she looked at Adam. "No." Her gut twisted, cramped. Rage started to pulse, pound, inside her as the enormity of what he was getting at hit her.

She'd never once questioned what she'd been told at that cabin. That soft, steady voice, those calm eyes. Relaying the words she'd thought had come from Judge Max, a man she trusted implicitly. She'd been sick, in shock, scared. Somehow, those words, planted on such fertile ground, had taken root and she had never thought to question. Not anything. With those words delivered in such a guileless tone, with such a matter-of-fact tone, with such a compassionate face, she'd had no reason to doubt.

Or so she'd thought.

She rose and once more started to pace as that slow-burning rage flared back to life. "He'd told me that he'd trusted a friend . . . and then he said he'd trusted the wrong person. They were lies, Adam. All of this time, everything I've believed in . . . it's all been a lie."

He came up and caught her when she would have turned away.

His hands felt scalding against her icy skin and she wanted to jerk away, take off running. Find Max. Find answers. Were they still there? Could she find them? Force them to give her the answers that she needed.

"Look at me." Adam's smoky, soft voice cut through the fog in her mind.

She dragged her eyes to meet his. He let go of her wrists, shifted his hands to her face. One thumb stroked across her lower lip. "You didn't kill Diane," he said, his gaze intense. "She was alive when she left, because I don't see Max Shepherd shooting a woman who wasn't a threat to him and Diane couldn't be a threat to him on her best day. He would have made sure she stayed there—somehow—but he wouldn't have killed her. Then he would have had plans to go back and figure out how to handle her. So something else happened to her."

Something else . . . Lana closed her eyes. "Somebody else went back and killed her. Somebody else knows about that night, Adam."

Caine sat out on the porch, wrapped in the darkness of night, thinking.

Max Shepherd.

Caine didn't have a lot of use for that old man.

But then again, Caine didn't have much use for a lot of people.

Sybil. He did care about her, as much as he could.

And he liked the boy. He wasn't her son by blood, but that didn't mean he wasn't hers. Caine did care about Drew.

Caine respected Noah.

He even had a grudging respect for Adam Brascum, the miserable son of a bitch.

And his family here.

If he loved anybody, it would be Abraham, the man sleeping in the little house at the bottom of this hill.

The house was quiet now, but it wouldn't be for long.

Before dawn, that household would be moving, Abraham up as he always was, despite the fact that he was coming up on eighty years. His daughter, Sarah, almost forty, and unmarried. It was an uncommon thing among the Amish, but it seemed her heart was in caring for the farm and her father, who'd been widowed almost twenty-five years earlier.

Caine understood the need to care for somebody, to protect that person. Maybe that was why he was out here, brooding, thinking, when he ought to be trying to sleep. He never did sleep well, though. Not until he was about ready to pass out.

Sometimes, if he was wrapped around Sybil, he could find a little bit of peace. Beyond that, though, until he was worn-out, his mind wasn't calm enough to sleep, and he wasn't one for lying in bed while his thoughts spun in circles. So he sat out here, brooding. Or he was out in the garage working. Sometimes he crawled under that old truck of his and worked to keep it from falling apart. It was almost thirty years old. It had been old when it had come to him and he liked to think it was an odd mix of desperation, determination and just plain dog-headedness that kept that old piece of shit going. Spare parts for it were just about impossible to come by now, and at some point soon he'd have to just let it go. Then he'd have to start the tedious process of getting his hands on another truck.

And there he was, thinking about getting another vehicle instead of thinking about whatever in the blue fuck old man Shepherd might want.

Letting his lids droop, he slumped in the seat and stared up at the sky.

It could be any number of things.

For all he knew, the old bastard was pissy about the roofing job the boys had done on the garage last summer.

It didn't have to be anything important.

And maybe, just maybe, the sun would rise in the west and the Easter Bunny was real and Caine could get a nice, peaceful night of sleep before he saw the old man.

CHAPTER NINETEEN

The woman in the bathroom mirror looked like a stranger.

Lana should be used to that.

Logically, after all this time, the woman in the reflection should be who she *was*. She'd worn a mask for twenty years—shouldn't she *be* that grim-eyed stranger in the mirror?

But as the clock crept closer to 2:00 a.m., her eyes gritty and tired, she couldn't sleep and she found herself staring at a woman she didn't know.

A woman she didn't want to know.

Her hand shook as she reached out and opened the cabinet.

She'd seen the shears in there before, and now her fingers trembled as she pulled them out.

Back in school, her hair had been her vanity. She worked odd jobs, babysitting, walking dogs, helping with yard work, whatever she could to make money, and most of it went into the bank for college. But every two months she let herself have one frivolous thing.

She'd adored her hair.

And ever since then, she'd punished herself by stripping away that part of her identity, dying it that awful, boring shade of brown. Pulling it back into that tight braid to conceal the curl, growing it too long and keeping it untrimmed, everything that was going to make it *un*flattering.

Now she couldn't stand to look at herself and she was so tired of it.

Adam's words echoed in her mind as she raised the scissors with one hand, gripping her braid with the other.

You didn't kill Diane.

All this time.

She had to half-saw at the thick cable of her hair, and halfway through, she really was panting. Odd little noises emerged from her, and if she hadn't swallowed them down, she might have been sobbing.

A soft noise echoed out in the hallway just as she lowered the scissors, the mutilated remains of her braid hanging in her hand.

Turning her head, she stared at Adam as he moved into the bathroom.

He reached up and pushed his hand through her hair, not saying a word.

Then he stroked his hand down, took the rope of hair from her hand. Her breathing hitched as he tugged it away and tossed it into the waste can. She stumbled a little as he nudged her over, moved her to stand in front of the mirror.

His eyes met hers over her shoulder and then he leaned over, reached for the scissors, a comb.

She held still as he started to comb the strands, and her heart stuttered as he smoothed them out. "You always had the most beautiful hair," he said, shattering the silence.

"Not now."

His fingers brushed the nape of her neck. "The color isn't the only thing that made it beautiful." He tangled a hand in it, tugged. "Soft. I loved the curls. And the color will come back if you let it."

He straightened the uneven ends, using the shears like a man who'd done more than a few haircuts in his time.

"Since when were you a beautician, Adam?"

"Doesn't take a genius to straighten out crooked hair," he said easily. "I can't do much more, but you can go anywhere for that."

A few more minutes passed and she closed her eyes, tried not to think.

When he started to comb his hands through her hair again, she blurted out, "I don't know what to do. . . . I ran away because I couldn't remember what had happened, because I was led to believe I'd killed somebody. Because I was told that it was the best way to protect a guy who had already gone through hell. I've been gone for twenty years—I know how fucking guilty I look showing up, but I came back because I wanted to make sure everything actually *stopped* this time. Now . . ." She let her voice trail off. Sighing, she opened her eyes and stared at Adam in the mirror. "Now I don't know what to do. What do I do now, Adam?"

He had no immediate answer. He put the comb down, the scissors, feathered his hands through her hair once more and brushed his broad palms across her shoulders, snippets of hair drifting to the floor.

Then he leaned in, his arms coming around her as he caged her in. "I think right now the one thing you need to do is sleep, darlin'." He nuzzled her neck, pressing his lips where it curved into her shoulder. "It's late and you never look like you sleep as well as you should. Tomorrow is soon enough for you to worry about how somebody else's tragedy has to ruin your life."

"It's already ruined mine." Slowly, she turned around and lifted her hands, curling them in the soft, worn material of his shirt, pressing her head against his chest. The smell of him flooded her head. Warm man, something spicy—the soap he wore or aftershave—she liked it. Rubbing her cheek against him, she murmured, "It's ruined my life for twenty years and I'm tired of it. I don't want to let it ruin my life anymore. That's why I'm trying to figure out what to do next."

"I already told you. Sleep." He rubbed his lips against hers and then said quietly, a thread of steel in his voice, "Tomorrow, we find answers. For now, though . . ."

He slid his hands down her back, cupped them around her hips. He boosted her up, and when she twined her legs around him, it was a sweet, sweet bliss. "Maybe the answer to that is think about *you*. You've lived your life day by day, always thinking about keeping your secrets. We need to figure out how you can reclaim your life, but you can't do that in the dead of night. So for now . . . think about you. What you need."

He dipped his head and caught her lower lip between his, bit her lightly.

"What do you need, Lana?"

A slow shudder racked her body and he decided he liked it. As he lifted his head to peer down into her eyes, she stared up at him, her gaze cloudy and heated. "Are you suggesting that maybe the answer to this lies in getting naked?"

"A temporary answer."

A sweet smile curved her lips and she tucked her head against his shoulder. "Maybe that's not a bad idea. Not a bad idea at all."

Moonlight fell across his bed as he laid her across it.

His bed.

And his woman . . . for now.

If he had his way about it, she was going to be his for always.

He'd find a way to take the shadows from her eyes, and maybe he couldn't fix all the hurts, take away the pain the past twenty years had put on her, but he could make sure the rest of her life was better.

Coming down across her, Adam tangled his hands in the shortened strands of her hair and took her mouth, slow and soft.

When she tried to hurry, he held her back.

Moonlight and darkness wrapped around them and he stripped her naked, watching as the pale silvery light painted its way across her body, long, lean and strong. He caught one nipple between his teeth, tugged lightly, watched as she arched and reached for him.

"What's your hurry?" he asked, catching her wrist and pressing his lips to the soft, sensitive skin on the inside.

"I'm empty," she said, her voice stark. "I've been empty for too long. I hate it."

The plan had been to make this last.

But that was an unspoken plea he couldn't ignore.

Sometimes an emptiness went too deep, cut right through the soul. Adam understood that—he'd been living with it for too long himself. Settling back on his heels, he held her eyes as he peeled his shirt off, tore open the button of his jeans. She never looked away.

He left the bed long enough to unzip his jeans and shuck them off, grabbing one of the condoms he'd gotten on the way to the bedroom.

Then he came to her, tearing the foil wrapper open.

She took it from him and he held his breath, enjoying each excruciating little pleasure as she unrolled it, her fingers steady and sure. As she lay back, her hair fanned out around her. "I want to see you like this in the sun," he whispered, coming down over her. "I know a spot on the river. . . . I can take you there. We can go fishing, have a picnic . . . wait there until the sun starts to set and I'll make love to you there. All night."

She wrinkled her nose. "Bug bites."

"It would be worth it."

"Yeah . . ." She looped her arms around him and tugged him close. "It would. Make love to me, Adam."

Tucking the head of his cock against her entrance, he caught her gaze, and as he sank inside, they watched each other. Her pussy was a silken, snug fist and he didn't stop until he'd buried himself completely inside.

A moan echoed in the room—he didn't know if it was hers or his. Didn't care.

He only knew that she was here . . . with him.

"Stay with me," he panted, pressing a hot, open-mouthed kiss to her neck as he surged against her.

"I'm here." Her hand stroked up his back as she rocked to meet him.

He didn't dare say he meant for more than this.

It wasn't time for that . . . not yet.

But the time would come. And he'd probably be ready to beg.

"You look like a man with heavy thoughts."

Caine had managed maybe two hours of sleep, but he'd gotten by on far less and he sat down at the table across from Abraham, ready to have a cup of coffee, ready to go and face whatever demons he had to face.

If he had to destroy those demons, then so be it.

He should have done it a long time ago.

"*Heavy thoughts* doesn't quite touch what's going on in my head, sir," Caine said, summoning up a smile for the quiet man who sat at the head of the table. Abraham Yoder had been the head of his small household for nearly sixty years. He would be eighty in a few short months. And now, save his daughter, Sarah, and Abraham, his household was empty. His wife was gone. Three years ago, one of his sons had died. Paul had been diagnosed with cystic fibrosis early in life and he'd always been prone to illness. That year, the flu had hit their small community and Paul had caught it. Abraham had no male children left. There were numerous nieces, nephews and cousins. But none of them lived here.

Abraham had Caine and Sarah.

Really, the old guy deserved more.

A lot more.

But Abraham had been the man to teach Caine that they all made do with what they had.

Abraham was actually happy with what he had.

Over the mug of his coffee Abraham studied Caine with faded, tired eyes. Abraham's simple, wire-framed glasses couldn't hide the speculation in that shrewd gaze, and Caine decided he should have spent a little more time focused on his breakfast. If he had, Abraham wouldn't have had a chance to glimpse all those secrets Caine had never been able to hide.

"Something is troubling you."

Caine shrugged and looked away. "I have to go see Max today."

A thick grey brow rose. "Ahhhh. I see. And you don't wish to go."

"I don't see the point."

"Then why go?" Abraham sipped his coffee and then put the mug down.

"Because he asked me to."

"Well." The old man nodded, reaching up to stroke his beard, thinking that through. "Max is not a man to ask for things without reason. You must make the decision on your own, but he wouldn't ask if it wasn't important."

Caine didn't respond.

"You've already made that decision."

"There's no decision, really." Caine folded his hands together, the way he might if he were the kind of man to pray.

Resting his chin on them, he stared at Abraham. "We both know there aren't many reasons he'd make the request."

"Sometimes you can cling to the past too tightly, son. That's a lesson neither of you ever learned."

Caine rose. His plate was untouched in front of him. Sarah could eat his food. Anything he tried to eat would sit like a stone in his belly anyway. "My past is like a chain to drag me down. I can't get away from it."

"Perhaps it's time that you break those chains," Abraham suggested gently.

Max smoothed his wife's hair down and smiled at her. "You look lovely, Miss Mary."

"Oh, stop." For a minute she looked at him with something that looked like recognition in her eyes, and then she frowned, gazing around with confusion. "We need to get some new drapes. Where is my sewing machine? We can get some new material. Something bright and cheerful. It would brighten up this drab room, don't you think?"

"Of course." He bent down and kissed her cheek, caught her hand as she continued to fuss about the bedroom. He'd painted it lemon yellow a few years ago, hoping the bright color would help cheer her up. It hadn't. The change seemed to confuse her even more, but now he worried that changing it back would only make things worse.

How much worse could things get?

Two days ago she'd woken up before he had and somehow she'd managed to undo all the locks he'd put on the front door.

He'd caught up with her on the porch.

His heart hurt with the knowledge.

He was going to have to consider having her put in a home.

If she'd gotten much farther . . . or if she'd gone out the back door, to the river . . .

Swallowing around the knot in his throat, he put the thought aside for now. He'd go with her. That was all there was to it. She wouldn't be alone there. He'd already been researching, and there were a few places where they could even share a room. Be together, as they'd always been.

A knock at the door had both of them looking up.

"If it's that Benningfield boy looking for some work to do around the yard, I don't want him near my flower gardens," Mary said, her voice cross. "He uprooted my daffodils, thinking they were weeds! How do you mistake daffodils for weeds?"

"I'll make sure he stays away from them, Miss Mary," Max said. Patting her shoulder, he rose. His knees popped and creaked as he headed down the hall. Caine was earlier than Max would have expected. Caine didn't usually show his face in town until noon or so. And Miss Mary would have been tired enough for a nap. . . .

But Max couldn't dictate the time for this confrontation and he knew it.

It was going to happen.

It had to happen.

Rubbing his face, he paused a minute, said a prayer for strength.

Yes.

This had to happen.

It was past time.

Then he leaned in, checked the Judas hole. Madison was a small town, but Max had spent too many years outside this small town and he'd spent too many years sitting on a bench, serving this small town—he knew for a fact that bad things did happen in his small, supposedly safe little town.

The sight of the person on the porch had Max frowning.

Not Caine.

Not whom Max had expected to see at all.

He opened the door, aware of the crossness in his voice as he demanded, "Why are you here?"

"I'd like to speak with you, please." No smile, no sign of emotion, crossed that dour face.

"It's early and I need to get breakfast for my wife."

"I wouldn't be here if it wasn't important."

Max blew out a breath. "Very well." He stepped aside, listened as shoes clodded on the floor. Down the hall, Miss Mary appeared in the hallway, a thin little wraith, her flowered sundress flapping around her thin calves, a smile on her face.

"Is it Noah? He is working so hard to save up money for that car he wants," Mary said, smiling.

"No, Miss Mary—"

The words froze in his throat when he saw the gun. He lunged, but he was old. He was strong for a man who'd seen eight decades come to pass. Strong, yes. But strength alone wasn't enough to stop a bullet.

The bullet caught him in the chest and he staggered, crashed into the wall.

And the last thing he saw was the blood blossoming on Mary's chest.

She didn't even scream.

Together, he thought dully. *We'll be together. . . .*

CHAPTER TWENTY

"I can't believe I'm doing this."

Jensen strode up to the door, Thorpe at her side.

"It's better to do it now than tomorrow," he said, his voice steady.

"Tomorrow?" She slid him look, then stopped, shook her head. "Son of a bitch. His wedding. I want to bitch-slap Layla."

Thorpe gave her a hangdog look. "We have to do it. She gave us his name, and if we don't take him in, ask the questions, it's just going to look worse."

Jensen wanted to find the nearest hard surface and just pound her head against it. It wouldn't be hard to clear him. All she needed was to alibi him for the murders and everything would be cool. And besides . . . this was Noah Benningfield. Preach, for crying out loud.

But her gut was still a nasty knot when she lifted her fist to knock on the door.

And it was an ugly tangle when he answered the door. His eyes met hers, moved to Thorpe's.

"We need to ask you a few questions, Noah." She smiled. It was her cop's smile.

And Noah's eyes went icy, because he recognized it. "Do you now?"

"Yes. Why don't you grab yourself some shoes? Ben can come in with you if you don't mind. We'll go down to the station, get this squared away." Her gut twisted so tight, it hurt. "It won't take long."

His face was shuttered.

That twisting in her gut went even tighter, because as sure as he recognized the cop's smile on *her* face, she recognized the look on his. He had things he really didn't want to talk to them about.

Noah hadn't had a cop at his door in ages.

The nerves never really went away, though, he realized. He hadn't done anything wrong, and it didn't matter.

Even as he met Jensen's cool eyes, Thorpe at her shoulder, Noah stared at them and realized he was about two steps beyond nervous and he hadn't done anything. Oh, he hadn't given them the information they wanted about Caleb or Kevin, but that wouldn't amount to anything. Confidentiality covered a lot of things, and while the cops could make his life annoying for a while they couldn't do much more. And Caleb didn't really know anything.

But . . .

A sick feeling spread through Noah as he realized there was another reason entirely for their presence here.

Lana.

Sliding his eyes to Benjamin Thorpe, Noah lifted his chin in silent invitation and then turned on a bare heel. As he headed into the house, they walked by the suit he'd bought to wear to his wedding.

His wedding.

Tomorrow.

He had to go to the police department.

He passed a hand over the back of his mouth.

"Mind if I make a call?" he asked.

"You can do that at the station," Ben said, his voice apologetic.

Noah stopped and turned, stared at Ben in the middle of his hallway. "I'd just as soon do it now." Looking from Ben to Jensen to the suit, Noah crossed his arms over his chest. "You see, you all know just as well as I do that I've got an important day tomorrow. When I'm seen in the police car, word is going to travel, and I'd like to let Trinity know before she gets word through the gossip vine. You can give me that courtesy."

"Sir—"

"Shove it," Noah said, biting the words off and turning away, pulling the phone from his pocket. From the corner of his eye, he saw Thorpe advancing.

"Ben." Jensen's voice was low, firm. "Let him make the damn phone call. Preach, be fast, okay?"

He curled his lip at her as some of the temper he struggled so hard to keep in check came spilling out. "Yeah, well, I'm not exactly looking to drag this out, Detective Bell."

"No alibi."

Sorenson stood at the window and dragged his hands down his face as he peered through the tinted glass at Noah Benningfield. He'd give the man credit—if he was a cold-blooded killer, he had every fucking person in town fooled.

He looked pissed, he looked frustrated and he looked worried.

Beyond all of that, Noah also looked tired.

"Not for two of the murders . . . he was picking up his suit the day Quimby was killed, but he doesn't know where the receipt is. He did give me the name of the store in Louisville. I'm calling—they might remember him," Jensen said, shoving a hand through her hair. "He didn't pay cash, but you know, I'm going to bet on somebody remembering him. He said the lady who helped out was named Pearl, she was a grandmother with two grandsons and both of them were getting married. People remember Noah. We can track this lady Pearl down, check his credit card statement."

"And he was alone the night Troyer was killed? He's engaged—why the hell is he . . ." Sorenson stopped and shook his head. "This is Preach we're talking about."

"What do you want me to do?"

"What's your gut say?" Sorenson's gut said there was no way that man in there killed those men. He knew for a fact that Benningfield could be violent. He'd seen it. Many people in town had.

But that was years ago.

"My gut says Layla Chalmers is playing us like a damn fiddle," Jensen said flatly. "She's been chasing after Noah for years and he does nothing but say no. She sees a chance to get him back and she takes it."

"You think she send him to jail because he won't sleep with her?"

Jensen snorted. "This would never hold up in court, Chief." She turned her head, met his gaze. "I'm telling you now, if we get a warrant, we won't find any evidence. If we question her again, her story will change. Maybe a little, maybe a lot. She'd never hold up for long. But he will, because he didn't do it. But . . . we have her statement and if we don't follow through?"

He blew out a breath.

"I want the time of death on Willie T. I want Noah to tell us just what in the hell he was doing yesterday," Sorenson said softly. "And I'm going to put that to the test. I'll talk to Layla, see how her statement holds up when I question her, and once it's mentioned that lying to an officer of the law isn't exactly considered kosher, we'll see how she holds up. If she's jerking us around, she's going to pay for it."

He turned on his heel and headed for the door.

He paused only long enough to gather up the information for Layla Chalmers and to look once more at the information that had come in overnight.

He'd hoped this would simplify things—give them a focus, at least.

Instead, things were just getting worse all the time.

Reaching out a hand, he touched the folder that held the preliminary reports for the Jane Doe found down in the cellar of the old Frampton place.

Sorenson's predecessor had been one lousy-ass cop—although Sorenson had his suspicions about just *why*—because the evidence for that night was all but gone.

But Sorenson already knew who was in that cellar.

The tests had pegged her to be in her mid-forties. She'd been healthy enough when she died. Her death hadn't been accidental or related to natural causes. No, there had been a rather aggressive strike to the back of her head, as evidenced by the X-rays provided. There were other X-rays, of the ribs, showing scrapes along the bones, possibly from a knife. Somebody had hit her in the back of the head and then stabbed her.

There was somebody out there who wanted to make sure Diane Sutter stayed dead.

No, there was no definitive ID yet . . . they were working on getting some mitochondrial DNA, although without a blood relative that would be difficult. But the Jane Doe had been wearing a wedding set. It hadn't been immediately obvious, thanks to the decay, the swelling. But their girl had a set of rings. Once the crime lab had gotten them off, Sorenson had been able to see the pictures.

And he'd spent a great deal of time going through old microfiches.

The rings matched Diane's.

To a T.

Tossing the file down, he turned to leave his office. His gaze sought out Sally, the part-time receptionist, sitting behind her desk. "Get Layla on the phone. I want her in here now."

"That won't be hard." Sally rolled her eyes and gestured to the small waiting area. "She walked in while you were in the office. All sad eyed and serious, Chief. She asked to speak with Jensen."

"Well. She won't be speaking with Jensen."

Answers . . . no more waiting around. We're finding answers today.

That was the one thing on her mind as Lana woke up.

Finding answers.

She showered, her mind on the task ahead.

She'd been in a dull state of near shock when Max had told her what he had to tell her, and she hadn't asked the questions she needed to ask.

"Shock," she snorted. "No, you were stupid."

She'd been operating on a level just above stupid for a little too long now and it was time to stop it.

The first thing she had to do was talk to Max again.

She needed names and she needed to know where to find the family who'd taken care of her. She hadn't been there long, and when she left she hadn't exactly been in good shape.

She shouldn't have been on the road, a fact she could easily acknowledge now. It made sense, too. *Max* wouldn't have put her out on the road when she was recovering from the injuries she had back then. He was too . . . anal. Too much in control. Too cautious.

So she needed to figure out just who had sent her away.

The blurred and hazed memories hadn't really cleared up until sometime after she'd left Madison. Whether it was shock or trauma—or both—she didn't know. But three days after she'd been declared missing, she'd found herself in a hotel, in a room paid for with cash, and she'd flirted up a storm with the clerk to even get that room. That had been in Gary, Indiana.

The Internet had been in its infancy then and news about her disappearance, about David and his parents, hadn't even made a ripple.

What little she learned had come from watching news channels, and there had been very, very little information and all the focus had been on the Sutter family.

Next to nothing was mentioned about her.

It had made it easier for her to disappear.

Over the years, more and more information made it online and she was able to research the case as it was archived, but none of that would help her, because only a handful of people really knew what happened.

Max was one.

And if she wanted to rebuild her life, it started with *finding answers.*

Adam was still asleep when she slipped out of the house. She left a note, told him where she went. He'd come with her, if she just asked, but he wasn't responsible for this mess she'd created and some part of her felt she needed to find these first answers on her own.

As she walked down the street, odd glances came her way.

Some of them paused, lingered.

Abruptly she remembered her glasses. . . . She wasn't wearing them.

She came to the intersection at Main Street and somebody bumped into her. Looking up, she found herself staring into a pair of familiar eyes—dark brown, velvety soft and intense. The man looked away and then abruptly he looked back at her. "Hey . . ."

Tate.

Oh, shit.

Tate Bell.

She gave him a vague smile and started across the street.

He caught up with her on the other side of the street. "Do I know you? You look really familiar."

Lana just shrugged. "Maybe."

She wasn't going to lie, but she wasn't ready to start renewing acquaintances yet, either. With another vague smile, she continued her walk. The house off Clifty Drive was still a bit of a walk, and she was so anxious to get there, she felt like taking off and running.

It felt like hours before she found herself on his porch.

A big, rambling old truck was parked there, a Lincoln Town Car. The windows were open, curtains fluttering in the breeze. Taking a deep breath, she lifted a hand, knocked.

No answer.

She knocked again. "Max!"

Deflated, she turned away and pushed her hair back, staring out over the river, squinting against the bright sunlight reflecting off of it. Part of her wanted to continue to bang on the door, but she'd already knocked. Maybe he was helping Miss Mary. Maybe they were around back.

"Shit." Lana looked back at the door. Frustrated, she moved closer, peered through the narrow windows that bracketed the door on each side. They were covered with sheer curtains, but maybe she could at least see if he was there. If he was there, she would just park her ass here until he opened the door.

She squinted, straining to see in the dim house. Nothing moving.

Her gaze bounced off the thing on the floor twice without really seeing it.

But the third time, she looked back. Stared.

Pale.

Thin.

Hair sprayed around the skinny body like a fan.

Sucking in a breath, she backpedaled.

"Turning into a Peeping Tom, sugar?"

Spinning around, she stared at Adam. "You . . ." She gulped. "You were sleeping."

"I was. Now I'm not. What are you—hey!"

She caught his arm, nervously digging her nails into his skin. "Look."

He stared inside and she knew the second he saw.

He jerked back, moved in front of the door, and she got the answer to an ages-old question.

No, it really wasn't as easy as one-two-three to kick a door in. It took him three tries, but Adam did manage to kick the door in and they both rushed in, only to damn near trip over themselves as they caught sight of Max lying just a few feet in front of the door.

It had been Mary they'd seen.

But Max had been hurt, too.

"Check Max," Adam said, moving down the hall, pulling his phone out, his gaze scanning the house.

Lana reached out and her heart practically stopped when she touched warm flesh. Warm . . . but cooling.

"Max."

No answer. But under her fingers she felt a faint, faint pulse at his neck.

She looked up, saw Adam bent over Mary. He shook his head.

"I have to call nine-one-one."

Lana slowly lifted her head, stared at Adam.

"I can't wait. If you're going to leave . . ." His voice trailed off.

"Call them." She brushed Max's snow-white hair back

from his face and then eased him onto his back, staring helplessly at the wound in the mid-section of his chest. She had no idea how to help him. "I'm not leaving."

He was so pale.

She remembered how he'd looked that night, like a tired old avenging angel. But still strong.

He was a broken one now.

"Lana—"

"Call them. Now." She looked back at Adam. "I'm done running."

Adam held her gaze, nodded once.

There were cops everywhere.

Cops. It looked like every uniformed officer in town was running around and he caught sight of Lieutenant Shaw Kramer standing just the right of the doorway, his dark face grim, his grizzled gray head bowed as he talked onto his phone.

Caine Yoder had about as much use for cops as he had for preachers, doctors and other so-called trustworthy souls.

He didn't trust them any further than he could throw them.

There were very, very few people he trusted in this life.

And one of them lived inside that house.

No, Caine didn't have much use for Max Shepherd, but he did trust the old man, and his heart hammered as he strode across the manicured lawn. Over the years, Max hadn't been able to keep up with the yard the way he liked. So Caine had done it.

Once Max had tried to pay him for it.

Caine had ripped the check into shreds, left the pieces fluttering in the wind as he walked off.

He had no words he wanted to offer the man, and Caine wouldn't forgive him for a lot of things.

But Caine knew the old man had tried to help.

And now . . .

Something inside Caine died a little as a couple of the uniformed officers turned to look at him.

"What's going on here?" he asked, pasting that blank, polite smile on his face. It had been the mask he'd hidden behind for twenty years now.

Not a soul had ever seen past it.

But then again, nobody had ever really tried.

As much as he hadn't wanted to spend the morning dealing with Layla Chalmers, this was even worse.

He'd just been sitting down to start going over her statement when Dispatch put through the call from Kramer.

A call from Kramer was going to be an important one, one he had to take. He'd been prepared to hear there was another murder, maybe. So close on top of Willie T.'s, well, it would have been a shock.

But he hadn't thought to hear that it would have been Miss Mary or that Max would be clinging to his life.

Now he was sitting in the hospital, trying to get answers from a woman who had no interest in giving them to him. It was like trying to get water from a stone. She'd given him her name—he didn't know if he believed her.

It was possible. Weirder things had happened—weirder things, crazy things, *evil* things were happening in his town, but that didn't mean he was just going to believe such a bizarre story without so much as a by-your-leave.

Lana Rossi. Here. After all this time, and just in time to save Max.

Or at least give him a fighting chance?

He didn't think.

And unless Max made it through surgery, he wasn't even going to be able to ask the old man, either.

"I think," Sorenson said, leaning forward, his elbows

braced on his knees as he studied the woman's face, "that maybe we should take this from the top."

The woman calling herself Lana didn't even seem to hear him.

Her face was ghostly white, her dark hair falling forward to frame her features as she stared down the hall. He recognized that expression. It was the look he'd seen any number of times. Like if a person stared at those doors long enough, hard enough, the doors would talk and tell them what they needed to know.

The look of a woman in shock. But a lot of things could put a person in shock. Coming across a person near death. Or killing a person.

"Ma'am." He put enough force behind the word that his voice echoed in the quiet, chilly hall. Churches and hospitals, sometimes they carried an eerie, almost surreal sort of silence. He thought it was almost a hallowed sort of ground, people carrying on serious, solemn tasks . . . tasks that sometimes ended in death. Or life.

She swung her head around and he found himself staring into a pair of pale-grey eyes.

It could be, he mused. It could very well be Lana Rossi. Jim Rossi had eyes like that—they could pin a person in place, darken from the color of the mist to pewter in a blink. Her hair was dark, but if he wasn't mistaken, the roots were starting to show and those roots weren't as dark as the rest. He tried to picture it, how she'd look twenty years older. Harder. Sadder.

She blinked and looked back down the hall, like she just had no use for him. No time to think about him, no time to entertain his question.

She'd have to make room in that mind of hers for him. All there was to it.

"You want me to believe," he said, making his voice as

caustic as possible, "that out of the blue, Lana Rossi shows up, just in time to save old Judge Max."

"I don't give a flying fuck what you believe," she said, looking back at him. Her voice was pitched low, husky. And her eyes were full of disgust, frustration and fury. None of it was directed at him, but he felt the impact just the same. "And I've been here for a while. Not my fault none of you can take your thumbs out of your ass to notice."

"Been here awhile, you say." He stroked his jaw as she looked away, dismissing him yet again. He had a feeling he wasn't going to get a lick of cooperation out of her until she had news on Judge Max.

Sorenson's gut told him she hadn't been the one to hurt Max. He couldn't go by his gut, though. He had to go by what he could prove. Just then, there was precious little of that.

While he admired the loyalty, he needed to get some information out of her so they could *find* who'd hurt the old goat and killed his wife. Poor old Mary. The woman had been helpless and harmless.

"You realize," Sorenson said, trying a different tactic, "what it's going to do to him when he wakes up and realizes that somebody took his Mary from him. She was his world. The reason he got up in the morning. And somebody killed her."

A sigh shuddered through Lana.

"I know that," Lana said softly. She covered her face with her hands. Moments passed. Then she looked up at Sorenson, and the vulnerability on her face stabbed at him, right in the heart. And he saw it, clear as the day, the girl she'd been.

It was her, all right.

Which only opened up an entire world of more questions, questions he didn't want to look at. Not considering some of the information he was sitting on. The last person likely to have seen Diane Sutter, David Sutter, Pete Sutter, was sitting in front of him.

And she was also wearing Max's blood.

Those grey eyes didn't seem to hide a cold-blooded killer.

But . . .

"I need you to take me back through what has happened today." He kept his voice genial. Calm. Tried not to think about anything else. "Start with when you decided you were going to go see Max. And why."

Lana opened her mouth, but just then Adam stepped up, covered her shoulder with his hand.

Sorenson decided then and there he just needed to pound his head against a hard surface. Stupid tired, running on no sleep, and the shock of seeing one of his oldest friends dying in front of him—no excuse. None.

"Don't say anything," Adam said, his voice flat. "You got a cop looking at you like that, you say nothing without a lawyer."

"If she's done nothing wrong, there's no reason to need a lawyer," Sorenson said. And he knew it was a lie. Whether Lana had hurt Max or not, she needed a lawyer, and bad.

Adam's mouth curled in a sardonic smile. "Yeah, well, why don't we just save that chat for when she *has* a lawyer, Chief?"

"Maybe we should just have it now. She can get herself lawyered up and we can get this done." Sorenson was fed up with this bullshit. Rising from the chair, he pinned Lana with his gaze. He was no small man and she stayed in the seat, looking tired and worried, but she didn't look at him. "Lana? You hear me? You can either talk to me about what happened today or we can just head on down to the station and talk about today, talk about twenty years ago. Talk about a lot of things that need to be talked about."

She slid him a look from those foggy grey eyes. Her lashes dropped low, shielding her gaze from him. "Talk now . . . or you'll haul me in and . . . what? Make me talk about what, exactly?"

He took his time crossing the floor, well aware of the fact that she watched every step. She didn't squirm or look away, and something about the way she watched him made him think she'd had more than one or two run-ins with the law before. She slid a brow up and leaned back in the chair, smirking at him.

"How about what happened at the Frampton house twenty years ago, Ms. Rossi? You were there. You know it. I know it. And as of right now, you appear to be the only survivor of whatever happened that night. I have at least one dead body that I'd like to discuss with you. So . . . we can either talk about Max. Or we can talk about the Sutter family. Pete, Diane, David. How do you want to do it?"

The tread of booted feet came striding up the hallway, close and getting closer.

Lana stared at him, an insolent smile on her face. "Get your questions together. I'll have my lawyer answer them."

Sorenson straightened up. "I guess you just have to do this the hard way. We'll have that talk, Lana. I'm going to find out what happened to the Sutter family."

"I guess—" She shrugged, looking away in mid-sentence.

And the final words died on her tongue.

Caine had pictured finding a lot of things when he got to the hospital. Kramer wouldn't tell him shit. He'd caught a few bits and pieces from the uniformed cops, but nothing had been concrete and he hadn't wanted to waste time.

He'd imagined finding people gathered around, already grieving.

He'd imagined finding yet *more* cops who wouldn't tell him anything.

He'd been almost positive he'd find Noah there, and that was what Caine had hoped to find, because Noah *would* tell him something.

But Noah wasn't there.

The cops were, just a few of them, gathered around Kramer in one waiting room. The big guy himself, Sorenson, waited in another one, a bit farther down the hall. He glared down at a dark-haired woman as he prattled on, the words connecting but not making sense.

". . . right now, you appear to be the only survivor of whatever happened that night. I have at least one dead body that I'd like to discuss with you. So . . . we can either talk about Max. Or we can talk about the Sutter family. Pete, Diane, David. . . ."

Brascum had a hand on her shoulder.

As Caine's boots rang on the floor, gazes cut his way and then bounced off.

Adam saw him and tensed.

Sorenson looked at him and then back at the woman.

The woman glanced up.

Twenty years fell away.

Her pale-grey eyes locked with his. She stared at him, her jaw dropping.

"Lana," he whispered, coming to a halt like he'd been jerked on a chain.

Staring into those dark-blue eyes, Lana slowly rose to her feet. Sorenson was still glaring at her. Adam stood at her back, his hand tightening on her shoulder.

"Damn it, Rossi, are you listening to a damn thing I'm saying?" Sorenson said, his voice edgy.

"No," she said, faint.

Then she took a step forward.

A second later, she lunged for the man standing in the middle of the hall.

Sorenson reached for her, but Adam cut between them and a moment later she was caught in David Sutter's arms.

"David," she whispered.

He said nothing. Twenty years ago, he'd been six inches taller than her, and all arms and legs, almost painfully skinny. There had been signs of muscle starting to show, but now . . . a tall, powerful body all but shook as he hugged her against him.

Long, silent moments passed, and then finally she eased back, staring up at him. His eyes were exactly the same.

Absolutely nothing else was.

The plain, simple clothing couldn't hide the fact that David was completely, utterly beautiful. Even if his eyes were all but icy. A watery laugh escaped her as she studied him, from the straw hat to the toes of his brown shoes. "Geez, you decided to stay there, huh? What did you do? Go completely Amish? Did you do that Rumspringa thing and everything?"

He grinned, his teeth a white flash in his face. "Nah. It just keeps people from looking twice."

He flicked a glance past them and Lana tensed.

He squeezed her shoulder. "It's okay, Supergirl. You're done trying to save me, okay?"

As they turned to face Adam and Chief Sorenson, she saw the appraising look on the faces of both men. Adam had already figured it out. Sorenson, though, was still glaring at her. "Now that you're done reacquainting yourself, Ms. Rossi, grab your things. You've got questions to answer," he bit off.

"About?" David said quietly.

"Caine, this is no concern of yours."

"Oh, I don't see how." He reached up, tugged off his hand, ran a hand through his hair. "I overheard some, you see. You asking Lana about the Sutter family."

He smiled, and a hard light glinted in his eyes. "If you wanted to know about my parents, Chief, all you had to do was ask. I've been here for twenty years."

CHAPTER TWENTY-ONE

She couldn't get in to see Max.

Lana stared at her short, ruthlessly clipped nails and fought the urge to bite at them.

She'd never been a nail-biter, but the urge was strong. If for no other reason than because she had nothing else to do.

She had things she *wanted* to do—David sat in the chair across from hers, his face serene, composed. Everything about him threw her—his face, the strength of him, those plain, simple clothes, the hat that sat on his knee. Hell, everything about him threw her off-balance, but she guessed that was why he'd done it. He looked nothing like the skinny kid who'd been just this side of veering into manhood. David Sutter had dressed in designer clothes, driven a Mustang that was just a few years off the lot, and he'd been sullen and moody and anger had simmered just below the surface.

He went by the name Caine now. Caine Yoder. People looked at him and saw a simple Amish man with a peaceful countenance and a calm demeanor and eyes that skimmed the surface.

People were stupid.

His eyes came to hers and she watched as his mouth hitched up in a faint smile.

As the questions threatened to bubble up inside she jerked her eyes away and focused on the clock on the wall. The second hand seemed to sweep by with excruciating slowness, and she groaned, turning her face and pressing it to Adam's shoulder. "What is taking so long?" she whispered.

He shifted and slid his arm around her.

There was a hesitancy to it, something that she wasn't used to from him, and she pressed herself more firmly against him. If they hadn't been in the middle of the waiting room, she might have climbed onto his lap and wrapped herself around him, clung to him. She so desperately needed that contact, that reassurance. "Max is an old man, sugar," Adam said, nuzzling her temple. "He's a stubborn goat, but he's still an old man. Even under the best circumstances, I don't think he had what we could call a minor injury. They are trying to keep him alive."

Curling an arm around him, she fisted her hand in the worn fabric of his shirt, felt the heat of him, the strength.

Then she opened her eyes and stared at the wall opposite her, not seeing the boring textured wallpaper, the pamphlets on grieving or how to see if you were at risk for heart disease or how to cut your cancer risks. She was seeing how Max would watch his Mary, how he'd smile when she'd smile at him. How the light in his eyes would die when the old woman would look at him and not know him.

"Why?" Lana asked quietly.

Feeling Adam's confusion, she pulled back and rose from the couch, moving to stare out the door.

They all watched her. Sorenson, Adam and David. Caine. Whatever he called himself now.

And now several of the people who'd been waiting in the hall were watching her, too.

"He won't want to be here without Mary," Lana said, staring down the hall, wondering what happened behind those doors marked: *Hospital Personnel Only*.

"The judge isn't a quitter."

That came from Sorenson.

She shot him a glittering look.

He stared back at her from under heavy brows, his mouth twisted in a scowl, his arms crossed over a thick, heavy chest. She didn't know him. He had moved to town not long after she'd left, from Otisco, a small bit of land out near Charlestown. Otisco made Madison look like a booming metropolis. She didn't know much about him, but she could read the look in his eyes, had learned enough about him in the past few hours, since they'd settled down to wait. He was a cop. He wasn't one who made her want to keep a witness with her at all times. And he was the kind who'd dig in and wait her out, too.

So she would be getting a lawyer, and she had better find a good one.

But being a good cop didn't make Sorenson an expert on the human condition.

She looked back at the doors that separated them from Max. "It isn't about being a quitter. Max had one person in this whole world . . . just one. And that was his wife. Miss Mary was his everything. Why he got up in the morning, why he worked so hard to keep those flowers blooming even though he hated them." Lana thought about a time years ago when she'd seen him cussing a bed of petunias out—he was allergic, a fact not that many people probably realized, because Judge Max hid his weaknesses and he hid them well. But the bright and happy colors had Mary happy.

So he made sure she had them. Always. Even though Lana had seen over the past weeks how Mary had slid into a place where she didn't even recognize Max at times.

"So you think he'll just give up since she's not here."
Sorenson shook his head. "That's being a quitter."

"No. If she was here, he'd have something to fight for.
There's a difference between *fighting* for something . . .
and just letting go. It doesn't make you a quitter if you're
just tired." Lana thought of the weight she'd seen in his
eyes and she knew it was the truth. Max *was* tired.

But she also remembered his words.

The gravity in his voice as he said, *I'll find answers.*

She didn't know if that was enough to pull him through
this.

Warm arms came around her. The scent that was
Adam surrounded her and she turned, pressed her face to
him. It was amazing how easy it had become to lean
against him.

A jangling sound filled the room, loud and shrill, and
she jolted.

Lifting her head, she watched Sorenson pull the
phone from his belt, silencing the old-fashioned ring-
tone. "I'll have to take this," he said, addressing the room
at large.

"Don't let us stop you from important cop work," David
said, a sardonic smile twisting his lips as he spoke to Sorenson's back.

Sorenson didn't bother to look back at them as he
pushed through the door and headed into the other private waiting room across the hall. He wasn't in there even
a minute before he came out, spoke quietly to one of the
officers and then headed down the hall.

Adam's phone started buzzing and he pulled it out,
sighing. "It's Trinity again. I need to call her." He rubbed
Lana's back. "I hope she hasn't heard about Old Max. She
doesn't need this right now. Her and Noah have had
enough. They ought to have their wedding in peace."

"Excuse me."

All three of them focused on the door.

The nurse there smiled and immediately her attention shot to Adam. Lana might have been a little bit put off, but then the nurse glanced down the hall and slipped inside. "You know I can't really tell you anything. But . . . well. None of you are family." She grimaced and then checked the hall one more time. "He's a tough old bastard, though." Then she winked.

After that, she was gone, moving down the hall, her long blond braid bouncing against her back.

"Hey!" Lana went to go after her, but Adam caught her arm.

"Celia can't say anything else," he said, shaking his head. "She can lose her job if she says anything to people that aren't family. It's risky enough that she even said what she did."

"But—"

Adam dipped his head, pressed his lips to Lana's. "He's going to be fine. She wouldn't have said what she did if he hadn't pulled through."

Then Adam squeezed her arms and stepped away. It was a force of will that kept her there.

That and David's blue eyes, resting on hers as Adam and moved to the door to make his call.

Like a lot of the teenage boys, David Sutter had had something of a crush on Lana Rossi.

She'd been part angel, part demon, all whirlwind.

People had either adored her or just outright abhorred her. She'd been all about causes before having a cause was even understandable. She'd gotten a C in her Honors Biology class because she hadn't wanted to do the dissection labs, but then she'd proven to the teacher that she understood more about the anatomy of a frog *and* any other animal he could think of.

When David had mentioned it to her during their tutoring classes, thinking to poke fun at her and just get her to leave him alone, she'd just shrugged it off: *Hey, biology is easy. You want to see me freeze up, quiz me on chemistry.*

He hadn't quizzed her on anything. For the first three weeks of the tutoring—which had been set up by the principal and his parents had approved it—David had said as little as possible. Lana had been required to do it as part of the community service that had been set up after another one of her *incidents*. He couldn't even remember what she'd done. She might have stolen all the frogs for a dissection class. It might have been when she left condoms and pamphlets in the girls' *and* boys' bathrooms, along with notes about safe sex—*safe sex is more than just abstinence or pulling out, kids . . . be smart!*

Since she was a smart kid, they tended to have her do tutoring or work with other kids as part of the community service, even though some parents protested that after the condom stunt.

David's dad had said, *You'd be a good influence on her.*

Peter Sutter couldn't have been more wrong.

The son of a bitch didn't live long enough to wish he'd hadn't okayed the tutoring. Within a week, Lana had realized there was something very wrong.

Within two weeks, she'd seen deeper than anybody else ever had.

Within a month, David had told himself he needed to pull back.

Not long after that, he'd started to believe Supergirl when she told him they could make a difference.

She told him how.

She told him what to do.

She got him the cameras, told him how to set them up.

It had hurt his gut to know that she might watch the video feed, but she promised him, from the beginning, she never would and he believed her. Supergirl was too honest to lie to him, and the way she looked when she talked about stopping everything . . . Yeah, he could believe it. Supergirl wanted to save the world.

Instead, they'd just ruined their own.

Looking at her through a filter of twenty years, Caine tried to align the woman he saw now to the girl she'd been.

He tried to align himself, the man he was, to the boy he'd been.

David had been just his side of scrawny, a gawky kid just on the verge of growing into the man he'd become. He was six four now, weighed two hundred even. His back was marred with scars and there were some on his soul that cut even deeper. Once, a brutal backhand from one of his "handlers" had knocked him into the wall and he hadn't seen straight for three days.

Now he could pick that man up by the neck. Caine could probably *snap* the man's neck, if he so chose. He'd imagined it. Had fantasized about it. Daydreamed about it.

Even now, with the cop standing out in the hall, talking in a low voice about what a fucking waste it was that somebody had hurt a helpless old man like Max, had killed a sick old woman like Mary, rage pulsed inside Caine.

He wasn't in the club anymore.

Max wasn't the only one who'd paid some nocturnal visits over the years. Yeah, Caine knew about that. He'd figured out what was happening almost right away and resentment had burned inside him as he sat by, waiting for his chance.

It had taken Caine years to get strong enough, fast enough. Then it had taken him a while to find the mean inside him. Years more to learn who else had been involved.

But he'd done it.

And that cop out there, sorrowfully hanging his head and commiserating with other cops, had been Caine's first nighttime visit.

He'd bled red, just like the boy Caine had once been.

His dick was a mutilated stump. He'd seen specialists in Louisville, but Caine had been thorough—the damage, much like the damage done to Caine, was permanent.

Nobody had heard his screams, a fact that Caine had seen to—he'd wanted to hear those screams, but he wanted, even more, to know that man who'd raped him would live in fear, never knowing the name of the man who'd come at him in the night, never knowing if he'd return.

And he had.

Several times.

The stable base of the Cronus Club had faltered because Max had killed the older members and Caine had stalked the others. The only ones who remained were the younger, weaker idiots who hadn't had the sense God gave a goat.

Caine had used the information his father had calmly given him over the years, during his indoctrination. That information had been used to destroy the stable group that had remained even after Pete's death.

Our brothers are everything. Brotherhood *is every-thing. We trust nobody but the brotherhood. You'll be one of us and we have to be able to trust you, son. You have to trust us.*

It had taken years for Caine to be able to think of that without feeling the bite of the whip.

He'd used those words on the nights he slid inside a

house, into a trailer, the night he was waiting in the back
of a truck's cab. He'd whispered them in the ears of men
and watched as they pissed themselves in fear and now, as
he watched one of them, he wondered if he shouldn't have
just killed them all.

He didn't believe in the cops. He didn't believe in
justice. Not for him. Maybe it was going to work out for
the kids now. Times had changed, some. And there were
people working for the city now who were different—
they didn't have his father whispering in their ear
and they didn't have crooked cops guiding their steps,
either.

Taking them out had been the crucial steps, Caine realized.

Although there were others. He hadn't known it had
continued like this.

The one in front of Caine had him curling his hand
into a fist and he imagined getting up, crossing the floor,
slamming that fist into the man's face, gone doughy now,
soft with age—

A hand touched Caine's arm.

He fought the urge to react, and react with violence.

Caine had been forged in the fires of hell. Physical
touch wasn't welcome. There were only a very few he allowed to touch him.

As Lana sat down beside him, he had to force himself
to relax.

She was one of the few.

"David—"

He closed his eyes.

A quiet sigh escaped her. "I guess you prefer *Caine*
now."

He gave a minute shake of his head. "I have no prefer-
ence, really." It was a lie, though and he knew it even as

he said it. He'd killed the child he'd been, buried him the day he got his first taste of blood.

The man out in the hall had been Caine's first, in more ways than one.

He'd been the first to rape David, while his father stood by and watched in silent approval.

And he'd been the one Caine had gone after first.

It had all started after he'd pulled Caine over for speeding, too. The memory flickered, burned bright in his mind.

"You have a look in your eye."

He knew the look. It was a look that spoke of a need for blood, a need to hurt. Closing his eyes, he reached for that inner calm that Abraham had spent years trying to teach him. Caine had never learned it, but he'd learned to fake it. Once he had the mask in place, he looked over at Lana. "Sorry."

She laughed softly and leaned forward, her elbows braced on her knees.

A raised voice from the hallway caught her attention and she frowned for a minute, studying Adam. Then she shrugged and glanced at Caine. "I'm not. . . . Sorry, I mean. You used to scare me. I was worried I'd find out you'd just jumped off the bridge or just hung yourself in your room. Now . . . well." She shrugged. "You look like you want blood, but it's not your own you're after."

He managed to keep from scowling, but just barely. She still saw just as deep as always. Before he could figure out what to say to that, though, Adam's voice, clear and furious, echoed from the hallway: "Just what the *fuck* do you mean, *Noah* is in *jail*?"

The two of them were on their feet in a heartbeat.

So much for seeing how things were going.

Granted, she hadn't really wanted to talk to Sorenson anyway.

The chief bothered her.

He looked at her like he saw right through her, and she hated that.

But they hadn't even had ten minutes' worth of time to talk before he'd up and told her they'd have to finish up later.

Later . . .

Shit.

Layla hadn't even had a chance to ask him what she wanted to know.

So she'd go looking for it elsewhere.

If Noah had been taken to the station somebody would have seen it, and she knew all the right places to talk gossip in town. The best place was Shakers. The next best? The coffee shop. She'd sit down, get a cup of coffee and then loiter there, wait until Sorenson called her back.

Since she'd had such a rough night, she didn't spend much time with her appearance that morning. She pulled her hair back, a simple, easy ponytail, then took the needed time to put on light makeup, frowning as she saw how deep the lines around her eyes were getting. It wasn't a bad thing for what she had to do—she wasn't supposed to look *happy,* for fuck's sake, but she was thirty-six. She wasn't supposed to look like she was already forty.

She took a few more minutes than she liked and then checked her clothes. A T-shirt, boring hair, barely any makeup. She still looked good, damn good. Flat belly, great boobs, and her ass was almost as tight as it had been in high school. So what if she had a few lines around her eyes?

She looked tired and stressed. Who wouldn't be, considering what she'd been through, right?

She barely wasted a minute's thought over what they'd do when they realized she was just jerking them around. There wasn't any evidence against Noah and she knew that, but there wasn't anything saying he *hadn't* done it, either, she figured.

Otherwise . . . well.

She shrugged it off and hit the door, pulling a cigarette from her purse and lighting it up as she headed down the street. They didn't have anybody, which meant they didn't have any evidence. If they had jack shit, they would have arrested somebody and they wouldn't have spent so much time asking *her* questions yesterday.

About Noah.

Again, for fuck's sake.

The guy had turned into a fucking Boy Scout, but they thought he could have killed somebody?

What the hell ever.

Served his ass right, though, she thought. Giving her so much grief, looking down his nose at her.

Her gut twisted as she thought about the way he'd looked at her. Sad, kind of. Like he'd meant it when he told her to be happy. If he wanted her to be happy, he could take her to bed. *That* made her happy.

Pushing all of that out of her head, she shoved through the door to the coffee shop and paused, looking at all the people packed inside. It was elbow to elbow and all the voices were low, somber.

Making her way to the counter, she arched a brow at Cassie, one of the two college kids Louisa had hired to help out in the mornings. "Damn, who died?" Layla asked.

Cassie flicked a look at her, the diamond stud in her nose winking in the light. She shrugged. "Some old dude. You want the normal?"

Layla nodded and looked around, frowning. *Man. Everybody was in here talking about Willie T.?* She hadn't thought that many people would care. Moving down to the end of the counter, she paid for her latte, using one of the twenties she'd swiped from Willie T.'s house to pay for it, as she looked back over the crowd, trying to catch a snippet of conversation. The closest group of people was a group of busybodies from the Methodist church, and when they caught her looking at them, the youngest just rolled her eyes and looked away, but Mona Grimes gave her a tentative smile. "I . . . I guess you heard the news."

Layla just grabbed her coffee and headed for the door.

Heard the news? Her belly started to pitch around on her. She needed a smoke. No. She needed a hit. Something to settle her nerves would be better. She'd *found* him. How many times had she felt him on top of her? And he'd been one of those monsters.

"Screw this," she muttered.

Whoever had killed him was a fucking hero.

She thought of Noah, wondered if maybe she should just let this all go.

She bummed a ride off Trick Thomas, cradling her latte in her hands and jamming her earbuds in so she didn't have to listen to him yap. The trip up the hill didn't take long, but it seemed to drag on endlessly. Sipping at her drink, she blocked out the scenes from yesterday and brooded.

Maybe if she ever found out who'd done this, she could sneak him in some cigarettes, but she didn't need to drag this on.

Not really.

Trinity could handle mad.

She'd been mad before. She'd been furious before.

She'd had her world ripped out from under her and she'd gotten through it with a cool smile.

She'd watched the father of her child across a courtroom

as she testified against him, and she'd managed to do it without shedding a tear.

But as she stood in the waiting room of the small police department in Madison she wondered if she'd ever been *this* angry.

"What do you *mean* I can't talk to him?"

The receptionist looked unhappy. "I'm sorry, Mrs. Ben—ah, Ms. Ewing. It's still Ewing, right?"

"Yes. The wedding is tomorrow." She tried not to grit her teeth. She was getting married in less than twenty-four hours. And her fiancé was sitting in a room somewhere in this police station and they wouldn't let her talk to him. "Why can't I talk to him?"

"He's still being questioned."

"For *what*?" she demanded.

A bell jangled behind her and a rush of hot air blasted against her.

She didn't care if Santa Claus had come in. It could have been her ex for all she cared. None of it mattered, because until she saw Noah she wasn't leaving. But then she saw the way the receptionist—her name tag read: *Sally*—looked past her shoulder. Sally's face drained of color and she bit her lip, her precise white teeth catching her lower lip in a way that would have done many a romance heroine proud, Trinity thought. "Ah . . . Ms. Ewing, I'll tell you what. You can wait in . . . um, well, maybe Chief Sorenson's office. Okay? And I'll, um, go see what I can find out?"

The sudden capitulation would have made Trinity ecstatic.

If it weren't for the nerves that practically bled out of the woman.

If it weren't for the way Trinity could feel her skin crawling.

Slowly, she turned.

When her eyes met Layla's, Trinity couldn't even say she was surprised.

Running her tongue across the inside of her teeth, she debated. She could do one of two things. She could do the wise thing. Go into the chief's office, wait. See what happened.

Or she could call Layla out, because Trinity knew damn well that Layla was behind this.

It was there, written in those purple eyes—that purple was as fake as the mock concern that spread across Layla's face.

"You." Trinity balled one hand into a fist.

"Oh, honey." Layla shook her head. "I am so sorry."

"Whatever you did, you better undo it," Trinity warned, taking one step forward. "Or you're going to find yourself in more trouble than you can even begin to imagine."

Something cool and calculating entered the other woman's eyes. "Oh, really? What can you do, city girl?"

A door opened somewhere behind them, but neither of them looked away from each other. Layla moved forward, a look of false sympathy on her face. "Look, it's gotta be tough. He must have just gone off the deep end at some point. We all thought he'd gotten better when he stopped drinking. But after he lost his girl back in high school . . . You heard about her—"

"Layla," Sorenson said, his voice carrying down the hall. "That's enough."

But Layla was on a roll, her words tripping over themselves in order to be heard. "Either David Sutter killed her or they ran off together or something. Whatever happened, it must have just snapped something inside him, and then this all comes to light—these kids he loves, they were all he had for so long, you know. Now he sees they were hurt so bad, and he couldn't protect them and I guess he thought he had to do something!"

Slow, mocking applause started.

Layla stopped, caught off-guard as Caine Yoder moved out of the small sitting area. Trinity blinked at the sight of him.

A dark-haired woman was at his side and Adam Brascum stood just behind her, a hand resting on her shoulder.

Both Caine and the woman were staring at Layla.

"Fascinating story," the woman said, her voice low and soft. "I hadn't heard that twist, David."

Lana could have kicked herself the minute his real name fell from her lips, but he didn't seem to notice.

David shrugged, still not taking his eyes from the woman standing in the doorway.

Lana had heard her name.

Layla.

Layla Chalmers. Back in school, she'd been the girl to try to steal everybody's boyfriend. She'd bullied the smarter kids into doing her homework or threatened— whatever had worked.

Lana had gotten into two actual *fights* when she'd been in school. Both times had been with Layla.

Her eyes—made purple by contacts—moved to meet Lana's, confused.

Lana smirked, still holding Layla's gaze. "I always heard that I'd been the one to kill everybody and then run off. But now you're the bad guy?"

"Well, that might not be all that far off, Supergirl." Caine slapped his hat against his thigh and then glanced over his shoulder at her, then at Adam. "What do you two want to bet that we can thank Layla for Noah's current situation?"

Adam said nothing.

"Well, I've been gone awhile." Lana stared hard at Layla. "But I'm willing to bet she isn't here to bring the boys donuts."

Layla curled her lip. "Who the fuck are you?"

"I'm hurt you don't remember me." Lana took a step forward. "You'd think you would. I'm the girl who broke your nose in tenth grade."

A choking gasp escaped her. "Lana."

The harsh intake of breath was echoed by the slim, elegant blonde standing by the desk. Lana shifted her attention to the blonde. Noah's soon-to-be-bride. Swiping her damp hands down her jeans, Lana arched her head. "I hear you and I share something in common. Trinity, right?"

"You . . ." Trinity squeezed her eyes shut. "I'm kind of confused. I'd heard you were . . ."

"Dead?" Lana smiled caustically. "Yeah. Dead, missing or a killer. Those are the rumors. What's the saying? 'Rumors of my demise have been greatly exaggerated.' Twain, I think. I'm not dead."

"If you're not dead, then you never should have come back," Layla snapped, color coming into her face, her eyes bright and hot. "The cops are going to lock you up. Gone, all these years. If you didn't kill David and his folks, you're the only one who has answers and you ran to keep them quiet. And you always thought you were the smart one."

Lana turned her head and looked up at the tall man standing silent at her side. She arched a brow.

"Layla always heard all sorts of shit." He shrugged. "But she never really did listen to anything."

He shifted his attention back to her. "I never left Madison, Layla. I've been here all along."

"You . . . what?"

It was so quiet, a pin drop would have echoed like a shotgun blast.

In the doorway across the room, Jensen whispered, "Son of a bitch."

CHAPTER TWENTY-TWO

Layla crumpled.

Sorenson put her in one of the smaller rooms, sat across from her and pinned her with a hard look.

Then he put a recorder in front of her. "I'm recording this. If anything you say conflicts with what you told Detective Bell, you are going to want to think long and hard about getting yourself a lawyer. We are looking at obstruction of justice here, at the very least, Ms. Chalmers, and I don't have the time or the patience for this shit. So think hard before you continue with this." He paused. "You and I both know you aren't being honest here. So think on that before you waste my time and try to tarnish the name of an innocent man. But if you insist, you better make sure you can keep your story straight. If you fuck up, even once, you'll be charged. Or you can just let this all go."

She stared at him.

And one thing he knew about Layla was that she was a decent judge of character. She could read a mark. Most people like her could. It was how she knew who to sucker and who to walk away from. It was why she'd never tried to pull her shit on certain people in town and why she'd managed to get by rent free on others. He'd heard rumors that she'd once lived in Trick Thomas' garage apartment rent free for a year. Of course, the way Trick had told it, she'd paid him in other ways. . . . Trick liked to think he'd gotten the better end of the deal.

But Sorenson wasn't a man to be led around by his dick.

And those big lavender eyes of hers didn't mean jack to him.

Reaching out, he tapped the button and waited.

"Fine," she bit off.

He crossed his arms over his chest and waited.

A few minutes later, he let her out. She crossed her arms over her chest and stormed off, tottering on toothpick heels for a second as she spun around to glare at him from the door. "You find out who killed Willie T., let me know. I'll buy that fucker a beer."

He arched a brow, but she didn't say anything else. She disappeared through the doors and he blew out a breath before turning to look at Sally. "Is Detective Bell still with Noah?"

Sally looked at him, nodded sorrowfully.

"Call her out."

They no longer had a witness against him.

Noah could go home.

Which was nice. The man had a wedding.

And Sorenson had a woman who'd been missing for twenty years. Who knew where she had been?

Sorenson turned and looked at the two men and the woman in the sitting area.

No, what he really had was a fucking mess.

The man at her side—Caine . . . Caine Yoder. Really David Sutter. Here in Madison all these years.

"You two have any idea how much more trouble you've just thrown onto my desk?"

The woman was the one who answered. She shrugged

and said, "Well, I guess I could have stayed away. But since I know who was buried in the Frampton house, I'd actually have thought coming home would make it *easier* on you. Not harder."

Sorenson felt every muscle inside him start to quiver. "You . . . you know who it is."

She brushed her hair back from her face and looked up at Caine—*David,* Sorenson told himself. *It's David.* That would have to be verified, he knew. But looking at the man, Sorenson suspected it was the truth. He didn't think he was being lied to.

David reached out and rested a hand on Lana's shoulder. "I know who it is, too, Chief," he said. "I just didn't see any point in speaking up."

"You didn't see the point," Sorenson said slowly.

"No." David's eyes were cold as ice. "You see, it's my mother. And for all I care, she could have rotted down in that hole for all of eternity. It's more than she deserved anyway."

David slid into the ICU.

He knew the rules.

And if the medical personnel started to argue the rules, he'd just turn around and walk away.

But he needed to see the old man.

David didn't make it to Max's bed.

Charity Whitlow intercepted him and he stopped, stared at her. "Caine?"

He just waited.

"You . . . I guess you want to see Max."

"I need five minutes."

"You're not family," she said gently.

"I need five minutes and I won't leave until I have them or you call the police," he said. "What's going to be more disruptive?"

A militant look came across her face. "You're going to get me in trouble."

"You call Security right now. I'll leave the minute they show up," he promised.

He'd already spent half the day talking to the cops. If he had to do it all over again, so be it.

He edged around her and placed himself at Max's side.

The old man looked fragile under the sheet, with tubes and wires running all over the place.

David was a basic sort of man. He'd never had the option to go to college, and he'd finished his high school education with more alternative methods. The only reason he'd finished at all was because it had mattered to Lana. He'd thought, all these years, that she had run away, that she could be anywhere, dead even, because she'd tried to help him, and that he'd ruined her life.

He was still trying to process just what had happened, and the man who might hold those answers lay in front of him, his life perched on a precarious edge.

Reaching down, David covered Max's hand with his.

"She's home, old man. I know you already know. You know everything, sometimes even before it happens, it seems. But she came home." Then, even though it was an ugly wrench in his gut to do it, David bent down and murmured, "You probably already know, in your heart, what's happened. If you're too tired to keep this up, most of us are going to understand. You're a tough old bastard, but you shouldn't have to hold on just because people here want you to."

He straightened and turned to go.

He'd moved a few steps before he stopped and turned back.

"I know. And I understand why . . . all of it."

Fully aware of Charity's confused stare, he left the ICU.

He needed to get back to his place and just lock himself away from the world.

While he could.

But a piece of the world followed him back.

Sybil Chalmers was sitting on his porch.

She wore one of those sexy little skin-skimming numbers that drove him crazy, and her hair fell down her back in a waterfall of black.

Her lips were red as sin and her eyes were soft on his, full of sympathy. "I heard about Max. I'm sorry."

Caine brushed past her, or tried to. She just followed him inside. "I never did much like that grouchy old bastard. Why are you out here apologizing to me?"

She slid her arms around his back and he went rigid.

"You can fool just about everybody else. But you can't fool me." Sybil was a tall woman, and with the heels she'd put on she was tall enough to press a kiss to his nape. The soft touch snapped his control and he spun around, grabbed her around the waist.

"I don't want to fool you," he growled against her mouth. "I want to fuck you."

He yanked the hem of her skirt, working the tight cloth up, found her naked underneath. Crowding her up against the door, he boosted her up and reached down, freed himself.

Here, with her, like this, he almost felt whole. The rage, the need to outrun himself, sometimes, when he was with her, it disappeared.

Right now the rage was still there, and he caught her thighs, spread her wide, shoved inside. She caught her breath, her mouth falling open. "Don't scream," he said, his voice level, steady. He might have been ready to explode inside, but none of it showed on the surface.

Her lashes fluttered and a broken moan escaped her lips.

He let go of one leg and covered her mouth. She bit his hand and he felt her clench down around him. "You can't scream," he warned again. Abraham's house was down the hill and those were explanations Caine wouldn't make. He would never be the son Abraham might wish, but he wouldn't disrespect the man that way, either.

She bit him instead, the muscles of her pussy clutching and gripping at him like a fist each time he thrust inside her, and he could feel the climax already rushing in on them both. Sliding his hand around, he stroked her between the cheeks of her ass, teased the dark pucker there and pressed his mouth to her ear. "Next time you come to me wearing this dress, bring me something so I can turn you to the door and fuck you here. I want to fuck you and know you're screaming on the inside, ready to fly apart as I take you there."

She shuddered and he pushed the tip of his finger inside. Some of the darkness in him edged back.

It was like when he spilled this part of himself into her, he claimed a piece of his broken soul back.

But he could never claim enough of those pieces.

His soul had been shattered too many years ago.

Snarling, he shifted, moving them from the door to the simple broken-down armchair a few feet away. It was the only one not near a window and it creaked when weight was placed on it, but the bed was too far away.

There was a wet, sucking sound as he pulled out, and Sybil whimpered under her breath, then gasped as he turned her around, bent her over. He pushed inside, using one hand on her hip to steady her, eying the round, white curve of her ass, the black dress that still covered her from the waist up. Tangling his other hand in her hair, he used his hold on her to tug her up. Her spine bowed, arching up. He twisted her head around, taking her mouth and tangling tongues with her as he shafted her, sinking his dick deep, deep, deep inside her pussy.

Slow, deep, easy, letting this time with her wash away some of the hell.

She climaxed once, a second time.

But he couldn't.

It was almost a snarl, trapped inside him, unable to break free.

And then . . . she braced her weight on a hand, slid the other down. Catching his balls between her hand, she squeezed, tight, taking him just over the edge of pain.

Dark, brilliant pleasure, edged with pain, washed through him.

And he fell.

David had to hurt before he found his release.

Sybil was the only woman who'd ever understood that.

And sooner or later she just might understand why.

It was probably better to end it, he thought, sometime later, before that happened.

He didn't want to see the disgust or, worse, the pity in her eyes when she realized what a complete, and fucked-up, mess he was.

There probably wasn't anybody who understood that man's moods like she did.

When he pulled away from her, she was prepared for him to say or do something stupid.

She could see it in the set of his shoulders, the flat line of his mouth.

Still wet from him, she told herself she wasn't going to let it hurt. Whatever *he* said, it would be because *he* was hurting.

It didn't matter what he said about Max. She knew Caine loved the old goat. She could see it, and more, she could feel it, in the pit of her belly. He was already pulling away, getting ready to shut down.

Nobody shut down the way he did.

But to her surprise, he didn't say anything stupid.

He didn't do anything stupid.

He came to her and turned her around. He caught the zipper of her dress and tugged it down. As it came free, he undid her bra, brushed both the wiggle dress and her bra straps down her arms until she could step out of them. She was still wearing a pair of heels, the ankle straps holding them on.

He caught her in his arms and swept her up, surprising a laugh out of her. The wide ridge of his chest bulged with muscle and she made an appreciative sound under her breath as she stroked her hand across his shoulders. "I figured you'd want me to leave before anybody noticed my car," she said, keeping her voice down.

"It won't be an issue much longer," he said obliquely.

And then he carried her off to his room.

He still didn't let her scream. And it was that much more amazing, catching all those sounds, biting her lip, his shoulder, *him,* just to keep from making noise as he took her to the edge and back, time and again.

Adam found her in the middle of his kitchen.

Arms wrapped around herself, her gaze on the floor, Lana looked lost and confused.

He came up behind her and caught her in an embrace, pressing his lips to her neck. "Why the lost face?"

"Maybe because I feel lost," she said, sighing. "I don't know what to do now. I've always known what to do. Now . . . now I don't."

He pressed his cheek to hers. "What do you mean, you've always known?"

"I had to hide. That was the goal. Stay hidden. Then I had to come home. Then I had to find answers. Answers, yeah, still looking there, but I had to put some of this in your hands, in Noah's hands, in David's. Even in the hands of a cop." She wrinkled her nose as she said it, like the word tasted bad. "Now I'm here and I don't know what to do."

She turned in Adam's arms and lifted her eyes to his. The grey clouded and he could feel the misery coming off her. "And I can't stop thinking about Max."

Adam brushed a hand down her hair. "He pulled through surgery. He may be okay."

"Even if he is, what then? Mary is gone. And if we figured out about what he's been doing, others will, too."

"Don't borrow trouble." Adam rubbed his mouth against hers and then slid his hands down to cup her butt, boosted her up. "Come here."

She boosted herself up, wrapped her legs around his waist. "Can't get much closer."

"Sure you can." He walked them over to the wall, rocked against her. "We can get naked. I can get inside you. Then we're as close as we can get."

A faint smile curled her lips. "That . . . sounds perfect."

He pumped his hips, watched her eyes go opaque. Letting go of her hips, he took the few seconds needed to strip her jeans away, but when he would have reached for her she evaded him and reached for the hem of his shirt. "Naked, you said," she reminded him. Obliging, he ducked his head and let her strip his shirt off.

He went to join her, but her hands against his chest stopped him.

"The dates—"

A ragged gasp escaped her lips and he looked down as

she traced her finger over the first series of numbers inked onto his flesh. "Adam," she whispered, her voice a choked murmur. "That was when—"

He caught her hand, pressed it to his flesh.

"That was when you left me." He dipped his head and pressed his mouth to her neck. "I want to get another now. At the bottom, marking when you came back."

A shudder rippled through her and he lifted up, cupped her face in his hands. "Don't cry," he murmured, even as the tears were already rolling down her cheeks. "Don't."

"You marked yourself over me."

He rubbed the tears away with his thumb, rubbed his lips over hers and leaned in. "I did a lot of things because of you, and many of them were stupid. Drinking, stupid-ass fights just to keep myself from thinking about all the shit I didn't want to think about. I did this after I finally started to pull myself back together," he said, lifting his head and catching her gaze. "That was the date you left. The next date the day my parents died."

He guided her hand to the phoenix and the date beneath it. "And this when I'd been sober a year. I marked myself because I needed to, not because of anything you made me do."

Lana twisted her hand away and he let her, held still as she ran her fingers along the wings of the winged, flaming bird. "Why the phoenix? Were you ready to rise from the ashes?"

"Not until I saw you from the river." He braced his hands over her head, watching her, hunger and want and need blistering inside his blood while love ripped at his heart. "I crawled out of the bottle, but I needed other ways to forget. I couldn't be alone in my head and stay sane, so I fucked every woman I could get my hands on."

Her lids flickered, her gaze falling away.

"No secrets, Lana. You called me a man-whore." He

grimaced while she winced. Reaching down, he fisted a hand in her hair, guiding her gaze back to his. "It's nothing but the truth. I couldn't escape my demons so I tried to fuck them away."

"Did it work?"

"No. Not until I put my hands on you." He pressed his brow to hers. "The only time I've felt any kind of peace in the past twenty years was with you."

"Peace." A slow, reluctant smile curled her lips. "That's just what a woman wants to hear from a Lothario. She makes him feel all nice and peaceful."

"Well, you also make my dick hurt."

A bubble of laughter gurgled out of her. "That's better." Then she sighed and leaned against him, looping her arms around him. "Peace is good, though. I haven't felt that in years. Haven't felt safe, either. I do here. With you."

They stood there, like that, for a moment. Then he slid his hands down, cupped her hips. "Let's not forget that part where you make my dick hurt."

She leaned back and caught the hem of her shirt. "How silly of me."

"Let me." He guided her hands down.

Adam stripped her shirt away, and in moments they stood naked in the doorway that joined his hallway to the kitchen. "I think this is the first time I've ever been naked in this part of my house," he whispered, pulling her back against him.

"We should christen each room."

"Later." He lifted her and groaned as she wrapped her legs around his waist. "Now, this."

"This." She shuddered as he pushed against her.

And he swore as she yielded, then opened for him. Words trembled inside him. He wanted to beg her to stay. Wanted to tell her everything he'd kept trapped inside for longer than he could remember.

Instead, he hooked an arm around her neck and arched her head back, taking her mouth hungrily.

She groaned against him, her sleek, strong body arching against his. Sweat formed between them and he could feel the muscles in her belly flex. He shuddered as she tightened around him. Her eyes locked on his, the grey almost black. Need and hunger shimmered in her eyes. *And maybe,* he thought, *maybe the beginning of something more.*

More . . . fuck more.

He wanted everything.

Flexing his hand, he tugged, watched the mist clear from her eyes. "Tell me you won't leave," he murmured.

"Adam." The word was a broken plea and she clutched at him, the demand clear.

The lazy, almost gentle moment passed as desperation settled in. "Tell me," he urged. He caught her lower lip between his, bit her lightly. "I fucking waited for twenty years. I . . . Fuck, I can't lose—"

The truth of it slipped out, hung there.

And she stared at him. She reached up, touched his cheek. "I waited twenty years to come home. This is where I want to be."

It wasn't enough.

But for now, it would have to work.

Slanting his mouth over hers, he clutched her tight . . . and lost himself in her.

"You waited, Adam?"

She felt him tense against her late that night.

He'd had to leave for a couple of hours and she'd quietly roamed the house, feeling like a caged bird while she waited.

When he came back, she'd taken one look at him, thinking they should talk.

But one look had led to one kiss and one kiss had led to her jerking at his clothes and him ripping at hers, and they had ended up christening the carpet on the living-room floor.

Nearly five hours had passed since he'd dropped that rather startling announcement.

And she needed more.

I waited. . . .

She'd eaten a sandwich while he was gone. He'd had supper while he was out—after all, rehearsal dinners usually involved dinners.

He had to be up early. The wedding was a simple affair, but they did plan on having a best man, a ring bearer.

Adam had come home with an invitation.

For Lana.

She'd read it.

She hadn't said anything, but they both knew she'd go.

Now they lay in bed and she waited for an answer.

A sigh escaped, the puff of air teasing her hair. He skimmed his fingers down her hair and she shivered a little as goose bumps popped up in the wake of his touch.

"You should go visit your dad again. Things are . . . well, not settling, but you can at least let him know it's working out some, right?"

She closed her eyes. "I don't know if that's what this is, but it's not going to hell in a handbasket yet. I'll go tomorrow. After the wedding."

"He'll be there. Noah stayed in touch with him."

She smiled sadly. "That sounds like Noah."

"You still love him."

"The girl I was a long time ago still exists inside me, somewhere. *She* still loves him. The woman I am now? I don't really know him. But neither of us are the people we used to be. I can't love a man I don't know. And he is in love with a woman who makes him happy." Lana sat up, turned to stare at Adam. "I want him to be happy, Adam. He deserves it."

Then she reached out, touched the tip of her finger to Adam's lower lip. "I didn't spend twenty years pining for him. Maybe that makes me a terrible person, but I was too busy trying to just forget things . . . then I was trying to get my life back together. I spent a long time trying to destroy myself. I had no room left to pine after the boy I loved."

Adam curved his arm around her waist. "He spent a lot of time pining after you."

"He spent a lot of time *worrying* . . . grieving. I knew he was okay. It was easier to let go, knowing that. I didn't give him any closure. It's harder that way."

Adam stared at her, his eyes turbulent. "You think I don't know that?"

"I'm sorry," she said softly. "I'm sorry for what I did, what I put you through."

Something unhappy shifted through her and she looked away. Noah had spent years grieving—that was what had made it harder for him to let go. Something about the way Adam watched her had an awful, wonderful, terrible thought forming in her mind, but she didn't know if she wanted to give voice to it.

Looking away, she focused on the wall. "What do you mean, you spent twenty years waiting?"

"What do you think?"

Unable to put it into words, she just waited.

He moved then, shifting around and tucking her under him. "You know, your dad never liked me."

She frowned, thrown off.

Adam didn't seem to notice. Catching a lock of hair in his hand, he rubbed his thumb across it, lifted it to his nose, like he wanted to breathe her in. "I think he knew."

"Knew what?"

Adam looked back at her, then. "That I'd fallen you, almost from the beginning."

The words hit her with hammer strength and her heart started to race, pounding against her heart, brutal and fast.

"I started to realize what, and why, in high school. You were too young for me, and it was crazy and wrong and I knew it. I was in ninth grade when I realized you were growing breasts." He skimmed his thumb across the curve and she felt heat crash through her. "You'd been my friend, this funny kid . . . and all of a sudden, you were a girl."

"You stopped talking to me!"

"And why do you think that happened?" he said, shrugging. "The older I got, the older you got, the worse it became. And the worse I felt about it. And then, all of a sudden, it wasn't such an issue. Maybe you were fifteen and I was eighteen, but that's not such an issue, right? Except Noah was there. And he was . . ." Adam trailed off, staring at her while the feelings of inadequacy raged inside him. "Noah was everything I'm not. He made you laugh and I'd been an ass for the past few years. He had scholarships lined up. I was going to be taking over my parents' place and I'd barely gotten through school with Bs and Cs. You two fit. And I was just . . ."

She closed her eyes.

The sting of rejection settled in.

But before he could turn away, she slid her arms around him, pulled him down.

"We might not have fit . . . then." She turned her face into his neck. "But we've established I'm not who I used to be. I can never fit with him now. This, though . . . this feels like a fit."

Maybe she hadn't said, *Adam, I've been in love with you all my life. . . .*

But she clung to him like she needed him.

And that mattered.

Gripping her to him, he settled down in the bed.

"It's a fit," he whispered.

CHAPTER TWENTY-THREE

It was a simple wedding.

Set along the banks of the Ohio with the water glimmering like a ribbon of silver at their back, Trinity Ewing walked away from her old life and began a new one with Noah Benningfield.

And she didn't walk down the aisle alone.

Noah had said he was taking them both and he wanted both of them to join him.

So Micah was there with her, for that first walk.

He held his mother's hand as she walked to join the man who had become their everything.

Adam stood at Noah's side, ready with the ring, watching . . . waiting. He felt like he perched on a razor's edge, the events of the past few weeks all piling up to some climactic event that was just going to set the entire town ablaze.

Not here, he thought, the closest he'd come to praying in a long time. *Please don't let it happen here.*

Maybe it worked.

More likely, the guy upstairs was just fond of Noah and wasn't going to let anything rain on his parade. The wedding passed without a hitch.

Caine—no, it was David—came in quietly.

Adam was going to have to undo fifteen years of thinking. The man hadn't really started mingling around town until five years after David's "disappearance" and he'd changed a lot.

David didn't talk to anybody, and so far nobody was paying him much attention. Adam suspected the town gossips hadn't heard the news yet, but that wouldn't last long.

David sat in the back, close to Lana, and the two of them didn't once look at each other.

They both watched the wedding, like they were determined to see it through.

The same as Adam.

He didn't know if they somewhat expected Layla to show her face or the cops or what.

He just knew he'd feel better once that line *I now pronounce you man and wife* was said.

As Noah pulled Trinity against him, almost everybody there started to clap. There was laughter and wet eyes, but under it all the happiness had a sharp edge.

Adam caught David's eye as he moved off to the back of the crowd.

And they both knew.

It wasn't over.

Nowhere near.

As the crowd gathered around, wishing the couple well, Lana moved in close to Adam, slipped her hand into his.

"You look grim."

He looked down, pressed his lips to hers. "You should be the one looking grim. Judging by all the sidelong looks you're getting, word is out. People will start rushing you soon."

She shrugged. "It's going to happen. I'd rather it not be here." Then she rested her head against his arm. "Why the heavy look?"

"Because it's not over."

Lana squeezed his hand. "No. I don't think it is. How can it be? No answers about Max. Still too many of the men from Cronus out there. But today isn't the day for this sort of talk." Then she tugged on him. "Come on. I heard there's going to be dancing. It's been twenty years since I danced, big guy. I've got a lot of catching up to do. Maybe if I stay busy, people will leave me alone . . . at least for a day."

"So you're using me, huh?"

"No. I'm thinking more along the lines of . . . keeping you." She paused and smiled at him. "Is that okay?"

He caught her up against him, pressed his mouth to hers. "Since that's kind of what I planned, yeah. More than okay."

Not everybody was at the wedding.

He'd gone over the information for the murder and attempted murder of the Shepherds. Heads would roll over that one, and if Max survived—and it looked like he was going to pull through—the murderer wasn't going to be pleased. Whoever shot Max should have made sure he was dead, because he wouldn't rest until he saw justice for his Mary.

That was just one of the cases he had to handle. He was walking through a damn minefield these days. Just then, he was focused on what little information he had on the events from twenty years ago. He had his own notes and he'd have to interview everybody, all over again. Now, at least, he had two witnesses to question.

Tugging on his lip, he studied the mitochondrial DNA report. David Sutter had agreed to give a DNA sample when he'd given his statement. He had more questions for that man, that was for certain.

He'd threatened every single soul in the station, and for now they were all keeping it quiet.

That wouldn't last, though.

He couldn't control Layla, and even if she didn't talk, word would get out.

If everything added up the way Lana and David claimed, then what he had here was an epic clusterfuck and the whole town was going to be shaken. They'd spent twenty years with the Sutter family on a pedestal.

That pedestal had to come down.

No.

Not come down.

Be shattered, completely.

And it was going to take David Sutter being willing to do what he couldn't do before—tell the truth about what his father had done to him and possibly countless other boys. David had no names, just a few suspicions, but those suspicions gave him a starting point.

Reaching across the desk, he picked up a picture, stared at it.

Then he rose and crossed the room, pinned the picture to the fresh board he'd started.

It was time to start thinking this through all over again, from the ground up.

They danced.

Flowers and lights and music filled the air, and laughter rang out.

There was one person who didn't laugh, though. No reason to laugh. No reason to smile.

Only watch.

As they danced.

The laughter was like a needle to the ear, a scrape against the soul, a knife in the side.

No way to escape it, though.

How could they all be so happy?

How could they all be so full of smiles and cheer?

Especially him.

Didn't he understand?

Didn't he know?

They should all be shaken and hopeless inside. Desperate and needy.

Broken.

A soft, desperate sound filled the air. But it was lost under the sound of a love song, lost under the music and the laughter.

DARKER THAN DESIRE

It was a slow, mostly silent walk, especially the first twenty minutes. They stopped at a cross street and David looked at Sybil for the first time when she pulled her hand from his.

She gave him a rueful grin as she tugged something from her coat pocket. "It's a good thing I know you."

That didn't click until he saw her pull out a narrow pair of slipper-like shoes from a pouch that she swapped out in place of her heels. She put the stilt-like shoes in one hand and then took his hand, sighing a little in relief.

"We could have taken your car," he said as something he recognized as guilt worked through him.

"Difficult." She slid him a sideways smile. "I caught a ride with Trinity and Noah. I . . ." Her words trailed off and she shrugged. "Well, I figured you'd be there and I wanted to be with you in case you needed me."

This time, he was the one to stop.

In case you needed me.

Words rose in him, trapping in his throat as he turned to face her.

They were still close to two miles from the little house where Max had lived all these years. Brilliant streams of sunlight shone down around them and cars passed by but all he saw was her. Reaching up, he threaded his fingers through her hair, cupped her face.

He opened his mouth, trying to figure out the way to say everything pent up inside. He wasn't a man who *cared* about words—they meant little, in his mind. Except what she'd just done proved him wrong. A few gentle words could somehow slash into him and yet flood him with something . . . *indescribable*.

Leaning in, he pressed his mouth to her forehead while an internal war waged inside him. He thought back to the first time he'd seen her, the fury that had lit inside him when he realized what he'd come across. The defiance and fear and anger he'd seen reflected in her eyes. The way she'd smiled at him the next time they met. Then, the third time, when he'd thought he was being casual about it and she gave him that slow, *I see what you did there* look.

It started then, he realized.

When he started to feel again—he'd thought it was just lust and he'd welcomed it. Lust was a *normal* thing. He hadn't felt it, not really, until she'd given him that slow, sure smile of hers and he'd thought about covering that red-slicked mouth with his own, fantasies that he hadn't entertained in . . . never. He'd never had them.

He'd fed that hot, hungry feeling then, let it consume him, but he'd never really noticed everything that grew along with it. The obsession. The *need*.

"You're in my blood, in my soul. I can't remember a time anymore when I didn't needed you," he whispered, the words slipping from him without him even realizing it.

Sybil tensed, a startled sound slipping from her.

He lifted his head and watched her from under his lashes. "I made Samuel put in that bid that bid on your studio," he said.

Well, well, well. Sybil walked into the studio and all but dropped her jaw. Okay, yes, she'd known the group the contractor had gotten for most of the construction was one of the Amish families out of Switzerland counties, but Caine was on it?

What were the odds?

He hadn't so much as looked at her, but she recognized him—would recognize him, no matter what, whether it was a dimly lit street and he was striding down the street with more confidence than any man should have, or if he was here, among the rest of the quiet, soft-spoken men, like a wolf among sheep.

In that very moment, he looked up and like he was surprised to see her, he blinked and cocked his head, then just nodded.

But she saw it, in just that moment, that he wasn't surprised.

He'd known this was her place. Once they were done, it would be her studio and she planned on making something of it.

She smiled back and lifted a brow.

He kept his face blank, a shutter falling across his features, but she didn't let it get to her.

He was here.

What to do about that?

That memory, more than a dozen years old, slammed into her and she reached up, curling one hand into the thick, woven material of the black sweater he wore. It was scratchy-soft under her hand, the heat of his skin like a furnace.

"Samuel?"

He shrugged restlessly, a gesture that was out of place on him. "He was Tom's father. Used to head up the crew before I took over. Tom is going to be taking over now, I guess. I asked Sam to take the job. Actually, I convinced Abraham to talk him into it."

"And why did you do that?"

He pressed his face into her hair and she shivered at the feel of his breath teasing her skin. He mistook it for cold and wrapped him arms around her, pulling her close. "Because I wanted to be around you. It was a weird thing for me. I never cared if I was around anybody or not—no. That's not right. I preferred *not* to be around people, but on that job, I tried to get the inside work as much as I could. Abraham heard about it, thought maybe I was . . ."

Sybil turned her head slightly toward him, rubbing her cheek against his when she felt the rasping brush of his stubble. "Getting better," she murmured. "But there's no getting better. It's not like you had a cold, is it?"

"More like cancer."

"They're the cancer." She stiffened and lifted her hands to his face, forcing him to meet her eyes. "*Them*. Not you."

Volatile emotion sparked in her gaze but for the first time in he didn't know how long, he had a hard time meeting her eyes. *Them* . . .

Sometimes he deliberately fooled himself, especially lately. Always with her. She'd known—always known. Now, aware of her vivid stare, as the ugly realization slammed into it, he let some of the bitterness he felt spill out.

"Yeah. They were a cancer. And they spread it around." He caught one of her wrists, dragged it down as he continued to watch her, stroking a finger across the inside. "You see so much, Syb. You always did. When did you figure everything out? How long have you known?"

She blinked, looking confused.

He advanced on her, moving his hands to her waist and urging her back, back, back until she bumped up against the brick wall of the building behind her. "Did you just look at me that first time, the second time, or was it the third time when you realized how completely fucked up I was inside?"

"Exactly where are you going with this?" she asked, her voice level.

"When did you know?" Bracing a forearm on the wall by her head, he dipped his head until their eyes were on level. He'd never been able to figure it out, why she could stand to be around him, put up with him. He'd never figured it out.

Her gaze met it. Then she angled her chin up and narrowed her eyes. "I figured something pretty shitty had happened to you the first time we had sex. Those scars all over your back didn't exactly happen because *boys will be boys*, right?"

Something twisted inside him and he swallowed his throat. "You didn't know . . ."

Sybil heaved out a breath, the motion causing her breasts to rise and fall. "Hell, David. What did you think was going on here? Some sort of marathon session of pity fucks?" She curled her lip as she said the words and they fell distastefully from her lips.

One hand clenched into a fist. "It's occurred to me."

Sybil reached up, slid her fingers inside the neckline of his shirt, the tips splaying out until she could trail them over the topmost edges of the scars. She never once moved away. "I don't *pity* you. Something in me breaks knowing what was done to the boy you were. You're not him anymore. Either they killed him or you did. But you're *not* him. You're you and I wake up every day wanting you, needing you. Don't think otherwise, not for one minute."

Some of the tension he felt drained out of him and he dipped his head, buried his face in her hair.

"I'm sorry," he said, his voice hoarse.

Sybil hooked an arm around his neck as she turned into him. "We've established the fact that you're fucked up. I figured that out a while ago, but I don't think you're fucked up so much as . . . pulled in. You only let pieces of yourself out in small doses."

Eyes closed, he listened to the rhythm and cadence of her voice as he let the words sink in slowly. Not fucked up. Oh, hell. Yes he was.

If he was smart, he'd pull free of her and stay away.

But that was one thing he couldn't seem to do.

After a moment, Sybil nudged him with her hands and he eased back, staring down at her. A car went blasting down the street, stopping at the stopsign with just a squeal of the brakes before speeding off down the street like a bullet. Neither of them even looked away from each other.

"I don't pity you," she said again. "That doesn't mean I can't hurt for what was done. To you, to God only knows how many others."

He let his hands fall away as a torrent of bitter anger rose inside him. He fought to keep it trapped. Letting it explode out of him wouldn't hurt anybody but Sybil.

"God." He spat it out as some of the rage leaked free. Spinning away, he stared down the street. He laughed and even that felt like acid boiling up his throat.

The sound of that laughter, ugly and broken, was like jagged glass on her skin. Sybil stared at his averted back, every line of his body rigid. "God knows how many?" he echoed. Then he turned and looked at her. "There is no God, Sybil. God wouldn't allow the things that happened here *to* happen. So not even *He* knows."

A wave of sadness rolled through her.

Sighing, she moved up and stroked a hand down his back. She might not have the kind of faith that somebody like Noah did—his could probably move mountains. That was the saying, right? But she did believe in something higher than herself. It seemed kind of sad to think this was it, that there was nothing else.

"David," she said, sliding her arm around his body. "This isn't about the things God *allows*. He gave us life, free will. That means the sons of bitches who choose to act in evil ways are going to do it. At the end of it all, they'll answer for it."

"Fuck," he muttered, his voice thick with derision, the word all but lost in a derisive snort. "You know how many times I cried? Prayed? Begged for help? It never came. I was alone. I've always been alone."

Sybil moved around him, then, cupped his face in her hands. "You're not. I'm here. I've been here a long time. I won't go away unless you make me and even then, you'll have a fight on your hands."

His lids flickered. "That's not . . ."

She rose up on her toes. "Shhhh. I know. This isn't anything I'm trying to change your mind about. You have to decide for yourself anyway. I just don't care to believe that it all ends here. And regardless of any of that, you're not alone. You've got me."

"Do I?" His arms came around her, banded tight, sliding yet again against under the heavy, long material of her coat. One fist tangled in the material of her dress while he buried his face against her neck.

"Always." The words she really wanted to say remained trapped.

Somehow, she knew this wasn't the time. The place.

But one day soon, she'd tell him. Whether he wanted to hear it not.

She stood there, holding him close while he practically

clutched her to him. Every line of his body was tense, so tense, she could almost imagine him vibrating. After a moment, his lips rubbed against her neck, the slight movement sending an electric thrill racing through her. How many years had she been with him? Not enough. She could spend a century, taking as many of these stolen moments as she could, and it wouldn't be enough.

His lips found her ear and she shivered as his breath ghosted over her skin. "Where's Drew?"

"Staying with his friend, Darnell." She forced a smile and shrugged. "I called Taneisha—you met her at the hospital, I think. She took care of Max. Anyway, I wanted to be here . . ."

He lifted his head, pinning her with an intent stare as her words trailed off.

"I wanted to be there if you needed me. Going to . . ." She trailed off, uncertain what to say. *Your place? Max's place?*

"It's too far." He dipped his head and rubbed his lips across her neck. "Your studio."

She caught her breath as he slid his hand around and up her torso, cupping her breast in one palm. Her coat shielded the action from view, but it still felt so very . . .

Wicked.

Wonderful.

And not enough.

"Let's get there, then."